I0667404

Dixie's Tale

H.E. Joseph

Dixie's Tale

By

H.E. Joseph

Typeset Book size Palatino Linotype size 12
H.E. Joseph, Dixie's Tale
An *Eleven-11* Book

1-3-0-6-2-0-0-5

www.hejoseph.eu

Author's Note

Although all the locations in this tale are situated in recognisable English postcode districts, it is important to state that they are all nevertheless purely imaginary in nature. In a similar way, none of the characters in the tale are based on real people – either living or dead.

For Joseph & Friends

Contents

-CHAPTER ONE-

The Carmichaels Meet Dixie

Dixie was born on a warm July afternoon. His parents, Jupiter Sue and Spartacus III, were both owned by Phil and Jill Candy, who had been in the dog-breeding business for twenty or so years by this stage.

Phil and Jill found it easy to secure new homes for Dixie and his brother and two sisters, although it would be another few weeks before the pedigree West Highland Terrier pups met their new owners.

When that day eventually came, Jill Candy diligently prepared the pups and their associated paperwork for this monumental occasion. She understood the importance of those first few moments shared between each pup and its new family, and she was careful to ensure that everything went as smoothly as possible. Phil, Jill's husband and business partner, had already liaised by phone and online with the pups' new owners, and it had been agreed which pup would go where, once monies had been exchanged, of course: John and Mary Cocker, both retired teachers in their sixties from Luton, would take a male and female pup, now that their children had (eventually) fled the nest; Abigail West, a wealthy forty-something single mother-of-one from Brighton, would take a female pup for her eight-year-old daughter, Coco; and Ray and Susan Carmichael, cosmetic dentists at an exclusive London clinic, would take the last male pup.

'I *told* you to take that left turn after the roundabout,' Susan Carmichael snapped at her husband. 'For God's sake, Ray, you've had ages to plan this journey – so how come you always seem to leave everything to the last minute?'

'Susan, just calm down, will you? I mean, I know you're anxious and excited about meeting the dog; but the poor thing will run a mile if he catches a whiff of your stress hormones.' Ray swung the car (dangerously) in the opposite direction.

'Wonderful. You might as well kill us both off before we even get there. Did you not see that jeep? Or was it not quite big enough for you?'

Ray bit his tongue at this stage, knowing that to do otherwise would be very *un*wise.

'Look!' Susan exclaimed. 'There's the sign for *Candy Pups* on the right!'

At this, Ray Carmichael veered sharply across the main road, only just making it onto the elusive lane they had been searching for.

'Did you remember to bring the credit card, by any chance?' Susan asked Ray after a long pause.

'Of course I did,' Ray replied calmly. 'So can we just chill a little now? I mean, let's enjoy meeting the pup, Susan. This day was meant to be about positive new beginnings, after all, wasn't it?' Ray reached over and lightly squeezed his wife's hand.

'OK, OK,' Susan said, as she suddenly glimpsed a building she suspected belonged to Candy Pups. 'There it is!' she cried, smiling broadly for the first time in a very long time.

'Well, thank goodness for small mercies,' Ray muttered under his breath, before turning to look at Susan's face, which appeared strangely yet pleasantly unfamiliar to him, now that it was suddenly beaming with happiness. Ray had become more accustomed in recent years to looking at pain and disappointment etched on his wife's face.

'Oh shit,' Susan said nervously. 'Do you think he'll like us, Ray?'

'Susan, pull yourself together. I mean, you're a successful cosmetic dentist and businesswoman. It's about time you had a bit more self-confidence; instead of worrying about what a dog's opinion of you is going to be.'

'That's easy for you to say.'

'Look,' Ray reassured her. 'I know you've taken a lot of knocks recently, what with your health and that. And I know that this is always the worst day of the year for you. But trust me. This dog is going to make life much happier for you – I just know it will, Susan.'

Susan looked at her husband tentatively, as he finally drove the car through the gateway that led into the yard belonging to Candy Pups. Ray Carmichael parked the car and took the keys out of the ignition. 'Come on Susan. Let's go and meet the new member of the family, shall we?'

Susan took a deep breath, before she finally turned and got out of the car.

As Ray and Susan Carmichael walked across the wide, concreted, empty courtyard in this leafy Buckinghamshire setting, their worries back in London seemed a million miles away. Susan felt an immediate sense of release from the stresses that had plagued her for the last number of years. It was as though her physical body was dissolving, due to a sudden blast of relief provided by the trees and skies that surrounded her now.

'I think it must be through this door,' Ray said, as he reached out and pulled the large green handle on the red door in front of him.

Susan marched purposefully past Ray into a small Reception Area, which was not particularly tasteful in its décor, Susan thought, and could have done with a few more plants and paintings. She wouldn't have chosen the sickly pink wall colour either, nor did she like the tacky red and green 'Candy Pups' signage above the untidy Reception Desk.

'This place looks nice,' Ray said cheerfully, as he approached Susan, who was standing by the empty reception desk. Susan fired him a look that only Ray understood the meaning of, before a door suddenly opened to save him from the verbal onslaught.

'You must be the Carmichaels! Our last appointment of the day!' a small middle-aged woman with cropped, dyed yellow hair exclaimed, as she waddled curiously towards Susan and Ray.

Susan found herself uncharacteristically silenced by the vision of the woman before her, whom she thought resembled some kind of retro sweet packaging, what with her unnaturally yellow hair and pink and green uniform.

'I'm Jill Candy! You dealt with my husband, Phil, on the phone earlier. He's just out back at the kennels. You guys must have had a bit of trouble finding us, did you? You're a bit past your appointment time, aren't you?'

'Sorry, Jill – all my fault,' Ray said, reaching out his hand to shake Jill's, once she had finally stopped asking them questions.

'Never mind, lovies!' Jill said cheerfully. 'I just like to make sure all my clients get lots of attention when they come to pick up their new doggies! I like to stagger appointments so that there are no overlaps or clashes – I'm sure you understand, don't you? So you have the whole place to yourself! That's great, isn't it?'

'Great!' Ray replied, a little overwhelmed by Jill's positive vibes, and very wary of his wife's stony-faced silence.

'Now, let's go out back, shall we? And introduce you both to your dog?' Jill sensed a bit of an atmosphere between the couple standing in her Reception Area. They were both about forty years old, she thought. She could tell the man was the steady, reliable type; fair-haired and blue-eyed; average in appearance and stature, but probably his wife's pillar of strength.

Her though – definitely a steely character. Seems to be hurting emotionally. Very good-looking, but has weight issues. A definite Size Sixteen, Jill guessed. Probably having difficulty conceiving. That's why she wants the dog, of course.

Jill had encountered every breed of dog and every breed of dog owner throughout her professional life, and she could grasp their personality and back story within an instant of meeting them; from the solitary pervert to the party-going socialite, Jill knew who they were and what they were like from their particular choice of dog – be it cute, huge, designer, ugly or athletic. 'So you're both dentists to those trendy types in London, I hear!' Jill said merrily as she escorted Ray and Susan through the door she had initially entered, down a long pink corridor, into a small room at the back of the premises.

'Yes, I'm afraid so!' Ray said, ushering his wife into the room ahead of him.

'Well, here's your little darling waiting for you over here!' Jill said, gesturing towards a hutch-like structure in the corner of the room. Jill walked over, carefully lifted its roof off, and took out its occupant, handing him directly over to Susan Carmichael, who let out an immediate squeal of delight.

The little white hairy face and dark eyes looking up at her was one of the most breathtakingly lovely sights she had ever seen before, Susan thought. She pressed her chin against the dog's and burst into floods of tears.

'It's OK, Susan,' Ray said tenderly. 'I told you he'd like you, didn't I?'

'Oh, Ray,' Susan sobbed, unable to find further words to express her feelings.

Definitely fertility issues this one, Jill Candy thought to herself. She and her husband Phil had never tried for children themselves: their dogs were their lives. 'What are you going to call the little darling then?' she asked Susan.

'Dixie,' Susan replied, wiping tears from her eyes. 'I had my appendix out a month ago and Ray said he'd get me a dog to help my recovery. That's how we came up with the name Dixie.'

'How nice!' Jill Candy said, intrigued. 'Now, why doesn't daddy Ray here come with me to see Phil so that we can sort out Dixie's birth certificate and other paperwork in Reception?'

'Is that OK, Susan? You want to take him back to the car with you?' Ray asked his wife.

'OK. See you in the car then,' Susan replied, totally engrossed in her new companion.

*****

And so marked the beginning of Susan Carmichael's love affair with Dixie. From this day onwards, Dixie was the cornerstone of Susan's life. It was not as though this little dog cancelled out all the negative events of the previous few years for Susan – her miscarriage, her numerous failed attempts at falling pregnant after this, not to mention the operation to have her appendix removed – but he certainly did a lot to ease the pain caused by the raw wounds bequeathed by these events.

In the three years that passed after Susan acquired Dixie, she never gave up her dream of motherhood, and she somehow felt that the loyal and lovely Dixie was destined to keep her company until that moment came. She couldn't contemplate life without him now, and she viewed Dixie more as a god than a dog. Susan was fiercely protective towards him, and she was loathe leaving him in the care of anyone other than Ray.

'We can't leave him with that moron – no way!' Susan said one Monday evening to Ray, as they were curled up on the sofa, drinking red wine.

'What harm could come from it, Susan? We'd only be asking him to pop round to feed Dixie and take him for a stroll around the back garden – and it would only be for this weekend.'

'Even so, Ray. He's really giving me the creeps these days – what with his mysterious phone calls, and always slipping off to do one of his so-called *little messages*. Steve's a prick and I don't trust him with anything - never mind Dixie.'

'He *has* been our business partner for over ten years, Susan. I mean, it's not as though he's that untrustworthy.'

'Don't be so naïve, Ray! He's a total sleaze ball. And to think of leaving Dixie with him, while we go off trying to procreate, puts me off the whole idea entirely,' Susan said, feeling a little queasy already.

'It's just that you've always said that you feel much more at ease in the countryside. I thought we could maybe stay at the Eden Resort - you know that lovely castle we saw in Buckinghamshire, the day we got Dixie?'

Susan began to think for a while. 'Well. I don't deny that I'd love to spend a weekend away there,' she said, softening her voice a little. 'But I'm still not happy about entrusting Dixie – not to mention the entire dental practice – in the hands of Steve Morgan.'

'For God's sake, Susan. He did provide the financial input needed to get the practice up and running in the first place – even if he's not the most professional dental surgeon on the planet. He's still got a stake in keeping the business afloat without us for a couple of days, you know?'

'You mean his *wealthy wife* provided the money. *Not* her idiotic husband. God knows what the woman saw in him,' Susan snapped.

'Whatever. Look, I know out of everyone at dental school he was the least likely person we'd ever have chosen to work alongside. But life just has a funny way of throwing people together sometimes, doesn't it?'

'Don't remind me!' Susan said, glugging down some wine. 'The Morgans only offered to involve us in the practice because we'd done so well professionally ourselves, and had worked up a brilliant reputation. Steve knew that we would help him make more money in the long-run, than he could ever have done alone - what with his dodgy reputation for surgery.'

'Well, it's worked out well for us financially too, hasn't it?'

'I suppose so,' Susan conceded, a little weary now.

'So how's about it then? Let's go away for a few days and make a baby! Leave the prick in charge of the practice for a while – what's the worst that could happen?'

'Don't even start me with that one. And anyway - what about Dixie?' Susan was beginning to slur her words a little now.

'Steve will be fine looking after the dog too. We'll just tell him to come around and feed him in the mornings and afternoons, and take him for a little walk. And anyway – Buckinghamshire is not too far away. We can keep in contact constantly with Steve while we're at the Eden Resort – and come back home immediately, if we need to.' Ray was trying his utmost to win Susan around to his idea.

'It's also the thought of giving him a key to our home, Ray. God knows who he'll bring round here with him.'

'Susan, I'm sure he'll be able to temper his sexual urges for a few short moments in the day.'

'I wouldn't bet on it. I just know he's at it with that Singleton woman. All that nonsense he tells us about her so-called nerve problems. Perv. problems, more like. Those big long slots he books her in for are all a ruse, you know?' The wine was beginning to make Susan very tired now; it only took a couple of glasses to get her very tipsy these days.

'That's not our business, Susan,' Ray said firmly.

'It *will* be our business when Madeleine Singleton's lawyer husband presses charges against the practice for inappropriate conduct though, won't it?'

'That won't happen, Susan. Look. Are we agreed that we ask Steve to look after Dixie? I mean, it seems a brilliant opportunity to get away from here – for the first time in ages – not to mention what could result from it. When exactly will you be ovulating?'

'Friday 7th October. Although I wish you wouldn't make me sound like some egg-laying chicken, Ray.'

'Sorry. I didn't mean to. Well look, that's perfect then, isn't it? We could leave here on Thursday morning, take two days off work and be back Sunday evening. We can tell Steve tomorrow morning and OK it all with him.'

'Well. Maybe. Although it's probably the wine talking now,' Susan mumbled.

'Great! Now why don't you go up to bed - you look knackered. I'll phone the Eden Resort and book us in for the weekend. I can't see there being any problem getting a vacancy.' Ray stood up and put his glass of wine on top of the small table positioned at the side of the sofa, and took Susan's half-empty glass from her. After placing it on the table beside his, he pulled his wife up from her curled position on the sofa, locked his arm around her waist, and carefully manoeuvred her upstairs to their bedroom.

Susan was asleep by the time Ray slumped her onto the top of their bed. He managed to take off most of her clothes, before he tenderly pulled the duvet cover around her. He lightly kissed her wine-stained lips and went downstairs to make the phone call to the Eden Resort.

As Ray had suspected, he was able to book a suite for the weekend with no difficulty whatsoever. He poured himself one more glass of wine to toast his success in persuading the usually mule-like Susan to come away with him. She was a difficult woman to convince, once she had made her mind up about something, and Ray admitted to himself that he had cheated slightly by using the wine – but he was convinced that he had been entirely justified in his methods.

Susan's strong opinions and forthright ways concealed the fact that she was a scrap yard of emotions. Their several unsuccessful attempts at making babies since their marriage, ten years ago, had destroyed much of Susan's self-confidence and joie de vivre, Ray realised; and he was desperate for his wife to be happy again.

It had all started so promisingly, Ray contemplated, as he took a drink of wine. Falling so easily pregnant on their first attempt; it had all seemed so easy and straightforward. Those first few weeks of Susan's pregnancy had been magical – the happiest they had ever shared together. Susan had been dancing on clouds with happiness, until the unthinkable happened. Ray could feel sadness and anger welling inside him now, as he recalled the events of that day, just over eight years ago.

Miscarriage. It hadn't even been a word in Ray's vocabulary until then. Susan lost their son at twenty three weeks' gestation, when she went into premature labour with Jacob. Ray felt he lost his wife that day too. Images of the feisty, witty and gorgeous Susan flashed in front of his eyes now – the Susan he had first known when they met at the Metropolitan School of Dentistry twenty-odd years ago; but who had become reclusive, defensive and depressed in more recent years. Ray still glimpsed bursts of Susan's former fire at times, but he was still more likely to find her alone, deep in thought. She didn't even like socialising any more – the Susan who had once loved going out to bars and restaurants. Ray couldn't believe they were both about to turn forty, early next year.

Anyway, Ray thought. At least she's prepared to try for another baby again, after all the failed attempts at pregnancy during the last number of years. 'I suppose you have to take some credit for her recent change of heart, Dixie,' Ray said playfully to the dog dozing contentedly at his feet. 'She said you were sent to look after her and make her strong again. No pressure there then, pal! I hope you've had more luck in that department than I've had recently!'

Ray suddenly realised how tired and woozy he was feeling. He put the guard on the fire, lifted Dixie and turned out the lights. He carried Dixie slowly upstairs and placed him in his basket at the foot of his and Susan's bed, just as he did every night. Ray undressed and got under the covers beside Susan, who was by now snoozing heavily. Sleep came easily to Ray, and he drifted off straight away.

Meanwhile, Dixie had stirred from his slumber. He was thinking deeply in his basket.

He had worked hard over the last three years to help Susan out emotionally: that had been his destiny, after all. Dixie recognised, however, that Susan's focus would soon change; and he knew that he was not to play as significant a part in the next stage of her life plan. He had other life journeys to sort out too.

This is it, Dixie thought with a smile. *Nearly time for me to move on.*

-CHAPTER 2-

The Morgans

'Absolutely! That's no problem at all, Ray,' Steve Morgan said, with more than a hint of excitement in his voice.

'And you don't mind popping in to look after Dixie a couple of times a day either, do you?' Ray Carmichael asked.

'Certainly not!' Steve replied enthusiastically, much to the suspicion of Susan Carmichael, who was listening attentively through the door of her surgery to her husband and Steve talking.

Tuesday mornings were always rather quiet at Epsilon Dental Spa, the exclusive London practice owned and managed by Steve Morgan and the Carmichaels. The partners had gained an excellent reputation over the years for their surgical expertise, and the Carmichaels in particular had built up a substantial book of clients – most of them affluent, many of them famous.

The surgery was situated in London W8. It had been tastefully and immaculately designed by Susan Carmichael, who had succeeded in achieving a clinical yet homely and luxurious feel in both the Reception Area and the three surgery suites.

Unlike the Carmichaels, Steve Morgan preferred not to burden himself with too many patients. He had provided the capital to get the practice up and running in the first place, after all. Steve liked to devote more of his time to fewer clients, ensuring that he could offer those clients lots of personal attention. He tended to attract a very female client-base, which he didn't complain about, and he would often dismiss his dental nurse from her duties, to ensure that his clients got his undivided attention. In fact, Steve had built up some very intimate relationships with a select set of regulars over the years, earning him the affectionate title 'My Thriller Driller', with his current favourite, Madeleine Singleton.

Steve had a rather easy-going relationship with Ray Carmichael, although he tended to steer away from Susan as much as possible. The vibes from those quarters were not good at all, Steve thought. Susan was not the type of woman Steve felt comfortable around. Too bloody serious and uppity, he felt. He knew that Susan looked down on him from her perch-on-high. She made him feel like a stupid little boy. *Happy Days!* Steve began to think gleefully to himself as he talked to Ray Carmichael at the Reception Desk, although he could sense the 'Ice Maiden' lurking somewhere in the background, listening with intent. *A couple of days away from her supervision is just what I need right now,* he thought. 'This Eden Resort is supposed to be outstanding, Ray – I'm jealous!' Steve enthused.

'Yes. We drove past it the day we went to collect Dixie, three years ago. I can't wait to go, to be honest, Steve. This place has been hectic recently.'

'Business is great!' Steve replied. 'We have a lot to thank High Definition T.V. for, Ray! They're all going mad, trying to out-do one another in the gnashers department nowadays!'

'I know!' Ray laughed. 'The number of requests we're getting for smile makeovers is unreal! To think that they placed any emphasis on decay, cavities and tartar at dentistry school seems absurd now!'

'Funny enough,' Steve responded. 'I watched a game show from the 1980s last night, and I was looking at the presenter's teeth, thinking – they're yellow and rough-looking – and then I realised they were perfectly good and healthy teeth! We're just all so accustomed to the whiter-than-white unnatural look these days!'

'Emmm. Sorry to interrupt this fascinating conversation,' Susan Carmichael interjected sharply: she had listened to enough irrelevant drivel by this stage to last her a lifetime. 'Aren't you meant to be discussing *Dixie*?' Susan glared at Ray. Her head was still a little fuzzy from the wine the night before, and she wasn't in the mood to be humoured. In fact, she was angry with herself for agreeing to go away and leave Dixie at all this weekend.

'We did discuss Dixie, Susan!' Ray reassured his wife, a little nervously. 'Steve said he'd love to look after him for a few days! And he said it was no problem shifting our Thursday and Friday appointments to another time. He's even offered to take them himself, as scheduled, if that's what the client wishes!'

'Absolutely Susan!' Steve exclaimed.

'How kind of you,' Susan said, trying not to sound too insincere. 'Look, Steve,' she continued firmly. 'You do understand how important it is to look after Dixie properly, don't you?'

'Of course I do, Susan! I know how much Dixie means to you, and it will be a privilege to take care of him for a few days – don't you worry!'

'Well, I hope you *do* know how much he means to me,' Susan replied, slightly menacingly.

'Absolutely! That's sorted then!' Steve was beginning to enjoy watching Susan Carmichael squirm a little. He didn't think she had a vulnerable side or an Achilles Heel up until this point in time. *Good*, Steve thought: Susan would have to be civil to him for the next couple of days, and that would suit his plans just nicely.

Susan walked back into her clinic, unimpressed and unconvinced by what she had just listened to. By this stage, Steve Morgan was on the phone to Madeleine Singleton in his private surgery, and Ray Carmichael was checking the Appointment Page on the computer screen in Reception (Epsilon's dental nurses and Receptionist always came in slightly later on a Tuesday, due to it being traditionally quiet). Ray could see that he had a client booked in at 10.00 a.m., while Susan had a set of veneers to fit shortly after that. Steve's schedule appeared to be clear until 2.00 p.m.

Ray knocked on the door of Susan's surgery and entered to find her sobbing at her desk. 'For God's sake, Susan – what's the matter?' he asked, as he walked towards his wife.

'I just get a really bad feeling about all of this, Ray. I want you to phone that Eden place and cancel the booking. I'm not going, and that's that,' she said decisively.

'Listen,' Ray replied firmly, as he took a seat beside Susan. 'We're going, and that's final, Susan. We both need a break away from here, and the booking has been made and a deposit paid.'

'But I'm not happy about leaving Dixie with *him*.'

'Oh, pull yourself together, Susan. The dog will be fine,' Ray said, gesturing to the huge notice board above Susan's desk, which was plastered with photos of Dixie. 'No matter how low your opinion of Steve is, he's perfectly capable of administering a few dog biscuits. It's not exactly rocket science, is it?'

'Well, you had better be right, Ray. Or I'll *never* forgive you.'

'Right.' Ray was determined to make their weekend break go ahead. 'Now go and sort yourself out before your first appointment arrives. And please just start looking forward for a change, Susan.' It still made Ray Carmichael feel very uneasy, watching his wife get herself into such emotional states; although he was conscious that this particular week of the year was always a very challenging one for Susan.

* * * * *

Steve Morgan pulled into his gravel driveway at 6.30 p.m. that evening. He drove in the darkness towards his luxurious, double-fronted Victorian detached residence, which was located at an exclusive address in London TW9.

Steve had finished work at 3.00 p.m. that day, after his only appointment; but he had met Madeleine Singleton in a nearby hotel for drinks, before eventually returning home.

Steve's wife, Amanda, recognised the crunch of her husband's Land Rover wheels on the driveway. She was making her way around the kitchen's granite work surfaces with anti-bacterial spray and a cloth when she spotted him pulling up at the garage across from the kitchen's large glass conservatory annex. Steve's arrival did not particularly fill Amanda with excitement; it hadn't done in about nineteen years – only one year short of the entire duration of their marriage. Amanda knew that Steve was a rampant womaniser and adulterer, but she had given up on caring much about what he did now. She had only really stuck with him this long for the sake of their nineteen-year-old daughter, Charlotte; but Amanda felt that Charlotte was old enough and strong enough now to cope with her parents' marital breakdown – so it would probably only be a matter of time. Now that Amanda and Steve had both recently turned forty, Amanda was resolved to steer her life in a new direction.

'I'm home!' Steve announced, as he walked through the back door, into the Morgans' large kitchen area. 'God, Amanda. This place smells more like a clinic than the dental surgery,' he said, screwing up his face.

'Well it's better than living in a pig sty, isn't it?' Amanda retorted. Steve's wife was obsessed with cleanliness and hygiene, although she had relaxed a bit in recent times – allowing the odd bunch of flowers into the house. Amanda's former psychotherapist, Adam, had helped her work out that her hygiene obsession had stemmed from her difficult childhood: the fact that her mother had died when Amanda was only six, leaving her an only child, and reliant on her millionaire father, Sir Horace Montgomery, owner of a large London department store. Sir Horace immediately offloaded Amanda onto his wife's sister, Matilda, whose sudden death, when Amanda was only nineteen, left her bereft – so much so that she found herself in the arms of the charming and handsome Steve Morgan, then a First-Year dental student.

Amanda married Steve only a year later, and they were madly in love with each other for the first few months of their marriage – until things started to go wrong. Steve began to distance himself from Amanda, although he still loved being hitched to Amanda's massive wealth, not to mention having the most stunningly gorgeous, platinum-blonde, blue-eyed, confident, well-bred woman in London by his side throughout dental school. Those Montgomery connections certainly ensured that Steve sailed through all his dental exams with minimal effort. He repaid the favour by starting a string of extra-marital affairs shortly after Charlotte's birth.

'What's for tea?' Steve asked Amanda.

'Sally left a pot of King Prawn Curry on the AGA for you,' Amanda replied, referring to the Morgans' full-time cook and house keeper.

'Is Charlotte at home?'

'Upstairs.'

'Great! I have a nice surprise for her.'

'What sort of surprise?' Amanda asked suspiciously. Amanda knew that Steve was up to something, but she couldn't quite put her finger on it yet. 'I'll tell her when she comes downstairs,' Steve replied. 'Charlotte!'

There was a pause. Amanda threw her husband a look of disgust as he started tucking into his King Prawn Curry.

'Charlotte!' Steve shouted loudly again.

'What?' an impatient voice yelled from an upstairs bedroom.

'Come here! I need to talk to you!'

Shuffling and thumping noises could now be heard above the kitchen, as Charlotte began to make her way out of her bedroom, where she had been updating her *MyVaneSpace* profile, and checking her messages on the *Twopenniesworth* website: she was an avid social networker.

'Whatever you're up to, Steve, you're not involving Charlotte,' Amanda snapped.

'I'm not up to anything,' Steve protested. 'I've sorted out a bit of work for her, that's all'.

'She already has a job.'

'You mean the ten hours a week she stands behind a cosmetics counter in your father's store? You call that *work*, Amanda?' Steve laughed.

'You bloody hypocrite!' Amanda snapped back angrily. 'You haven't done a day's work in your life – you lazy, freeloading waste of space!'

'Yeah, yeah, yeah,' Steve mocked. 'She should never have been allowed to walk out of her A Level studies half way through. You've always been far too easy on her, Amanda.'

'You moron!' Amanda snarled quietly, sensing Charlotte's imminent approach. 'Of course I'm easy on her. I love her. I'm her mother, you know? But then you're such a self-centred prick you wouldn't have a clue about caring for anyone other than yourself – would you?' Amanda was furious: she really felt like strangling her husband at times like this.

'What do you want?' Charlotte demanded of Steve as she entered the kitchen.

'Don't speak to me with that tone, Charlotte.' Steve was becoming increasingly annoyed by his daughter's dismissive attitude towards him. 'Sit down and I'll tell you what I want,' he said, more calmly this time.

Charlotte glanced over at her mother, who rolled her eyes in solidarity with her daughter. The two women were staunch allies – especially when it came to Steve. Although Charlotte did not really know about her father's womanising ways, she was nevertheless fiercely protective of her mother, whom she realised had raised her practically single-handedly. Amanda had always been determined to lavish her daughter with all the maternal love and protection she had missed out on after her own mother's death.

'I have a bit of a treat for you!' Steve announced.

'Oh?' Charlotte replied, unimpressed, albeit curious.

'Ray and Susan Carmichael are going away for a few days this weekend, and they'd like you to look after their dog – Dixie – for them!' Steve enthused.

There was a stunned pause from Steve's daughter and wife.

'What?' Charlotte yelled in disgust.

'You heard me, Charlotte!' Steve said, trying to sound natural. 'Ray and Susan's dog – Dixie – they'd like you to take it for walks and feed it while they go off for a break this weekend. Thursday to Sunday.'

'Why the hell would they ask Charlotte to look after their dog?' Amanda snapped.

'Because she'd do a brilliant job. And she's free on those days. That dog means the world to Ray and Susan, you know?' Steve was trying to sound genuinely concerned about the Carmichaels.

'Well I don't want to look after their stupid dog! I don't even like dogs,' Charlotte protested.

'You don't have to like dogs to look after dogs, Charlotte,' Steve said, trying to sound philosophical.

'Since when did you give a shit about Susan Carmichael, Steve? Never mind her dog?' Amanda asked suspiciously.

'Amanda, it's like this. The Carmichaels have told me they're going away for a few days. I have to keep the practice afloat. Someone has to look after the stupid dog, because Susan wants it to stay in the comfortable surroundings of its own home.' Steve was getting rattled. He had realised he would be up against it when he hatched his plan on the journey home that evening. It was always two against one in the Morgan household; and Steve and Amanda were never on the same team. Steve was accustomed to using underhand methods to get his own way. He knew he was unanimously unpopular, and he soon tired when his nice-guy approach didn't work. 'Charlotte. You're looking after the dog, and that's that,' Steve said, irked.

'For God's sake!' Amanda was appalled.

'It's OK, Mum,' Charlotte laughed. 'So what's in it for me then, dad? Are the Carmichaels *paying* me for my services?'

'*I* would agree to pay you a fee to look after the dog for them. What would you like?' Steve's only way of connecting with his daughter tended to be through bribes and buy-offs. He didn't seem to know Charlotte very well: he had always been busy at work. Steve would have liked to have known her better, he thought at times. Charlotte was so like her mother had been, when Steve first met Amanda, at the same age. The two women - even now - looked more like glamorous sisters than mother and daughter. But Steve knew that he had burnt his bridges with both of them. He didn't have a look-in.

'I want a bedroom makeover,' Charlotte announced.

'OK,' Steve stated nonchalantly. He always criticised his wife for over-indulging Charlotte and encouraging her high-maintenance ways. *Like mother, like daughter*, he thought dismissively. *Trot mare, trot foal*. Although Steve did admit to enjoying the finer things in life himself; it was just that he worked hard for them, in his opinion.

'And my computer needs a colonic,' Charlotte added.

'What do you mean your computer needs a *colonic*?' Steve was genuinely puzzled.

'It's all bunged up or something. I think its memory is full up.'

Steve rolled his eyes in despair. This was exactly the reason why he had wanted Charlotte to continue at school. His daughter had a good grasp of beauty terminology and text language, he conceded, but she had certainly not exceeded academically. If Charlotte and her mother had spent a bit less time socialising, networking and preening themselves, Steve thought, trying to justify his absence in the Morgan household over the years, they might have been a bit more interesting to be around.

'So you'll be very busy at the Dental Spa over the next couple of days, you say?' Amanda enquired of Steve: she always had a keen interest in the business.

'Absolutely!' Steve replied, trying to sound convincing. He began to walk over to the fridge to fetch a bottle of sauvignon blanc to settle in for a night's television viewing.

'You'll not know what's hit you then. You're so accustomed to letting Susan and Ray steer the ship for you.' It had been Amanda's idea to involve the Carmichaels in the Epsilon Dental Spa venture when it first launched, just over ten years ago. Steve would have been a vulnerability acting as a stand-alone dental surgeon by that stage of his career: his laziness meant that he needed professionals working alongside him, if the business was to succeed. It annoyed and angered Amanda to think about that fact. Steve had once been academic, intelligent and diligent; but marrying into Montgomery wealth had led him to be complacent, arrogant and idle. Steve secretly recognised this himself, and it sometimes irked him, but he soon brushed these thoughts aside when they entered his head.

Amanda had a good business head. This came from her Montgomery genes. She had realised back then that investing part of her inheritance money into a cosmetic dental practice would make good economic sense, given the times they were living in. She credited a lot of the practice's financial success to the Carmichaels, of course. Amanda realised they were smart, level-headed people, and it was a cause of some embarrassment to her that Ray and Susan had to tolerate Steve and his ways, even though the Carmichaels had profited from their position as business partners in the practice.

Ray was very steady and easy-going, Amanda thought. Susan was a tough character– she was so forthright and smart. Amanda was glad to have Susan at the helm to keep Steve and the business in check. She thought it a pity that Susan had piled on so much weight since her student days, having been such a slim-line brunette beauty back then. Amanda also felt sad that Susan had lost her baby all those years ago, having lost one herself. She even tried to understand Susan's ever-so-over-the-top obsession with her dog, Dixie; although she found it a bit unhygienic that Susan displayed so many pictures of him in her surgery. Even Amanda, as proprietor of the Dental Spa, didn't fancy the thought of having her teeth done with all that dog hair on show, and it worried Amanda that it might put off some of the practice's wealthier clients. 'Are you sure you're OK with looking after the dog?' Amanda asked Charlotte, as Steve disappeared from the kitchen with his bottle of wine, leaving his half-eaten dinner on the kitchen table.

'No I'm bloody not!' Charlotte grumbled, staring intently into her mobile phone at her updated MyVaneSpace page. 'But it will keep *him* off my back, won't it?'

'I guess.'

'Do you really think the Carmichaels asked for me to do their dog-sitting?' Charlotte asked Amanda, who was by now busy clearing up Steve's dishes and wiping down the table Charlotte was slouched at.

'Of course they didn't! It's just that your father is too sodding lazy to walk the dog himself. God knows what he'll be up to while the Carmichaels are away – it certainly won't be work.'

'Right mum. I'm going round to Ebony's house for a while. I'll be back around nine.' Charlotte suddenly got up from the kitchen table.

'OK Charlotte,' Amanda replied, a bit annoyed at herself for having lashed out so much against Steve in her daughter's presence. 'I'll see you later then. I think I'll go upstairs and have a nice bath and put a face mask on. I'm going to Flic's art exhibition in town tomorrow.'

'Lucky you. I have to work tomorrow morning,' Charlotte said resentfully, as she fetched her designer leather coat from the stand beside the conservatory doors.

'I would treat you to lunch tomorrow afternoon Charlotte, except I have an appointment I have to keep.'

'No worries, Mum. I think I might do some shopping then anyway. See you later.' Charlotte exited the conservatory door.

'Take care, darling!' Amanda shouted, as the door shut behind her daughter.

Amanda continued to disinfect the kitchen work surfaces for another few minutes before she went upstairs for the evening.

As she cleaned, she began to think about how she would find the right time to finally end her marriage to Steve. She was finding it more and more difficult to bottle her negative feelings towards him, and she realised that Charlotte was increasingly picking up on this. Amanda sensed that Charlotte would be ready and able to cope with her father's absence in the house by this stage of her life; although Amanda needed the perfect opportunity to make this happen; to allow Amanda to move forward, exonerated. She also needed time to discuss her new choice of companion with Charlotte, and it was this aspect that worried Amanda the most. She loved her daughter more than anything else in the world, and she wanted to protect her from as much hurt and harm as possible. Amanda was very confused, however. If Charlotte didn't like the idea of her new companion, it would have to end: Amanda was resolved on this.

*****

As Amanda Morgan prepared for her bath, mulling over all of these thoughts in her head, Susan Carmichael was watching a documentary called *Rogue Solicitors*, at her elegant Edwardian detached home in TW9, only three streets away from the Morgans' house.

Dixie was sitting peacefully and contentedly on Susan's lap. He secretly smiled at the events that had just occurred in the Morgan household, as he sensed the grand design slowly but surely unfolding.

-CHAPTER THREE-

Dixie's Challenging Day

Susan Carmichael awoke the next morning with profound sadness in her heart. It was Wednesday 5th October, and she should have been celebrating her son Jacob's eighth birthday.

Susan dreaded this day of the year more than any other. Although her son had been born too early, on a warm morning in early June, Susan had always considered October 5th as Jacob's real birthday: it had been his due date.

As long, angry tears rolled heavily down Susan's face, Dixie was already sitting upright in his basket at the foot of her bed, prepared for a challenging day ahead.

He had first entered Susan's life on this exact day, three years ago. It had been Dixie's destiny to do so. Some would say that Dixie had drawn the short straw by getting paired with Susan Carmichael – but he certainly didn't view it like that. He had known Susan before he even met her, and he had been fully versed on all the traumas she had been through.

In comparison to Dixie, his three siblings had been given relatively easy challenges: John and Mary Cocker from Luton were boring, predictable types, and demanded very little in the way of emotional support from Millie and Billy; while Coco Wright simply wanted a companion to chat to while her socialite mother entertained her business associates at home in Brighton – a cinch of a role for Angelica.

Dixie understood Susan's predicament totally. He knew that she was suffering from a terrible form of grief.

It had all begun when Susan lost her son, Jacob.

Those looking down on her from the invisible realms had reckoned that Susan would successfully conceive and deliver another baby within a year of this terrible event, but it had not been foreseen that she would take Jacob's loss so badly.

Susan's confident and forthright exterior completely belied the fact that she had a very brittle interior; so brittle, in fact, that her soul had almost completely shattered when she discovered that Jacob had gone. Susan's ability to cope with such a loss had been grossly miscalculated, it was clearly recognised now.

Many attempts had been made to intervene and help Susan since Jacob's passing to the invisible realms, but none had really worked. Nobody seemed to have been able to say the right thing to her; to encourage her; to cajole her into recognising that Jacob had simply had to leave because his physical body was too weak. Surely Susan would see that and move on?

And yet, Susan had found herself in such a dark and hopeless place after Jacob's passing - she was unable to read any of the signs, or recognise any potential for a happy future.

That's why Dixie came on the scene. It was decided that Susan needed more than just human intervention to help her move her life forward: she required an animal guide too.

The seed for this plan was deliberately planted in Ray Carmichael's mind three years ago, when his eyes were drawn to an article in a magazine he was reading, as he sat in a hospital waiting room. Susan was undergoing emergency surgery to have her appendix removed at the time. Outside, it was a cold and wet September day.

The article Ray was reading was entitled 'Animal Therapy'; and it discussed how animals could be used to help people grieve the loss of a loved one. Fortunately, Ray was reliably responsive to this deliberate prompt. He subsequently convinced Susan to get a dog – an idea she had previously fought against – thanks mainly to her sudden bout of appendicitis, which had (conveniently) rendered her weak and more open to persuasion.

Susan eventually decided that she would like a West Highland Terrier pup – mainly because they were small, manageable, and could live happily within the confines of the Carmichaels' elegant Edwardian home and its modest-sized walled back garden.

Ray went on an immediate Internet search for a prospective pup, before Susan could change her mind, and he was automatically drawn to the 'Candy Pups' website, simply because he had always had a sweet tooth.

Surely enough, a litter of pedigree West Highland Terrier pups had been born at Candy Pups only a month or so previous, and they would be ready to be re-homed in a matter of weeks. *Perfect!* Ray had thought, as he lifted the phone to call Jill and Phil Candy, who happily informed him that one male pup had yet to be found a home. Ray placed his order for the pup there and then, and he gave his details to Phil Candy, who, along with his wife Jill, played their part in ensuring that Dixie and Susan Carmichael's lives became joined over the next few weeks – so ending their involvement in the plan.

And so Dixie's destiny was sealed: he was to console Susan Carmichael during her darkest hours as she continued to grieve for Jacob, and listen to the outpourings of her broken heart and soul. Although Dixie realised that he would never fully touch the depths of Susan's despair, at least now she would have someone to talk to; to cuddle; to love her; to listen to her – when she couldn't find the words to talk to another human being.

Dixie knew how Susan felt, more than anyone else on the planet, but he was to fulfil an even wider role during his short life on earth – a life that was about to end soon.

At the age of thirty-nine, Susan Carmichael was still destined to have children (two of them, in fact), but she had to grasp that opportunity soon, before she missed her chance entirely.

Dixie had been rather pleased with the progress he had made with Susan thus so far, and Ray had done sterling work in persuading Susan to go away and leave Dixie with the Morgans this weekend – albeit that he *had* cheated by using the red wine.

It was now up to Dixie to put the final pieces of the scheme into place, however. Susan and Ray Carmichaels' happiness depended on it - but the happiness of other lives was also at stake. Dixie had always known that the next phase of his existence would be just as significant as the three years he had just spent with Susan Carmichael – just in a different way, perhaps; and now that the Morgans had eventually been brought on board, it was time for the remaining players to engage in the plot. Timing had to be perfect, given the delicate nature of the plan that was afoot, not to mention the variety of people involved. Everything had been synchronised perfectly up to this point in time, and it was felt that Susan Carmichael was (at last) ready to embrace her future.

It was no coincidence that Wednesday 5th October was chosen as the day to kick-start the series of future events that were about to unfold. Dixie knew full well how emotionally sensitive Susan was on this day of the year, so if anything was going to affect her soul profoundly, it would have to occur on this day.

Dixie jumped onto Susan and Ray's bed, and immediately proceeded to walk up to Susan's face, which was by now sore, red and damp from crying. Ray was still snoring – it was still rather dark at 6.30 a.m. in the morning – so Susan could feel comfortable confiding her feelings to Dixie now.

'Oh Dixie,' she whispered. 'This should have been Jacob's eighth birthday today.' Susan stroked Dixie's lovely white face, as his eyes gazed tenderly into hers. She almost felt as though Dixie understood what she was telling him. 'I miss him so much, Dixie. *Why* did all of this have to happen?'

Dixie tenderly mopped up Susan's tears with his gristly pink tongue, bringing an immediate smile to her face.

'Do you think Jacob knows it's his birthday today, Dixie?'

Dixie immediately let out a little yelp.

'Do you really think so?' Susan stroked Dixie's fur in gratification and relief at his response.

At this point, Ray awoke. He looked at the silver watch on his wrist, which told him that it was 6.45 a.m. Ray turned around to find Susan being comforted by Dixie beside her, and he immediately joined in, by wrapping his right arm softly around Susan's broad shoulders.

'Are you O.K. Susan?' Ray asked gently.

'Jacob would have been eight today,' Susan replied, still cuddling Dixie.

'I know, Susan. I know.'

'Do you think he's alright Ray? I mean – Jacob does know that we still love him, doesn't he?' Susan turned her face away from Dixie's and towards her husband's. Before Ray had a chance to reply, Dixie had already begun to bark cheerfully. Susan and Ray both looked at each other and laughed. 'I think that's your answer, Susan. That dog seems to know more about this life than we do,' Ray said philosophically.

'I know.'

'Listen, Susan,' Ray said, more seriously this time. 'I know this is the worst of days for you – and me. But let's try to be more positive about it this year, shall we? I mean, I'm sure Jacob would want us to be happy on his birthday. So why don't you treat yourself to an afternoon shopping – instead of coming back here after work and being alone and sad?' Ray was now treading very carefully, into very sensitive territory. Susan always took the afternoon of Jacob's birthday off work. She liked to go in to the surgery in the morning to feel useful, but for the remainder of the day, she preferred to be at home, alone.

Dixie began to bark enthusiastically and lick Susan's face.

'You see,' Ray said, smiling. Even Dixie thinks you should go out and enjoy yourself.'

'Are you trying to tell me something, Dixie?' Susan asked, half laughing, half concerned.

'Susan,' Ray said tenderly. 'It's O.K. to enjoy yourself, you know? You have nothing to feel guilty about today.'

Susan looked at Ray, unconvinced. She always felt guilty and inadequate - especially on this day of the year. Guilty: that she had perhaps done something wrong to make Jacob go. Inadequate: that she couldn't even function as a woman should, and   produce   a   baby.

Dixie knew that no-one would ever fill the huge and painful void left in Susan Carmichael's life after her son Jacob's departure; not even her potential future babies, in fact. Yet he did know that Susan *could* feel happiness in her life again - although Susan needed to go out this afternoon, to ensure that future events would unfold in the way they were destined.

Dixie had to think fast. It would look too suspicious if he started doing somersaults and back flips to get Susan's attention at this stage of their relationship, so he had to think of a more subtle approach.

Dixie quickly scanned the Carmichaels' bedroom, where he spotted Susan's handbag lying on top of a wooden rocking chair. He immediately pounced across the room and landed beside it, panting and barking for a more dramatic effect.

'Ray – look!' Susan exclaimed, sitting upright in her bed.

'I think the dog is trying to tell you something, Susan!'

'You clever dog! Do you want to go out with me this afternoon?' If anyone brought out Susan's soft, maternal side, it was Dixie.

'Well. I think you've been as good as told, Susan!' Ray laughed.

'OK then. I suppose I do have to get a few things for going away tomorrow.'

'Great!' Ray was genuinely delighted that his wife had decided to live a little, on a day when she had traditionally, for the last eight years, withdrawn so deeply inside herself. Ray had to admit that Dixie had to take most credit for Susan's change of heart on this occasion. It was almost as though the dog knew something, he thought.

As Susan and Ray got out of bed to prepare for the day ahead, Dixie lounged on top of Susan's tear-stained pillow and congratulated himself on a job well done.

'Dixie is such a special dog, Ray,' Susan said reflectively.

'I know. We were meant to have Dixie, I think. It's three years today since we got him, isn't it?'

'God – yes!' Susan suddenly recalled how nervous and anxious she had been when she first met Dixie, all those months ago. She had felt particularly weepy and emotional on that occasion – given that it was Jacob's fifth birthday. 'Oh Ray,' she suddenly said in a worried tone of voice. 'Do you really think Dixie will be OK with Steve Morgan?'

'Of course he will, Susan,' Ray said. 'Won't you, boy?'

Here we go again, thought Dixie. He barked and did a cute little roll on Susan's warm pillow to convince her that she was right to entrust him to Steve Morgan the next day. It seemed to work, as Susan turned to Ray in amazement and relief and laughed. 'Well. I suppose that's my answer then!' Susan trusted Dixie's opinion more than anyone else's.

*****

When the Carmichaels eventually left their house for work that morning, it had been agreed that Susan would return there after lunch to collect Dixie to go shopping. Dixie made Susan feel close to Jacob, for some reason, and it was Jacob's birthday, after all.

As the door slammed behind Ray and Susan, Dixie walked over to his porcelain water bowl on the Carmichaels' marble-tiled kitchen floor, and took a long drink from it.

He went upstairs again to his basket at the base of Ray and Susan's luxurious king-size bed, and snuggled in for his regular morning nap.

Before he eventually drifted off, Dixie began to think about the moments and days that lay ahead. He did feel slightly guilty about the fact that he had persuaded Susan to leave him with Steve Morgan. She had been right to worry that something might go wrong with her dog while she went away for the weekend, but it *had* to happen for her future happiness – not to mention the happiness of the other individuals Dixie had yet to be fully introduced to.

Sleep, Dixie told himself. He knew the afternoon that lay ahead would be a very significant one.

*****

Susan arrived back at home at 1.30 p.m. She entered the elegant hallway to her house, and hung up her coat on the mahogany stand by the front door. She had only been through the door a few seconds when Dixie came bounding down the stairs to greet her. 'Hello pal!' Susan said excitedly. 'Are you ready for our shopping trip this afternoon?'

'Woof!' Dixie replied, eager to convince Susan not to change her mind.

'OK then! We'll just grab some snacks and leave soon.'

Susan carried Dixie into the large open-plan kitchen at the rear of the house. She was particularly fond of this room, as she had designed and created it herself. In fact, Susan had a real talent for interior design. She had poured her entire self into decorating and furnishing her home: the project had kept her occupied over the last number of difficult years. She felt safe and cocooned in this space.

Susan had also developed something of a passion for gardening in recent years – thanks mainly to Dixie, who had introduced her, through his walks, to the 'great outdoors'. She loved to spend time with Dixie out in their back garden, where Dixie had a special fondness for a particular large Oak, which he would lie under on sunny days. Susan had planted several 'Jacob's Ladder' plants nearby the Oak tree. She had happened upon these plants one day when she was attending a car boot sale, at the nearby Unity Park. Susan had never heard of this plant before – but when she saw that it was called after her son; and that it bloomed beautiful bell-shaped, lavender-blue flowers, every year, at around the time Jacob was delivered – in June – Susan had to buy the several Jacob's Ladder plants the eccentric-looking, very talkative lady seller had on offer that day. When Susan had paid for the plants, the lady informed Susan that the particular type of Jacob's Ladder plants she had purchased were called 'Stairway to Heaven'. This had made Susan smile, even though Susan wasn't a very spiritual person. When the lady then went on to tell Susan that 'Jacob's Ladder' was the ladder to heaven, as described in the Book of Genesis – Susan almost began to think that her son was trying to tell her something; although she realised this was probably just wishful thinking.

As well as Unity Park, Dixie had also led Susan to explore several other lovely locations, such as the highly manicured Regal Park. It was as though Dixie had allowed Susan to feel glimmers of sunlight in her soul again, when he led her into nature.

Susan fetched some food for Dixie from a cupboard beneath the kitchen sink and placed it in a bowl for him. As he munched into it, Susan got her handbag and put some doggie treats inside it for later. She grabbed a large piece of banana cake from the larder and ate it quickly, before grabbing her bag from the marble work surface, and walking towards Dixie. 'Come on boy! Let's get this on you.' Susan took a red, yellow and black tartan dog lead from her handbag, which had Dixie's name elaborately embroidered on it with white silk thread. She linked the lead's golden hook onto the red leather collar around Dixie's neck, which also had Dixie's name etched on a smart gold band in the centre. Susan had numerous leads and collars for Dixie – all different designs and colours. She felt it only proper that Dixie should have ample changes in outfit, just like any other person did.

Susan lifted Dixie from the kitchen floor and put him under her left arm, swinging her handbag over her right shoulder. She walked into the hallway once more and placed her bag on the parquet wooden floor, as she got her coat from the stand beside the front door and put it on. Susan then lifted her bag again, took a look at herself and Dixie in the large hall mirror, and went out the front door to start her short walk to the shops.

Dixie was well used to this routine when Susan went shopping. He understood that Susan didn't care much for being out in public now – except really when she was working. She had felt a bit paranoid and self-conscious since losing Jacob, and she much preferred to stay within the safe confines of her own home or work place – although she did like to go walking in quiet parks and other nature locations with Dixie. Susan was also well aware that she had gained some weight due to comfort-eating over the years, and she tended to dress conservatively, so as not to draw too much attention to herself. Dixie knew that Susan was inclined to make all of her public outings as short as possible, so he realised that he had to act quickly and decisively this afternoon to ensure that things went according to plan.

Susan's preferred shopping street was only a few minutes' walk from her home. She always liked to carry Dixie most of the way to the shops, almost as though he was a comfort blanket. When she did place him on the ground to walk at times, he would totter alongside her at a lightening pace. Susan was tall and ample in stride, so Dixie's short legs had to work rapidly to keep in tow with her.

Susan viewed shopping as a 'must-do' exercise, as opposed to a pleasurable past time. She always went to the shops with a carefully drawn-up list, and she rarely, if ever, digressed from this. She had worked out that she only had three places to visit today: the pharmacy, for some multivitamins for herself and Ray; the pet shop, for some weekend snacks for Dixie, which she would give to Steve Morgan tomorrow; and the post office, to buy a couple of stamps. Susan liked to keep things practical when it came to shopping - plus, she wasn't able to bring Dixie into most shops, which suited her fine.

After she had bought her stamps and purchased the dog biscuits, Susan scooped Dixie into her arms and entered the pharmacy – her last shop of the day. She paid for her multivitamins at the counter by the door, after incurring a few dirty looks from the cashier for bringing Dixie into the store, she knew. Susan exited the pharmacy, placed Dixie on the ground again, held his tartan lead, and began to walk in the direction of home.

Dixie knew he had to act soon. He needed to introduce Susan to someone nearby. This was to be a 'chance' meeting for Susan – although Dixie fully understood that there was really no such thing as 'chance' or 'coincidence'. In fact, the encounter that was (hopefully) about to happen had been planned by those residing in the invisible realms many weeks back, unbeknown to Susan and her new acquaintance; and it was (hopefully) to have profound implications for each of their future lives.

As Susan marched purposefully towards the road that would eventually take her home, Dixie suddenly ceased to trot behind her. It took all his might to pull against the momentum Susan had built up in her stride, to make her realise that she had to stop in her tracks. 'What's up, Dixie?' she asked him as she turned around, a little perplexed.

Dixie had stopped directly outside a dog-friendly café that he and Susan had visited occasionally in the past. Although Susan did not particularly enjoy going out socially any more, Dixie knew that she liked 'Paws for Thought' because it was a little dowdy, very relaxed and completely unpretentious. She felt comfortable in her own skin in this place, and she could enjoy quality time with Dixie there too, without feeling very self-conscious at all. 'Come on, Dixie!' Susan said, tugging lightly at his tartan lead.

Dixie resisted. He began to pull Susan in the direction of the café, and although he did not have a mission of actually pulling her one millimetre from her spot, she nevertheless realised where her small companion was trying to lead her. 'You little rascal!' Susan laughed, thinking that Dixie simply wanted her to bring him into the café for a sugary snack, as she had done before on occasions.

Dixie knew that he had to mount a massive charm offensive soon if he was to convince Susan to go into the café. Her head was full of thoughts of Jacob at this time, and she desperately wanted to go home to cry. 'Whimper, whimper,' Dixie said, pulling the cutest doggie expression he could muster.

Susan melted, in spite of herself. 'Well. OK then. I guess a few more minutes won't hurt.' Susan scooped Dixie firmly from the pavement and cuddled him under her left arm once more, before marching into the café with him.

Result, Dixie thought.

As Susan made her way through the front door of Paws for Thought, she immediately noticed that it was unusually busy today; so busy, in fact, that there didn't appear to be a spare table in the place.

Just as she was about to turn on her heels and make a quick exit, Dixie sprang into action. He gathered as much power as he could into his hind legs, and pushed himself away from Susan's clutches. Before she had time to react, Dixie had sprung across the floor and made his way over to a table near the window, where he took an empty seat opposite the person he had been anticipating meeting.

The plan had been perfectly executed so far, Dixie thought to himself. It had been correctly reckoned that Susan would only ever talk to this individual – who was a complete stranger to her, and vice versa – if she was forced to make contact with him. It just so happened (purely by coincidence, of course) that a group of international tourists had been scheduled to have afternoon tea in a hotel nearby that day, but the hotel had unfortunately been forced to close due to a sudden power cut (another coincidence). The tourist contingent had therefore been relocated to Paws for Thought, which had delighted them, as they found it quaintly British, and therefore a very authentic tourist experience. They had filled every table in this rather small establishment - except for the one by the window that had already been occupied by Matthew Rourke, earlier that morning.

Matthew was now sitting directly opposite Dixie Carmichael.

'Come here right now!' Susan Carmichael ordered Dixie, flustered by the busy and noisy environment she now unexpectedly found herself in.

'Woof!' Dixie replied, refusing to budge an inch from his seat by the window.

'Come here!' she ordered, a bit rattled.

'Woof! Woof!' Dixie answered back, defiantly.

Susan was reluctantly forced to walk over to the window to fetch her dog.

'He's a determined little thing, isn't he?' Matthew Rourke said cheerfully to Susan Carmichael, as she stood by his table, beckoning to her stubborn, mischievous West Highland Terrier. 'He doesn't usually do this sort of thing,' Susan replied, bewildered - and very eager to get away from Paws for Thought as soon as possible.

'Woof! Woof! Woof!' Dixie insisted. He was really beginning to irritate Susan now.

'Listen,' Matthew Rourke said. 'Why don't you sit down with him and order something? I don't mind sharing a table.'

'Woof! (multiplied by four!)' Dixie responded, sensing (hopefully) that Susan might have to stop on a while.

Susan Carmichael was so beside herself by this stage, she hardly knew what she was doing or saying. She wasn't fond of small, crowded rooms. Susan much preferred spending time in large open spaces with Dixie – like in gardens, parks or woodland areas.

Matthew Rourke immediately sensed Susan's panic and vulnerability. He stood up and gently guided her into his now empty chair. 'Are you OK?' he asked kindly, as he bent down beside her.

'Em, yes,' Susan replied. 'I just get a bit panicky in noisy, enclosed spaces.' Susan was feeling light-headed. She hadn't even looked at Matthew Rourke's face by this stage of their encounter.

'I'm going to go and get you a glass of water,' Matthew said, a little concerned at Susan Carmichael's greyish pallor. 'Wait here.'

As Matthew Rourke walked up to the counter at the far end of Paws for Thought, Susan sat on at the table and began to compose herself. She became dead to her surroundings, and thoughts of Jacob began to fill her mind once more. Dixie decided to let her have this quiet moment to herself. *I should be celebrating his eighth birthday with him today*, Susan thought sadly. She could hardly believe that those eight years had passed by at all, and yet, they felt like a lifetime to her at the same time. All a horrible cold and empty blur.

'Here you go,' a caring voice said to her. 'Drink this.'

Susan looked up at Matthew Rourke, as though she was just coming out of a daze. 'Thanks.' Susan took the glass of water from his hand. 'I don't know what came over me.'

Matthew took the seat opposite Susan, beside Dixie. 'I think you were about to faint,' Matthew said. 'You should blame this little fellow here!'

Susan took a sip of cold water from her long glass and swallowed hard. After she had begun to feel a little less light-headed, she looked up at Matthew Rourke properly for the first time. 'This place looks like an airport today,' Susan said, like she had just been suddenly and mysteriously transported to a distant, faraway location against her own will.

'HaHaHa!' Matthew laughed. 'It's just a bunch of tourists! The waitress told me they had to be relocated from 'The Enigma' – earlier. A power cut or something.'

Susan's eyes were immediately drawn to Matthew Rourke's teeth. She noticed that he had a lovely, genuine smile. A real smile. Not a flash-of-the-teeth, whiter-than-white, I've-just-had-my-veneers-done-smile; but a smile that suddenly made her smile too.

Susan also began to notice the rest of this man now. He was only in his early thirties, she thought; handsome; quite tall and well-built; fair-haired; blue-eyed. He spoke with slight regional accent – Yorkshire or Cumbrian, Susan thought. Most of all though, Susan somehow felt drawn to him; she felt warm in his presence. She almost felt as though she had met him somewhere before. Her soul felt as though it had just begun to thaw. 'Do you own a dog?' Susan suddenly asked Matthew.

'What?' he asked puzzled, reaching over for his half-drunk mug of black tea.

'Do you own a dog?' Susan repeated. 'It's just that I only really come in here because it's dog-friendly.'

'Oh, right! No, I don't. My wife wouldn't allow it.' Matthew was now stroking Dixie, who was sitting to his right.

'So what are you doing in here today?'

Matthew was a little taken aback by his companion's rather forthright manner, but he was quite happy to answer her question, all the same. He didn't know this woman, so he thought he may as well confide the truth in someone. 'Well, it's like this,' he said reflectively. 'I was told I'd lost my job yesterday. I was manager of a designer shoe store in the centre of town – but it's just gone bust,' he said smiling, trying to look for a bright side to his story.

'I'm sorry,' Susan replied, genuinely annoyed for the man.

'I was too chicken to tell my wife last night, so I'm pretending to be at work today – see the suit?' Matthew laughed and pointed at his smart light-grey jacket. 'I thought this was probably the last place I'd bump into anyone I know. '

'That's awful. You're not having a very good day then?'

'No, I'm not!'

'Me neither.'

'And it's my birthday, to boot!'

Susan looked at Matthew meaningfully, as tears began to well up in her eyes. She couldn't believe that she suddenly felt compelled to confide in this stranger. She somehow felt safe, as though she had nothing to fear or lose, by discussing something she never usually discussed with anyone other than Ray or Dixie. 'It's my son's birthday today,' she announced.

'Wow! What age is he?'

'Eight.'

'Are you having a party for him later?' Matthew was a bit curious about why the woman sitting opposite him appeared to be getting very emotional all of a sudden.

'No,' Susan replied. 'He died just before he was born.'

Matthew's face filled with compassion. 'I'm so sorry.' Matthew hardly knew what to do with himself. 'You're having a much worse day than me then. What is your son's name?'

'Jacob,' Susan replied, taking a sip of water.

'Well, I'm sure Jacob loves you being his mum.'

Susan looked up at the man opposite her, hardly able to take in what he had just said. 'Do you really think so?'

'Totally,' Matthew said quietly.

Nobody had ever referred to Susan in the present tense as Jacob's mum before. It was music to her ears. She had never had the chance to really feel like Jacob's real mum – until now. It was as though Jacob was actually still there. She suddenly felt more complete as a person; as a woman; as a *mother*.

'Do you have any other children?' Matthew enquired.

'No.'

'You will,' Matthew stated.

Once again, Susan's companion had taken her aback completely. And for the first time since losing Jacob, Susan actually believed that she *would* have more children. For the first time, she believed that she perhaps even *deserved* to. 'Thanks,' she replied, eternally grateful that she had somehow managed to find herself in the company of this kind and handsome stranger. It was as though he had opened a magical door to her future, Susan thought. She strangely felt like he had been *sent* to meet her that day.

'You'll make a great mum,' Matthew said, with another warm smile.

Susan's face exploded with a radiant smile. She could see it all now. Her future. Her children. Her happiness.

Her entire life had just clicked into place. 'You've just made my day,' Susan said, underemphasising the reality of what she actually meant by her statement.

'You're welcome.' Matthew did not fully understand his companion's meaning.

'Oh, and Happy Birthday!' Susan added. 'What age are you?'

'Thirty-three.'

'What do you think you're going to do – about your job, I mean? And your wife?'

'Well, I suppose I've just got to trust that it will all work out the way it's meant to. I'm a firm believer in the power of fate,' Matthew said philosophically. 'And in invisible forces!'

'Photograph please?' an animated voice interjected.

Susan and Matthew looked up to see a male tourist with a camera around his neck, gesturing towards them and Dixie. 'Photo?' the man repeated in a strong foreign accent, pointing especially at Dixie.

Susan and Matthew looked at each other and giggled. 'Shall we?' Matthew asked Susan.

'Why not!' she laughed, hardly able to believe that she was laughing on this day of all days.

They smiled for the man's camera, but he excitedly insisted that they get up and stand with Dixie beside the Paws for Thought billboard at the door of the café.

'I'm going home now anyway,' Susan said to Matthew, rising from her seat.

'Me too,' Matthew replied with some apprehension in his voice. 'I guess I have to go home and face the music some time.' Matthew got up from his chair and passed Dixie over to Susan Carmichael. 'Nice collar and lead,' he said, referring to Dixie's tartan lead and red collar.

Matthew, Susan and Dixie followed the grateful tourist with the camera out the door of the café, and dutifully stood beside the billboard that had so caught his attention. 'Smile!' he encouraged them.

Susan Carmichael and Matthew Rourke smiled for the camera, as Susan clutched Dixie between them. An audience of around fifty smiling, chatting tourists was now watching on. Susan Carmichael felt as though she was having a weird out-of-body experience.

'One more please!' the photographer demanded.

Susan suddenly felt the need to take her phone out from her handbag. She impulsively handed it over to one of the other international tourists, who took a photo of the happy scene, and handed Susan's phone back, nodding and smiling to her.

Susan and Matthew stood a while longer, giggling like teenagers, before the photographer announced, 'Thank you!' and dismissed them. The entire group of happy tourists then proceeded to walk towards their large coach, which had just pulled up in front of the café, waving and clapping and generally. enjoying themselves.

Susan turned to Matthew, hardly able to believe the series of strange events that had just occurred. 'Well. I guess I'd better start making my way back home again,' Susan said. 'Listen,' she continued. 'I really hope things work out for you.'

'And you too,' Matthew replied, still smiling.

'Goodbye then,' Susan began to turn in the direction of home.

'Bye,' Matthew replied. 'I've quite enjoyed my day people-watching as it happens! I always used to do it as a child. I think I'll go back inside here for one more cup of tea, before I make my way home. Although I could probably do with something a little stronger right now!' he laughed.

Susan Carmichael walked away, smiling. After a short time, she put Dixie onto the pavement and walked beside him, holding his lead. She glanced down at the photograph on her phone, feeling a bit surreal. She somehow knew that this man – this angel – had changed her life forever. *God*, she thought suddenly to herself. *I didn't even find out his name.*

As Dixie walked alongside Susan, struggling to match her pace, he knew that she was deep in thought and oblivious to his presence. He also knew that the photograph Susan was gazing at would be the last one taken of the both of them together.

But Dixie's thoughts had moved to the future already. He recognised that Matthew Rourke had assisted him in sorting out Susan Carmichael's life at last; but it was now up to Dixie to sort out the mess that Matthew Rourke had got his life into. Not to mention Amanda and Charlotte Morgan's, too.

-CHAPTER FOUR-

It's Good to Talk

As Susan Carmichael returned home from her eventful shopping expedition on Wednesday, October 5th, Amanda Morgan was attending an appointment she had made the previous week, at an address in London W5.

She was sitting opposite her psychotherapist, who was listening to her words, and making occasional brief notes.

Amanda had secretively attended similar counselling sessions some eight or so years ago, when she had reached a crisis point in her marriage, after several very unhappy years with Steve. She had been referred to a psychotherapist back then by her private family doctor, Mr. Wells, who had informed her that medication would not sort out her particular personal predicament at the time. Amanda had found those psychotherapy sessions incredibly enlightening, and her then therapist, Adam, had helped her come to terms with her unfulfilling marriage. Adam had in fact suggested that Amanda should perhaps think about breaking up with Steve, but she had resolved nevertheless to stay with Steve, to tolerate his presence – for the sake of their daughter, Charlotte.

Now that she had just turned forty, however, Amanda had decided that enough was finally enough: she wanted a fresh start – without Steve.

Amanda's only problem was that she still worried about Charlotte's feelings. She had concealed the details of Steve's infidelities and wrongdoings from her daughter in the past – to protect Charlotte's happiness, and to allow her to have some sort of a relationship with her father. Steve had blown that opportunity spectacularly, however. He had frequently 'forgotten' to turn up on family occasions in the past; he had stayed away too many nights; he had never turned up for Charlotte's birthdays; and he had generally behaved like the irresponsible, immature prat Amanda realised a long time ago she had married.

Amanda recognised that her family wealth and connections meant that she could dispose of Steve very easily, but she was still somehow anxious about breaking away from him, once and for all. Although Amanda was an outgoing socialite, with multiple acquaintances, she had few real friends or confidantes. Amanda needed someone impartial to help her through this new crossroads in her rather empty life. She could sniff a happy and fulfilling future for herself, just around the corner, and yet, she was still too afraid to grasp it fully with both hands. For some strange reason, she still felt as though she needed to justify ending her marriage. Amanda hoped that her new therapist, Ruth, could help her work towards her (as yet) elusive goal of happiness.

'It sounds as though that made you very angry, Amanda,' Ruth said, three-quarters of the way through Amanda's one-hour appointment.

'Well of course it made me bloody angry. Would it not make *you* angry? – your so-called husband going off to start a whole string of affairs, when you had just given birth to twins – and lost one of them on the very day they were born?'

'That must have felt incredibly difficult for you,' Ruth suggested calmly.

'Steve destroyed me when he did that. I needed him. But he was never there from the moment Matilda - Charlotte's twin - died. I named Matilda after my late aunt.'

'*Destroyed* is a very strong word, Amanda. How do you feel that Steve *destroyed* you?'

'He made me feel like dirt. Like Matilda's death was all my fault. Like I just wanted someone to hold me and take care of me – but nobody was there.' Amanda burst into tears.

Ruth leant forward in her chair. 'Would you like *me* to hold you now, Amanda?'

'Yes please,' Amanda said, sobbing and patting her eyes with the tissue she had just taken from a box on Ruth's desk, which was otherwise bare, except for a small black ceramic pot, containing a dead, cobwebbed cactus plant.

Ruth moved towards Amanda and embraced her for a few moments.

'Thanks,' Amanda said quietly, when Ruth moved back into her chair. For much of her adult life, Amanda had not experienced much in the way of real physical or emotional support: that had all ended a long time ago with Steve.

'You said that Steve made you feel like it was all *your* fault - that your daughter Matilda died?'

'I thought he suddenly hated me – despised me – because he thought I'd done something wrong. Steve always seemed to think that I was just some sort of air head who provided the money. I mean, I know I don't have as much in the way of formal qualifications as he does – but at least I've grown up a bit over the years. Unlike him. He completely underestimates me.'

'You sound as though you want to *prove* yourself to Steve.'

'No. I don't want to *prove* myself to him. Steve is so self-centred and selfish these days – he's lost most of the common sense he was born with. And I'm done with beating myself up over losing Matilda too. I know what happened to her was tragic – but I know now that *I* didn't kill her. *He* should have supported me. He didn't, and I just want to get away from him now.'

'Do you feel as though you need to *justify* leaving Steve?'

Amanda paused for a while before she continued. 'I just need to feel that what I'm doing is right.'

'It sounds as though you think that breaking up with Steve might *not* be right?'

'No, no, no. I'm not really sure. Breaking up with *him* isn't really the problem – I don't think,' Amanda replied. 'I really *do* feel that I could work through that one with Charlotte right now. It's just talking to her about the next bit that I'm worried about.'

'The *next* bit?'

There was another pause. 'I've found a new companion,' Amanda stated guiltily.

'You sound as though you feel *guilty* about that fact.'

'I suppose I do.'

'And *why* do you think you feel guilty about having a new *companion*, Amanda?'

Amanda paused again before she replied. 'Because I can't believe it has happened. That I've found somebody that I feel I can finally trust and confide in. I just want Charlotte to understand that. I'm afraid of Charlotte's reaction when I tell her. I don't want to lose Charlotte. I love her too much. And I don't even know if it's worth taking the risk of telling Charlotte – in case nothing comes from it all.'

'It sounds as though you feel you'd be taking a massive *risk* if you told Charlotte about your new companion.'

'Yes.'

'Do you fear that Charlotte might *reject* you if she finds out?'

'Yes.'

'There must be a reason *why* you feel Charlotte might reject you, perhaps?'

'There is,' Amanda paused. 'But I don't want to talk about that right now.'

Ruth rested her notebook and pen on her lap before speaking to Amanda again. 'Maybe we should think about wrapping the session up now, Amanda?' Ruth suggested, smiling.

'OK.' Amanda was very relieved not to have to pursue these issues any further right now.

'We've made good progress today – do you think?'

'Yes. Thank you.' Amanda was deep in thought once more.

Ruth continued to round off her session with Amanda Morgan, who left her psychotherapist's rather cramped office some minutes later, only a little bit clearer about what she would do in the future.

Amanda descended the narrow set of steps from Ruth's office, which was situated above a bakery, onto the main shopping street beneath. She began the five minute walk back to her car, which would take her to her home a short distance away.

Amanda enjoyed her psychotherapy sessions. It was good to have someone neutral, calm and trustworthy to talk to – although Amanda wouldn't ever tell anyone that she attended these appointments. Living with Steve had made Amanda intensely protective of her deepest thoughts and emotions. She had attempted to lay her feelings bare to her husband, after her daughter, Matilda, died tragically from sudden heart failure, one hour after she was born - but Steve hadn't responded to her cry for help back then. Steve's indifference and distance towards Amanda had made her feel ridiculed, cheapened, and totally undermined as a woman and as a new mother at the time. Amanda was left to look after Charlotte practically single-handedly from the moment Steve had stood by her hospital bed and looked blankly at Amanda, as she held Matilda's tiny body in her arms, and cried broken-heartedly to her young husband.

Steve had said nothing to Amanda on that occasion. *Nothing*.

Steve's frequent AWOL episodes from this point onwards in their marriage had rendered Amanda confused and angry. She threw herself into her role as Charlotte's mother, which she loved; and she ensured that she socialised and networked as much as possible to keep herself occupied. The only adults Amanda had been able to trust or feel close to during all this time, however, had been her psychotherapists, Adam and Ruth; and more recently, her new companion.

Ruth had been correct. The thought of telling Charlotte about the new person in her life filled Amanda with terror. She wanted somebody to help her know that she was making the right decision about Steve and her future. She wished her daughter Matilda was here to help her right now. It was at times like this that Amanda missed Matilda the most.

*****

Meanwhile, as Amanda Morgan got into her car to make the journey home that afternoon, Ruth, her psychotherapist, was filing paperwork away in her office. As she worked, Ruth noticed that a lot of cobwebs had gathered around her office shelves. She would have to complain to her cleaner about this tomorrow morning, she thought.

Ruth had worked as a stand-alone counsellor (or psychotherapist, to all her wealthiest clients) on the premises she rented above 'The Cookie Jug' bakery for almost five years now.

At the age of thirty-five, Ruth felt that she had heard everything there was to hear about failed relationships, obsessions, addictions, phobias, disorders and complexes. She demanded complete and utter professionalism and dedication from herself, and she had never broken any of her clients' confidences.

Although Ruth had only started working as a counsellor six years ago, after having been a hospital receptionist for several years, Ruth's spirit had been well and truly eroded by the demands of her job. She realised that she should have sought help from one of her counselling supervisors at least a couple of years ago, but she had chosen not to. Ruth always managed to keep her composure during her consultations (she knew that she had to if she was to maintain a healthy income), but when she got out of work, the problems began.

Ruth's husband, Matthew Rourke, had found it increasingly difficult to please his wife in recent years. Ruth had become aggressive, needy, demanding, disillusioned and unreasonable – as though she had absorbed all of her clients' worst habits and behaviours. She certainly wasn't coping with the pressures of her job,

Matthew thought, and she had become too stubborn and angry to admit this to anyone – especially to herself.

Ruth preferred to blame Matthew for her unhappiness. She complained (amongst other things) that he was too nice; too boring; too predictable; not ambitious enough; uninspiring, and too safe. Matthew admitted to being most of the above, although he knew that these were the very qualities Ruth had said she married Matthew for, six years ago.

Ruth's driving force now was *money*. Matthew still desperately wanted to placate his wife – to please her – but this only drove her madder still. Ruth resented her husband for not earning quite enough to give her a taste of the lifestyle most of her very affluent clients appeared to enjoy. Her referrals always tended to be from private doctors, so Ruth had developed something of a taste for the excitement, complexity and drama that appeared to comprise life for the wealthier sections of society. She now felt as though she had missed out on life – and this made Ruth angry.

*****

As Matthew Rourke arrived home from Paws for Thought at 4.00 p.m., on Wednesday 5th October, he dreaded the evening that lay ahead.

He knew he had to break the news of his redundancy to Ruth, but he clearly recognised that his wife would not be applying any of her counselling skills when dealing with *his* problems and emotions that evening.

At 4.30 p.m., the front door of Matthew and Ruth Rourke's modern two-bedroom apartment shut with a thud. Ruth Rourke entered the apartment's stylishly decorated hallway, where she took off her coat and threw it onto a chair. She checked her reflection in the floor-length hall mirror, and admired her recently dyed long blonde hair; her tiny, pinched-in waist; and her long slender legs. Ruth thought she still looked good at the age of thirty-five, and indeed she did. She had always turned heads, with her designer clothes, good looks, and the very high-quality make-up and perfume she always wore - much of it bought on credit.

Ruth began to make her way towards the kitchen at the back of the apartment. Before she reached it, however, she suddenly heard a noise coming from one of the bedrooms. Ruth froze to the spot, convinced that there must be an intruder in the apartment. A million thoughts raced through Ruth's mind about what she should do next – but she didn't have time to do anything, as a voice unexpectedly spoke to her from the bedroom area. 'Ruth?' it called. 'Ruth – is that you?'

'Who the hell is there?' Ruth demanded angrily.

'What do you mean-?' the voice replied, sounding confused. Matthew Rourke suddenly appeared in the corridor in front of his terrified wife.

Ruth's heart was still pounding like a terrified puppy's. She initially thought that her husband was playing some kind of sick joke on her – although that would be completely out of character for him, she quickly realised. 'What are you playing at, Matthew?' she screamed. 'What are you doing here?'

Matthew realised already that he had got off to the worst of starts with Ruth. 'Sorry, Ruth. I didn't mean to frighten you. I got home early – that's all.'

'You nearly frightened me to death.' Ruth pushed past her husband to get to the kitchen.

'I'm sorry,' Matthew repeated, following her into the kitchen.

'How come you're home early anyway?' Ruth demanded impatiently, deliberately deciding not to wish her husband a *Happy Birthday* now.

'Well,' Matthew said rather solemnly. 'I need to talk to you about something, Ruth.'

Ruth paused for a while, and then swung around to look at her husband. She hadn't liked the tone of his voice one bit. She knew something must be up. 'Go on,' she snapped, making Matthew feel even more intimidated than he did before: Ruth had the ability to cut her husband in half with one fell swoop of her tongue.

'Can you sit down at the table with me?' Matthew suggested nervously, pulling out a chair for her.

'Oh my God,' she said mockingly. 'What the hell have you done?'

Matthew immediately realised that his wife would *not* be sitting down with him at the kitchen table. He took a deep breath before he finally plucked up enough courage to speak to Ruth again. 'I've been made redundant.' The colour drained from Matthew's face.

There was another long pause before Ruth eventually responded to Matthew's news. 'What? What do you mean you've been made redundant?'

Matthew had already prepared the answer to this question in advance, as he had sat in Paws for Thought, earlier that day. 'The shoe business has not been doing as well recently, Ruth. More and more people are getting their old shoes repaired and renovated – as opposed to buying new ones.' Matthew hardly knew what he was saying – he was in such a state of dread by now.

Ruth looked at her husband in disgust. 'Is there a chance they'll ever take you back again?'

'No. The entire shop – business – has completely folded.'

Ruth's jaw dropped in disbelief. 'And how the hell are we supposed to live now, Matthew? We can't live and pay the mortgage on my wage alone – can we?'

'No. But they've given me a decent redundancy package, which will keep us secure for a few months until I get another job.'

'And what makes you so sure you'll get another job?'

'I will. And you never know, Ruth – this could actually be a blessing in disguise.' Matthew was trying to appeal to his wife's optimistic side: not that he was exactly sure Ruth had one any more.

'Do you know what?' Ruth said. 'I could do so much better than this, Matthew. I don't deserve this second-rate crap in my life.'

'Ruth, you've never have to make do with second best,' Matthew protested. 'I mean, look at where we live,' he said, gesturing around at the beautifully decorated London apartment they were standing in. Matthew had earned a very handsome wage in his managerial position at 'Snaub's Foot Boutique' in Central London. It had been enough to enable him and Ruth to purchase an apartment with a very desirable TW9 postcode, when they first got married, and his wife had certainly seemed more than happy with her lot back then. Matthew thought that Ruth had loved him once - even during the first year or so of their marriage; but she had grown increasingly cold and resentful towards him recently. He could remember how Ruth used to compliment his dress sense, his looks, his achievements and his kindness towards her – but he couldn't seem to do anything that pleased her these days. It was as though Ruth had given up on him; but Matthew still did not want to give up on Ruth. What Matthew didn't realise, however, was that Ruth had only really 'loved' Matthew because he had once appeared to provide her with a ticket to a more affluent and exciting way of life. Ruth knew now that Matthew would never likely be able to bring her the happiness she so craved. 'Listen, Matthew,' Ruth said. 'You might be content to sit back and be happy with your lot. But I'm afraid that's just not good enough for me any more. I need to know that life can get better; more... *exciting*.'

'I will get another job, Ruth.'

'Whatever.' Ruth looked at her husband very sternly now. 'I expect more than this, Matthew. Much more.' With this, Ruth brushed past Matthew again and walked out of the kitchen. She went directly to her and Matthew's bedroom, where she sat down hopelessly on the bed and began to cry. Ruth felt as though her life couldn't get much worse than it was now. She was miserable. Her husband's limp-wristed, nicely-nicely attitude was driving her insane. Matthew bored the life out of her now, she realised.

As Ruth contemplated life with her husband, Matthew Rourke reached for a beer in the fridge beside the kitchen table, and opened it with his key ring. He took a swig from the bottle, as he threw the lid into the bin, and proceeded to walk into the hall corridor, towards the lounge. Matthew listened briefly at the door of the bedroom Ruth had entered, and heard the sound of his wife crying.

As he took a seat on the sofa in the lounge, he began to feel very angry at himself. Matthew felt sick at the thought that he had perhaps let Ruth down. He had always tried his best to be the model husband to her, but perhaps he hadn't been ambitious, daring or outgoing enough in the past; perhaps she did deserve someone better than him. It had been a terrible thirty-third birthday for Matthew. But he deserved no better, he thought now.

Although Matthew realised that money would have to be spent more prudently in the Rourke household - until he would secure another job - he resolved there and then to treat Ruth to an extravagant present this weekend. He would sweep her off her feet again; convince Ruth that he could be 'exciting'.

Matthew also swore that he would secure a dream appointment at the 'Retail Management Recruitment Fair' he had seen advertised in a newspaper in Paws for Thought, earlier that day. It was to take place at a venue only one tube stop away from Paws for Thought, and two from his own home, this coming Friday, October 7th.

Matthew took another drink of beer, feeling very determined and very ambitious about proving himself to Ruth, once and for all. *If a little dog can manage to get his own way so effectively,* Matthew thought, reflecting on the feisty West Highland Terrier he had encountered earlier that day; *then so can I.*

-CHAPTER FIVE-

Goodbyes

Susan Carmichael awoke on the morning of Thursday October 6th knowing that a monumental day lay ahead.

It was 5.30 a.m., and darkness still reigned outside. Susan lay in bed with her eyes wide open, her thoughts jumping from one thing to another. Before she had even realised it, she awoke once more to find that it was 8.00 a.m. and much brighter. Her husband, Ray, was already awake and dressing himself beside the large set of fitted wardrobes opposite their bed.

Ray had his back to Susan, so he was not yet aware that his wife was awake. Susan decided to maintain a little more thinking space for herself - before she would speak to Ray, and break the morning's silence.

She closed her eyes peacefully and let her mind drift happily to wherever it took her. Susan felt much calmer and more centred than she had in a very long time. She recalled the curious events from the previous day: Dixie's mischievous behaviour, the fair-haired handsome stranger, and the group of international tourists – and smiled wryly to herself. Susan still didn't quite understand why these events had spoken to her soul so profoundly; all she knew was that they had.

Her thoughts now focused positively on the day ahead. Susan contemplated the fact that she would be leaving Dixie with Steve Morgan, later in the afternoon; but for some strange reason, she didn't feel the same sense of dread about the prospect of that any more. She realised that she must say goodbye to Dixie for a while this weekend, if her life was to begin to move on: Dixie had as much as given her his blessing on that one. Susan sensed somewhere deep inside her that this weekend would signal the beginning of a wonderful new chapter in her life, although her negative experiences in the past meant that she would not let her mind get too carried away with any wild hopes or dreams just yet.

Before Susan was about to open her mouth to say her first 'good morning' to Ray and Dixie (who was still snoozing happily in his basket at the bottom of the bed), she suddenly recalled a dream she'd had - during her second wind of sleep that morning.

She remembered that in her dream she had been walking in a beautiful park, on a bright, sunny day, with the handsome stranger she had met in Paws for Thought, the previous afternoon. They were laughing and smiling – very much like they had when the friendly tourist took their photo outside the dog-friendly café. For some reason, Susan and the stranger then decided to sit at a picnic bench, which had been laid out lavishly for lunch, with all sorts of cakes, pies, drinks and fruit. After only a moment or so, Susan recalled watching, as a young couple – a man and woman in their late teens or early twenties – came walking towards them, accompanied by a young boy. There were then a few blanks in the dream, but Susan thought she could remember Dixie appearing on the scene. She even recalled Steve Morgan's wife, Amanda, sitting beside her at the picnic bench at one stage.

Susan shook her head as she lay in bed: she realised that her dream was clearly just a mish-mash of thoughts and memories from the last few days. She sat upright and stretched her arms in the air with a yawn, before Ray spoke first. 'It's not like you to sleep on this long Susan. You must have been having lots of sweet dreams!'

'I must have!' Susan replied mysteriously. 'What time are you aiming to leave for Buckinghamshire, later?'

'Well. I thought about two-ish. Steve told me he'll be coming around at lunchtime to collect the keys to the house, and to familiarise himself with Dixie's routine.'

'Right.'

'I think he said he wants to bring his daughter Charlotte with him – to show her the ropes – just in case he gets caught up with an emergency appointment during one of Dixie's feeding times.'

'A likely scenario, I'm sure,' Susan said ironically.

Ray looked at his wife as she began to get out of bed. There was something different about Susan this morning, but Ray didn't quite know what yet. She appeared contented, relaxed – even blasé: a strange phenomenon for Susan, especially on the day when she was about to leave Dixie in the incapable hands of Steve Morgan. 'Are you OK, Susan?' Ray enquired.

'Yes,' Susan replied. 'Why do you ask?'

'Oh, nothing. It's just that you seem very laid-back or something.'

'Well I *am* going away for the weekend, aren't I? I *should* be feeling laid-back, shouldn't I?' Susan laughed.

'I guess so,' Ray replied, a little suspiciously.

Susan proceeded to walk across to the wardrobes to choose her outfit for the day. She reached in to the wardrobe nearest the window, and grabbed a smart magenta-coloured jersey dress and belt, which she only ever wore on rare and special occasions. Ray glanced sideways at Susan's choice of clothes. He was delighted to see that his wife was going to dress positively today – albeit that he was still very wary of her uncharacteristic behaviour. Susan was a fabulous-looking woman, Ray thought; although he longed for her to allow herself to shine much more – just as she had when she was younger. 'You haven't worn that one in a while,' Ray said curiously.

'I know. I'm just in the mood to wear it today.'

Just then, Dixie raised his head and sat upright in his basket. 'Good morning, Dixie Wixie!' Susan said happily, as she hung her jersey dress on the back of the wardrobe and bent down to cuddle her beloved dog. Dixie loved it when Susan called him that name. 'Woof!' he replied, in gratitude.

'You know we're going away for a few days today – don't you, sweetheart?'

'Woof!'

'And you'll be OK until we get back on Sunday evening – won't you, darling?'

'Woof!' he reassured her.

'Good boy!' Susan said, rubbing Dixie's ears, as she drew her face towards his shiny black nose for a kiss.

'Do you have much packing to do this morning, Susan?' Ray enquired.

'Only a little,' Susan replied, standing up again. 'Although I need some time alone - *after* I pack. I have something I need to do before I leave for Buckinghamshire today.'

'Oh – OK,' Ray said, intrigued. 'Shall we go downstairs and get some breakfast now? It's great to have a morning off to relax a little – isn't it?'

'Yes – it is!' Susan said cheerfully, as she put on her dressing gown.

Ray, Susan and Dixie made their way out of the bedroom and onto the hall landing a few moments later. As the three of them began to descend the stairs, Ray Carmichael continued to wonder at his wife's sudden sense of inner calm. Susan definitely hadn't started to take medication – she would have informed Ray, he knew; but it certainly appeared as though *something* had given her a much-needed lift in spirits.

*****

The Carmichaels enjoyed a hearty cooked breakfast, prepared by Ray, before Susan went back upstairs alone to pack. She had offered to do Ray's packing for him too, which he had gratefully accepted: packing wasn't Ray's sort of thing at all.

As always, Susan had diligently prepared for this occasion by compiling an exact list of the items she and Ray wanted to take with them on their weekend away. The exercise would not take very long, therefore.

Susan opened the large wardrobe in her bedroom that contained all of her and Ray's luggage options. She pulled out her husband's stalwart black suitcase, before pondering her own choice of bag. It was so long since Susan had been away anywhere, she hardly knew which one to choose. She initially contemplated bringing her large, flowery-patterned designer weekend-bag, which she adored, but she decided that it was not quite big enough to carry everything she wanted to take to Buckinghamshire. Susan therefore settled for her bulkier red suitcase, which would hold all of her clothes, footwear, toiletries and towels: Susan had always found the idea of using second-hand hotel towels a bit disgusting.

She conscientiously packed everything she and Ray required into the two suitcases, before closing them. Susan then got dressed into her magenta jersey dress and went downstairs for a cup of coffee with Dixie and her husband.

It was almost 11.30 a.m. by this stage, so Susan knew she only had a short time to complete the other thing she needed to do, before Steve Morgan would arrive with his daughter at lunch time. 'I'm going to have that time alone now,' she announced to Ray, as he reclined on a sofa in the Carmichaels' lounge, with Dixie on his lap. Ray loved having days off, and he found relaxing a very easy thing to do. 'OK,' he said, looking up curiously at Susan, as she took Dixie off his lap, and walked out of the room with him.

As Susan entered her bedroom once more, and shut the door behind her, she paused for a moment in thought, contemplating the task that lay ahead. She had taken Dixie with her for moral support and company: Susan thought that she would probably need both of these, right now. She put Dixie down on the bedroom floor, and he toddled contentedly over to his basket by the bed, where he curled up cosily. Dixie understood what was about to happen, but he knew that only his presence was required by Susan on this occasion - although he would take his cue to action if and when necessary.

Susan walked over to one of the large fitted wardrobes, opened its door, and lifted out a small blue cardboard box from one of the shelves inside. She placed the box carefully down on top of the bed, where she sat alongside it, and stared at it quietly for some time, before finally lifting its sturdy lid.

Upon looking at the box's contents, Susan immediately began to sob. She had known that she was going to cry on this occasion; she did so every time she looked inside *Jacob's Box*.

Although Susan had never been able to obtain a birth certificate for her son, she had kept as many mementos of him as she had been able to gather around the time of his birth. She had wanted to be able to remember as much about Jacob as she possibly could.

As she carefully began to lift out the first item from the box, Susan smiled and wept in equal measure. She was holding the one and only scan photograph she had of Jacob; the one given to her by her obstetrician, only ten weeks before Jacob's death and birth. She looked at the grainy grey-and-white image now, and made it come alive again inside her head.

Tears streamed steadily down Susan's face, as she smiled, and remembered that first encounter with her son. It had been a beautiful spring morning in late March, more than eight years ago. Susan had obviously known she was pregnant at the time, but it wasn't until her eyes had focused on the little figure, bouncing about on the monitor in front of her, that Susan had *really* known there was a baby growing inside her.

She recalled watching Jacob's tiny heart pumping; his right arm waving at her; his mouth opening and closing to say hello to her – and Susan Carmichael fell head over heels in love. She couldn't believe what her obstetrician was pointing out on his monitor – she just giggled and giggled like an immature schoolgirl on a first date – and she didn't give a damn about how her silly behaviour might be perceived.

Susan floated out of Memorial Hospital that day inside a lovely bubble. She was unable to stop smiling down at the little scan picture her obstetrician had given her – the one Susan was now holding in her hand. She suddenly recalled that she had attended the scan alone that day, because Ray had unfortunately been forced to work, due to Steve Morgan calling off 'sick'. It hadn't bothered Susan much at the time, because she knew that there would be another scan in a few weeks' time that Ray could attend. But that was unfortunately never to be the case, she knew now. Susan lost Jacob the day before she was due to have her second scan. Susan always regretted that Ray had never seen his son alive.

Susan placed Jacob's scan photo back inside the box, her heart still throbbing with love for her baby boy.

She then lifted out the next item.

It was a white newborn baby-gro. Susan had bought it for Jacob on her way home from the hospital, after that first and only scan. She remembered she had felt so elated and overwhelmed by her experience, earlier that day, she had decided to buy her baby an impromptu present – to welcome him (although she didn't know her baby was a 'him' at the time). The baby-gro had a little baby penguin embroidered on it, with fine white silk thread, which Susan now touched lightly with her long fingers. She held the baby-gro up to her face, and wiped her tears with it, before placing it back inside the box.

Susan paused before she took out the final item she had kept to remind her of Jacob.

It was a photograph the hospital had taken of her son, shortly after he was delivered. Her Jacob. Susan did not hold back any tears now, as she looked at her son's face. He had been so tiny when he was born; so fragile and gentle and lovely.

Susan recalled the moment she saw Jacob for the first time, after he was born, in the nearby Memorial Hospital. He had been placed inside a little wicker basket, which had been lined with a fine, white muslin fabric. The nurses had thoughtfully placed the heads of two flowers at the top of the basket, near Jacob's head: chrysanthemums; one yellow and one violet. Susan now glanced over at a picture frame that was sitting on top of her bedside cabinet. Inside it was those same two chrysanthemums that had adorned Jacob's crib. Susan had pressed them and kept them as constant reminders of her son.

She looked at Jacob's face again and smiled. Her son was smiling back at her. He had been born with a heavenly smile on his face.

Susan now recalled the agony she had felt, when she looked at Jacob for the first time, after his delivery. She hadn't been able to reconcile Jacob's still and silent body with the vibrant, joyful image she had seen on her obstetrician's monitor, only ten weeks previous.

Susan's heart and soul were crushed completely, the day she went into premature labour with Jacob. It was 8th June. It had been a nightmare. It still felt like a nightmare, eight years later. Ray, standing crying at the door of Susan's private side ward, as medics surrounded her. Susan had been able to watch the horror of it all unfolding on the face of one the young nurses, as Susan pushed, and Jacob was delivered. Susan could not believe that her bubble of happiness had been burst so brutally. Jacob never got to wear the little baby-gro she had bought for him – and that still broke Susan's heart.

Susan placed Jacob's photo tenderly back inside the box, along with the two other items, and looked closely at it one more time. She knew that she had to say goodbye to Jacob for now: that's why she had wanted time alone with him, before she left for Buckinghamshire. Susan realised that she had been holding on too tightly to her son's memory. She realised that this had likely prevented her from conceiving another baby. Her womb could no longer be Jacob's empty tomb, she recognised. Susan needed to move forward with her life: that's what the handsome stranger in Paws for Thought had made her understand, yesterday.

As she thought about all of this, Susan could somehow sense that Jacob was in agreement with her, but she decided to call upon Dixie for validation nevertheless. Susan always trusted Dixie's opinion. 'Come here boy!' she said to her dog.

Dixie immediately leapt out of his basket and joined Susan on top of the bed. 'Can you help me say goodbye to Jacob, Dixie?' Susan asked. 'He knows why I have to say goodbye – just for a little while – doesn't he, Dixie?'

'Woof,' Dixie replied solemnly. He recognised the monumental nature of Susan's decision not to look at Jacob's Box 'for a little while'. Dixie had witnessed the anguish Susan had endured, every time she encountered mothers, babies or pregnant women, ever since Dixie had become part of Susan's life. He fully realised that Jacob's Box had been the only thing that had allowed Susan to feel like she was still Jacob's mum – until yesterday, that is. Matthew Rourke had magically shown Susan that she would always be Jacob's mum, but she needed to move on – for the sake of her future babies.

Something inherent inside Susan now told her that Jacob wanted her to release her tight grip on him – to let him go his own way, and let Susan continue along her own path on earth. Dixie cradled his head in Susan's lap, as she placed the lid slowly and gently onto Jacob's Box.

Susan had stopped crying by now. She would visit Jacob's Box again someday, she knew; but for now, she had other pressing issues to attend to. Dixie lifted his head from Susan's lap, to enable her to walk over to the wardrobe and place her box back onto its shelf. She closed the wardrobe door behind it, and paused for a moment, before looking over at Dixie for moral support. Dixie tilted his head sideways, and barked once at Susan. He knew that his time with her was nearly over; his mission almost completed.

*****

Steve and Charlotte Morgan arrived at the Carmichaels' house at 1.15 p.m. that afternoon.

Ray Carmichael invited them into the kitchen, where Susan immediately began to brief them on Dixie's needs and wants. As a Pedigree, Dixie did not tolerate second best with anything, Susan understood.

Dixie had not left Susan's side since the moment she placed Jacob's Box back onto its shelf. He wanted to spend every minute he could with her now.

'So you're both clear about all of that?' Susan Carmichael asked in a rather matronly fashion, after she had carefully outlined Dixie's daily requirements - again. Susan and Ray Carmichael were sitting opposite Steve and Charlotte Morgan at their kitchen table. Steve felt as though he was being vetted by the authorities. 'Absolutely, Susan!' Steve Morgan replied. 'You're clear on that too, Charlotte – aren't you?' he asked his daughter, who was seated next to him at the Carmichaels' large kitchen table. Steve had coaxed his daughter into going along with the story that he and Charlotte would be *sharing* responsibility for Dixie in the Carmichaels' absence: Steve had promised his daughter more hair extensions in return for her compliance on this occasion.

'Yes,' Charlotte answered, unimpressed. Charlotte didn't do dogs. She did not have a dog-ternal bone in her body. In fact, it quite disturbed her, right now, the intimate display of affection between Susan Carmichael and her hairy white dog. Charlotte couldn't believe that a woman would actually hold a dog up to her face and allow it to *lick* her. *Gross*, Charlotte thought to herself. *God knows where that tongue has been in the past.*

'Dixie sleeps upstairs beside our bed,' Susan continued matter-of-factly. 'But he'll come running downstairs to greet *you* when you come through the front door.' Susan was directly addressing Steve Morgan. 'So you *won't* have any reason to go *upstairs.*'

Ray Carmichael twitched a little nervously. He thought his wife was being a little *too* pertinent in the presence of Steve's daughter.

'Absolutely!' Steve enthused, not really catching Susan's meaning at all.

'Do you have any other questions?' Susan asked – sounding a bit like a teacher addressing a class of pupils.

'What brand is he?' Charlotte enquired.

There was a stunned pause. Susan and Ray Carmichael looked at Charlotte, puzzled by her question.

'Sorry guys!' Steve interrupted, laughing, albeit a bit embarrassed. 'I think Charlotte means what *breed* is he! My daughter and wife are very into their brands and labels!'

'Right,' Susan said, curious. 'He's a Westie. A West Highland Terrier.'

'Does he bite or anything?' Charlotte asked. She had no experience with dogs whatsoever.

'No. He's very friendly,' Susan said, defending her dog.

'OK,' Charlotte said.

Susan was beginning to get a little suspicious about Charlotte's questioning – as though Charlotte might perhaps be the *only* one looking after Dixie in her and

Ray's absence. While Susan could clearly recognise that the very beautiful and glamorous Charlotte wasn't exactly the most academic kid on the block, she did think that she had a certain warmth, kindness and intelligence about her – qualities that her father clearly lacked. Charlotte was definitely her mother's daughter; so in a funny kind of way, Susan felt rather reassured by the thought that Charlotte, and not Sleazy Steve, would be tending to Dixie's needs while she was in Buckinghamshire with Ray.

'OK!' Ray Carmichael said. 'I think that just about covers everything – don't you, Susan?'

'I guess so,' Susan replied, a bit shocked to suddenly realise that she was actually about to go away for the weekend.

'OK folks!' Steve Morgan said cheerfully, as he leapt from his chair. 'I think Charlotte and I will love you and leave you both now! Business as usual for me this afternoon back at the practice!'

Ray kicked Susan under the table to make sure that she didn't give a smart retort to Steve's last comment. 'Thanks Steve,' Ray responded quickly, as he got up from the table. 'So you've got a set of front and back keys, Steve – and you're happy about Dixie's regime?'

'Absolutely!' Steve enthused again.

Charlotte rose from the table now. She knew now what her mum had meant about Susan Carmichael. Susan *was* a bit scary – but nice at the same time, Charlotte thought. *And* she was very pretty – if not a bit on the fat side.

'Thanks Steve,' Ray said. 'It means a lot to know that Dixie will be OK while we're away – doesn't it, boy?' Ray addressed Dixie, who was still being held tightly by Susan at the kitchen table.

Dixie did not reply to Ray's question. He was deep in thought.

As Ray Carmichael escorted Steve and Charlotte Morgan to the front door, and closed it behind them, Dixie curled himself protectively into Susan's lap.

'That went well – didn't it?' Ray said cheerfully to Susan, as he re-entered the kitchen.

'As well as could be expected, I suppose,' Susan replied pensively, before she stood up from her chair and hoisted Dixie up into her arms. 'OK, Dixie!' Susan said. 'I'm going to have to put you down now – so that I can get ready to leave for Buckinghamshire.' Dixie jumped out of Susan's arms as she bent down towards the floor with him. He walked over to his large armchair by one of the kitchen windows, and cuddled himself contentedly around one of its plump cushions.

*****

At 2.25 p.m., Susan entered the kitchen with her coat already on. Ray Carmichael was just outside, packing the last case into the boot of the car. He had already fed Dixie, and let him have a little walk outside in the garden.

'OK, Dixie,' Susan said. 'We're about to leave now, fella.' Susan knelt down in front of Dixie's large armchair and began to rub his face affectionately. Dixie lifted his head and looked deeply into Susan's eyes. 'Now, you know everything will be OK, Dixie, don't you?' Susan reassured her dog. 'Someone will come to feed you and walk you later this evening – and again tomorrow and the next two days.'

'Woof!' Dixie responded.

'Good boy!' Susan said, relieved and smiling. 'I'll miss you, Dixie – but I'll see you again on Sunday – won't I? And I'll bring you a special doggie treat back from Buckinghamshire too!'

'OK, Susan – are you ready?' Ray interjected, as he walked into the kitchen once more.

'Yes – I suppose so.' Susan rose to her feet.

'We should try to leave now to beat the rush hour traffic later,' Ray suggested sensibly, as he checked his coat pockets again for his keys and toffee sweets.

'I know.' Susan looked down at Dixie again. She never remembered him looking as lovely as he did now. Except perhaps for the day she saw him for the first time, at Candy Pups.

'OK Dixie – see you Sunday then, mate!' Ray said happily, as he approached Dixie and gave him a friendly pat on the back, before turning to make his way out of the kitchen. 'I'll see you in the car, Susan. Everything's locked up already.'

'OK.' Susan turned to look at Dixie one last time. 'Goodbye Dixie,' she said, as her dark eyes gazed into his. 'I don't know what I'll do without you this weekend.' Susan Carmichael gave Dixie one more kiss and cuddle. She turned and walked out of the kitchen, leaving the door opened behind her to allow Dixie to roam freely through the house in her and Ray's absence.

As the front door shut behind Susan, Dixie listened to the silence filtering through every room in the house. He would remain in his chair in the kitchen, he contemplated, until Charlotte Morgan would come later to feed him, and let him into the back garden for a while. Then he would spend his last night alone in his basket upstairs.

Dixie had loved his time with Susan and Ray Carmichael, he thought peacefully to himself now; but it was time to move on. He realised, more than anyone else did at this stage, that much of his tale had yet to be told.

-CHAPTER SIX-

The Beginning of a Long Day

Charlotte Morgan set out on foot from her family home on Friday 7th October, dressed from top-to-toe in designer clothes. Charlotte had arranged to meet her friend, Ebony Glazier, later that morning, for some shopping, gossip and a facial; so she had decided that she would nip in briefly to the Carmichaels' house to do her dog-sitting duties, before she would eventually make her way to the nearest tube station, and finally into town. The weather wasn't looking too promising, so Charlotte wanted to make her visit to the Carmichaels' as short as possible.

Charlotte entered the Carmichaels' Edwardian residence on Friday morning, fully expecting to be met by their West Highland Terrier.

On the previous evening, Dixie had come bounding out from the kitchen to greet Charlotte in the entrance hallway, although he hadn't barked or behaved too exuberantly on that occasion: Dixie had thought it best not to intimidate Charlotte – given her complete inexperience with the canine race. Charlotte had been quite shocked to find that the Carmichaels had not individually measured out Dixie's meals for the proceeding few days, and she had been appalled by the fact that she was forced to handle disgusting-looking and foul-smelling dog biscuit things.

After Dixie had eaten his dinner, Charlotte then dutifully let him wander about the Carmichaels' back garden for a few minutes, while she checked the Twopenniesworth site for any updates. She then let the dog back inside the house, before locking up and leaving a short while later. Susan Carmichael phoned Charlotte's dad, Steve, later that night, to check up on Dixie. Steve informed Susan that the dog was 'perfect'.

Charlotte now stood in the Carmichaels' front hallway, listening for dog noises. She reached into the fur-lined pockets of her expensive cropped down jacket and took out a pair of disposable white latex gloves – given to her that morning by her shocked mother, Amanda, after Charlotte had informed her about handling dog food the evening before.

Upon hearing no sounds whatsoever inside the Carmichaels' house, Charlotte now proceeded to walk into the kitchen to see if she could find the dog there. She could see Dixie's empty feeding bowl on the kitchen floor, which she had filled yesterday, but there was no sign of the dog at all.

A little irked at the unexpected delay, Charlotte decided to fill Dixie's bowl with food nevertheless – although she forgot to fill his drinking bowl with fresh water from the tap. She had forgotten to give Dixie his water on the previous evening also.

As she was just about to exit the Carmichaels' front door to make her way to the tube station, Charlotte's conscience and curiosity suddenly got the better of her. She recalled how Susan Carmichael had told her dad the previous afternoon that Dixie slept in a basket at the bottom of her bed (*how disgusting*, Charlotte had thought to herself at the time); so she decided to go upstairs to see if she could find Dixie there, and let him into the garden for a 'walk'.

Charlotte marched up the elegant stairway that led to the first floor of the Carmichaels' five-bedroom house, taking in her surroundings as she moved. Everything looked very classy, she thought, although the smell-of-dog kind of detracted from the Carmichaels' expensive and tasteful fixtures and fittings.

As Charlotte reached the top hall landing, she paused and called out to the Carmichaels' dog: 'Pixie! Pixie!' - but still there was no sound or movement inside the house. Charlotte was very perplexed by now. 'Stupid mutt,' she grumbled out loud. Charlotte proceeded to look into each of the upstairs rooms to see if she could locate the dog: she supposed he was more than likely asleep, inside the Carmichaels' bedroom.

After opening her third door, Charlotte eventually discovered Dixie lying inside his basket at the base of Susan and Ray Carmichaels' king-size bed. 'Pixie!' she shouted – but the rigid-looking dog strangely did not respond. 'Get up you lazy dog!' Charlotte said, still wearing her white latex gloves for protection.

As the Carmichaels' dog continued to lie stubbornly static in his basket, Charlotte began to move furtively closer to inspect him. It was by now 9.26 a.m. 'Oh shit!' Charlotte exclaimed impatiently. She touched the dog a couple of times with her right foot to satisfy herself that he definitely *was* dead. 'For God's sake!' Charlotte snapped out loud: she was due to meet Ebony at 11.00 a.m. and her facial was booked for noon. Charlotte took out her mobile phone immediately, and dialled her dad at the Dental Spa.

It took some minutes for Steve Morgan to accept the call at his end. Steve had kindly told Epsilon's Receptionist and dental nurses to go shopping for the day. He had banked on Amanda not checking up on him, since he had heard her saying to somebody on the phone, this morning, that she was booked in for several beauty treatments, at a location several miles away from the dental surgery today.

Steve had been busy in his surgery with Madeleine Singleton, and he had to rearrange some of his clothes, before he eventually entered the Reception Area of the Dental Spa to lift the phone. 'Epsilon Dental Spa. Steve speaking. How may I help?' Steve said in his politest voice, as he eyed Madeleine Singleton's bare legs on the reclined dental chair, just through the door of his private surgery room.

'Dad?' Charlotte said sharply at the other end.

'Charlotte?' Steve replied, massively irritated. 'What the hell are you doing phoning the surgery, while I'm – working?'

'The bloody dog's only gone and died – hasn't it?' Charlotte snapped back.

There was a stunned pause at Steve's end. 'Whaat? - Please tell me this is sick joke, Charlotte!' Steve yelled in disbelief, hardly knowing where to place himself.

'Listen dad,' Charlotte continued in a business-like fashion. 'You're going to have to come over here and bury him yourself – because I'm meeting Ebony at eleven, and I've an appointment after that.'

There was another stunned pause. 'I can't go over there to bury a sodding dog today!' Steve screamed hysterically at his daughter, causing Madeleine Singleton to immediately reach for her clothes: she clearly sensed that something must be up. 'For God's sake, Charlotte – what the hell am I going to tell Ray and Susan? I've just told Susan Carmichael over the phone that her dog looked great when I fed him this morning! This is a bloody nightmare for me!'

'Tell me about it! This place is *stinking* of dog – even worse than usual!' Charlotte said in disgust, pinching the end of her perfectly-structured nose.

'How the hell did the dog die anyway? Did you *poison* him or something?' Steve was a little bit maniacal now. He wasn't particularly good in a crisis. And he knew that this was most definitely a crisis.

'No I didn't bloody poison him!' Charlotte was twirling a strand of her long platinum-blonde hair. 'He was out cold by the time I got here.'

'Is there blood on him or anything?' Steve's panic levels were increasing rapidly. 'I mean – you don't think anyone else got in and murdered the dog? No sign of a break-in or anything?'

'Who got murdered?' Madeleine Singleton now asked excitedly, as she stood (dressed) by Steve Morgan's side in Reception.

'Shhhhhh!' Steve ordered Madeleine impatiently, hardly throwing her a glance.

'Who's that?' Charlotte asked Steve.

'Nobody!' Steve insisted, shooing Madeleine Singleton away from him. He was desperately trying to establish how he could get himself out of this dilemma. 'Right, Charlotte,' Steve said, attempting to convince himself that he had thought of the best possible solution at last. 'Put the dead dog into some sort of bag – or hold-all – or something like that – and bring it to Mike Gordon's Veterinary Surgery – you know where it is - it's only one tube station away from where you are now – '

'*What*?' Charlotte interrupted him, appalled. 'Are you *mental* dad?'

'No, Charlotte. I'm *not* mental. Although I *will* be dog shit when Susan Carmichael gets back from her weekend break.' Steve felt very worried and sorry for himself.

'I'm not *touching* that dog, dad – never mind bring him for a walk – when he's *dead*.'

'I'm afraid you have no choice on this one, Charlotte. Mike's a good mate of mine. I'll phone ahead to let him know you'll be arriving with the dog later this morning. He'll know what to do with it.' Steve was trying to reassure himself.

'DAD – '

'Charlotte – please. You *have* to do this for me. I really do promise that I'll make it worth your while. Name *anything*. I'll get it for you,' he begged, rather pathetically.

'And what if somebody stops me when I'm walking about with a dead dog? What do I do then?'

'Nobody will stop you, Charlotte – don't be so stupid. Now I need to get off the phone if I'm to call Mike and explain all of this to him before you arrive at his surgery. God – this would just have to happen to me – wouldn't it?' he grumbled.

Father and daughter both hung up their phones at this stage.

Steve Morgan was so angry and flustered, he immediately demanded that Madeleine Singleton leave Epsilon Dental Spa, before he made the phone call to Mike the Vet, informing him that Charlotte was on her way to his Surgery, with Susan and Ray Carmichaels' (dead) dog. Madeleine duly did as Steve said – but she felt *very* scorned by his treatment.

Meanwhile, Charlotte stared down at Dixie in his basket. He was curled in a conveniently compact manner, she thought, so he shouldn't be too difficult to fit into a bag – as long as the bag was big enough, obviously. Charlotte also guessed that Dixie was about a stone in weight – meaning that he shouldn't be too difficult for her to carry either. Charlotte's only motivation at this stage was the Mediterranean holiday she would demand from her father in return for the favour she was about to carry out for him. She stood for a second or two in disbelief at her morning so far, tutted to herself, and proceeded to walk towards Susan and Ray Carmichaels' wardrobes to look for a suitable bag.

After opening several large wardrobes containing all sorts of things – from clothes, to shoes, to cardboard boxes and golf clubs – Charlotte eventually hit upon a wardrobe containing various types of luggage. Staring out at her immediately, at the top of the pile of bags and suitcases, was a designer weekend-bag, with a pretty red-and-blue floral pattern, shoulder strap and handles. 'Perfect!' Charlotte said, anxious to leave the Carmichaels' house as soon as possible. She carried the large weekend-bag over to Dixie's basket, and opened it beside him. Charlotte was more than satisfied the dog would fit neatly inside the bag.

Dixie's soul laughed and chortled, as it looked on at Charlotte Morgan's attempts to manoeuvre a dead dog into a flowery-patterned designer weekend-bag.

Dixie had 'died', at the very premature age of three, from sudden heart failure (he hadn't felt a thing). Dixie had thought that as apt a way as any to go; although he worried that Susan Carmichael might fear that her dog had died from a broken heart, in her and Ray's absence. Dixie would work on reassuring Susan that that had not been the case, at some later date.

Dixie had been careful to slip away only after he had positioned himself sufficiently compactly for Charlotte Morgan to lift and position him into Susan Carmichael's favourite bag. Luckily for Charlotte, she had kept her white latex gloves on from earlier, when she had put the dog food into Dixie's bowl (what a waste of time *that* had been, she thought to herself now). By this stage, Charlotte had turned the air in Susan and Ray Carmichaels' bedroom the same shade of dark blue as the collar Dixie was currently wearing. Susan had attired her dog in this particular collar before she had departed for her weekend break, because she had always thought it made Dixie feel calm and reassured.

Once Charlotte had eventually managed to place the dog's body into the bag, she took off her latex gloves and threw them in after him, zipping the bag as quickly as possible, so as not to have to look at the dog or smell him any longer. She then lifted the bag by the two handles, before swinging it over her right shoulder. The bag was quite heavy, Charlotte thought, but luckily she only had a five-or-so-minute walk to the tube station; and then just a very short walk at the other side, to Mike Gordon's Veterinary Surgery.

Charlotte began to walk downstairs towards the Carmichaels' spacious front hallway, her bag resting heavily against her right hip. By the time she had reached ground level, her right shoulder was quite uncomfortable, so she placed the bag on the hall's parquet floor for a rest. Charlotte then lifted the bag onto her right shoulder once more, and walked over to a large hall mirror to look at her reflection: she wanted to make sure that it did not look as though she was carrying a dead dog about with her. Satisfied that she looked perfectly normal, Charlotte went out the Carmichaels' front door, closed it firmly behind her, and began her short walk to the nearest tube station. It was by now 10.15 a.m.

As Dixie continued to look on at this scene, he felt pleased at the events that had unfolded so far. He was very much enjoying his new state of being. It was great to be able to sit back and watch things happen, without having to run about and get tired all the time. Dixie was also able to pop in to see Ray and Susan, at the Eden Resort, in Buckinghamshire, when he wanted (they were having a great time); although he did dread the future scene on Sunday, when Susan would discover that he had gone. But that was for another day, Dixie thought now.

In the meantime, he would observe Charlotte Morgan unwittingly assist him in the final part of his mission on earth. Dixie admired Charlotte's practical way of thinking. Only she would have agreed to carry a dead dog around London with her, in order to secure a holiday abroad. Plus, she was the only person Dixie had met on earth who had been better groomed than him. Who better then to help him reach his final destination?

*****

Only one tube stop away from Charlotte's, and two from Mike Gordon's Veterinary Surgery, Matthew Rourke was setting out from his apartment to attend the Retail Management Recruitment Fair he had read about in a newspaper in Paws for Thought on Wednesday.

He had spent all the previous day scouring recruitment sites on the Internet – but to no avail. Despite Matthew's excellent C.V. in Retail Management, as well as his track record for reliability, dedication and excellent people skills, there just didn't seem to be any suitable employment opportunities out there for him at the moment.

Matthew was desperately pinning his hopes on the Recruitment Fair today. Ruth, his wife, had barely spoken to him since he broke the news of his redundancy to her on Wednesday evening. She had withdrawn further away from Matthew in the last couple of days, and she had even asked him to sleep in the spare bedroom.

Ruth had arrived home from work very late last night. Matthew had suspected she was out drinking with one of her friends – or was perhaps even with her sister, Eva. Ruth always tended to steer in Eva's direction when she was at a particularly low ebb, although she barely had time for her otherwise. Eva was a very kind, considerate sort, Matthew thought.

As Matthew now straightened his silver-grey tie at his hall mirror, Ruth eventually emerged from the bedroom. It was by now 10.15 a.m.

Ruth never accepted appointments from any of her psychotherapy clients on a Friday, insisting that a four-day week, consisting of three one-hour sessions, was quite enough for her to cope with psychologically. Ruth deeply resented the possibility that she might have to work more hours in the future, given her husband's recent unemployed status; so she had decided, last night, to make the most of her free time, given that she might have to get up early next Friday morning.

'How are you feeling?' Matthew asked Ruth, as she brushed past him in her pyjamas.

'Fine,' she answered abruptly.

'What time did you get in last night? I don't think I heard you.'

'Two or so.' Ruth entered the kitchen.

'Were you with Eva?'

'She was there at the beginning of the night, but she had to leave at 8.00 p.m.'

'Oh. Who else was there then?'

'Clare. And Deborah.'

'Right.' Matthew decided not to pursue the topic any further. When Ruth went out with Clare and Deborah Silvestri, she tended not to remember much about her evening. Not that Matthew frowned on Ruth's partying at all: he would just prefer if his wife asked *him* to go out with her from time to time. 'You remember I'm going to the Recruitment Fair this morning – don't you?' Matthew asked from the hallway.

'Oh yeah,' Ruth replied, remembering; as she turned towards her husband, who had by now followed her into the kitchen. 'What time do you have to leave?' she enquired, as she took a large drink of orange juice from a glass she had just poured.

'Now.'

'Oh. What do you think your chances are of getting something out of it?' Ruth asked, throwing a couple of painkillers into her mouth, and swallowing them down whole.

'Very good. I honestly get a good feeling about today, Ruth.'

'*Do* you?' Ruth was unconvinced.

'Listen, Ruth. I know things haven't been easy between us recently. And the news of the redundancy has come as a bit of a blow. But please don't give up on us yet.'

Ruth looked at Matthew blankly. Her head was thumping with pain from the alcohol she had consumed the night before. 'Not now, Matthew,' she said, shaking her head.

'I know, I know. But just think about it – will you?'

'OK. OK.' Ruth just wanted Matthew to leave her alone now, so that she could go back to bed.

'Right then – I'm off!' Matthew announced. 'Wish me good luck?'

'Yeah,' Ruth replied, trying to muster as much enthusiasm as she could. 'Good luck.'

Matthew Rourke approached his wife, put his right hand on her left shoulder, and kissed her tenderly on the forehead. Ruth looked up at her husband, but could barely sustain eye contact for even a moment.

'Bye,' Matthew said, turning to leave.

'Bye,' Ruth replied, as she continued to stand with her glass of orange juice in the kitchen.

As Matthew Rourke shut the front door of his apartment behind him, and began the five-minute walk to his nearest tube station, Ruth made her way back to bed.

She felt absolutely dead inside. Ruth knew deep down that she was probably depressed, but she did not want to admit this to herself fully, in case it affected her job. She chose instead to blame all her negative feelings on the world around her – and especially on her husband. She would only find happiness away from Matthew, Ruth convinced herself now, as she fell quickly into a deep slumber.

*****

The train pulled into Matthew Rourke's tube station at 10.36 a.m. – within just a minute of Matthew's arrival. He was able to get a seat immediately, which was an unusual experience for Matthew, since he had been so accustomed to travelling during the very busy morning rush hours when he had worked in the designer shoe store. These ten or fifteen minutes seated would give him ample time to gather his thoughts before the Recruitment Fair, he reflected, inwardly admitting to himself for the first time that he was very uncertain about his chances there today. Matthew couldn't have told that to Ruth, of course, but he knew that times were very grim in the retail sector. If he were to be offered a job today, he realised, it would be a pretty miraculous thing.

As the train moved away from the station, Matthew began to feel a mass of nervous pressure building up inside him. He hadn't expected to feel under so much strain today, but the situation at home with Ruth had really begun to take its toll on him by now. Matthew couldn't contemplate his marriage with Ruth ending. It was never meant to end, he thought now. He must do something to please her – to convince her that he was worth holding on to. He had to secure a job today. Or he had to at least surprise Ruth with an expensive present this evening – to cheer her up –

and to make their weekend together at least bearable. Matthew began to try to calm his nerves by focusing on the designer footwear of a smartly-dressed businessman seated opposite him. This technique was so effective, Matthew hardly noticed the other passengers getting on and off at the next stop. It was by now 10.42 a.m.

Charlotte Morgan was one of the passengers who boarded the train at this stop – along with Dixie Carmichael, who was tucked neatly inside the flowery designer weekend-bag Charlotte was carrying. Charlotte took the seat of a smartly-dressed businessman, who was by now marching purposefully to his office, Matthew Rourke thought (slightly resentfully) to himself.

As the train moved away from the station once more, Charlotte Morgan's heart was dancing about inside her ample chest. She had slightly misjudged the train times, and she had been standing around at her station for around twenty minutes before the train arrived to take her to Mike the Vet's place. This delay in her schedule had unnerved Charlotte, to the extent that she now felt like a murderer, transporting the remains of her latest victim about, in a designer weekend-bag. She now placed the bag containing Dixie Carmichael's body between her two feet; clamped firmly, as though the dog inside it was still alive and might escape at any moment.

Of course nobody on the train even suspects you're carrying the body of a dead dog about with you! Dixie tried to reassure Charlotte from afar, as he looked on at the scene on the train, very much enjoying himself.

Charlotte's breathing began to deepen as the train proceeded further along the line. She desperately tried to settle her nerves by convincing herself that she only had a very short way to go with her 'doggie bag' now: there was only a couple of minutes left of the train journey; a short walk to the top of the escalator when she arrived there; and Gordon's was only two doors up from that.

As all of this was going on inside her frantic mind, Charlotte suddenly shifted with some alarm in her seat, as she noticed a smartly-dressed, rather good-looking man, staring at her bag. He was seated opposite her, and he would just *not* stop staring. *Oh my God*, Charlotte thought, beginning to panic even more. *Maybe this wasn't such a good disguise. Is the dog's tail sticking out or something?* she began to wonder.

And all the time, the smartly-dressed man opposite did not once lift his head to make eye contact with her.

*****

Matthew Rourke was feeling especially anxious as his train eventually pulled into his stop. It was by now 10.48 a.m. He lingered behind the other passengers getting off the train, and he was amongst the last to step onto the platform. As the train doors thumped behind him, Matthew began to move towards the escalator, just behind a glamorous, platinum-blonde female, who appeared to be struggling to carry a large bag she had slung awkwardly over her right shoulder. For some reason, Matthew felt strangely compelled to help this female; he thought it might take his mind off the Recruitment Fair. 'Would you like some help with that?' Matthew asked her pleasantly, as she stopped again to place her bag onto her left shoulder this time.

'No thanks. I can manage,' Charlotte Morgan replied timidly.

'Here – it's no problem!' Matthew Rourke said agreeably, lightly grabbing the bag from Charlotte. 'Do you have far to go at the top of the escalator?'

'No. Just a couple of doors,' Charlotte barely answered back, her eyes glued to the bag. She was certain at this stage that the man must suspect something, and was about to arrest her or something. Charlotte also thought that he must be foreign: he had a strange and unfamiliar accent.

'Well, let me help you then. It won't inconvenience me at all!' Matthew smiled warmly at Charlotte, but she refused to look directly at him.

Charlotte began to walk alongside Matthew Rourke, who was by now carrying Susan Carmichael's dead dog, Dixie.

'My goodness!' Matthew exclaimed. 'What have you got in here? It's no wonder you were struggling!' This thing's very heavy!'

Charlotte had to think on her feet now, although she didn't even think it was worth her while lying to the man at this stage. 'Oh – just some of my things. I'm moving to a new flat – that's all,' she mumbled.

'Ah – right!' Matthew smiled again at the female, who kept looking twitchily around her at everyone passing by.

Three-quarters of the way up the escalator, Matthew Rourke asked, 'Which way do we go at the top?'

'Right,' Charlotte said abruptly, still checking the bag with her eyes to see if there was anything unusual-looking about it.

'OK.' Matthew was curious about why this female would not look directly at him.

As Charlotte looked down to catch her step at the top of the escalator, her body tightened with anxiety at the thought of the next few moments. She just wanted to get the bag back now and get rid of it at Mike Gordon's place.

Charlotte now turned towards her gentleman helper, who had by this stage made his way quickly past several pedestrians on the street to the left. Charlotte stood dumbfounded at the top of the escalator, frozen to the spot, hardly knowing which way to turn, as the man disappeared from sight with Susan Carmichael's bag and its contents.

Charlotte glanced one more time over her shoulder towards the street where the man had just disappeared, before walking down the steps to catch the next train into town, and her rendez-vous with Ebony Glazier. Charlotte was late already, although she had briefly texted Ebony at the last station to explain her unexpected delay.

As she approached her platform, Charlotte suddenly began to laugh-out-loud nervously – to the mild bewilderment of a few passers-by.

Didn't he look stupid, she thought. *A man in a grey suit – running about with a flowery weekend-bag!*

-CHAPTER SEVEN-

Matthew's Story

Matthew Rourke had never intended to steal Charlotte Morgan's bag. As he slowed his pace to a steady walk now, satisfied that he had not been pursued by the female at the tube station, Matthew could hardly believe what he had just done. He could feel a cold, clammy film of sweat develop all over his body. Matthew was sure that his skin must be the colour of ash.

He looked over his shoulder once more. Everything looked normal. Every*body* looked normal. So why did Matthew suddenly feel so removed from the realities and certainties of the world around him? He continued to walk along the street he now unexpectedly found himself on, remembering that he was meant to be attending the Recruitment Fair in the opposite direction. Matthew supposed that he could go there later – once he had sorted out the bag situation. He needed to stop somewhere; to gather his thoughts; to establish what had just happened, and to figure out what he would do next. Matthew caught sight of an alleyway ahead, between a bookmaker's shop and a convenience store. He decided that he would stand in there for a while – to take stock of his situation. Matthew was not particularly familiar with this area.

Once he had reached the alleyway, he placed his bag on the ground between his feet, and took his mobile phone out of his jacket pocket, to make it look as though he had stopped to text somebody. As Matthew stared blankly at the screen of his phone, pretending to tap in a message, he suddenly began to recall his split-second decision to grab the bag from the glamorous-looking female he had offered to 'help' at the tube station.

Matthew recalled that he had genuinely wanted to assist the female. She had so obviously been struggling to carry her bag; it had seemed only right to come to her assistance at the time. Matthew remembered looking at the female's designer footwear on the train. She had taken the seat of the smartly-dressed businessman, who had been sitting opposite Matthew. The female had immediately grabbed Matthew's attention for that reason alone. When Matthew later encountered the female on the platform, after disembarking the train, he had felt naturally compelled to approach her – even though it was never the kind of thing he would normally do.

Matthew remembered noticing how well-groomed the female was: she was evidently very affluent. She was dressed from top-to-toe in designer clothing. Matthew recognised all the expensive labels and designs she was wearing from the wealthy clients he had assisted while he was Manager at the designer shoe store. He recalled estimating that the female's ensemble was worth almost as much as he would have taken home in his monthly wage packet from that establishment.

And then Matthew remembered panicking. He didn't have a monthly wage any longer. He didn't know if or when he would ever have a monthly wage again. He didn't know how he could possibly convince his wife, Ruth, that he was worth sticking with. Matthew always seemed to mess up *all* of his relationships, he thought now.

The female hadn't even looked into his face - ever since Matthew first came to her assistance on the platform. She would never remember him, therefore. And that had been his rationale. This extremely wealthy girl would never miss a few of her expensive possessions. She would have the money to easily replace them. Matthew would sift through the contents of the bag, and present Ruth with something special this evening.

He must have been mad, he now suddenly realised. Matthew hadn't even thought about the presence of all the CCTV surveillance at the tube station. What had he just got himself into?

Matthew looked down at the bag clamped between his two feet. He noticed for the first time that it had a flowery-pattern on it. *God*, he thought. *I must have looked stupid – running about with a flowery bag.*

He felt ashamed. It was a terrible thing he had done. He had never done anything like this in the past. Matthew thought he must definitely be going insane. He wanted to go back immediately and undo what he had just done – but he knew that he couldn't. He would therefore have to go along with his plan to present Ruth with something nice this evening. Matthew believed in the power of fate. This was probably all meant to be, he thought to himself now. He would simply go somewhere secluded to retrieve the contents of the flowery bag, transfer them into another, less conspicuous bag, and go to the Recruitment Fair. *Who knows?* he pondered. *This could be my lucky day.*

Matthew picked up the weekend-bag by its two handles. He looked at the time on his mobile phone (it was 11.15 a.m.), before slipping it back into his jacket pocket. Matthew decided to go into the convenience store next door. He wanted to purchase some things, in order to gain ownership of a large plastic bag. *Preferably opaque*, he thought logically.

Matthew walked into the convenience store and grabbed some items from the shelf: a tin of chicken soup, a large box of breakfast cereal, and a bag of sugar. He thought that these items would secure him the large plastic bag he needed. Matthew gave the items to the cashier, who handed them back to him inside a large, opaque blue plastic bag. Matthew noticed the young female cashier staring at the flowery bag, which was now slung over his right shoulder. He would have to get rid of it soon, he realised.

Just as he was about to exit the convenience store, Matthew was suddenly stopped in his tracks by a familiar voice. 'Matthew!' it shouted, whereupon Matthew turned around to see Ruth's sister, Eva, standing beside him in the shop.

'What are *you* doing here, stranger?' Eva asked curiously, as she approached Matthew at the door of the convenience store.

'God. Eva – Hi!' Matthew replied, very taken aback. 'I'm – em – just attending a Recruitment Fair a few doors away from here – I just came in for some things,' he answered, flustered.

'Ah – yes,' Eva said, feeling terrible now. 'I'm so sorry, Matthew. Ruth told me you lost your job.'

'Thanks,' Matthew replied, a little embarrassed.

'Nice flowery bag!' Eva teased, trying to lighten the conversation. She was holding a bag of apples she was just about to pay for at the till.

'HaHaHa!' Matthew laughed nervously. 'This is just an old colleague's. She forgot it in work the other day. I'm just returning it to her at the Recruitment Fair today,' he lied. He felt terrible lying to Eva.

'Suits you!' Eva said playfully.

Matthew had always liked Eva. She was two years older than Ruth, but she had never got married. Eva and Matthew had always got along well – ever since he first met Ruth, six years ago. Eva was very pretty, just like Ruth; although she had somehow always been more centred, grounded and safe in her own skin than Ruth. Eva worked as a professional gardener. She had set up her own small business in NW1 five years ago, after having worked on a private estate in Bournemouth for eight years. Eva was quiet and understated in demeanour. She liked to dress casually, in warm, earthy tones that always seemed to match her shoulder-length chestnut hair and her hazel eyes. Eva always looked as though she was ready for contact with nature, Matthew thought. There was something magical about her. 'How come you're in this neck of the woods today anyway?' Matthew asked Eva, a little self-consciously.

'Oh, I was asked to come down to lend some of my horticultural expertise to a friend who works at Unity Park,' Eva explained. 'New bulbs they're planting for next spring.'

'Right!'

Eva smiled warmly at Matthew. There was something not quite right about him today, she thought. Matthew didn't seem his usual relaxed self. Although that was probably due to his redundancy, Eva realised. 'Well, I guess I'd better get back to work in NW1 – and let you get to where you need to be,' Eva said. 'I really hope you get a positive outcome today, Matthew.'

'Thanks, Eva. Will you be seeing Ruth later?'

'No – I have other plans this evening. But tell her to give me a ring and let me know how you get on at the Recruitment Fair – won't you?'

'Of course. Bye then Eva!'

'Bye Matthew!' Eva gave Matthew another smile, as she walked towards the till to pay for her apples.

Matthew exited the shop, glancing back once more at Eva, who was by now standing looking at some magazines beside the till. He was glad he had met her so unexpectedly today. Unity Park would be the perfect location to transfer the contents of the flowery bag into his newly-acquired plastic bag, he thought. He had forgotten all about the existence of Unity Park until Eva had helpfully reminded him about it.

The park had large areas of woodland, bog land and open green picnic areas. More importantly, it was located at a crossroads only a few hundred yards from where Matthew was now. He would go there and find a secluded place; retrieve the contents of the flowery bag, and go to the Recruitment Fair. Matthew reckoned that he could simply leave the plastic bag and its valuable contents in a safe at the hotel where the Recruitment Fair was being staged.

It was fate that he had encountered Eva, Matthew realised.

As Matthew continued to make his way to Unity Park, Dixie's soul looked on at the choices Matthew had just made. It could have gone any way at the tube station, Dixie realised. Charlotte Morgan had almost been on the brink of panicking and abandoning the bag with Matthew, as she had approached the start of the escalator. If this had happened, Matthew would likely have left the bag at 'Lost Property'. Charlotte's nerves had held intact – somehow.

On the other hand, Dixie also knew that the likelihood of Matthew Rourke stealing anything, yet alone a young female's bag, had been almost completely improbable – up until the moment he eventually cracked. Dixie recognised that Matthew had most definitely experienced several moments of 'madness' in the last hour or so.

It was well known in the invisible realms that Matthew had spent too much of his young life pleasing others, and blaming himself for things that were beyond his control. It would (unfortunately) take something quite traumatic to jolt Matthew's soul in the right direction once more; to make him come to terms with events from his past, and to ensure that he lived the future he had originally intended for himself. That's why Dixie Carmichael had entered Matthew Rourke's life at this time. Dixie had presented Matthew with the opportunity to shift his life in a different direction – whether Matthew realised this or not – and Matthew had grabbed it (quite literally) with both hands. Dixie did not look forward to the moment when Matthew would discover his cold and rigid body inside Susan Carmichael's weekend-bag, but he knew that even Matthew would recognise why these events had perhaps needed to happen – some day soon.

*****

Matthew Rourke entered Unity Park at 11.55 a.m. He hadn't noticed the weather until this time – he had been so preoccupied. Matthew could see now that it was a rather cold day for this time of year. He was dressed in the grey suit he had intended to wear to the Recruitment Fair, so he hadn't worn an overcoat for walking outdoors in October. It was rather grey and ominous-looking overhead, and Matthew realised that it might start raining at any moment. He would therefore have to move quickly, so as to get back to the Recruitment Fair without getting drenched. He hadn't brought an umbrella either.

Matthew scanned the park ahead, as he walked through its large double gates. He walked along the wide tarmac driveway for a few moments, looking left and right, for a suitably secluded area. The park was quiet. Eerily quiet, Matthew thought. Not one picnic bench on the wide area of grass was occupied. Matthew wondered what section Eva had been working in earlier that morning. Nobody appeared to be about now: *they must either know it's about to rain, or they've all gone for their lunch-break early,* Matthew contemplated. Either way, that suited him just fine right now.

Matthew suddenly spotted an area of woodland just to his left, a few yards ahead. He looked around to ensure that nobody would see him disappearing into the woodland, and then casually ambled towards it with his two bags. Matthew felt disgusted with himself. He couldn't believe what he was doing. He must be going insane, he thought again. He checked over his right shoulder once more, before treading his way through long grass, and into the area of woodland.

After walking a short distance, Matthew began to recognise the trees that comprised the area of woodland. They were the trees of his childhood: Silver Birches, predominantly; with some yellow-berry Rowans interspersed. Matthew also caught sight of a large Oak up ahead. He would go there, he thought, to sift through the contents of the flowery bag.

As he approached the Oak, Matthew suddenly began to recall how much he had loved being in nature as a child. He would have spent hours and hours roaming freely in the countryside surrounding his parents' home, oblivious to any worries or concerns. Since he had moved to London, however, and married Ruth, he had hardly spent any time outdoors. Ruth preferred towns and people to countryside and animals.

Matthew crouched beneath the large Oak, and placed his two bags on top of the knotty slope that contained its large, impressive root system. Rain began to tap lightly against the blue plastic bag, so Matthew knew that he had to work quickly. He tugged at the zip of the flowery bag, which began to slip easily along its indented track. Matthew looked around again at the trees and grass that surrounded him, to ensure that he was completely alone, before finally pulling the zip to the end of the track.

*****

Matthew's mind screamed at the image of the dead dog inside the flowery bag. He stared at it in stunned horror, as his stomach began to contract, and sharp-tasting vomit trickled out of his open mouth.

Matthew had been asleep up to this point, he suddenly realised. It was as though he had been walking around in a daze all morning, and had just become fully, terribly conscious for the first time that day. He couldn't piece together how he had suddenly found himself in this position. It was all madness. This couldn't possibly be happening, Matthew thought.

But then he remembered. The Recruitment Fair. The female at the tube station. The flowery bag. Ruth. Eva. It had all been real. It wasn't just a terrible dream.

Matthew didn't know what to do next. He looked at the dog inside the bag again. There was a pair of white latex gloves lying on top of the dog. What the hell had an affluent female been doing, walking about London with a dead dog? It just didn't make any sense, Matthew thought angrily. Was this some kind of sick joke? he wondered, feeling suddenly paranoid, like he had perhaps been set up.

He stared once more at the dog, hardly able to believe it was there at all. Matthew could clearly see that the dog was white in colour. It looked like a West Highland Terrier. Very much, in fact, like the dog he had encountered in Paws for Thought on Wednesday. But it couldn't possibly be – could it? *No*, Matthew thought decisively. That dog had been wearing a red collar. This dog had a blue collar. There were hundreds of similar West Highland Terriers out there anyway.

Matthew looked at the time on his mobile phone. It was 12.15 p.m. He had already missed the first hour of the Recruitment Fair. This was his karma for stealing the female's bag at the tube station, he knew. There was no way he would be able to go to the Recruitment Fair now. He wasn't in any fit state of mind. No job. No expensive present for Ruth. He had messed up everything in his life - *again.*

Cold rain was now tumbling steadily down on Matthew's patch of woodland. He could feel his clothes getting wetter, but he didn't know which way to go next, or how to proceed. Matthew was once again the inadequate, stupid, self-loathing seventeen-year-old he had been, back when he had killed Christian.

Christian. His only brother. The only sibling Matthew ever had. Christian was only six when he died. Matthew had loved him so much. He had been his 'Bud'. Until the day Christian was killed in the car accident that had so nearly claimed Matthew's life too.

Matthew put his face in his hands now and began to cry hard tears of anguish. He was being punished again for messing up so badly in the past – he knew it.

He hadn't meant to kill Christian. Matthew had been driving his brother home from a birthday party, one cold day in mid October, when their family saloon unexpectedly slid on a greasy section of road, and tumbled into a field. Matthew woke up in hospital a few hours later with no memory of the accident. He had sustained a few cuts to the face, a broken right leg, and had been rendered unconscious for a time; but Christian had *died*. Matthew was informed of this by his parents the next day. They had reassured Matthew that the accident hadn't been his fault. It was just a terrible, tragic 'accident'. Christian had banged his delicate head so badly as the car had tumbled over, he never woke up again. Matthew hadn't even been able to remember the last few moments he had spent with his vivacious little brother; as he stood looking into Christian's grave, as they lowered his small white coffin into the ground.

No matter how hard Matthew's parents had tried to convince him that they didn't blame him for Christian's death, Matthew remained sure that they must despise him. He grew cold towards them. Matthew didn't want them to waste their time on him any longer. He didn't deserve their acceptance or forgiveness.

Matthew left home for university two years later, to pursue his degree in Retail Management. He chose to study in London, several hundred miles away from his home in the Lake District. His parents tried to support Matthew as much as he would let them at the time, but he hardly saw them from this point on in his life.

When Matthew met Ruth, a Londoner, some years later, he loved the fact that she knew very little about his background. Matthew chose not to tell Ruth about Christian or the car accident. He informed her that he simply wasn't very close to his parents. Matthew had been relieved that Ruth had never asked him too many personal questions when he first met her. She was a psychotherapist, and she preferred to accept people as she found them, she informed Matthew.

Ruth had thought Matthew perfect in the beginning. He was successful, attractive, kind, considerate, and eager to please Ruth in every way he could. Matthew cut off all ties with his family in the Lake District. He and Ruth married in a London Registry Office, alone, within a year of their first date, and their first couple of years of marriage were fine. Until Ruth began to complain that Matthew was too 'nice'; too 'predictable'.

But Matthew had conditioned himself to be 'nice and predictable'. He didn't want to mess up – like he had messed up with Christian and his parents. Matthew sought to place his needs and feelings second to those of Ruth – always. He was lucky to have her, Matthew frequently told himself. He was lucky to have anyone who wanted to be around him. It was his fault that Ruth had changed so much recently. Somehow, he had messed up his life again. He was being punished for his past – again. Matthew still hated himself. He deserved to be punished, in his opinion.

He needed a strong drink now.

Matthew looked down one more time at the dead dog and the white latex gloves inside the bag, before zipping it closed again. He had to bury it somewhere, he thought – not that the rich girl at the tube station would ever likely come looking for it. Matthew lifted the flowery bag by the handles and walked towards a pile of rocks and stones he had spotted - just over from the large Oak – near a group of Silver Birches. He walked back to retrieve his bag of groceries, and set them down beside the dog's bag, before reaching in for the tin of chicken soup. Matthew used the tin of soup to scrape away as much earth as he could - to dig a hole for the flowery bag. He couldn't even remember exactly why he had bought the chicken soup now (not to mention the breakfast cereal and the sugar) – but he was just glad that he had.

Matthew dumped the flowery bag and its contents into the hole and attempted to cover it with the soft brown earth he had just scraped away. He had made a hopeless effort of it, he realised. Noticing the rocks and stones beside him once more, Matthew began to lift some of the smaller, more manageable ones, and dumped them on top of the bag, one by one.

When he was finally satisfied that he had concealed the flowery bag adequately, Matthew stood back and looked at the impromptu tomb he had created.

He was soaked by this stage, and the rain continued to fall steadily on him. Matthew could see that his grey suit was a little dirty - from when he had knelt on the ground and lifted the rocks and stones against his buttoned jacket. He felt as though he wanted to stay here – amongst the safety and peace of the trees, the rocks and the grass – but he knew that he would have to leave soon, to return to the chaos of his human life.

Matthew began to contemplate what he should do with the soup, cereal, sugar and blue plastic bag. After initially thinking that he might take them with him, and dump them in the nearest litter bin, he eventually decided that he couldn't be bothered with the hassle of all that. Instead, he tore open the box of cereal and scattered its contents on the ground for the birds to feed off. He did the same with the bag of sugar (even though he wasn't exactly sure if animals or birds ate sugar), and he then hurled the tin of chicken soup deeper into the area of woodland. Matthew placed the empty cereal and sugar packaging into the blue plastic bag, and buried it under some more rocks and fallen tree foliage. He thought he was thinking logically at the time.

Matthew walked out from the shade of the trees the same way he had entered, just over half-an-hour ago - except this time he was empty-handed. He surveyed the large open area of parkland he was now faced with, before quickly approaching the tarmac driveway just beyond it. There was nobody about, except for a group of schoolchildren and their adult guide, who were far enough in the distance away from Matthew for him not to worry about their presence. The rain had now slowed to a gentle drizzle.

As he eventually made his way onto the wide driveway that had first led him into Unity Park, Matthew slowed his pace down to normal walking speed. He saw the park's large open double gates ahead, and he simply couldn't wait to get beyond them. Matthew resolved to find the nearest bar to get a drink. He reached the Unity Park crossroads, and began to walk back up the street, towards the tube station. The street was even busier than it had been this morning, Matthew quickly realised. It was just before 1 p.m., so a lot of people were out for their lunch. This suited Matthew well. He would simply go into a bar and merge with the lunchtime crowd until they left. Then he would leave too.

Matthew spotted a drinking and eating establishment up ahead, just to his left. He approached it and entered, going first to the gents to clean himself off and dry himself down.

He returned to the generous-sized bar and lounge area, which had around twenty people sitting in it right now, and he ordered and paid for a drink: a cold pint of 'Rising Dawn' beer – the establishment's home brew. Matthew sat with the pint at a table, alone, and took several large mouthfuls, to settle his nerves. He felt himself becoming light-headed very quickly; he never usually drank alcohol at this time of day. But today was an exception, he told himself. Matthew thought he would sit at the table in the bar for as long as was required to gather his thoughts – although he didn't quite know how long exactly that would take, or where exactly his thoughts would take him.

Matthew was also unaware, as he sat drinking in 'The Rising Dawn', that it would only be a matter of time before Dixie Carmichael's body was discovered nearby.

-CHAPTER EIGHT-

From Bad to Worse

Steve Morgan was sitting at the computer in the Reception Area of Epsilon Dental Spa. Madeleine Singleton had taken her leave of the premises earlier, when Steve had unceremoniously chased her away, after his daughter, Charlotte, had unexpectedly dropped the bombshell of Dixie Carmichael's untimely demise.

On the previous evening, after having consumed several glasses of sauvignon blanc (whilst watching re-runs of 1980s and 1990s game shows), Steve had decided to amuse himself by updating Epsilon Dental Spa's website. He had wanted to deliberately antagonise Susan Carmichael – now that she was off Steve's back for a few days.

Steve's reluctance to work meant that he was always on the lookout for other opportunities to expend his pent-up intellectual energy. Plus, he was a strong believer in the maxim; 'While the cat's away ...'

Steve had (incorrectly) assumed that Susan would be beholden to him the following week - for looking after her beloved dog so well this weekend. He had also (incorrectly) assumed that Susan and Ray would be in such a good mood after their break that they would take a more laid-back attitude to his mischievous nature.

Steve had often fought with Susan in the past about the 'tone' of Epsilon's website. Susan preferred a sophisticated, professional approach, while Steve had always argued that they should use catchier, tabloid-style phrases: he thought that these would appeal to the wider, aspiring classes, whilst still amusing Epsilon's more discerning clients. Needless to say, Susan had always got her way over this issue in the past, and Susan always had Amanda Morgan's full backing when it came to the business. Susan insisted that Epsilon was *not* some second-hand car dealership – and so too did Amanda.

So, on the previous evening, Steve Morgan decided to completely overhaul the practice's website, in Susan and Ray Carmichael's absence. He deleted much of Susan's considered, articulate phrasing, and replaced it with slogans such as: '*Get your teeth into these wedding deals!*'; '*Cop a mouthful of these veneers!*'; and '*Treat yourself to a Gnasher-Flasher Special!*'.

Now; as he sat in Epsilon's Reception Area, frantically attempting to undo his previous evening's handy work, Steve Morgan suddenly realised that he must have consumed too much alcohol on that occasion. Susan's absence had definitely gone to his head, he clearly recognised. Steve was desperately looking at the practice's printed brochures beside him, trying to reinstate their phrasing and prices onto Epsilon's website. He knew that Susan Carmichael would definitely *not* be easily humoured upon her return next week, now that her dog had died. He really wished now that he *had* offered to take Susan and Ray's appointments this Thursday and Friday, instead of cancelling them all until some time after the Carmichaels' return from holiday. Everything that could have gone wrong so far for Steve this weekend had gone wrong. Not only had he messed up the practice's website, but Susan Carmichael's dog had died, and he had perhaps even scuppered his well-laid plans with Madeleine Singleton too.

As Steve continued to work at the computer, the phone on the Reception Desk suddenly began to ring. It was 1.30 p.m. 'Epsilon Dental Spa. Steve speaking. How can I help?' Steve said politely.

'Oh yes. That's it. Go on – you *bastard!* – You're all sweetness and politeness and light now – aren't you?' the voice said at the other end.

'Em - Madeleine -?' Steve Morgan enquired tentatively.

'So you *remember* my name – do you?' Madeleine Singleton had already consumed several brandy-and-gingers to settle her nerves after her ordeal with Steve this morning.

'Madeleine – I can explain,' Steve said smoothly – convinced that he could still wangle his way with Madeleine this weekend.

'You don't have to explain anything! Except to my husband!'

'Eh – what do you mean, Madeleine?' Steve wasn't sure if he wanted to hear Madeleine's response at all. He had known he had taken a bit of a gamble when he began his fling with Madeleine Singleton, two months ago. Madeleine had a lot of suppressed energy (Steve knew); but more importantly, she had been married to seventy-two-year-old Douglas Singleton, a top London lawyer, for twenty-seven years now. Steve had (incorrectly) reckoned that he would have the performance power and charisma to go the extra mile with the beautiful, fifty-two-year-old, mother-of-two-sons, Madeleine. He had somehow believed that she would never inform her husband of their affair. Steve knew for a fact that Douglas Singleton preferred to spend much of his time cavorting with younger legal types in nearby courtrooms and hotels, and he realised that this was one of the main reasons why Madeleine had needed a dentist in the first place. He also knew that Singleton and Singleton Solicitors were possibly the most money-ruthless 'legal' set-up in London. Douglas Singleton was notorious for preying on educational and health institutions, suggesting possible claims opportunities to students, patients – or anyone else who happened to pass through the doors of these establishments. What Steve Morgan didn't fully realise, however, was that Madeleine Singleton had even more 'issues' than he could ever begin to understand.

'I *mean* – you're scraped-out tooth decay – you – *BASTARD!*' Madeleine slurred and shouted, trying to sound metaphoric at the same time.

'Now, now, Madeleine,' Steve replied, realising that he was potentially in big trouble. 'Please meet me this afternoon so that we can discuss this – darling.'

'Get stuffed!'

'Now – that's not a very nice thing to say – is it, Madeleine? You didn't *really* tell your husband about us – did you?'

'Yes!' Madeleine announced. '*Nobody* treats me like that!' she shouted proudly, before slamming down the phone.

As Steve Morgan began to absorb the possible implications of Madeleine Singleton's outburst, he realised that his day couldn't possibly get any worse.

He set the phone back on its cradle on the Reception Desk; but within a few minutes, it had begun to ring again. 'Madeleine?' Steve asked optimistically, believing that he could still convince Douglas Singleton's wife not to 'betray' him.

'Steve?' the voice said at the other end of the phone.

'Who's that?' Steve asked, rattled.

'It's Mike Gordon.' the voice replied.

'Mike? - Oh – MIKE! Sorry, mate – I was miles away.'

'Is everything OK, Steve? I mean – I take it there's been a change of plan?'

'What do you mean?' Steve asked, feeling very paranoid: he hadn't confided in Mike about his affair with Madeleine Singleton yet.

'I mean – the dog?'

'What about the dog? Did you find out why it died?'

'Hardly,' Mike replied. 'I haven't even seen the dog.'

There was a baffled silence at the other end of the phone. 'What do you mean – you haven't seen the dog?' Steve asked – getting very anxious.

'I mean – Charlotte never came here with a dog today, Steve.'

'But she should have arrived ages ago – before 11 o'clock – I was expecting you to phone any minute to let me know why the bloody thing had died!' Steve was beginning to hyperventilate.

'Sorry, mate – but she never arrived here – and I've been at the surgery all morning.'

'This cannot be happening to me!' Steve Morgan yelled, as he flung himself dramatically out of his seat, and began to shut down Epsilon's computer. 'Listen, Mike – can I phone you back later? I need to call Charlotte now to find out what the *HELL* she's up to!'

'No problem, mate. Talk to you later.' Mike put down the phone.

It took Steve Morgan three attempts before his daughter, Charlotte, eventually answered her mobile phone. It was by now 2.00 p.m.

'What?' Charlotte demanded impatiently: she had seen that the incoming call was from the dental surgery.

'What do you mean – *what?*' Steve shouted. 'Where the hell are you, Charlotte?'

'In town – where I told you I'd be.'

'Did you take the bloody dog with you then? Mike told me you never went to the vet's with it.'

'Don't be such a moron, dad. Why the hell would I take a dead dog to a facial? - It got nicked.'

'*What* got nicked?' Steve thought that he must have heard Charlotte wrong.

'The dog,' Charlotte stated nonchalantly, as she rolled her eyes at her companion, Ebony Glazier, who was sitting beside her at an upmarket coffee shop, called 'Fateful', in Central London. The two nineteen-year-olds were drinking skinny lattes and discussing 'things'.

'Who the hell would want to steal a dead dog, Charlotte? Are you taking the piss out of me?'

'Well – let's see,' Charlotte said sarcastically. 'I'm guessing that the person who stole the dead dog perhaps didn't realise that there was a dead dog inside the flowery bag. What do you think, Ebony?' Charlotte laughed over at her skinny latte partner, who tee-heed back at her.

'So you think this is funny, Charlotte? Do you know how much trouble I'm in at the moment?' Steve was about to explode. 'And what's this about a flowery bag?'

'Never mind the bloody bag. None of this is *my* fault - *is it*?' Charlotte snapped back angrily. 'If you'd looked after the stupid dog yourself, it might not have got stolen - at a tube station. I should sue you for trauma.'

Charlotte's last comment riled Steve. He began to imagine himself standing in court, with Madeleine Singleton and his daughter hurling charges at him. 'You ungrateful Miss.' he snarled. 'After all I've done for you, Charlotte.'

'Don't kid yourself, dad – you've never done anything for me – so don't expect any favours in return.' Charlotte was angry now.

Steve didn't really know how to respond to Charlotte's last comment. All he could do at this stage, he thought, was attempt to establish exactly what had happened to Dixie Carmichael. 'OK, Charlotte. Let's be civil about this – shall we? Can you please tell me who took the dog, and where they took it from – *please*?'

'It was at the tube station beside Mike Gordon's – when I got off the train. I didn't look at his face.' Charlotte was bored now, and just wanted Steve off the phone so that she could get back to her conversation with Ebony Glazier.

'*His* face,' Steve said excitedly. 'So *he* was a *man*?'

'Well done, dad,' Charlotte said, examining her nails.

'Can you describe him then?'

'No.'

'What do you mean – NO?' Steve was getting riled again.

'I mean *no* – I didn't really look at him closely. He was probably just some tramp or other. I think he might have been a foreigner. He talked strangely. Probably German. Or Scottish.'

'GREAT!' Steve said hysterically. 'Thanks for all your help, Charlotte!' And with this, Steve Morgan hung up on his daughter.

Charlotte immediately turned off her phone to ensure that she didn't have to talk to her father again any time soon. She *did* remember more about the man who had stolen Susan Carmichael's dead dog, but she wasn't going to tell Steve: it was hardly likely that her dad would go bumping into him – was it?

'I thought you said the thief was fit?' Ebony Glazier said to Charlotte, laughing.

'He was.'

'So how come you didn't describe him to your dad then?'

'Because I like winding my dad up – and anyway, I didn't get *that* close a look at the man. I just remember that he was fit, and wearing a suit – and foreign.' Charlotte liked to play cat-and-mouse with Steve. She enjoyed swimming against her father's tide – mainly because it grabbed his attention. It annoyed Charlotte that Steve had never taken much of an interest in her as she grew up – except when she misbehaved or answered him back. It was pretty much the same with Steve now – as Charlotte entered adulthood; and this was one of the main reasons why Charlotte had decided to walk out on her A Levels, a couple of years ago. She had known that her decision would really annoy Steve, and would give him ample opportunities to come and argue with her.

Charlotte couldn't quite understand why her father had chosen to stay away from her and her mum for much of Charlotte's life. She had often wondered if it had been her fault – that Steve had perhaps wandered off because Amanda had been too busy with her new baby daughter. Charlotte's mum had always insisted to her that this had not been the case; that Charlotte had not been to blame for Steve's absences.

And yet, none of it ever made any sense to Charlotte Morgan. She could never get her head around the fact that her mother was so beautiful and kind, and yet her father had never shown any interest in Amanda at all. Charlotte loved Amanda dearly, and it annoyed her to see her mother on her own so much – except for when Amanda was out at social events with 'The Botox Brigade' (which was Steve's smart-ass title for Amanda's social circle).

'Do you think your dad will still let you have the bedroom makeover, hair extensions and holiday – now that the dog has died and gone missing?' Ebony was laughing: she loved hearing tales of the Morgans' insane, super-wealthy existence. Charlotte and Ebony got on like they were close sisters.

'He'd bloody better!' Charlotte exclaimed. 'He can't say that I didn't fulfil my side of the agreement!'

'I guess not!' Ebony responded. 'So what are you going to wear to '*PolkaPolka*' tonight – the new cat suit or the mini-dress?'

'Mmm – I think I'm in a cat suit kind of mood,' Charlotte replied, as she gazed into one of the four designer bags at her feet. Charlotte Morgan wanted for nothing – materially-speaking, that is. While Charlotte's parents had inherited much of their wealth, Ebony Glazier's parents were both professional musicians. Ebony's dad, Julian, was a concert pianist, whilst her mother, Jo, was a cellist with the London Philharmonic Orchestra. Charlotte and Ebony had been friends ever since Ebony joined Charlotte's private girls' college in Sixth Form, only a couple of years ago. Although Charlotte had decided to drop out of her A Level courses early into her studies, she had maintained a close friendship with Ebony, whom she found both fascinating and lovely. Charlotte secretly envied Ebony. To her, Ebony had it all: a happy, secure family; a sister who was only a year older than her (called Melody); and a career that Ebony knew she dearly wanted to pursue (in classical music).

Charlotte had always wanted a stable family life; a sister she could be close to, and something she could be good at. She loved art – but Charlotte had never been much good at drawing or painting. She would have loved to have been able to do something like that for a career. Instead, Charlotte had contented herself with the cosmetics counter at her grandfather's department store. At least there she could indulge her creative side a bit, and pretend that she was an artist (of sorts). Charlotte couldn't have stood one more second at school. She hated being told what to do.

'Shall I get Melody to pick you up at around 8.30 tonight?' Ebony asked. Charlotte always liked to get ready to go out to nightclubs at the Glaziers' house: it was always such a laugh. 'That would be brilliant – thanks.'

'Do you think Pippa will go?' Ebony asked.

'God knows. She's a bit too obsessed with Andrew at the moment to know what she's doing.'

'Did you see her MyVaneSpace page?'

'Oh my God! Did you see that she's even referring to her and Andrew as *AndyPip*? I mean – get a life.'

'Does she talk about him as much at work?'

'She would if I let her – but I've started to run to the other end of the counter when she approaches me. She's even got me stock-taking and serving customers now.'

Pippa Parsons was twenty-years-old, and she worked full-time in the cosmetics section of 'Montgomery's Department Store' in Central London. Pippa and Charlotte were friends, although Pippa's relationship of one month, with Andrew Singleton (Madeleine and Douglas Singleton's twenty-six-year-old son), had driven a bit of a wedge between the two women recently.

'Any more O.M.P.s in recently?' Ebony asked Charlotte, sipping the last of her skinny latte.

'Not really. Although the Christmas season will be starting soon – unfortunately.' Charlotte referred to any male over the age of thirty as an O.M.P. – or 'Old Man Pervert'. She had developed something of a distaste for most males since starting work at Montgomery's. Charlotte had noticed – much to her distaste – that many of her so-called gentlemen clients, who claimed to be purchasing presents for their 'partners' – tended to spend most of their time ogling and flirting with her, Pippa and the other glamorous ladies her grandfather, Sir Horace, had strategically positioned in his store. Charlotte was not flattered by the attention of these men. It only reminded her of her horrible suspicion that her father, Steve, was also an O.M.P.

Charlotte and Ebony chatted about 'things' for another fifteen-or-so minutes, before they decided to leave Fateful at 2.45 p.m. and make their respective ways home by tube. The two women would hopefully meet up later that evening, at the Glaziers' house.

*****

Meanwhile, back at Epsilon Dental Spa, Steve Morgan was just completing his first (and last) appointment of the day. George Burrell – a fifty-three-year-old Architect – had just had some work done.

Steve felt much imposed upon by George's presence in the surgery. George was one of Steve's few male clients, and Steve did not enjoy George's company at all. Steve could always tell what George had been eating for the last several weeks by the festering food lodged between George's back molars, and the smell of his breath. 'OK George – see you again soon!' Steve exclaimed, as he handed George Burrell back his credit card upon payment at Reception. 'And don't forget the brushing and flossing!'

'Thanks, Steve – will do.' George was holding his swollen left cheek, which was still throbbing from Steve Morgan's dental handy work. George could feel a lot of gritty material inside his mouth now – as though there were still bits of his drilled tooth swilling about.

'Bye George!' Steve said, willing his client to leave the premises with immediate effect.

'Bye Steve!' George Burrell replied, eventually exiting the door of the dental surgery.

Steve Morgan immediately lifted the phone in Reception and dialled Mike Gordon's Veterinary Surgery. He had been unable to call Mike before this, to explain about the stolen dead dog: George Burrell had ungraciously arrived at the surgery just after Steve hung up the phone on Charlotte, earlier. It was by now 2.55 p.m.

'Gordon's Veterinary Surgery. Lisa speaking. How may I help?' the polite, softly-spoken receptionist said at the other end of the phone.

'Hi. I need to speak to Mike. Tell him it's Steve.'

'I'm sorry, sir,' came the polite voice again. 'Mike has an Open Surgery this afternoon. Would you like to leave a message and I'll get him to call you back later?'

'Listen, sweetheart,' Steve Morgan said, with a hint of lunacy in his voice. 'This is an emergency. Mike needs to speak to me - NOW!'

'Please hold the line, sir,' Lisa said, unnerved by the strange man at the other end of the phone.

There was a pause of about three minutes, before Steve Morgan heard anything else.

'Steve?' Mike Gordon said, very annoyed that he had been summoned away from his examination of Derek Bustard's tabby cat.

'Mike!' Steve replied, very relieved to hear his friend's familiar voice. 'I need you to meet me, mate. As soon as possible.'

'What the hell is going on, Steve?' Mike Gordon asked impatiently, trying not to let the clients sitting in his waiting room hear his phone conversation.

'Somebody's nicked Susan Carmichael's bloody dog!' Steve said frantically.

'So it's not dead then?' Mike enquired, confused.

'Oh yes. It's dead alright,' Steve replied. 'But some lunatic's only gone and stolen it from Charlotte. She said he was a foreigner.'

'Are you taking the piss, Steve? I mean – you do know that I'm working. I don't have time for jokes at the moment.' Mike was becoming more and more irritated by the phone call.

'I swear to you, mate – I'm not taking the piss. You have to help me out of this one, Mike. Susan Carmichael is going to rip my privates off when she finds out about this.'

'OK, OK Steve – I get it.' Mike realised that Steve Morgan was on the verge of having a nervous breakdown. Indeed; *he* would be having a nervous breakdown if he was faced with telling Susan Carmichael that her beloved dog had died. And been *stolen*. 'I'll be finished here at half-past-four. Meet me in 'The Rising Dawn' – just up from here – shortly after that. I have to go now,' he added, smiling pleasantly over at a middle-aged lady, who was holding a rabbit on her lap in his waiting area: Mike had suddenly realised the woman was listening intently to his phone conversation.

'Thanks Mike – you're a life-saver.' Steve Morgan quickly put down the phone at his end.

Steve Morgan and Mike Gordon had been cronies ever since their university years. They had pulled each other out of many a tight spot in the past – and Steve Morgan desperately hoped that Mike would come good again on this occasion. Steve decided that he needed a stiff drink – now. He turned to grab his coat from the hanger behind the desk in Reception, and swung it under his right arm, accidentally clipping Susan Carmichael's tall umbrella plant as he did so. The plant toppled over on the floor – its soil spilling everywhere onto the carpet behind the Reception Desk. 'Sod it!' Steve said, before kicking the fallen plant, grabbing the keys to the practice, and exiting.

Steve locked the practice door behind him. He was only just about bothered to operate the electric shutters at the front of the premises, before he eventually began to make his way down the busy High Street, towards the car park, where his top-of-the-range Land Rover was stationed.

Steve now began to formulate his plans for the evening. He thought that he would drive to the private car park owned by one of his dental clients, Harriet Harper, which was located down a private alleyway, just behind Harriet's bookmaker's shop. Harper's was just a few doors away from 'The Rising Dawn', where Steve was due to meet Mike Gordon at 4.30 p.m. Steve thought that he would simply leave the Land Rover at the car park overnight, and get the tube home, after he had had a few drinks. Harriet never minded when Steve asked her for a favour: he was confident that she would comply with his wishes on this occasion, therefore.

As Steve pulled onto the High Street to begin his short drive to Harriet Harper's car park, he regretted the day he had ever agreed to dog-sit Dixie Carmichael. He couldn't believe that such a small and insignificant dog had created so much havoc, for so many people.

-CHAPTER NINE-

The Rising Dawn

Matthew Rourke had been sitting in 'The Rising Dawn' for over three hours. He looked at the clock behind the bar, which told him that it was 4.25 p.m.: he knew he had definitely missed all of the Recruitment Fair by now.

Matthew had lost count of the number of pints of home brew he had consumed since first entering The Rising Dawn at lunch time, but he guessed that it must be around five or six. He knew that he must be intoxicated, but for some unknown reason, he felt strangely in control of all of his faculties. It was almost as though the alcohol streaming through Matthew's body had slowed his mind down to such an extent that he was now able to enjoy a magical stillness within; something that he hadn't felt in a very, very long time.

For Matthew, time had now *frozen*.

As he sat in his bubble of timelessness and calm, he felt completely protected from the world around him. Matthew somehow sensed that an invisible force had removed him from all of the realities and difficulties that comprised human life – for now, anyway. He would relish every moment of this sensation, he resolved. Matthew looked around The Rising Dawn. He could see that it was relatively empty now – compared to when he had first arrived; but even stranger than this, Matthew Rourke felt as though he was *invisible* to everyone there.

He was able to observe the other clientele: there was a group of three smartly-dressed businesswomen eating bar snacks at a table near the window; three barmen; a waitress; two young men, chatting whilst playing slot machines near the bar; and a gentleman of about forty-years-of-age, sitting alone at a table, drinking a bottle of white wine. While Matthew knew that he was able to observe all of those around him, he had the distinct feeling that they were completely oblivious to his presence – for as long as Matthew needed that to be the case.

All noise now filtered completely away from Matthew. All he could hear was stillness and silence. Any degree of self-consciousness or anxiety he had experienced since his arrival at The Rising Dawn completely left him now. It felt almost as though Matthew was looking over his own shoulder at his life; like he had become detached from his own physical body, and was able to observe things with more clarity and sense. Matthew was alone; at peace; frozen in time and space.

He suddenly found himself back at the area of woodland, inside Unity Park. He could smell the muskiness of the Silver Birches, Rowan and Oak above him, and feel the dampness of the grass beneath his feet. Matthew didn't feel frightened or panicky – as he had earlier – but rather he was calm and observant. He felt as though the trees and grass and sky had taken on a life-force of their own; as though they were now his companions and friends.

Matthew stood and looked down again at the flowery bag at his feet. It was zipped closed, but for some reason, Matthew felt compelled to open it again.

As he pulled the familiar zip once more along its indented track, the only sound he could hear was the soft swish of the breeze amongst the branches above his head. Matthew looked into the bag. It was empty. The dog had completely vanished.

Before he could react to this discovery, Matthew suddenly realised that he could hear voices deeper inside the area of woodland – just ahead. He decided to walk further into the trees, to investigate who these voices belonged to.

As Matthew approached a large Oak, he was able to see the figures of two people just beyond it: a small boy, and his older, taller-looking male companion. Matthew came closer to them now. He stared hard at them. He recognised who they were. He was looking at his younger self – and his brother, Christian.

The two boys were laughing and talking happily. The sun was shining down on them through the branches of the trees above, onto the clearing where they were playing.

Before Matthew was able to observe this scene from his youth any longer, he suddenly found himself transported elsewhere.

He was sitting behind the wheel of a car. He wasn't actually driving the car; but he was *watching* his younger self drive it. As Matthew looked on at this scene, the vision gradually began to widen, until he was able to see his brother, Christian, sitting beside him in the front seat of the car. Matthew could hear the happy conversation they were having:

'So what else did you get up to?' Matthew asked Christian.

'We played policemen and robbers. And Jamie hit Gary. And Gary's mum shouted at him,' Christian replied.

'I hope you didn't get involved!'

'No. Me and Richard just went over to the table and got more sweets.'

'Would you like to go to the cinema with me tomorrow? To watch *The Spider Mystery*?'

'Really?' Christian was very excited. 'Do you mean it, Matthew?'

'Of course I do! We're best mates, after all – aren't we, Bud?' Matthew said, glancing over at Christian beside him.

'Yeah!' Christian said proudly. 'I love being your best mate, Matthew!'

All of a sudden, Matthew Rourke now found himself sitting behind the wheel of the car - he had – up until now – just been observing. He looked deeply into the eyes of his younger brother. They were sparkling with life; happiness; joy. They were vibrant green. Christian was beaming with childhood happiness. He was as happy as any child could ever hope to be on earth, Matthew could see.

Then everything stopped.

Matthew Rourke began to sense himself hurtling backwards into darkness. He had no control now over his movements or his whereabouts. He couldn't see or hear anything. He let himself fall freely, until he eventually stopped, and found himself sitting back at the table inside The Rising Dawn.

Matthew could feel the heaviness and form of his physical body once more. He could see the people sitting around him, inside The Rising Dawn. He could hear the noises inside the bar again. He looked at the clock behind the bar, which told him that it was still 4.25 p.m.

As Matthew took hold of the pint glass sitting on the table in front of him, he gripped its base tightly, to ensure that it was real. He lifted the glass up to his mouth, and took three long, heavy mouthfuls of the stale-tasting liquid inside it. Matthew felt thoroughly disorientated by the realities of the world that surrounded him now. He felt overwhelmed by the noises, the smells, the tastes, touch and sight of everything inside the bar. Matthew had to get out. Now. He had to get out into some fresh air, to figure out what had just happened to him.

Matthew placed his pint glass back onto the table again. He looked up, in an attempt to take in his surroundings, before he would eventually stand up, and walk out of The Rising Dawn.

As he focused, he watched a tall, burly-looking man walking past his table, towards the forty-something-year-old-man Matthew had noticed earlier; sitting alone at a table, drinking a bottle of white wine. The burly-looking man was about forty-years-old, Matthew thought. He was dark-haired, moustached and perma-tanned. Matthew watched, as the man took a seat beside the gentleman with the bottle of white wine. The two men flashed their super-white teeth at one another; but they were soon deep in conversation. They looked agitated, Matthew thought; especially the gentleman drinking the white wine – who was rolling his eyes to heaven, and shaking his head. Matthew decided not to listen in on the two men's conversation. He needed to go now – to establish what had just happened to him, inside The Rising Dawn.

Matthew stood up. Before he began to walk towards the exit, he steadied himself by briefly holding onto his table. He walked out of The Rising Dawn, and onto the High Street once more. It was beginning to get dark outside. Everything still felt a bit surreal to Matthew – like he was still looking on at his own life. He decided to go back to the same tube station he had arrived at earlier that day. Matthew needed to go home now, he thought to himself; although he had no idea yet what would happen between him and his wife, Ruth, when he got there. Matthew Rourke began to walk towards the tube station. His mind was blank, except for a few passing thoughts about the white dog and the flowery bag.

*****

Meanwhile, back inside The Rising Dawn, the two gentlemen Matthew Rourke had been observing were still talking.

The burly-looking man had by now ordered himself a pint of stout, while the other gentleman had started on his second bottle of sauvignon blanc.

'So you're telling me that Charlotte just went off shopping – without even letting you know that the dog had been stolen?' Mike Gordon asked incredulously, as he took a large mouthful of stout.

'You have no idea what I have to put up with, mate,' Steve Morgan replied, shaking his head. 'My wife and daughter are from a different galaxy: the bloody Sulky Way.' Steve often talked about his wife and daughter in such flattering terms to Mike Gordon. He thought it would endear him to his 'mate'. Steve assumed that *he* must be the smartest in the Morgan household – simply because he had the most paper qualifications. He completely underestimated Amanda and Charlotte Morgan's intelligence.

'So what the hell are you going to tell Susan and Ray? I mean – it's obviously not Ray I'd be worrying about – if I were you. Susan's going to go ape when she finds out. She's capable of murder where that dog's concerned, you know?'

'Thanks for that, Mike,' Steve answered, a little irate. 'I was kind of hoping that you might actually be able to help me out here.'

'What? You mean you'd like me to craftily acquire another West Highland Terrier – and try to pass it off as Dixie Carmichael?' Mike laughed.

'Could you?'

'Catch a grip, Steve! You really don't think Susan Carmichael would recognise the difference between Dixie and another Westie? Come on – that dog was Susan's baby!'

'You're making me feel very positive here, Mike,' Steve Morgan said acerbically. 'Could you at least suggest how I might explain to Susan why her beloved three-year-old dog could possibly have died so prematurely? Especially when I told her this morning that he looked as fit as a fiddle?'

'Beats me, Steve,' Mike said, nonplussed. 'Unless the dog died from a broken heart in her absence maybe.'

'*Really*? So you reckon it was Susan's fault that the dog died?' Steve asked excitedly.

'For God's sake, Steve. Of course I don't! I'm afraid you're just going to have to be straight with Susan, and tell her you don't know what happened to the dog – Lord help you!' Mike was laughing again.

Steve Morgan glared over at Mike Gordon now. Steve was terrified. He had banked on Mike steering him out of the crisis over Susan Carmichael and her (stolen) dead dog. Steve hadn't a clue what he was going to do now. Mike had always been able to get him out of messes in the past – probably because Mike had been in so many messes of his own making during his adult life. Mike Gordon had been divorced by his wife, Janet, two years ago, when she discovered that he was having a long-term affair with Barbara Black, a twenty-three-year-old gym instructor. Mike was an ex-rugby player, and he still enjoyed working out at the 'Elite Physique' exclusive gym in Central London. He had always had form with the ladies, so being married with two teenage daughters (Louise, 14; and Sara, 13) hadn't changed Mike's lifestyle much at all. Mike now lived alone (except when he had 'company') in his smart bachelor pad, near the Carmichaels' Edwardian home. Up until this morning, he had been Dixie Carmichael's vet.

'Anyway,' Mike said. 'Who the hell is *Madeleine*?'

Steve Morgan paused before answering. He could probably do with Mike's advice on that one too, he thought now. 'A *client*,' Steve answered tentatively, as he took a large drink of white wine.

'OK. I get it.' Mike understood Steve's coded language perfectly. 'Madeleine *who*, exactly?'

'Singleton.' Steve took another large drink of wine.

Mike paused in disbelief before speaking again. 'Steve. Please tell me you are not talking about Madeleine Singleton – as in *Douglas* Singleton – *are* you?'

'Yes,' Steve said sheepishly, not quite understanding why he suddenly felt like the stupid school boy, explaining himself to the older school bully.

'You bloody idiot!' Mike exclaimed in disgust: Steve Morgan had just gone way down in Mike's estimation. 'For God's sake, Steve – are you on a suicide mission – or what? You do know she's called MAD–eleine for a reason - don't you?'

'No. What do you mean?'

'I mean - she's an absolute looper, Steve. She's been throwing herself at every bloke over the age of sixteen at the gym for the last few months – but they've all had the sense to run a mile in the opposite direction.' Mike Gordon proceeded to fill Steve Morgan in on Madeleine Singleton's many past antics: her recent nymphomaniacal tendencies (which Mike had heard Madeleine had learnt from her more-than-eccentric sister); her drinking bouts; not to mention her ruthless, money-grabbing lawyer husband. 'Please don't tell me there's any chance that *Dastardly Douglas* will get to find out about your fling with his wife.'

'That's the thing,' Steve responded. 'She told me this morning that she's already told him. But I don't know whether or not to believe her.'

'You've had it.' Mike Gordon sat back in his seat.

'THAT BLOODY DOG!' Steve Morgan shouted angrily, banging his fist on the table.

'Shut up! – will you?' Mike Gordon looked around at the almost-empty bar to ensure that nobody was listening to his conversation with Steve Morgan. 'How the hell can you blame the dog for this one?'

'Because I wouldn't have lost my temper with Madeleine – if I hadn't heard that the damned dog had died – *would* I?' Steve was irate; his face was a vivid shade of pink now.

'OK, OK – steady on, Steve. Don't take it out on me.'

'What do I do now, Mike?' Steve was desperate.

'I think you just sit back and wait, Steve. Weigh up your options and be ready to react when the Singletons hit you with the legal papers.' Mike paused before delivering his next piece of friendly advice. 'They could put Epsilon out of practice, you do realise that? These lawyer types are sniffing around professionals like you and I right now, looking for easy bucks, because they can't get it in the property market any longer.'

Steve Morgan felt physically sick. He had always looked up to Mike Gordon and his philandering ways in the past. Mike had always been a bit of a 'bloke'. He had always been able to have his cake and eat it – and that had been partly what Steve Morgan had aspired to as well. Steve had enjoyed endearing himself to Mike over the years: Mike, whom he had always followed around - a bit like a smitten puppy. Something now began to dawn on Steve Morgan, however. Mike Gordon didn't give a shit about him – nor had he ever likely given a shit about him. Steve knew that he was in it alone now. He was in it alone with Susan Carmichael and her stolen dead dog; and he was in it alone with Madeleine Singleton and her money-grabbing two-faced lawyer husband. Steve Morgan had never felt so alone and afraid in all his life. He began to think about Amanda and Charlotte. Amanda had always disliked Mike Gordon, Steve knew: she had warned Steve about Mike's 'type' on many occasions in the past, in fact.

'You've made your own bed this time,' Mike Gordon said, slightly smugly: he had always known he was the slicker, more professional cheat of the two. 'I thought you were smarter than that,' he added, slugging on his stout. 'You silly, silly boy.'

Steve didn't respond. He continued to drink his white wine in silence for some minutes, until Mike Gordon spoke again. 'Are you going to tell the Carmichaels about the Dixie situation tonight?'

'No way. It will be time enough telling them when they get back on Sunday evening. And anyway. I'll have Amanda to deal with tonight. I'm sure Charlotte has told her about the dog situation by now.'

'Probably,' Mike Gordon said.

Steve Morgan and Mike Gordon sat in The Rising Dawn for another two hours, before they eventually left for the tube station at 6.55 p.m.

The two men got off the train at the same stop. Mike Gordon walked home to his modern bachelor pad, while Steve Morgan began the walk home to his detached Victorian residence. Steve began to wonder if it would be his home for much longer.

*****

Matthew Rourke had arrived back in his apartment in TW9 at around 5.20 p.m. that evening. He had been thinking deeply ever since.

It was by now 7.26 p.m., and Matthew was sitting on the sofa inside his darkened lounge, drinking from the fourth bottle of beer he had opened since his arrival home. Ruth was out. She had been out since before Matthew's arrival at 5.20

p.m. Matthew didn't know where Ruth was, but for once, he didn't really care. He supposed that she must either be at a hair appointment, shopping or swimming at the local pools. He was hopeful that she wouldn't arrive home any time soon.

Matthew clearly recognised that something very profound had happened to him earlier, inside The Rising Dawn. He couldn't get the image of Christian's vibrant green eyes out of his mind. Matthew felt as though Christian had been trying to tell him something earlier – but he daren't yet think about what that possibly could have been.

Matthew now began to recall how he had re-entered the wooded area, inside Unity Park; as he had sat, zoned-out from his own physical body, inside The Rising Dawn. Matthew questioned the white dog's absence from the flowery bag on that occasion: Where had the dog gone? What did this mean?

But Matthew's mind kept returning to Christian.

Did I imagine everything? Matthew now wondered, as he took another slow drink from his bottle of cold, stale beer. Everything had felt so real; as Matthew had watched his younger self driving Christian in the car, chatting happily with him. But surely this had only been a vivid dream?

Matthew now recalled the conversation he had enjoyed with Christian inside the car. He remembered asking Christian about what he had been doing, earlier that day. Christian had been playing; eating sweets; messing about with his friends. It was as though Christian had just been to a *party.*

Matthew Rourke froze at this point. He thought he was about to vomit – just as he had earlier, when he first glimpsed the dead dog inside the flowery bag. Matthew instantaneously began to sob like a child. He suddenly recognised the scene he had revisited inside The Rising Dawn: it was the lost minutes before the crash that had killed Christian, sixteen years ago. Matthew had never been able to recall these moments, until now: except he didn't really feel as though he had recalled them - more like he had been permitted to *relive* them. Matthew had been able to stare into Christian's smiling eyes – as though Christian was still *alive.* Matthew had met his younger brother one more time.

As he continued to sit inside his darkened lounge, Matthew Rourke felt completely overwhelmed with emotion. He suddenly began to laugh. He didn't doubt what he had seen or experienced inside The Rising Dawn now. Matthew sensed that Christian had come to let him know that he was OK; that Christian and Matthew were OK; that they were still friends and brothers. The dead dog inside the flowery bag had somehow forced Matthew to remember his last few moments with Christian on earth.

*****

The front door of Matthew's apartment now closed with a bang.

Matthew hadn't heard it opening to begin with, but he assumed that it must be Ruth, as he rose from the sofa to turn on the lounge light. Before he had managed to do this, however, Matthew watched Ruth through the lounge door, as she crept past him, towards the direction of the kitchen. Matthew now walked into the corridor, and proceeded to follow his wife into the kitchen. He stood swaying in the doorway, looking at her. Ruth had her back turned to Matthew. She was busy tidying away a few groceries she had purchased in the nearby convenience store on her way home. Matthew sensed that Ruth must have been at the pool, since her long blonde hair still looked slightly wet. 'Hi,' he said casually.

'Oh my God!!!' Ruth cried hysterically, as she flung herself around to face Matthew. 'What the hell are you playing at, Matthew? This is the second time this week you've nearly scared me half to death!'

'I hardly did it deliberately – on either occasion,' Matthew replied calmly, with a slightly glazed expression on his face.

Ruth paused now, unnerved by her husband's strange demeanour: the Matthew she knew would usually be grovelling and begging for her forgiveness by now. 'Are you pissed, Matthew?'

'More than likely.' Matthew stared indifferently at Ruth.

'What the hell have you been doing all day? Were you not at the Recruitment Fair?'

'No. It didn't quite work out that way.'

'What's that supposed to mean?'

'It's supposed to mean that it didn't quite work out that way,' Matthew repeated, as he opened the fridge to take out another cold bottle of beer.

'Are you sure you should be drinking that?' Ruth felt a little uneasy now.

'Quite sure.' Matthew smiled, before leaving the kitchen.

'Get back here now, Matthew!'

Matthew Rourke chose to ignore his wife, much to her unease and horror. Ruth had no idea what to do next. *She* had called the shots in their relationship up until now - but Matthew somehow appeared to have forgotten that. Ruth didn't feel in control at the moment. She was used to controlling her compliant husband with her frequent foul moods. She needed a drink badly. She had to get away from Matthew, to gather her thoughts, and to figure out how to proceed with all of this. Ruth was sure that Matthew would repent for his unacceptable behaviour soon. He looked like a psycho now, Ruth thought. She would phone her sister, Eva, for moral support.

'EVA!' Ruth exclaimed when her sister lifted the phone: it was by now 7.45 p.m.

'Ruth?' Eva asked, slightly taken aback by Ruth's crazed tone of voice.

'Eva – I have to meet you – now! Matthew's gone mad!' Ruth was hysterical: she had watched a psychological thriller earlier that day, while she had lay in bed, recovering from her hangover from the previous night's drinking.

'What do you mean – Matthew's gone mad?'

'Trust me. He needs sectioned.' Ruth was whispering now.

'Why? What's he done?'

'He's sitting drinking beer by himself in the lounge. I think he's pissed,' Ruth whispered, as though she had just discovered she was sharing her apartment with a murderer she had just recognised from a T.V. crime reconstruction.

'Well that's a sure sign of madness – isn't it?' Eva replied sardonically: she was annoyed that she had apparently been disturbed for no real reason. 'The entire adult population of this country should be sectioned - if that's what constitutes madness, Ruth.'

'You don't understand, Eva. I know Matthew. There's something really different about him tonight. He's creepy and weird. You have to meet me. I can't stay here by myself with him!'

'But I've already made plans for this evening.'

'Oh. Right. Sure,' Ruth replied manipulatively. 'Do you really think I'd ask you to meet me on a Friday night if it wasn't an emergency?' Ruth was good at getting her own way with Eva; just as she usually was with Matthew.

Eva thought about what Ruth had just said, before replying. She did recall that Matthew's demeanour had been a little strange – perhaps even *dark* – earlier that day, when she had encountered Matthew inside the convenience store, near Unity Park. Eva had put this down to Matthew having lost his job – but she couldn't be quite sure now. 'OK, Ruth,' Eva said. 'I'll get on the next train and meet you.'

'Thanks, Eva. You're a life-saver. Meet me at 'The Twisted Corkscrew' – you remember it – the bar on Old Street.'

'OK,' Eva replied, before putting down the phone.

Eva was not happy. She had become increasingly fed up recently, running around after Ruth and her latest dramas. Eva had always been loyal and good-natured when it came to her younger sister in the past; but Eva was beginning to run out of patience with her now.

Eva lifted the phone once more, this time to cancel her previous plans for the evening. She knew that the person on the other end of the phone would be upset by this – but no more upset and angry than Eva was currently.

Meanwhile, Ruth Rourke crept past her husband, who was by now fast asleep on the sofa in the lounge. She grabbed some money from a drawer, and then walked back into the corridor, and out the front door.

Matthew did not hear his wife leave the apartment that evening, nor would he hear her entering again – shortly after midnight. He had drifted off into the dream realms, where he hoped he might meet his brother, Christian, again.

*****

As Matthew Rourke slept, Dixie Carmichael looked on, contented. He was pleased with the progress Matthew had made since discovering his earthly body inside the flowery bag. He knew, however, that Matthew still had a long way to go – before he would finally reach his desired destination.

-CHAPTER TEN-

The End of a Long Day

Steve Morgan arrived back at his detached Victorian residence at 8.32 p.m. on Friday 7th October – to find a police car at the front door.

Although he had arrived at his nearby tube station an hour previous, Steve had decided to have one more drink (a neat Scotch) in his local, 'The Dutchman', before he finally returned home to face the ire of his wife, Amanda.

While he had been at The Dutchman, Steve had received an incoming call from Susan Carmichael, which he had chosen not to answer. Instead, Steve forwarded her a text, which read: 'Hi Susan. Dog fine. Can't talk because I have diarrhoea.' Steve had once read somewhere that people never tended to question a person who claimed to have diarrhoea. The theory had appeared to hold true: Susan never texted or called back.

As Steve stood now, attempting to focus on the driveway in front of him, he began to imagine the worst. Steve supposed that the police were there to inform him that Madeleine and Douglas Singleton had decided to press charges against Epsilon Dental Spa. Amanda would be doubly unimpressed with him tonight, Steve feared.

Steve (eventually) reached the impressive front door to his home. He peered through its paned side panels to see if he could see anybody – but there was no activity at all inside the fully-lit, generously-proportioned hallway. Steve fumbled in his coat pocket for his keys; but before he had time to locate them, Amanda appeared in the hallway with two uniformed policemen. 'Sssshit,' Steve said out loud.

Amanda Morgan walked towards the front door with the two policemen, chatting and shaking her head, as if in disbelief. She opened the front door to let the two uniformed gentlemen leave, whereupon she stumbled upon her husband, who had been leaning against the door. Steve fell forwards into the hallway, knocking into the taller of the two policemen. 'Sorry about that,' Steve mumbled apologetically, as he steadied himself once more. Amanda Morgan glared at her husband. Steve had never been lower in her estimation than he was right now – and he had stooped incredibly low in the past. 'I'm sorry about this Officers Steele and Jenkins,' Amanda said, mortified. 'This is my husband, Steve Morgan.'

'Good evening, Sir,' the taller officer replied.

'Is everything alright then?' Steve asked, flashing his super-white teeth at Officer Jenkins.

'Oh yes, Sir. Just taking a routine statement.'

'Good! Absolutely! Thank-you folks!' Steve said, not really knowing what he was saying.

'You do know why they're here – don't you?' Amanda Morgan snapped angrily at her husband.

'Amanda. It meant nothing,' Steve blabbered. 'We can get the right legal team and it will all be fine!'

Amanda glared at her husband, and then at Officers Steele and Jenkins, who looked curiously back at her. 'How the hell is *the right legal team* supposed to retrieve a stolen dead West Highland Terrier? What the hell are we going to tell Ray and Susan when they get back on Sunday, Steve?'

'A stolen dead .... ? Oh – that?!'

'What do you mean – *Oh that*? What *else* did you think Officers Steele and Jenkins might be here for?'

'Oh – nothing! Nothing! I've just had a bit too much to drink this evening – Ossifers.'

'OK Sir,' Officer Jenkins responded dubiously. 'Well, Mrs Morgan. Do call us again if your daughter thinks she can remember anything else.'

'I will, Officer,' Amanda replied politely, as she ushered the two policemen past her drunken husband, and out the front door.

'Bye!' Steve shouted, as he flashed another smile in the direction of Officers Steele and Jenkins.

The two policemen walked towards their car, marvelling at how 'the other half' live. Steele and Jenkins would later put the 'stolen dead dog' case at the bottom of their 'to do' list: they weren't going to risk the ire of London tube staff, by requesting potential CCTV footage of a foreign male, running about in a suit, carrying a flowery bag – with a *dead dog* inside.

Amanda Morgan shut the front door with a bang. She turned to Steve, who was still grinning drunkenly. Amanda recalled how Steve used to have a lovely, warm smile: it was more of a face-stretching, veneer-revealing exercise nowadays, she thought.

'That went well!' Steve said hopefully.

Amanda was so appalled by her husband's behaviour at this stage, she didn't even dare to open her mouth in his presence – yet. She stormed past Steve, and marched straight into the kitchen, where her daughter, Charlotte, was still sitting at the large breakfast bar, where the two police officers had just interviewed her over Dixie Carmichael's theft. Steve shuffled immediately after his wife – not fully realising the extent of Amanda's foul mood this evening. It was by now 8.45 p.m.

'Just stay away from me, Steve!' Amanda yelled angrily, as her husband entered the kitchen. 'I will not be held responsible for my actions tonight if you as much as come near me.'

'What's the matter?' Steve enquired, raising and circling his arms like an air-traffic controller.

'You absolute asshole! How dare you ask what's the matter!'

'What have I done?' Steve asked, as though his soul was whiter than his veneers.

'How the hell could you think that it was OK to tell your nineteen-year-old daughter to haul a dead dog about London?'

'What else was I supposed to do?' Steve protested, ambling casually towards the fridge for a bottle of wine: the alcohol he had consumed – not to mention his relief that the Singletons hadn't pressed charges (yet) – had given Steve an inflated sense of confidence and security.

'You were meant to have been looking after the bloody dog yourself. You were meant to have gone straight over to the Carmichaels' yourself, when Charlotte told you about the dog dying! What the hell were you up to all day anyway?'

'You didn't mind – did you, Charlotte?' Steve asked casually.

'Of course I minded!' Charlotte shouted from her high stool at the breakfast bar. 'The only reason I did it was because you said you'd treat me to a holiday! Oh – and, by the way, I'm still holding you to that one. *And* the room makeover: *and* the hair extensions.'

'You are aware that your daughter got mugged today - by some foreigner – aren't you?'

'*And* I've had to ask Melody Glazier not to collect me until 9.30 p.m. – because of the police and that stupid dog.'

'You really are such an irresponsible prick-of-an-excuse-of-a-man.' Amanda added.

Something now snapped inside Steve Morgan. While the thought of explaining himself over the stolen dead dog had worried him somewhat, earlier, the alcohol streaming through his bloodstream had by now blocked any of his remaining rational faculties. Steve looked at his wife and daughter sitting side by side at the breakfast bar. They were evidently both dressed for a glamorous night out on the town. He knew for definite that Amanda had been out all day at beauty salons, preening herself. Steve was sick of feeling like the prick between the two well-maintained roses. He was sick and tired of everybody right now. 'Oh get stuffed – the lot of you!' he shouted.

'That's right, Steve. You just slope off – away from all your responsibilities – as usual.' Amanda was livid; she wasn't even thinking straight. 'Just like you did when your daughter died!'

There was a stunned silence.

Steve, Amanda and Charlotte Morgan glanced around at each other, dumbfounded, before Charlotte eventually spoke. 'What are you talking about, mum? What daughter died?'

Steve looked at Amanda, and Amanda looked back at Steve. Amanda recognised the look in her husband's eyes. It was that look that said *this is all getting a bit too much for me.* It was the exact look Steve had given Amanda when he had stood staring at her, as she held the tiny body of their daughter, Matilda, just moments after Matilda died. Just as he did on that occasion, Steve said *nothing* now. He turned and walked quickly out of the room.

'That's it!' Amanda shouted after her husband, with angry tears in her eyes, as Steve walked into his downstairs office with his bottle of wine. 'You go off now and pretend that nothing has happened. Leave me to fix it all by myself – *again!*'

'Mum!' Charlotte shouted. 'What's going on? What daughter is he talking about?'

Amanda was crying loudly by now. 'Charlotte!' she begged, as she reached over to hold her daughter. 'I had always meant to tell you. It was just never the right time. I didn't want to upset you. I didn't know how to talk to you about it,' she sobbed.

Charlotte pulled back from Amanda, still very frightened and confused. 'Tell me what?'

'Oh Charlotte!'

'TELL ME *WHAT*?'

'That you had a twin sister, Charlotte,' Amanda said softly. 'But she died – just after she was born.'

There was another stunned silence inside the Morgans' kitchen, as Amanda and Charlotte looked into each other's eyes. 'I have to phone Ebony,' Charlotte said calmly. 'I can't go out now.'

'Charlotte!' Amanda yelled as her daughter rushed past her, out of the kitchen, and upstairs to her bedroom.

Charlotte slammed and locked her bedroom door behind her, and threw herself face-down on top of her double bed. She began to sob uncontrollably. She reached over for her phone, which informed her that it was just after 9.00 p.m. Charlotte then texted Ebony Glazier to let her know that she wouldn't be going out that evening; and Ebony immediately called her back.

'What's wrong?' Ebony enquired, when Charlotte answered her call.

'I can't talk about it, Ebz.'

'Are you crying? Oh my God, Charlotte – what's going on?'

'Some other time, Ebony. Just let Melody know she's not to come around here tonight. I'll explain to you some other time – maybe. I'm sorry.' Charlotte ended the call immediately.

Charlotte Morgan now sat on the end of her bed, not really understanding what emotions she was experiencing. This day had been a complete disaster – from start to finish – and all because of a dead dog. She didn't know who to turn to any more. Charlotte would usually talk to her mum, Amanda, when bad things came her way; but Charlotte didn't even know if she could trust *her* any longer. How could Amanda not have told her that she had a twin sister? What had *happened* to her sister? What had been her *name*?

Charlotte began to cry uncontrollably again. She was furious. She was desperate to go downstairs to her mother again, but she needed to figure out what she would say to Amanda first.

'Charlotte?' Amanda's voice said at the door.

'Not now,' Charlotte ordered. 'Not yet.'

'OK, darling,' Amanda whispered softly. 'I'm so sorry. I can explain it all to you. Please come downstairs soon and talk to me – will you?' Amanda was still crying. She couldn't believe she was having this conversation with Charlotte tonight.

'OK,' Charlotte said abruptly. She then heard Amanda walk back downstairs again.

Charlotte had never felt so isolated in all her life. She had never really been very close to anyone – except Amanda. While Charlotte did have several hundred *VaneChums*, and although she was always *Two-ting* a huge network of Twopenniesworths; Charlotte Morgan had always sought to keep most people at arm's length – except perhaps Ebony and Melody Glazier. She had never really trusted anyone. Charlotte had always felt as though there was something missing in her life. She had always presumed that this might have been due to her father's neglect over the years. Charlotte was angry at Steve for constantly having fobbed her off with money and excuses in the past. She had never been able to figure out why Steve had been so glaringly obviously absent from her and Amanda's lives throughout the years. Charlotte had frequently blamed herself for Steve's indifference. The only way she had been able to grab her father's attention as she grew up had been through annoying him and disobeying him – even though she knew that this made him dislike her even more.

Charlotte had never been able to work out what had happened between Steve and her mother, however. She could clearly see now that Amanda didn't like Steve any more, and she could understand why – given Steve's irresponsible, selfish behaviour. Amanda had told Charlotte on numerous occasions that Steve was suffering from a serious case of 'arrested development', which had set in shortly after Charlotte was born. But what Charlotte really couldn't understand was why her parents had ever got together in the first place; why they had grown to hate each other so much; and why they had even chosen to remain together for this long. Amanda had always reassured Charlotte that none of it had been Charlotte's fault. She had even told her daughter that she shouldn't worry about anything like that – that she should just get on with enjoying her own life.

Charlotte had tried to do as her mother advised. She had created a whole family and network of friends around her – thanks mainly to MyVaneSpace and Twopenniesworth. Charlotte loved looking on at the lives of others; watching their dramas unfold; laughing at their stupid relationships and break-ups; hearing about their families, social lives and daily routines. But something was still missing for

Charlotte. She had recently begun to question 'the point' of everything. Charlotte sometimes felt as though she didn't even have any control over her own life. She did things – like buy clothes, get her hair done, socialise and work – but it all felt a bit boring at times (not that Charlotte would ever want to imagine a day where there wasn't any shopping, hair-dos or socialising). She wanted her life to be a bit more like Ebony and Melody Glaziers'. Charlotte wanted to know what she could be good at; what she could do to make all the other crap worthwhile. She knew that she had always done her bit for the community – by always updating her MyVaneSpace page, posting Twopenniesworths, and keeping up with everybody's lives – but she was bored with this community work now.

Charlotte needed to talk to Amanda. She had to find out about her mother's past, in order to begin to piece together her own future.

Charlotte took off her make-up and changed out of her designer cat suit, into her night clothes, before she ventured downstairs to confront Amanda.

The house was in complete silence – a bit like the Carmichaels' had been earlier. As Charlotte got to the bottom of the stairs, she could hear her father's laughter coming from his office. Charlotte knew that every time Steve was pissed he went back to his glory days – his student days – and watched old game shows and T.V. programmes from the 1980s and 1990s. She knew that her father had never really grown up: Charlotte had heard Amanda say that on numerous occasions.

Charlotte walked into the kitchen, and saw Amanda sitting alone at the breakfast bar, eating a bowl of something. Her mum was still dressed as though she was about to go out, although her make-up had been entirely messed-up by all the crying she had done that evening.

'Charlotte!' Amanda said, rising to her feet. Charlotte looked at her mum before starting to cry like a child. Amanda ran over to her daughter and embraced her, cuddling and swaying with her, telling her calmly and softly to *shhhh*.

After several minutes, mother and daughter looked at one another again, before Charlotte spoke: 'Did I really have a twin sister?'

'Yes,' Amanda answered sadly.

'What was her name?'

'Matilda.'

*****

For the next two-and-a-half-hours, Amanda and Charlotte spoke about all that had happened, nineteen years ago, when Charlotte and Matilda were born.

Charlotte Morgan discovered that she had been born only a matter of minutes before her twin sister. It had been a very long and arduous labour for Amanda, and Charlotte had appeared reluctant to be born at all. When Matilda was eventually delivered safely, all had initially appeared well with both babies – until Matilda suddenly died, only one hour later.

Charlotte found out about how her father, Steve, had been unable to face up to his responsibilities at the time; how he and Amanda had grown rapidly apart from this moment on – despite having been quite in love up to this point. Charlotte also heard Amanda describe how she had often blamed herself for Matilda's death, and for Steve's inability to cope with this. Amanda had offered her husband several opportunities to discuss the matter with her; to be part of Charlotte's life; and to move forward with Amanda and Charlotte as a family. Steve had, however, always chosen not to.

While Amanda now resisted the opportunity to inform Charlotte about Steve's many extra-marital affairs, she managed to convince her daughter, once and for all, that none of the mess had been Charlotte's fault. Nor had it been Amanda's fault (she had only realised this recently herself). In fact, it hadn't even been Steve's fault. It was simply the case that Steve hadn't chosen to confront the hard realities of adult life. Amanda and Steve hadn't been much older than Charlotte was now, when Matilda died – after all.

Amanda went on to explain how she met Steve on her 19th birthday (30th September), only four weeks after Steve's, and right at the beginning of his first year of studies at The Metropolitan School of Dentistry. She had been very vulnerable when she met Steve, as she had only recently lost her aunt, Matilda. Steve had been as caring and intelligent at the time as any nineteen-year-old man could realistically be expected to be. Amanda Montgomery needed somebody she could feel secure around, and Steve happened to fill that gap in her life.

Amanda and Steve got married on Amanda's 20th birthday, and Amanda got pregnant with Charlotte and Matilda a few weeks later, around the middle of October. Charlotte and Matilda were born the following June (22nd), just over nineteen years ago. Both babies had appeared perfectly healthy to begin with, until Matilda's tiny heart suddenly failed her. From this point onwards, the Morgans ceased to operate like a 'normal' family.

Amanda now told Charlotte that she regretted having put her life on hold all this time. She had only really stayed with Steve out of misplaced guilt over her daughter Matilda's death, and because of her naive assumption that Steve might finally grow up some day. Amanda was desperate for Charlotte to have both parents in her life, given that Amanda had lost her own mother at such a young age; and that she had always craved her father's paternal presence (which he had denied her). Amanda even gave Steve the opportunity to exercise his fatherly influence over Charlotte, by standing back when he made decisions over what Charlotte should and should not have: but Steve only really used these 'powers' for his own selfish ends; bribing Charlotte to keep quiet, go away or give him an easier time. Amanda regretted this now too.

Steve had remained with Amanda, she now believed, because it had been the easiest thing for him to do at the time, in a strange kind of way. Amanda provided the financial backing for Steve's increasingly expensive tastes, and he became more and more lazy and careless as time went on. Having a wife and daughter also gave Steve a respectable family-man image – as he went off with Mike Gordon and others like him, philandering and cheating on their partners (although Amanda did not tell Charlotte about this aspect of the story). The only thing that had kept Amanda sane throughout these years had been *Charlotte*.

'You're going to leave him – aren't you mum?' Charlotte asked now.

'I've already decided to, Charlotte. I've just been waiting for the right time to talk to you about it.'

'You don't need to talk to me about it. Just do it – you deserve a lot better than dad now.'

'I'm going to tell your dad tomorrow, Charlotte,' Amanda said calmly, looking directly into her daughter's eyes. 'As soon as he's awake and sober-looking.'

'OK,' Charlotte responded, realising the monumental day that lay ahead for her family.

'Thank-you for being so grown-up and understanding about all of this, Charlotte,' Amanda continued. 'I know this is all a massive thing to take in – and all in one night.'

'Thanks to that bloody dog,' Charlotte said angrily, wiping another wayward tear from her face.

'Well. Things have a funny way of working out sometimes. Poor Susan Carmichael when she gets back.'

'What time is it now?' Charlotte asked her mum.

Amanda looked at her gold wrist watch. 'It's just after midnight. I think your dad must be asleep. It's gone very quiet in his office. I'll throw a blanket over him and turn out the light to let him sleep if off. Anyway, Charlotte - would you like some chicken soup before you go to sleep? I heated some up earlier for myself. I was meant to be going out for a meal – until everything kicked off this evening.'

'No thanks. I'm exhausted.'

Charlotte and Amanda Morgan got up from their seats at the breakfast bar to leave the kitchen and go to bed. Just as Amanda was about to switch off the kitchen light behind them, Charlotte noticed a large bunch of pink roses, sitting on one of the kitchen's granite work surfaces. 'You've never been much into flowers until recently, mum.'

'No,' Amanda replied, a little embarrassed. 'I was told that pink roses are supposed to signify *new beginnings*. Maybe there's something in that, after all.'

Charlotte picked up her mother's meaning immediately. 'You can tell me about who sent them another time.'

'OK.' Amanda was relieved. She was not ready to discuss *that* topic - not after everything else that had happened today.

Charlotte walked upstairs and got into bed, after saying goodnight to her mum. Amanda Morgan then carefully took a rug from one of the drawers in the hallway. She walked into the large office downstairs and placed the rug over her sleeping husband. Steve was fully clothed and asleep in the large armchair in his office. He had barely touched the bottle of white wine he had taken from the fridge earlier: it was still sitting by his feet. Amanda switched off the Game Show Channel Steve had been watching, before turning out the light and walking upstairs to bed. She realised that it might be the last time she would ever spend another night under the same roof as Steve.

*****

As Amanda and Charlotte Morgan drifted off to sleep that night, Eva Kelly was leaving her sister, Ruth Rourke, back to her apartment. It was 12.25 p.m.

'I think he must be sleeping!' Ruth whispered loudly and drunkenly, referring to her husband, Matthew.

'Here he is,' Eva said calmly, as she turned on the corridor light and peered in at her brother-in-law, who was lying slouched asleep on the sofa in the lounge.

'Do you think I'm safe with him?' Ruth asked, with a hint of intoxicated madness in her watery, glazed eyes.

'I think so. Now just get into bed, Ruth. You need to sleep now.'

'OK, OK,' Ruth said, as she stumbled forwards towards her bedroom door. Eva caught her, and steered her sister into the bedroom, helping her to undress and get into bed. 'I'll call you tomorrow – if I'm still alive!' Ruth giggled drunkenly.

'Go to sleep, Ruth.' Eva closed the bedroom door behind her sister.

Eva walked into the corridor once more, before entering the darkened lounge. She looked at her sleeping brother-in-law. Matthew Rourke was still wearing his grey trousers and white shirt from earlier – although his jacket, tie and shoes had been thrown in a bundle at his feet, beside his empty beer bottles.

Eva had always liked Matthew. He had put up with a lot – living with Ruth over the last few years. Eva had listened to her sister's paranoid ranting all evening – the evening when Eva had hoped to put in place plans of her own. As she continued to look at Matthew, she knew instinctively that he wasn't capable of hurting anybody – no matter what nonsense Ruth had got into her head earlier. Eva realised that her brother-in-law was under massive stress right now. She knew that this had undoubtedly led him to behave and act uncharacteristically recently. Eva also recognised that Ruth was a deeply unhappy individual: her sister couldn't even get on with her own reflection at the moment, yet alone please anyone else she came into contact with. Eva felt only compassion for Matthew – but not in a patronising way at all. She deeply hoped that Matthew would find himself a job and happiness soon: whatever or whoever that happiness might entail.

Eva took a throw from one of the armchairs in the lounge, and tucked it carefully around Matthew on the sofa. She looked at him one more time, before leaving the darkened lounge, and finally exiting Ruth and Matthew's apartment. She went onto the street outside. Eva would have to get a taxi home now; the last train from the nearby station would already have departed.

As she headed in the direction of a taxi rank, a few minutes' walk away, Eva Kelly vowed there and then never to let her manipulative, drama-queen sister get in the way of her personal plans again.

-CHAPTER ELEVEN-

The Tables Turn

Dixie Carmichael could hardly believe that a whole day on earth had passed by since his 'death'.

Time didn't really appear to exist in his new realm of existence. Dixie almost felt as though he had been there for eternity.

Dixie's every thought now became an intense reality. Whenever he found himself thinking about a pleasant walk, there he was, drifting happily in a beautiful wooded park, bedecked with flowers from every imaginable climate and season. The sun was forever shining; the sky forever blue; the few fluffy white clouds there for purely aesthetic purposes.

Dixie had met up with a few old acquaintances since his return to this realm (not to mention a few new ones), although he hadn't quite cut off all of his earthly cords of attachment. Dixie's soul was still occasionally able to flit from scene to scene and from person to person back on earth. This always tended to happen when people Dixie had known on earth thought about him. It was almost as though they could still summon Dixie's attention with their earthly thoughts and emotions.

Dixie had been re-familiarising himself with the freedom and flexibility of movement in his new dimension, although his soul was still easily attracted to certain events on the denser earthly realms. Dixie had always been a rather curious dog when he had lived with Susan and Ray Carmichael back on earth – and this was certainly not going to change now, simply because Dixie had undergone a shift in consciousness.

In particular, Dixie was very sensitive right now to the thoughts and words of Matthew Rourke and the Morgans, as they struggled to make sense of their complicated human existence back in London, England. Dixie's spirit was keen to see the imprints it had made – and continued to make – on their earthly lives (Dixie still had a bit of a pedigree ego), although he knew that all of these individuals were destined to move in their own direction soon enough.

For the next few moments, however, Dixie's attention was not distracted by the thoughts of Matthew Rourke *or* the Morgans. Instead, he was drawn to a scene playing out at the Eden Resort, in Buckinghamshire, England. Susan Carmichael had just begun to talk about Dixie to her husband, Ray, as they sat together at a table by a beautiful window that overlooked gardens and lakes, eating a continental-style breakfast.

'Of course Dixie will be OK,' Ray Carmichael replied. 'Steve told you as much yesterday. So let's just allow Steve to get on with looking after him – shall we? And let's enjoy our last day here, Susan. We'll see Dixie tomorrow.'

'I know,' said Susan. 'It would be lovely if Dixie was here now though – so that we could take him for a walk around this gorgeous place on such a sunny day. I really don't understand why places like this operate a *no dogs* policy.'

'At least we know that he's happy where he is, Susan.' There was a brief pause. 'Are *you* happy, Susan?'

'Yes.' Susan looked radiant and glowing. She could feel the new life bursting open inside her.

Dixie felt like celebrating. Susan Carmichael's life was just about to begin for real, he sensed. Although Susan would undoubtedly endure some very difficult days ahead, upon discovering Dixie's death and theft, she would be carried through this trauma by thoughts of better days ahead; something Susan Carmichael had been incapable of thinking about until her 'chance' encounter at Paws for Thought, on Jacob's eighth birthday.

As Susan Carmichael glanced down now at her mobile phone, she smiled happily at the image staring back at her. It showed her standing by the billboard outside Paws for Thought the previous Wednesday, holding her beloved Dixie, and laughing into the face of the handsome lone stranger she had so unexpectedly encountered on that occasion. Susan began to fondly recall the events of that fateful day, when Dixie had mischievously insisted on sharing the company of the handsome stranger. She remembered the hustle and bustle of the normally quiet café; the buzzing tourists; and the warmth, kindness and life-changing words uttered by the gentleman whose name Susan didn't even catch. As she looked at his face now, Susan genuinely hoped that things would work out for him too.

*****

Dixie's attention switched immediately to the scene unfolding at Matthew Rourke's two-bed apartment in South West London.

It was 9.46 a.m. on Saturday 8th October, and Matthew had just begun to stir from his awkward slouched position on the sofa inside his darkened lounge. He opened his eyes, not fully recognising where he was at first. Matthew felt sick. His head was pounding with pain. His back hurt.

After a few confused moments, he attempted to sit upwards on the sofa. As he did so, Matthew pushed away the throw that was wrapped around him: he couldn't recall putting it over himself the previous night. He looked around at the room in front of him, and saw his jacket and shoes bundled on the floor, alongside several empty beer bottles. The sight of the beer bottles made him feel physically sick now. Matthew was afraid to move an inch further from his position on the sofa. He wanted to stay frozen there forever – to convince himself that yesterday hadn't even happened at all. Matthew's mind was dizzy with chaotic images from the previous day: the female at the tube station; the dead dog in the flowery bag; Eva; Unity Park; The Rising Dawn; Christian.

Oh my God, he suddenly thought to himself. *Where's Ruth?*

Matthew couldn't recall if he had spoken to his wife upon his return from The Rising Dawn yesterday evening. He could have done, he thought now; and then again, maybe he hadn't. Matthew stood up quickly – and fell back onto the sofa again. He tried once more, much slower this time, and made his way out of the lounge, and into the corridor. Matthew approached Ruth's bedroom door and opened it tentatively.

'What do *you* want?' his wife growled from under her bed covers, as the door squeaked to a halt. 'Keep away from me, Matthew.'

'I just wanted to see if you were OK.'

'As if you care. After your behaviour yesterday evening. You nearly frightened me to death.'

Matthew was mortified. He couldn't remember much after leaving The Rising Dawn. 'I'm sorry. I think I was a bit drunk.'

'A bit? A *bit*?' Ruth screamed, sitting up in bed now. 'I had to call Eva – I was so frightened.'

'*Eva*?' Matthew asked, confused. He recalled meeting Eva when he was carrying the flowery bag yesterday. 'What did she tell you?'

'What do you mean – what did *she* tell *me*? You mean what did *I* tell *her* – about your *psychotic* episode.'

'What psychotic episode?' Matthew was becoming very nervous and paranoid over what he may or may not have done or said to Ruth the previous evening. 'What did I do? What did I say?'

'Nothing! You were so bloody off-hand with me.' Ruth's head was throbbing even more than Matthew's.

'Oh – right.' Matthew was very relieved.

'Right?' Ruth screamed. 'Nothing's right, Matthew. Everything is very, very *wrong*.'

'OK.' Matthew began to walk calmly away from the bedroom door, towards the kitchen. He could hear Ruth shouting something after him, but he didn't really care now. All of a sudden, Matthew's mind suddenly recalled Christian's vibrant green eyes from the day before. He also recalled his younger brother's laughter, his words, his happiness and his presence – just like yesterday, when Matthew had been magically permitted to relive his last few moments with Christian, before the car crash that had so cruelly taken his brother's life.

Matthew now recalled sitting on the sofa in his lounge the previous evening, recollecting what he had experienced inside The Rising Dawn, earlier that day. He automatically began to feel lighter and more self-assured. Matthew smiled. He remembered sensing that Christian had come to visit him yesterday, to remind

Matthew that he and Christian were still brothers and friends. Matthew could almost feel Christian standing nearby him now.

As he began to pour himself some water from a bottle in the fridge, Matthew's mind suddenly and instinctively switched attention. '*The Spider Mystery*!' he said out loud, laughing.

'Oh my God,' Ruth said, as she entered the kitchen to demand that her husband grovel for her forgiveness. 'What the hell are you talking about now?'

'The Spider Mystery!' Matthew knew that he had to watch 'The Spider Mystery' - today. As soon as possible. He had forgotten all about that film – until Christian reminded him about it yesterday. It was released in cinemas around the time of Christian's death. Matthew had promised to bring Christian to see it – but they had tragically never managed to watch the film together. Matthew had forgotten all about the film's existence, in fact. He had to watch it today, Matthew thought excitedly. He would search for it online, and download it immediately.

'What *spider mystery*? Have you taken complete leave of your senses?' Ruth yelled. She felt horrendously sick after having drunk several vodka cocktails the previous evening. Ruth vaguely remembered her sister, Eva, leaving her back to the apartment after their night at The Twisted Corkscrew. She would have to phone Eva later, she thought, to piece together their evening. Eva always tended to remember everything about nights out: she rarely, if ever, touched alcohol.

'Don't worry about it, Ruth. Just leave me alone today – will you?' Matthew walked calmly out of the kitchen and into the lounge.

Ruth was seriously livid now. She had grown to expect much more in the way of courteous, submissive behaviour from her husband. She had often complained that Matthew's compliant attitude bored her to death in the past, but she still expected a certain amount of respect and courtesy. How *dare* he brush her off like that! 'Get back here, Matthew! What way is that to treat *me*? As if I don't have enough to put up with all week!'

Matthew didn't respond. He was too engrossed in setting up his laptop in the lounge. He needed to see if he could locate 'The Spider Mystery' online. Matthew knew that he was meant to watch it today – and nothing was going to get in the way of that now.

'Look at the state of this room!' Ruth was steadfast in the pursuit of the moral high ground; and relentless in the pursuit of her husband's attention. Matthew blanked Ruth out again. She had to turn up the heat on him a little more, she knew. 'Did you know that I was on the verge of leaving you last night?' she screamed at Matthew.

Matthew turned towards her suddenly and stared. 'Why didn't you then? I got the distinct impression you've been meaning to do that for quite a while.' He looked away from Ruth again and continued to click his way through Internet sites.

Ruth froze to the spot. She had no idea what to do next. *She* called the shots in their marriage – not Matthew. If the relationship was going to end, *she* would be the one to decide that outcome. Ruth realised that she had been unhappy with her marriage to Matthew for a long time. His passivity, up until this moment in time, had driven her distracted – bored out of her head. She was unnerved by her husband's sudden penchant for unpredictability, his desire to defend himself. She realised now that she had actually preferred it when Matthew had surrendered to her dark moods in the past. She had enjoyed feeding off his vulnerability. Ruth recognised that she had nowhere to go with her husband – for now, anyway.

She ran out of the lounge and into her bedroom – the one she had shared with Matthew up until recently, at her own insistence. Ruth grabbed some clothes from her wardrobe and began to pull them on. She didn't know where she was going to go – but she had to go somewhere, to figure out what to do next. Ruth put on her coat and grabbed her mobile phone and handbag. She would go shopping, she thought now. Her hairdresser might even be able to fit her in for a wash and blow-dry. She could go and have her make-up done professionally too. She would stay away all day, and make Matthew sweat a bit over her. Then she would go out that evening. She would phone Clare and Deborah (or, failing that, Eva) to arrange a night out on the town.

Ruth felt better about everything already.

*****

It was several minutes after Ruth had banged the front door of the apartment behind her that Matthew Rourke suddenly twigged she had gone. He had only just located 'The Spider Mystery' online, and his attention had been completely waylaid by his Internet search. What had he been thinking? He needed to contact Ruth now, to apologise for his unreasonable behaviour. Had he taken complete leave of his senses, as Ruth had suggested, earlier that morning?

Matthew grabbed his jacket from the lounge floor, and took out his phone from the inside pocket. He attempted dialling Ruth several times, before he resigned himself to a simple text, which read: 'Sorry.'

Ruth Rourke smiled in triumph as she read Matthew's brief message. She had just caught the 10.55 a.m. train from her station, which would take her to her favourite London shopping district within minutes. Ruth resolved to do all that she had promised herself, earlier (the shopping, hair and make-up) – except she would enjoy it doubly as much now. She would make a day *and* a night out of it. She would definitely call Clare and Deborah soon. Matthew would be all over her again tomorrow, Ruth knew; then *she* would consider her future with *him*.

As Matthew Rourke settled in front of his laptop with his headphones on, still dressed in yesterday's clothes, he thought only fleetingly about the previous day's insane sequence of events, before he was quickly able to immerse himself in 'The Spider Mystery'. It was by now 11.05 a.m.

*****

Dixie Carmichael's attention swapped immediately to the Morgan household, only a couple of miles away from Matthew and Ruth Rourke's apartment.

Charlotte Morgan had only just awoken. She was thinking about the dead dog she had carried around London yesterday – inside Susan Carmichael's flowery weekend bag. Charlotte was wondering what had become of the dog – and of the stupid idiot who had stolen him.

She lay on for another while, just thinking. Charlotte knew that this day was going to be like no other she had ever experienced before. She felt different already – as though her entire identity and history had changed with one swiftly-delivered piece of information: Charlotte had a twin sister.

Charlotte realised that in one sense, this piece of information didn't have the ability to radically alter her life at all – given that her sister wasn't around for Charlotte to talk to or be with. For some reason, however, Charlotte didn't feel as isolated any more. She didn't feel alone. It was probably silly, Charlotte thought to herself now, but it was almost as though just knowing about Matilda's existence meant that Charlotte *did* have a sister – after all. Charlotte had always secretly envied the closeness Ebony and Melody Glazier enjoyed. The fun, laughter, bickering and buzz at the Glaziers' home had always made Charlotte feel so lonely in the past; like she was missing out on something very wonderful. Now Charlotte didn't feel like that any more. She had a twin sister.

Charlotte's optimism now turned suddenly to grief. She was angry and sad that she would never get to know Matilda properly. Charlotte would never really be able to enjoy what Ebony and Melody Glazier had. Why had Matilda had to die anyway? What had been the point of *that* happening? Charlotte Morgan began to grieve for the sister she was never permitted to know. She had never had to think about anything like this in her entire life before.

All of a sudden, Charlotte heard raised and angry voices in the kitchen beneath her bedroom. It was her parents. A dreaded realisation now made its way inside Charlotte's mind, much against her own will. Charlotte realised that her parents were finally going to split up – today. As much as Charlotte understood the inevitability of her parents' break-up, it made her feel very sad and very alone. Everything in Charlotte's life appeared to have changed since yesterday. It was as though she had left her home the previous morning to go dog-sitting, but had returned in the evening to discover that her whole life was about to be turned completely upside-down, and inside-out.

Charlotte recognised that her mum had sacrificed her own happiness for Charlotte's – by putting up with Steve Morgan's selfish, immature ways over the years. Charlotte was furious with her father for not having given his family more effort and time in the past. She couldn't understand why her dad had chosen to walk away from Amanda, just after Charlotte's twin sister had died so tragically. What had been *wrong* with him?

And yet, as much as Charlotte resented and hated her dad right now, she still felt sorry for him. Charlotte knew that Steve was just a silly, stupid, pathetic man. She had always heard her mum calling him an 'overcooked adolescent' in the past. There was no way he would be able to cope without Amanda – and Charlotte knew that her mum realised that deep down too. Steve had been given numerous chances to change his ways, to grow up and step up – but he had deliberately and consciously chosen not to take the chances offered him. Her dad didn't really deserve Charlotte's sympathy at all right now – so why did she still feel pity for him? He hadn't even behaved like her dad.

Charlotte rose from her bed now. As her parents' angry voices continued to rise through her bedroom floor and into her head, Charlotte decided that she would not go downstairs to become involved in their break-up. Instead, she would sit at the top of the stairs and listen to their argument – just as she had on several occasions in the past, ever since she was a very young child.

She put on her dressing gown and crept onto the hall landing. The kitchen door was opened, so her mum and dad's words were easy to make out. Charlotte settled herself on the top step of the elegant flight of stairs – and *listened.*

'How was *I* meant to know that the dog would be stolen? And anyway – why the hell did you have to call the bloody police, Amanda?' Steve was still trying to fight his corner, despite the odds being stacked firmly against him.

'Because – in case it escaped your notice, Steve – your daughter was mugged yesterday! A crime was committed! Do you not think Susan and Ray Carmichael will go to the police over all of this, when they return home tomorrow evening? How would it look then, if we hadn't even bothered to report the whole thing?'

'I didn't really think of it like that at the time.'

'You never think, Steve. That's always been the bloody problem. You always expect others to clear up all your grubby messes.'

'That's not true.'

'Of course it's true. You've never faced up to anything remotely problematic for most of this marriage.'

'Keep your voice down, for God's sake, Amanda. My head is throbbing.' Steve Morgan still didn't quite realise the seriousness of the situation he was about to be confronted with.

There was a pause before Charlotte Morgan heard her mother speak again. 'I've had it with all of this, Steve.'

There was another pause. Charlotte realised that not even Steve could fail to realise the meaning behind Amanda's words and tone of voice now. 'What do you mean?' Charlotte could tell that her dad was frightened.

'I mean.' Amanda paused. 'I mean, Steve – it's over. I want you to take what you need – at least for the next few weeks, until we get all of this sorted out – and leave.'

The silence inside the house was tangible now. Charlotte Morgan huddled herself together on the top stair and began to quietly sob. It was all over. Charlotte had never felt so sad in her whole life. She suddenly wished that her sister, Matilda, was here to talk to. Charlotte sank her head onto her knees and curled her feet under her legs. She put her arms around the top of her bowed head, and closed her eyes. She rocked her body in the darkness, all the time *listening*. The voices and noises Charlotte heard were muffled now.

'Where do you expect me to go?'

'I don't care. You have a bank account of your own. Go wherever you want to go.'

'But this is my *home*, Amanda.'

'Well it's a pity you never *treated* it like your home then – *isn't it*?'

'Please don't do this, Amanda.' It was the first time Steve had really had the tables turned on him like this.

'It's over, Steve. Don't make it more difficult than it already is.'

Steve Morgan sounded beaten now. 'OK. What about the Dental Spa?' he asked anxiously.

'That's for another time, Steve. Not now. Please just go – I don't want a huge show-down – not when Charlotte is at home. At least do your daughter that favour.'

Charlotte Morgan huddled in darkness for a few seconds longer at the top of the stairs; just enough time for her to absorb her parents' conversation. She felt comforted in the dark cocoon she was enveloped in. Charlotte felt protected; cosy; safe – as though she was swimming in a warm and tranquil enchanted lake. Charlotte sensed a protective presence around her and beside her. She felt like she had experienced these strange and magical sensations before – although she couldn't quite remember where or when. Charlotte wanted to float in this bubble forever. She felt as though time didn't really exist in this bubble – like she could stay here forever, and nobody would even know or care. But most of all, Charlotte loved the sense of companionship and sanctuary in this place. She didn't feel alone any more. She almost felt as though she could reach out her hand – and touch somebody beside her. She didn't quite know what or *who* was allowing her to feel as she did now – but Charlotte Morgan would never forget this experience for the remainder of her lifetime on earth.

'What are you *doing* Charlotte?' Steve demanded impatiently, as he began to walk onto the first step: Charlotte's attention was suddenly jolted by her father's agitated presence at the bottom of the flight of stairs.

Charlotte pulled herself to her feet again, a little self-conscious, and very reluctant to leave the lovely existence she had been enjoying. 'Nothing,' she replied, moving out of Steve's way as he reached the top step. Charlotte watched, as her father entered his bedroom and shut the door firmly behind him. She then walked back into her own bedroom, and got dressed for the day.

By the time Charlotte re-emerged from her bedroom, it was 12.30 p.m. She walked downstairs to the kitchen, where her mother, Amanda, was speaking quietly on the phone to somebody. Amanda immediately looked up at Charlotte, and gestured for her to wait; she wouldn't remain on the phone for much longer. Charlotte fixed herself a snack. She poured a glass of apple juice and put two slices of bread in the toaster. Sally, the Morgans' housekeeper, didn't work weekends, so the house always felt even quieter on a Saturday and a Sunday.

'Hi sweetheart,' Amanda said to Charlotte, as she hung up the phone and began to approach her daughter.

'Hi mum.' Charlotte was busy buttering her toast.

'Are you OK?' Amanda asked, putting her arm around Charlotte's shoulders.

'Yes. Are you?'

'Yes. I've told your dad, Charlotte. He's in the process of getting ready to leave now.'

'I know. I heard.'

'Everything's going to be OK – you know that?'

'Yes.'

'And I'm so sorry you had to go through so much yesterday, Charlotte. About the dog. Your dad. And *Matilda*.' Amanda looked at Charlotte anxiously.

'It's OK, mum. I understand now.' Charlotte bit into her buttery toast.

There was movement on the stairs. Amanda and Charlotte glanced at one another tentatively. After several seconds, Steve Morgan walked into the kitchen. He looked at his wife and daughter, before breaking the very awkward silence that had materialised when he first stepped onto the stairs. 'That's me then. The taxi will be here any minute.'

'OK,' Amanda said matter-of-factly. She was determined not to let this become a slanging match in front of Charlotte.

'I called Mike Gordon. He said that I can stay at his pad for a while. Until I find somewhere else.'

'Fine,' Amanda said, tidying away Charlotte's spilt butter and crumbs from the granite work surface.

'OK then. I guess I'll go wait for the taxi at the door. I've left my two cases in the hallway.'

'OK,' Amanda replied. She looked at her husband briefly. He had put on weight in recent years. Steve's belly preceded him now. Although he always claimed to make regular trips to the gym, Amanda realised that Steve must never get any further than the private members' bar on these occasions.

All of a sudden, Charlotte Morgan began to cry. She was still standing beside the work surface, pretending to eat her freshly-buttered toast. Amanda immediately went over to Charlotte and held her close. Amanda looked over at Steve, hoping against hope that he might attempt some comforting words for his daughter now. Instead,

Steve Morgan stared blankly back at Amanda and Charlotte, and said *nothing*. He turned and walked out of the kitchen, grabbed his two cases by the front door, and walked outside, banging the door firmly behind him.

To his great relief, Steve's taxi pulled into his gravel driveway; although he wasn't sure if it was his gravel driveway any longer. 'Harriet Harper's car park – beside the bookmaker's shop, mate,' Steve announced to the taxi driver, as he slammed the taxi door behind him. He placed his suitcases on the back seat floor of the taxi.

'Late night, Steve?' the taxi driver enquired, laughing: he had done this same Saturday morning run for Steve Morgan on numerous occasions in the past.

'Something like that, Pug-nose.'

'What's with the cases then? Are you in the doghouse with the missus?'

'Don't ask, mate. Don't ask. And please don't mention *bloody dogs* to me this morning.'

Steve Morgan sat quietly in the back seat of Pug-nose's taxi for the duration of the journey to Harriet Harper's car park. Steve would retrieve his Land Rover there, and make his way back to Mike Gordon's bachelor pad. He didn't know what would happen after this.

As he looked out of the window of the taxi, Steve realised that he had bottled it again. He had thought fleetingly about saying more to his wife and daughter in the kitchen; he had even considered comforting Charlotte before he had left the house. But he had chosen not to. Just as he had chosen not to respond or react on numerous occasions like this in the past. Steve never knew what to do or say in awkward situations like these. It seemed easier to walk away and leave other people alone with their emotions. He would probably only make things worse if he did say anything, after all. At least, Steve had always thought he would have made things worse by saying something in these situations. He would never really know for sure now.

*****

Dixie Carmichael's attention switched back to the scene at Matthew Rourke's apartment. It was 1.22 p.m., and Matthew had just finished watching his second viewing of 'The Spider Mystery'. He was closing down his laptop, when he noticed the time on his phone. Matthew started to recall how he had just entered The Rising Dawn around this time yesterday, just after he had buried the dead dog and the flowery bag inside Unity Park.

Matthew now started to think about The Spider Mystery's storyline; the film he had meant to watch with his brother, Christian, all those years ago.

The film had told the tale of Octavia Creep – the most bewitching, powerful spider on Planet Arachno.

Octavia had once been a kind and gentle spider – until she came under the mesmerising spell of the Dark Web Palace – a place rich with every kind of jewel and precious stone and metal.

Octavia would lure servant spiders to the Dark Web Palace, promising to make them ruler of Planet Arachno, if they agreed to obey her every command.

Whole families of male spiders were drawn to Octavia's palace, where they all eventually died, when Octavia tired of them. She would inject each male spider with venom from her nasty fangs, and suck out their blue blood, until they were no more. Octavia gained in power with every spider she killed.

The terrible tales that circulated Planet Arachno about Octavia Creep did not stop another ambitious warrior spider, Janus Goldenweb, from wanting to be ruler alongside her. His family tried their best to stop him, but to no avail. Janus believed that he could prove to Octavia that he could be her King.

He was proven wrong. After enjoying the attention and riches of the Dark Web Palace for many Arachno years, Octavia threw Janus into a dungeon, where she would eventually kill him and drain his blue blood, whenever the time was right.

The word soon spread around Planet Arachno about Janus' plight. His family gathered huge armies of spiders – of every type, rank and colour – to go to the Dark Web Palace, and defeat Octavia Creep and her powerful spider army.

After many weeks of blue bloodshed, webs of deceit and spider trickery, Octavia and her army were defeated.

Janus Goldenweb returned to his family. He begged for their forgiveness, for ignoring their advice about Octavia Creep and the Dark Web Palace. Janus believed that he had been rightly punished for being so selfish and so foolish.

The head of the Goldenweb clan, Sylvie Tangleweb, a wise and elderly spider, did not agree with Janus' assessment. She told him firmly that he had not been punished for being foolish or selfish at all: he had simply made a poor choice in this instance.

Sylvie showed Janus that many bad things can happen to a spider during their lifetime; but none of these things are sent to punish; all are there to teach. Bad things can happen for many reasons - often beyond a spider's control - but they should simply be seen as positive opportunities to move life in a different direction.

Sylvie told Janus that instead of looking for more darkness in the shade, Janus should rather seek new ways to introduce light into his existence. Since, for every ending, there is always the potential for a new beginning.

Matthew Rourke began to think about his brother Christian again. He would have loved to have been able to watch The Spider Mystery with him, sixteen years ago. Matthew knew that Christian would have been spellbound by the action in the film – especially during the spiders' battle scenes.

As for Matthew, he had been fascinated and enthralled by the film. Its storyline had spoken to him – although Matthew had known it would, even before he had started watching it. Matthew also knew that he had been *meant* to watch The Spider Mystery today. His encounter with Christian had told him that yesterday.

Matthew Rourke smiled to himself now, as he curled up on the sofa in the lounge once more, and tucked a throw around him. He needed to sleep. Matthew closed his eyes and began to drift into the dream realms. The Spider Mystery's meaning had not been lost on him. Matthew had always believed in fate, after all.

*****

As sleep found Matthew Rourke easily, Dixie Carmichael melted into the background of earthly life again. He had other things to tend to on his own realm, before the earthly events of this Saturday evening would command his attention once more.

-CHAPTER TWELVE-

Saturday Night

By the time darkness had set in on Saturday 8th October, Amanda and Charlotte Morgan were already curled up on the sofa together at home, watching chick-flicks and eating pizza. They had decided to spend the evening together – alone.

Mother and daughter had spent the best part of the day talking about what had happened with Steve earlier, and discussing Charlotte's twin sister, Matilda. At lunch time, Charlotte had spoken briefly on the phone to Ebony Glazier, who had been genuinely concerned about Charlotte's wellbeing, after Charlotte had so uncharacteristically backed out of last night's outing to PolkaPolka. Charlotte agreed to meet Ebony tomorrow – for coffee – although Charlotte had already resolved not to tell Ebony about what had occurred with her dad earlier; or about Matilda. Not yet, anyway.

Amanda Morgan was exhausted after the events of the last few days. She was more than relieved to be spending the evening at home with Charlotte. Amanda had explained the recent developments in her complicated domestic situation to her new companion, who, as always, had offered Amanda complete support and understanding. It felt wonderful, Amanda thought, to know that she had someone who would never pressurise her. Amanda adored her new companion's easy-going nature; their ability to just go with life's unpredictable flow; to let events unfold naturally, at their own pace; and to enjoy each moment as it happened. Amanda's new companion couldn't have been more different than Steve Morgan.

*****

Meanwhile, Amanda's estranged husband had been trying all day to settle into his new existence at Mike Gordon's bachelor pad. Mike didn't mind Steve Morgan being there – for now, at least. The two men had spent most of the afternoon watching old 1980s cop films, drinking beer and eating Mike's speciality vindaloo curry, which was doing no favours for Steve Morgan's delicate stomach right now.

Mike had already planned to go to a new club in SW1 tonight, close to Elite Physique gym, where Mike and Steve were both members. Mike's Receptionist, Lisa, had told him about the opening night of 'Abandonment' at work, yesterday. Steve Morgan would have much preferred to stay in tonight and watch some game shows, but he nevertheless felt obliged to tag along with his host.

*****

'Abandonment' also happened to be Ruth Rourke's chosen venue for tonight. Ruth had managed to contact her friends, Clare and Deborah Silvestri, when she had been at the hairdressers, earlier.

Clare Silvestri was the same age as Ruth (thirty-five). The two women had met some years ago, when they trained alongside each other to become psychotherapists. While Ruth had entered the counselling profession because she had wanted to carve out a good career for herself, Clare had chosen this career path because she was fascinated with strange human behaviours: these ran strongly in Clare's family.

Clare still lived at home with her mum, Deborah, and her twenty-eight-year-old brother, Benito. Clare and Benito were both single. Clare told Ruth that she had been put off relationships for life, thanks to her experience as a couples' counsellor, as well as her own family history. Clare's father, Antonio, absconded back to Italy years ago, shortly after Benito's birth. From what Deborah had told Clare about her father, he had been the archetypal 'Italian Stallion', love-'em-and-leave-'em type. Clare couldn't remember much about Antonio herself – except his smoky breath and his Spaghetti Bolognese.

Clare's mum, Deborah, sixty, was a hairdresser, and a native Londoner. Deborah worked from a specially-adapted shed in her back garden in SW12. The elusive shed was situated beside Deborah's many rabbit hutches, where she housed her several cuddly pets. Although Deborah's shed salon catered for both male and female customers, she tended to better provide for the former group. Deborah always made sure that her male clients got more than their hair and whiskers trimmed when they visited her shed – *if* they handed over a suitable fee, of course. Deborah's buxom build, bleached-blonde hair, orange tan and gregarious make-up ensured that she was never short of paid-up male attention. If there ever happened to be any trouble with any of her clients, Deborah simply got her burly son, Benito, to 'sort them out' there and then, in the back garden.

Ruth Rourke always had a 'wicked' night out with the Silvestri women, who certainly knew how to be 'wicked'. Ruth had only been drawn to the two women in recent times, undoubtedly because they provided such a stark contrast to Ruth's 'boring', predictable husband, Matthew.

As Ruth sat in a taxi now, on her way to Abandonment to meet Clare and Deborah, her thoughts were still focused on events from earlier that day. It was by now 8.30 p.m.

Ruth had arrived home from her shopping and pampering session at 5.45 p.m. to find her husband, Matthew, lying asleep on the sofa with a throw around him. He was still wearing his clothes from yesterday, and the lounge stank of stale beer. Ruth initially chose not to wake up her husband. She wanted to unpack her new purchases first: these included many expensive items of clothing, which Ruth had paid for using her much-used credit card.

Once she had carefully made space for her new clothes in her very cramped wardrobe, and laid out her outfit for tonight, Ruth crept into the kitchen to pour her first vodka of the evening. She must have made too much of a racket when she fiddled in the cupboard for a suitable glass, because she suddenly became aware of Matthew's presence in the kitchen. 'Are you getting some sort of kick – sneaking up on me like this?' Ruth had screamed at him.

Matthew Rourke had remained calm, in spite of Ruth's attack. She was a little unnerved by her husband's quiet mood this evening. Matthew hadn't really said much to her at all, except to tell Ruth that he was going to have a quiet night in by himself, watching films and eating pizza. Ruth attempted on several occasions to draw Matthew into a confrontation, to extract a reaction or an apology from him, but she hadn't been quite able to latch onto him fully for some reason or other.

Thankfully, Ruth had better things to think about tonight. She simply got ready, had a few more vodkas, and called a taxi to take her to Abandonment. Matthew would wait until tomorrow.

Ruth's taxi pulled up outside Abandonment, just before 9.00 p.m. She had already arranged to meet Clare and Deborah somewhere near the entrance to the club. As she got out of the taxi and paid her fare, Ruth was immediately pounced upon from behind. 'BOO!' Clare Silvestri shouted playfully, as she wrestled Ruth from behind. Clare, like Ruth, had already consumed a few vodkas.

'Shit!' Ruth exclaimed, petrified at first.

'So – how's boring Matthew tonight?' Clare laughed.

'Still boring!' Ruth was still recovering from the shock of Ruth's sudden arrival.

'HAW! HAW! HAW!' Clare shouted, as though she was the evil villain in a horror film. 'Maybe Matthew *isn't* as boring as you've been saying! Maybe he's really a PSYCHO-KILLER!'

'Shut up!' Ruth just wanted to get inside Abandonment now, and forget about her dullard husband, not to mention the rest of her unfortunate life.

'Come on, ladies!' Deborah Silvestri called from the queue that had gathered outside Abandonment. 'Last one in is a virgin!' Deborah was dressed from top to toe in animal print: tiger print overcoat and stilettos; leopard print plunge-neck mini dress; zebra print earrings; all very mutton-dressed-as-lamb. Deborah's hair was luminescent yellow-blonde tonight, which contrasted sharply with her orange fake tan and garishly loud make-up. Her figure-hugging dress did her figure few favours, Ruth Rourke thought, as she eyed her 'friend' up and down now. In fact, Ruth wouldn't even be surprised if Deborah was refused admittance to Abandonment tonight.

'OK – Granny!' Clare Silvestri shouted over at her mum, as she grabbed Ruth's arm and led her to the queue. Ruth always knew that she could rely on Clare and Deborah to make her forget her everyday existence. Her friends' outlandish behaviour and dress sense always ensured that their nights out together were so unforgettable, they rarely ever remembered anything about them the next day. Clare always dressed ever-so-slightly less flamboyantly than her mother, although even she made Ruth look purer than snow, with her dyed jet-black hair, metallic make-up and skin-tight micro skirt and vest top. Ruth wouldn't normally be seen dead with people like this, but at least they took Ruth's mind off going back to work on Monday, as well as letting her forget about her own miserable head, and her otherwise dull existence with Matthew. 'Whose idea was it to come here?' Ruth was curious to know.

'Hers,' Clare announced, pointing at Deborah. 'How did you hear about this place anyway, mum?'

'I heard about it in passing yesterday!' Deborah was moving her shapely body to the 80s music playing inside the club. 'I thought it sounded like my kinda place!'

As the three women laughed together, paid their admission at the door, and handed their coats over, Steve Morgan and Mike Gordon had already ordered their first drinks at the bar inside. It was by now 9.20 p.m.

'Well, Steve – O! Here's to your first taste of life as a single man!' Mike Gordon clunked his bottle of beer against Steve Morgan's whisky glass.

'Thanks mate!' Steve replied, trying to sound as though he was enjoying himself. Tonight's themed 80s and 90s music night at Abandonment actually made Steve feel like he *was* back re-living his hey-day single life: except he didn't really want to be there for some reason. 'It's not very busy yet – is it?'

'Give it time, Steve! Give it time!' Mike reassured his pal, as he sucked on his designer bottle of beer.

'Do you fancy going to Elite Physique's Members' Bar – if it doesn't pick up in here later?' Steve's stomach was still feeling very delicate from his previous day's drinking, not to mention from the vindaloo curry he had felt obliged to eat earlier.

'For God's sake, Steve! Where's your sense of adventure gone? You're a single man now!' Mike enthused.

Steve Morgan surveyed Abandonment. The club was neither empty nor full. Its mainly 80s décor, lighting and sounds would usually be right up Steve Morgan's street, but for some reason, they didn't quite resonate with him tonight. Abandonment's customers all appeared to be around Steve's age, or older; albeit that there were a handful of young people there too. Everybody seemed to be in all-male or all-female groups. Steve didn't feel great at all, but he resolved to make this as good a night as possible. Steve was single, after all. 'Two shots please – barman!' he announced.

'Shit, Steve. It's not even ten yet!' Mike said disapprovingly to his amateurish drinking partner.

'Something to ease away the pain in my stomach, mate – and to make me forget about Susan Carmichael's return tomorrow!' Steve flashed his teeth at Mike Gordon and slammed back his two shots. 'HE SHOOTS! HE HITS!' Steve screamed, swivelling and gyrating his hips. 'Two more, barman!'

'Shit.' Mike Gordon shook his head in disgust.

Just across from the bar, and directly opposite Steve Morgan and Mike Gordon, Ruth Rourke and Clare and Deborah Silvestri were sitting at a table, tucking into their first round of drinks.

'Here's to an *interesting* night, ladies!' Deborah said, as she raised her glass of brandy and ginger in the air, before taking her first mouthful.

'That sounds – *interesting*!' Clare said curiously to her mother: she recognised Deborah's *I have something in my mind* tone of voice. 'Go tell!'

Deborah pointed triumphantly in the direction of the bar. '*He's* why I'm here tonight!' she announced.

'Who?' Clare demanded, taken aback.

'*Him*. The burly one. With the tan and the moustache!' She was referring to Mike Gordon.

'How the hell do you know *him*?' Clare took another drink from her vodka cocktail.

'He's my vet at the moment.' Deborah said proudly. 'Well – not exactly *my* vet - yet. He looks after my bunnies - when they're in need of attention.'

Clare and Ruth looked at each other curiously now, as Deborah continued. 'I heard his Receptionist telling him to come here yesterday - while I was sitting in his surgery with Buffy. He looks like he might be worth a penny or two – doesn't he, ladies? I'd like to give him my business card.'

Ruth Rourke was lost by this stage of the conversation, although Clare Silvestri had grasped her mother's meaning completely. 'Oh mother!' she said. 'Behave yourself!' Clare didn't mean a word of it. She knew her mother made a habit of travelling around different London vets to secure clients for her hairdressing business. Benito always drove. Deborah's many bunnies meant that she always had at least one poorly pet to justify her visiting a veterinary clinic.

'Absolutely not, Clare! I refuse to behave myself!' Deborah replied defiantly, as the two Silvestri women roared with laughter.

Ruth Rourke was nonplussed, out of her depth, without really realising it. 'Am I *missing* something?' she enquired, looking very confused.

'Not at all, sweetheart!' Deborah reassured her. 'It's all just a bit of fun. Really!' There were no back doors or side doors with Deborah Silvestri. She got up from her seat immediately and approached Mike Gordon and his companion at the bar. 'Good evening, gentlemen!'

Mike Gordon and Steve Morgan turned around to look at the vision-in-animal-print. She looked like something that had just escaped from the zoo, Mike Gordon thought to himself now; a tragic cross-breeding experiment, between a tiger, leopard and zebra.

'Would you like to join us?' Deborah Silvestri asked, gesturing towards her daughter and Ruth Rourke, who were both drinking heavily.

Mike Gordon looked over at the animal-print woman's two younger companions. 'Thank-you! We'd love to!' he replied, tugging at Steve to follow him.

Mike began to walk excitedly behind Deborah Silvestri with his drink, while Steve Morgan followed behind like a puppy. The two men pulled up two seats beside the three women already sitting at the small circular table. 'Good evening, ladies!' Mike said to the younger two women, as he mistakenly placed his seat beside the older woman – much to her delight.

Steve Morgan was now seated between Ruth Rourke and Mike Gordon at the circular table, while Deborah Silvestri sat between Mike and her daughter. Mike was devastated; appalled at his tragic positioning at the table. Steve Morgan was already chatting drunkenly to Ruth Rourke.

'So, darling!' Deborah said to Mike. 'My name's Deborah!'

'Pleased to meet you, Deborah. I'm Mike.'

'I couldn't help noticing your lovely dark hair and moustache as you stood with your friend at the bar,' she said enticingly.

Mike Gordon was immediately uneasy. 'Em – thanks.' He took a long drink of beer.

'It's just that I'm a hairdresser, darling. I can't help noticing people's hair!'

'Ah! – right!' Mike felt slightly relieved.

'How did you hear about this place?' Deborah asked, vetting Mike.

'Oh – my friend here told me about it!'

Liar, Deborah thought. 'How nice!' she said sweetly, taking a mouthful of brandy and ginger to soothe her mind. 'I heard about it at *my vet's*.'

Mike Gordon felt disturbed now. He looked more closely at the animal-print woman, with the mad yellow hair, orange face and plunging neckline. Where did he know her from?

'Don't you recognise me – *Mike*?' she asked mysteriously.

Mike was nervous. 'Em – I'm guessing that maybe you come to my *clinic*?'

'Correct!' she said. 'You were a little tensed-up yesterday – weren't you, darling?'

Mike Gordon's feathers were well and truly ruffled now. '*Was* I? Sorry – would you mind telling me who you are?'

'I'm very disappointed that you don't remember me – *Mike*.' Deborah gestured to her daughter to order her another brandy and ginger. She liked to play with her prey before eventually enticing them with her business card. Deborah began to suggestively touch her cleavage. 'I bring my bunnies to see you,' she said. 'I have twenty-two of them.'

Mike suddenly recognised the woman. He recalled that she had brought in one of her rabbits to his Open Clinic, yesterday afternoon. Except on that occasion, the woman hadn't been wearing nearly as much make-up, and her hair hadn't been quite as yellow. Mike remembered that the woman had tried to listen in to his telephone conversation with Steve Morgan, as Mike had stood at the Reception Desk. She had smiled up at Mike at the time, although Mike hadn't really paid her much attention later, when he examined her rabbit's congested right eye.

'Twenty-two! Wow – that's *a lot* of rabbits!' Mike was determined to grab Steve Morgan's attention, and get to hell away from this woman – and this nightclub – now.

'You're very attentive with your animals – aren't you, *Mike*?'

'Em, well, yes. It's my job.'

'I'm very attentive with *my* customers too - *Mike*.'

'That's great!' This was getting worse by the second.

'How about we do a little *return trade – Mike*?'

'Sorry?'

'My business card!' Deborah announced, pushing a small piece of paper towards Mike Gordon's large, manly, hairy hand.

Mike looked at it briefly. The business card listed *Shed Head*'s address, in SW12, and a mobile phone number. Mike was scared. 'Thanks!' he said nervously.

'And don't forget, *Mike*. If you don't call *me* – I still know where *you* are!' Deborah Silvestri took a long, suggestive drink from her brandy glass.

'Oh my God, mum!' Deborah Silvestri excitedly interrupted Deborah and Mike's exchange. 'Wait until you hear this!'

Ruth Rourke had just informed Clare about her drunken male companion's interesting chat-up approach. Steve Morgan had just gone to the bar for more shots.

'Tell her, Ruth!' Clare said, roaring with laughter.

Ruth giggled and took another slug of vodka, before speaking. 'He only sat down and told me he had his *dead dog* stolen yesterday! Inside a *flowery bag*! Then he asked me if I'd like to help him *look* for it!' Ruth was hyperventilating with laughter.

Dixie Carmichael's ears began to twitch. His attention was automatically summoned to events on the earthly realms again.

'I think your mate has a lot to learn about the dating game!' Clare Silvestri said to Mike Gordon, who couldn't quite believe that Steve Morgan had been so pissed and so naive as to tell a complete stranger about the Dixie Carmichael situation.

'Hi there, folks! Get these down you!' Steve Morgan announced, as he carried a tray-load of shots over to the table. 'Anyone want a boogie?' he asked, as he swung his hips clockwise to the disco beat.

'You wouldn't happen to be a *dentist? – would* you?' Deborah Silvestri asked Steve, very intrigued and serious all of a sudden.

Everybody stared at Deborah now, puzzled by the seemingly random nature of her question.

'What: is it the *mouthwash* - or the *hips* - that gives it away?' Steve joked, referring to the shots and his gyrating dance moves.

'It's the *dead dog*, actually,' Deborah replied, staring psychotically at Steve Morgan, as he stumbled to his seat and threw another shot into his mouth – much to his obvious discomfort.

Mike Gordon was very concerned by the middle-aged woman's current topic of conversation. Ruth Rourke and Clare Silvestri were a bit too pissed to take much notice yet.

'Why darling – do you like *dogs*?' Steve asked Deborah drunkenly.

'I'm into *rabbits*, as it happens,' Deborah answered intensely.

'Ever *boiled* any?' Steve knocked back another shot, delighted with his own sense of humour.

'You still haven't answered my question – clever dick.' Deborah was suddenly becoming very annoyed. 'Are you a *dentist*?'

'Yeah – I'm a *dentist*!' Steve laughed. 'What of it? You needing some *work*?'

'You *offering*?' Deborah asked, becoming visibly angry now – much to her daughter and Ruth Rourke's confusion.

'I'm *always* offering, sweetheart!'

Deborah Silvestri snapped. 'You BASTARD!' She stood up and tipped over the entire table, drinks and all, mainly over Steve Morgan.

Steve stumbled off his chair and fell to the floor. 'You bloody psycho!' he yelled at the animal-print woman.

'Mum! What the hell are you doing?' Clare Silvestri was hysterical. Ruth Rourke and Mike Gordon stood back in stunned disbelief.

Three burly bouncers now sprinted across the half-empty dance floor, and pushed their way past several people. Most of the people in Abandonment were now making their way over to the strange and chaotic scene unfolding around the figures of Steve Morgan and Deborah Silvestri. Deborah was lashing out with her fists at Steve Morgan, as her daughter and Ruth Rourke attempted to hold her back. Mike Gordon thought the scene reminded him of an ugly episode he had witnessed, several years ago, whilst training in a safari park in Kenya. On that occasion, several wild animals had to be put to sleep – although the mad bunny woman in the tiger, leopard and zebra skin outfit looked like a much more formidable beast than any of the poor Kenyan animals had then.

'Mum! What the hell are you doing?' Clare Silvestri yelled again, as Deborah continued to lash out – this time, against the burly bouncers, who now lifted her, kicking and screaming, into the air, ready to stretcher her out of the night club.

'You're STEVE MORGAN! – aren't you – YOU BASTARD!' Deborah screamed at a very dazed Steve, as he attempted to get to his feet once more. Deborah's eyes were beyond insane by this stage. 'You and your dead dog! You murderer! Madeleine told me about you!'

The three bouncers now marched Deborah across the night club, and threw her out the door, as her daughter and Ruth Rourke followed behind drunkenly. Ruth could almost *swear* that she had heard the name *Steve Morgan* before – but she couldn't quite remember where at the moment.

Mike Gordon now spoke angrily to Steve Morgan. 'Why the *hell* was she talking about *Madeleine*? Is she referring to *Madeleine Singleton*? Do you *know* that lunatic woman?'

'Beats me!' Steve Morgan replied, pie-eyed drunk.

Mike Gordon sprinted towards the night club door and caught a hold of Clare Silvestri's arm as she was collecting the three women's coats at the door.

Clare was taken aback by Mike's sudden arrival. 'What the - ?'

'Who is *Madeleine*?' Mike Gordon was determined to know.

'My aunt. Mum's sister.'

'What is Madeleine's surname?'

'Singleton. What's it to you?'

Mike did a double take before he spoke again. 'What was your mum talking about – when she mentioned a *murderer*?'

'How should I know? Sounds like your mate over there has issues though.'

Ruth Rourke arrived on the scene. 'Come on Clare! Your mum's behaving like a deranged animal out here!' Ruth Rourke was frantic: she could hardly believe the madness she had become embroiled in tonight.

'Steve didn't kill the dog,' Mike said in Steve's defence.

'So there actually *was* a dead dog?' Ruth Rourke asked in disbelief, as Clare Silvestri took the three coats and went outside to contain her mother.

'Yes. But Steve didn't murder it – like your mum just said.'

'She's not *my* mum,' Ruth said sharply, defending her designer image. 'And was the dog really stolen?' she enquired incredulously.

'Yes. In a flowery bag, apparently.' Mike wasn't really thinking about what he was saying now. 'We think the thief was foreign.'

'Shit!' Ruth laughed. 'The poor bastard could do with a good psychotherapist right now!' She found the whole idea hilarious beyond belief. Ruth then turned and left the club to join Clare and Deborah Silvestri outside. It was only 10.55 p.m.

Mike Gordon walked over to Steve Morgan inside the night club again. Steve was by now sitting at another table, nodding off to sleep. 'Come on!' Mike said angrily, grabbing Steve's arm. 'We're going!'

'Mike – my friend! Let's D.I.S.C.O.!' Steve stood up and gyrated his hips once more.

'Honestly, Steve. It's people like you that give alcohol the bad reputation it's got.' Mike was furious that his night had been cut so disastrously short. He hauled Steve across the club and out of the door, and got straight into a taxi with him. 'TW9 please, mate,' Mike ordered the driver.

Dixie Carmichael's ears were still pricked attentively.

'Steve!' Mike shouted, attempting to shake his friend awake in the back seat of the taxi.

'OK folks! Game over!' Steve chuckled deliriously. His stomach was still churning with pain.

'How the hell would Madeleine Singleton and her sister know about Susan Carmichael's dead dog? Steve?'

'Must be my deadly hips, mate!' Steve chuckled. 'I am the *Thriller Driller*!'

Mike Gordon sat back quietly in disgust. He had already had enough of sharing his apartment with Steve Morgan. Mike decided there and then that he would let Steve stay to the end of the week – tops – and then he would ask him to leave. In the meantime, Mike desperately hoped that he would never encounter the mad bunny woman in the wild animal outfit again, although for some reason, he knew that his and Steve's dealings with the two mad sisters was probably not over yet. Mike also realised that Steve would have to deal with Susan Carmichael's roar, upon her return from holiday, tomorrow evening. Mike Gordon knew that the crazed scene that had just played out at Abandonment would look like a kitten fight in comparison to the lions' brawl that would inevitably unfold between Steve and the Carmichaels, when they would find out about Dixie's death and theft.

*****

As Mike Gordon and Steve Morgan made their way back to Mike's bachelor pad that night, Steve's wife and daughter were slipping quietly and soberly off to sleep back at the family's Victorian residence in TW9. The two women had enjoyed a relaxing night together, building bridges, and talking about the future.

A few miles away, at an address in NW1, Amanda Morgan's new companion was also about to go to sleep.

Eva Kelly had spent her evening designing a new rose bed for one of her clients. Eva never felt calmer and happier than when she was thinking about nature and working alongside nature. Unlike her sister, Ruth Rourke, Eva had always preferred the *nature* to the *human*. Eva preferred plants, animals and the countryside, whereas Ruth had always been drawn to the chaos of towns and the human mind.

It was *nature* that had initially drawn Eva and Amanda together, four months ago. Eva had been recommended to Amanda by Amanda's father, Sir Horace Montgomery, who had once employed Eva as a gardener on one of his estates in Bournemouth. Sir Horace had been greatly impressed by Eva's gardening prowess back then – not to mention her feminine beauty and calm disposition. Amanda had 'hired' Eva in June, to do some planting for that summer. The two women had got on instantly well with one other, and they had met for coffee, lunch and dinner on several occasions after that.

Steve Morgan didn't know about Eva's existence. He barely ever noticed anything about Amanda's home or garden; and he had always presumed that gardeners were male anyway. On one occasion, Steve had happened to stumble over a heap of rocks that Eva had temporarily placed at the side of the Morgans' driveway. Steve had drunkenly entered the kitchen shortly after his fall to chastise Amanda.

'Tell bloody Mellors to clear up after him!' he had shouted. While Steve had watched the T.V. series, Amanda had gone to the trouble of reading the book * – but she hadn't been entirely impressed by Steve's analogy. Amanda and Eva's relationship was certainly *not* based on the physical.

Eva Kelly had known Amanda Morgan was a beautiful, warm and selfless woman – ever since the moment she first met her. Eva and Amanda's friendship blossomed instantaneously, and it grew from strength to strength during the warm summer months. Each woman's soul felt nourished by the other's company, to the extent that their friendship soon became genuine companionship.

Now that autumn had arrived, and winter was soon about to set in, Eva and Amanda had discussed putting down new roots together, perhaps early next year. Eva had been to the Morgan household recently – to plant new bulbs and trees for springtime – although Eva and Amanda preferred to spend their personal time together away from Amanda's home. Eva fully understood that Amanda was very anxious about telling her daughter, Charlotte, about her developing relationship; but Eva, more than anyone else, understood that healthy things always instinctively know the right season to grow and bloom. Nothing, therefore, was ever worth rushing unnecessarily, Eva believed.

Amanda Morgan had told Eva all about her history with Steve, including the recent, ludicrous dead dog situation. Eva sent Amanda pink roses, symbolising *new beginnings*, in an attempt to let her friend know that the future held many wonderful things – if Amanda chose to grasp them. Eva had an instinctive feeling that Amanda would.

As Eva curled herself up in bed, ready to sleep, her thoughts turned briefly to her sister, Ruth. It was now 11.35 p.m.

Eva had all but given up on Ruth – at least until her sister would begin to help herself out of the tangled web of unhappiness she had found herself in recently. Eva had encouraged Ruth on several occasions to pull herself together, to release herself from the spiral of drinking, partying and shopping she had got sucked into, and to seek some professional help.

Ruth Rourke had consistently ignored her sister's advice, however. Eva knew that Ruth could lose one of the best things that had ever happened in her sister's life – Matthew – if she didn't change her ways soon. Eva wouldn't blame Matthew if he chose to leave Ruth right now. She had, in fact, sensed that Matthew might just do that, last night, as she tucked the throw around her brother-in-law, as he lay asleep on his sofa. Eva had the ability to hear seeds growing beneath the ground. Her finely tuned intuition had permitted her to pick up on Matthew's latent thoughts and dreams last night, which had revealed that Matthew was undergoing a definite shift in attitude and emotions - not that Eva knew exactly what this shift might entail yet.

Eva had only agreed to meet Ruth last night because she had picked up something troubling about Matthew, at the convenience store near Unity Park, earlier that day, and she had been curious to know more. She had sensed that there was something not quite right about Matthew – and the story about the flowery bag certainly didn't seem to add up. Eva would never tell Ruth anything about her encounter with Matthew and his flowery bag, however: her brother-in-law had endured enough in recent years. Eva had always admired Matthew. She had always cared very deeply about him, too.

*****

By the time Eva Kelly had fallen asleep, just before midnight on Saturday 8th October, Dixie Carmichael had already slipped back into his new dimension in the invisible realms. Many new seeds had been planted since his departure from earth – only yesterday morning – and Dixie was hopeful that none of these would be destroyed or trampled on, before they would have the opportunity to grow.

Dixie knew that he would be coming back down to earth again tomorrow. An eventful and difficult day lay in store for Susan and Ray Carmichael.

Mellors was Lady Chatterly's Lover, from the novel of the same title, by D.H. Lawrence.

-CHAPTER THIRTEEN-

The Carmichaels Return

While the rest of England was either busy piecing together the events of the previous night, or fretting about the forthcoming week, Susan Carmichael found herself in a strangely wonderful, peaceful state of mind on the morning of Sunday 9th October. She had awoken in her suite at the Eden Resort in Buckinghamshire to discover that her husband, Ray, had ordered them a romantic breakfast in bed. Susan and Ray had laughed and talked, as they ate a full 'English Breakfast' and drank tea. Susan could not remember the last time she felt this contented. It seemed as though her life was stretching out happily in front of her at last.

Susan had texted Steve Morgan at 8.30 a.m., to let him know that she would be arriving back in London with Ray at around lunch time. She had been anxious that Steve hadn't contacted her yesterday, to update her on Dixie's wellbeing, although Susan realised that this had probably been due to Steve's dodgy stomach from the day before. Susan supposed that Steve's daughter, Charlotte, had been tending to Dixie's needs in Susan's absence anyway – in spite of what Steve had told her on the phone on Friday.

As Ray and Susan Carmichael now sat quietly in their car, only minutes away from home, Susan closed her eyes briefly in the passenger seat, and smiled contentedly to herself. She was thinking about the lovely weekend she had just spent with Ray at the Eden Resort, and thanking herself for agreeing to go away with him in the first place. Although Susan had missed Dixie, she was glad to have spent time away with Ray, alone. In fact, Susan had been enjoying herself so much yesterday, she only just remembered to locate the Eden Resort's gift shop, to purchase a present for Dixie – just as she had promised him before she left for Buckinghamshire on Thursday.

The gift shop had been small but well-stocked. Ray had immediately purchased several packets of the resort's home-made toffees, although Susan had taken some time to decide what she should get for Dixie. The shop did not have any gifts specifically designed for dogs, so Susan eventually chose to buy Dixie a packet of lily bulbs and a beautiful pink rose bush. Susan thought that she would plant these in a bed alongside one another, at the bottom of the garden, near Dixie's favourite Oak tree, and beside Susan's several Jacob's Ladder plants: she hoped that Dixie could enjoy all of the flowers every summer, as he relaxed under the shade of the Oak. Susan had particularly liked the names of the bulbs and plant she had purchased: the beautifully-coloured lilies were called *Stargazer lilies*, while the pink rose bush was called *Dream Time*. Susan thought these names captured the magic of the last few days she had just spent in Buckinghamshire with Ray.

'OK Susan. Wakey wakey!' Ray Carmichael said, lightly shaking his wife beside him in the car.

Susan Carmichael opened her eyes to find herself outside her Edwardian home in TW9. She must have dozed off for the last part of the car journey. 'God! Was I asleep for long?' she asked, still coming around.

'Only the last fifteen minutes or so. You looked so peaceful – I hardly wanted to disturb you at all!' Ray joked.

'What time is it?'

'One-thirty. Why don't you go inside first, and I'll get the cases from the boot. I could murder a cup of tea right now.'

'OK. I'll put the kettle on. I'll see you inside.' Susan moved to open the passenger door of the car, but Ray momentarily leant over and stopped her, by holding her right hand in his. 'Just before we go inside, Susan, I want to thank you again for the lovely time we had this weekend. I'm so glad you agreed to come away with me.'

Susan smiled over at Ray. 'I should be thanking *you* – for making me go in the first place!'

'We should do it again – some time soon.'

'I'd love that.' Susan reached over and kissed Ray on the lips, before she got out of the car and began to make her way to the front door of the house.

As she walked, Susan took the time to look around at the large, mature trees that were dotted around her neighbourhood. She noticed that their leaves were only just beginning to change colour for autumn; although if the weather continued to remain as cold as it was today, Susan thought, it would not be long before the street was covered in foliage of every imaginable hue.

Susan fetched her front door key from her handbag, and inserted it into the lock. She turned the key excitedly and pushed against the front door with her right shoulder, expecting to hear Dixie's friendly bark and footsteps straight away.

There was no sound inside Susan's front hallway. Susan left the front door slightly ajar for Ray, who was following behind her with the suitcases. 'Dixie!' she called. 'Dixie! We're home, sweetheart!'

Dixie Carmichael's soul was immediately drawn to Susan.

'Dixie!' Susan called, as she walked from the hallway into the kitchen. 'Dixie!'

Dixie wanted to jump into Susan's arms and cuddle her – but he knew that he wasn't able to. Although he enjoyed much more freedom of thought and overall movement in his current state of consciousness, Dixie was still finding it a little frustrating at times, not being able to grab people's attention on the physical realms; to let them know that he was still around. Dixie knew that he would have to work on this aspect if he was ever going to convince Susan Carmichael, during the forthcoming hours and days, that he was still happy and well.

'Ray – something's wrong,' Susan said, as her husband walked through the front door with their two suitcases, and placed them on the hallway's parquet floor.

Ray could see from Susan's face that she was very troubled. 'What do you mean, Susan – what's wrong?'

'There's no sign of Dixie – not down here, anyway.' Susan brushed quickly past Ray and began to run up the stairs to check for Dixie in their bedroom.

'He's probably just asleep in his basket!' Ray called after her, as he ambled into the kitchen to put the kettle on.

Susan thumped down the stairs again. She entered the kitchen, even more flustered than she had been before. 'He's not here, Ray! Dixie's not here!'

'Calm down, Susan!' Ray approached her and put his arms around her. 'Dixie's probably out with Steve or Charlotte for a walk! It's Sunday, after all!'

There was a pause. 'Do you really think so?' Susan looked up at Ray. She was trembling.

'Of course!'

'Well – I suppose he could be. I hadn't thought of that.'

'Look!' Ray said, gesturing to Dixie's empty drinking bowl, and his half-filled food bowl. 'He's already had a drink and a little to eat today, and now he's away for a little Sunday stroll!'

'OK, OK. I suppose you're right.'

'Of course I'm right! Now – take your coat off, relax, and have a cup of tea with me.'

Susan duly did as she was told, although she still felt a little apprehensive, in spite of Ray's reassuring words. She took out the packet of lily bulbs from her handbag and set them on top of the kitchen work surface, ready for Dixie's imminent arrival back from his walk. 'Did you bring the rose bush in from the boot?' she asked Ray, who was tucking into a packet of chocolate digestive biscuits. 'It's in the hall,' he replied, munching happily.

Susan walked into the hall and fetched the rose bush, and placed it alongside the packet of lily bulbs on the work surface. She didn't know what to do with herself now, she felt so fidgety and nervous. 'I think I'll go upstairs and start to unpack our stuff.'

Ray looked up at Susan as he continued to drink his tea and eat his digestive biscuits. 'OK. But let me carry the cases up for you.' Ray (reluctantly) left his tea and biscuits at the kitchen table and walked into the hallway, where he lifted the two suitcases and carried them upstairs into his and Susan's bedroom.

Meanwhile, Susan was still downstairs in the kitchen, pacing about. Why was she getting such a bad feeling about all of this right now? In her nervous state, Susan suddenly began to recall a dream she'd had about Dixie the previous night. It had been a very similar dream to the one she'd had last week, when she encountered Dixie alongside a young couple and a small boy, in a park of some sort. This time, however, Susan had been able to watch, as the small dark-haired boy ran about the park, laughing and playing. She also recalled seeing a field of lilies and roses during this particular dream, as well as a large Oak tree. Susan saw the handsome stranger from Paws for Thought; and she met Amanda Morgan too. Susan also, strangely, glimpsed Charlotte Morgan during her most recent dream, walking alongside the young couple.

Again, Susan recognised that all of her dream's fleeting images were strongly connected to her thoughts about Dixie over the last number of days – so she dismissed it automatically now, as she looked at the clock on her kitchen wall. It was 2.12 p.m. Ray re-entered the kitchen. 'That's that done!' he announced, as he sat down at the table again.

'Ray – I'm going to call Steve. I'm just not happy about all of this,' Susan said anxiously, as she lifted her mobile phone from the kitchen work surface.

'Honestly, Susan. He'll just be out somewhere with Dixie. Leave it and relax for a bit!'

Susan chose to ignore Ray. She called Steve Morgan's mobile number. There was no answer. Susan was just about to call him again, when there was suddenly a knock at the front door. Susan looked over at Ray, her heart beating rapidly now, before she sprinted out of the kitchen towards the front door. Ray walked after her into the hallway. Susan opened the door to find Steve Morgan standing there – alone. 'Where's Dixie?' Susan demanded angrily.

Dixie Carmichael desperately wanted to cushion Susan's fall in the next few minutes – but he was as yet powerless to do so.

'Susan. I need to come in and talk to you,' Steve Morgan said ominously, as he began to shuffle through the Carmichaels' front door. Steve felt horrendous after his eventful time at Abandonment, the previous evening. He looked as though he'd been sleeping out rough for the last few nights, and his stomach was killing him.

'What? What?' Susan screamed: she knew instinctively that something terrible must have happened to Dixie. Ray Carmichael put his arm around her waist. 'What the hell is going on, Steve?' he asked angrily.

Steve Morgan shut the Carmichaels' front door behind him. He couldn't believe what he was about to tell Susan and Ray. 'Guys,' he began. 'I can't believe I'm about to tell you both this – '

'WHAT?' Susan was hysterical.

'Dixie died,' Steve continued. 'Mike said it was probably a broken heart – '

'Oh my God!' Susan dropped immediately to her two knees on the floor and began to wail.

Ray Carmichael tried to comfort Susan, but he was in such a state of shock himself, he simply didn't know where to begin. Ray looked up at Steve, who was holding his head in his left hand. Ray thought that Steve looked shockingly ill. 'Where is Dixie, Steve? Is he at Mike's surgery?' Ray just wanted to get their beloved dog back home again.

'This is very complicated, Ray – ' Steve began.

Susan looked up at Steve Morgan now. She wanted to strangle him to death. '*What* is very complicated?' she growled.

Steve was petrified. He was only just managing to hold himself together. His stomach was in such pain. 'The dog got stolen.'

There was complete silence now inside the Carmichaels' front hallway. Susan momentarily began to think that Steve was taking the piss – in his usual warped mindset kind of way – and that Dixie might actually pop out alive from under Steve's long overcoat, whereby Steve would yell 'Surprise!' But the more Susan now stared up at Steve, the more she realised he was not joking. She rose to her feet, trembling with grief and anger. 'Where the hell is my dog? You bastard!'

'Susan!' Ray pulled his wife back from throttling Steve Morgan with her hefty fists. At this point, Steve stepped backwards in the hallway. 'The truth is, Susan – I don't know where the dog is. Charlotte was bringing his body to Mike's on the tube, but some lunatic with a foreign accent snapped him from her.'

Susan Carmichael had listened to a lot of crap from Steve Morgan in the past, but this really took the biscuit. 'And when the hell was this supposed to have happened?' she asked, in a complete state of shock.

'Friday morning,' Steve answered quietly.

Susan began to think back. 'Friday morning? You mean – the Friday morning when you reassured me that Dixie looked great, when you had fed him? And then told me how fit looking he'd been later that evening, when you texted me?' Susan could barely get her head around all of this madness right now.

Steve Morgan knew that he was sunk. He couldn't even respond to Susan, as she continued to yell at him. 'And anyway – how did your daughter manage to carry the body of a West Highland Terrier on a London train? How did Dixie die anyway? Why would anyone in their right mind want to steal a dead dog?' Susan's mind was a mess of images and thoughts.

'Ah – well, you see!' Steve said, finally delighted that he could answer one of Susan's questions. 'Charlotte put him inside a flowery bag – so we reckon the bloke who stole Dixie didn't really know he was in there at all!'

Susan couldn't stand looking at Steve Morgan any longer. She couldn't think straight at all. She couldn't even begin to contemplate what had happened to Dixie, or think about where he was now. Susan simply knew that her worst nightmare had just come true. Dixie was dead. Gone. She wouldn't even be able to bury him, more than likely. Susan didn't think that she could cope with any of this. 'Get him out of here!' she ordered Ray. 'Was it not enough for you to deny Ray the chance to see his son alive?' she shouted at Steve. 'Now you've killed our dog too!' Steve looked at Susan, stunned. He felt so sick, he didn't even know what she was talking about now. Susan began to walk quickly upstairs, as Ray wisely ushered Steve Morgan out the front door and closed it behind him.

Susan entered her bedroom and shut the door quietly behind her. She felt so tired and so sad, she hardly had the energy to know what to do, or how to react. She lay down on top of her bed and began to cry. Susan knew that she had been punished for going away and leaving Dixie alone this weekend. She should have known, when she was enjoying herself so much at the Eden Resort, that something terrible would have to happen to counteract her happiness. It had been the same with Jacob. It was as though every time Susan let herself go, and started to look forward to a happy outcome in life, something terrible happened to bring her back down to earth with an agonising THUMP. That's why she had hid away so much after losing Jacob, eight years ago. Susan had promised herself never to become too happy again. Happiness for Susan always appeared to be accompanied by a nasty after-bite. She must have taken leave of her senses, she thought now, when she agreed to go away with Ray this weekend. Susan must also have been an absolute fool for thinking that she would ever have children – just because some stranger had told her that this would be the case, inside a dog-friendly café.

She suddenly began to think about the previous Wednesday, when Dixie had introduced her to the handsome stranger, with the regional accent, inside Paws for Thought. Dixie had been so mischievous and so happy on that occasion – thinking about her beloved dog lying dead now – God knows where – made Susan feel nothing but contempt for herself. She didn't deserve to be happy. How had she been so foolish as to leave Dixie with Steve Morgan? She had known instinctively that it was the wrong thing to do; so why the hell had she done it?

Susan sat up on her bed and looked across at Dixie's basket. She began to cry out loudly again. She was in agony.

Ray Carmichael slowly opened the door to the bedroom. He walked in with a cup of tea, which he held out to Susan. She refused to accept it. Susan was almost as furious with Ray as she was with herself. 'You think a cup of tea is going to make me feel better, Ray? This is *your* fault. I told you that we should never have left Dixie with Steve Morgan. I'll never forgive you for this, Ray!'

Ray Carmichael knew there was no point in jumping to his own defence. He was devastated. Ray loved Dixie – but even more than this, he knew how much Susan loved Dixie, and he couldn't begin to contemplate his wife enduring any more suffering than she had already, in recent years. Ray had truly begun to believe that Susan's life was about to turn a new page. He could hardly believe that it had all gone so tragically wrong. Ray couldn't think about what else to say to his wife.

Meanwhile, Dixie had been conferring with others inside the invisible realms. It was imperative that Susan Carmichael didn't continue much further along this path of destructive and self-defeating thoughts. She needed to keep sight of the positive and happy future she had begun to create for herself this weekend. A spark of enlightenment needed to be placed in Susan's way, to reconcile her with the road to happiness and fulfilment, and to allow Susan to proceed positively along the route she most deeply wanted to follow. Dixie believed that he knew exactly what Susan needed to shake her to her senses again, although he would need someone to work alongside him on this project, to ensure that Susan grasped its full meaning.

Ray Carmichael spoke to Susan softly now, as she began to look at the photo frame containing the two pressed chrysanthemums that had once decked Jacob's tiny crib.

'I'm so sorry, Susan.'

Susan lifted the photo frame from her bedside table and held it against her heart. 'Just leave me alone Ray.'

Ray Carmichael left the bedroom and walked downstairs to the kitchen.

Susan looked at the photo frame again. She dearly wanted to go over to *Jacob's Box* and look into it, to know that Jacob was still with her at this time; to let her know that Dixie was alright. But Susan felt that she couldn't. She had made such a big deal and ceremony out of saying 'goodbye' to Jacob's Box before she left for Buckinghamshire on Thursday, she would feel more than stupid if she were to open it now, so soon after. Susan began to recall how Dixie had sat so patiently beside her, as she had put the lid back on top of Jacob's Box. Dixie had been Susan's constant companion during the last three years. She didn't know what she would ever do without him now. How could she have left him on his own like that? Susan Carmichael felt so alone. She deserved to, in her opinion. She owed it to Dixie to locate his body – wherever it happened to be.

Susan suddenly recalled Steve Morgan saying that his daughter had placed Dixie inside a flowery bag before he was stolen. She immediately went over to the wardrobe that held all her luggage. She knew it: her favourite weekend-bag had gone. Charlotte Morgan must have taken Dixie in the flowery weekend-bag. *Oh my God*, Susan thought. She felt sick at the thought of her poor dog, lying dead, inside a bag. Before she realised it, Susan was running into her en-suite bathroom to vomit. She felt so sick she thought she might actually pass out.

She suddenly decided she had to phone Steve Morgan again, to demand to talk to Charlotte, to ask her about what had happened to Dixie on Friday morning. Then Susan would go directly to the police to report her missing dog. Susan had to get Dixie back – one way or another.

She exited her bedroom and marched downstairs to the kitchen to get her mobile phone, which contained Steve's number. As she entered the kitchen, she saw Ray sitting at the table, talking on his phone. 'Who are you talking to?' Susan demanded crossly. Ray attempted to deflect his wife's attention by shaking his head, but Susan automatically realised that he must be talking to Steve Morgan. 'Give me the phone,' she said, grabbing it from Ray's hand.

'Susan – go easy with him – please!' Ray pleaded with her.

'Oh, get real, Ray.' Susan was disgusted that her husband was even *trying* to protect Steve Morgan's feelings, after he had neglected Dixie so badly.

'Right, Steve,' she said firmly. 'I don't actually want to speak to you at all. In fact, I would prefer never to have to speak to you again. But I do need to speak to your daughter – to find out what happened to Dixie. Can you please put her on the phone – now.'

'Sorry, Susan. But I can't. I'm not at home at the moment – '

'Listen, you lying prick. I want to speak to Charlotte *now*.' Susan was becoming very emotional again. Ray grabbed the phone back from his wife and hung up on Steve, before pulling his distraught wife close to his chest. Susan began to wail. 'I killed Dixie – didn't I,' she cried. 'Steve told us earlier that Mike said Dixie died from a broken heart. That means that *I* killed him – by leaving him alone.'

'Don't be silly, Susan. How could Mike have said that – he didn't even *see* Dixie.'

Susan stopped for a while. She couldn't make sense of any of this. 'Ray – I need to speak to Charlotte Morgan to find out what really happened to Dixie. I'm phoning Steve again.'

'Listen Susan,' Ray said in a serious tone of voice. 'There's no point in calling Steve's phone. I was trying to tell you earlier, but Steve and Amanda split up yesterday. Probably over all of this. Steve just told me over the phone. He's not living with Amanda and Charlotte any more. He seems in a bit of a mess at the moment – if you ask me.'

'Oh – God.' Amanda was taken aback, simply because she had never been able to figure out why Amanda Morgan had tolerated Steve for so many years. 'Did Amanda throw him out?'

'As far as I can tell. He's staying at Mike Gordon's for now.'

'Right. Then I'm calling Amanda – to ask her to let me speak to Charlotte. And then I'll find out what Mike Gordon has to do with all of this later.'

'Susan – go easy – will you?'

Susan Carmichael fired her husband one of her looks.

As Ray retreated into the lounge for sanctuary, Susan dialled Amanda Morgan's number. Susan rarely ever spoke to Amanda, unless it was to do with Epsilon Dental Spa, but this occasion necessitated direct contact between the two women.

'Hello,' Amanda's voice said over the phone.

'Amanda. It's Susan Carmichael. I need to speak to your daughter.'

Amanda Morgan informed Susan Carmichael that Charlotte was out with her friend, Ebony Glazier, and would not be back until much later that evening. Amanda therefore insisted that she would like to go over to the Carmichaels' house personally, to tell Susan all she knew about the Dixie situation, based on what Charlotte had told Amanda and the police on Friday evening. Susan agreed to this. Amanda Morgan was very sorry about what had happened to Dixie, and she offered a sincere apology on behalf of her (estranged) idiotic husband. Amanda went on to explain how she and Steve had split up for good, telling Susan that Steve would be living elsewhere from now on. Amanda also reassured Susan that new arrangements would likely be made regarding Epsilon Dental Spa – although it was too early to discuss that just yet. Amanda wanted to ensure that Charlotte was OK before anything else drastic happened in her daughter's life, and Susan was in full agreement.

'OK Susan. It's nearly four-thirty. Let's say I come over for a brief chat to explain as much as I can about Dixie in about an hour. Would that suit?'

'That would be fine, Amanda. I just need to be able to piece all of this together.'

'I'll see you in an hour then.'

'OK. Bye.'

Susan Carmichael stood alone inside her kitchen. She looked down at Dixie's feeding and drinking bowls on the floor. Susan walked over to the work surface and lifted up her mobile phone. She flicked through the photographs on her phone until she came to the one taken by the friendly tourist last Wednesday. She touched Dixie's face softly with her long fingers, as tears streamed from both her eyes. Susan could hardly recognise herself in the picture, smiling happily at the handsome stranger outside Paws for Thought. She flicked through some more photographs on her phone, taken by Ray during their break in Buckinghamshire this weekend. Susan couldn't bare this any longer. She put her phone down, trying to save herself the agony of looking at any more happy images, but she immediately caught sight of the lily bulbs and rose bush she had brought back from the Eden Resort. 'Oh Dixie!' Susan cried, as she looked outside at her back garden, towards Dixie's favourite Oak tree and the bed of Jacob's Ladder plants. Susan didn't think she would ever be able to pick herself up again, after this latest tragedy.

*****

As Susan Carmichael looked out into her back garden, Amanda Morgan was already making her way into her local supermarket.

Amanda had decided to leave home as soon as she had finished her phone call with Susan. She drove to a nearby shopping centre, in order to purchase some flowers for Susan, to tell her how sorry she was about her dog.

Amanda entered the large supermarket at the shopping centre, and went immediately over to the flower section to select a pretty bouquet. To her disappointment, Amanda immediately noticed that there was only one pathetic little bunch of flowers left, which weren't to her taste or standards at all. She decided that she would have to buy the flowers anyway, because there wouldn't be any other flower shops open in this area on a Sunday.

Amanda went to the till, where she complained to the cashier about the dreadful choice of flowers on offer. The cashier informed Amanda that one of the local hotels – The Enigma – had only just sent round some members of staff to buy up all the flowers in the supermarket. They needed them desperately because they were hosting a charity dinner tonight, but their flower delivery company had only just phoned to say that they would not be able to complete their order today. Apparently, the electric locks on the shutters to their large flower warehouse had suddenly and unexpectedly malfunctioned, and nobody would be able to get in there until an engineer came tomorrow. The only reason why the supermarket had one bunch left in their flower display, the cashier explained, was because a customer who had already picked up that particular bunch, before The Enigma staff swooped in, later decided at the check-out that she no longer wanted them: the flowers had therefore been placed back on the display. 'They must have been meant for you!' the cashier joked with Amanda Morgan, as Amanda accepted her story. Amanda only hoped that Susan Carmichael wouldn't be too insulted by her depressing little flower offering: she would simply explain that it was all the fault of The Enigma.

Amanda pulled out of the shopping centre car park, and began her short journey to the Carmichaels' house. She would only stay there for a short while this evening, she thought. Amanda wanted to get home in time for Charlotte's arrival back from her outing with Ebony Glazier, and she also wanted to phone Eva before bedtime.

She pulled up outside the Carmichaels' Edwardian home, took the bunch of flowers from the front seat, and proceeded to walk towards the Carmichaels' front door.

Susan took only a few seconds to answer the doorbell. She opened the door to find Amanda Morgan standing there, as glamorous and as beautiful as ever. But Susan's eyes were immediately drawn to the bunch of flowers Amanda was carrying. Susan wasn't even listening to Amanda's words, as Amanda apologised for her paltry bouquet of yellow and violet chrysanthemums.

Susan was mesmerised. She had never been so grateful for a bunch of flowers in her entire life. It was almost as though she had received this particular bunch of flowers by magic; like it had been Susan's fate to receive them today.

While Susan still felt massive grief over losing Dixie, Susan's thoughts, as Amanda Morgan went through the details of Dixie's theft, at the hands of the fair-haired foreign man, kept returning to the bunch of chrysanthemums. Susan strangely knew, although she would never tell anyone this, that Dixie – and Jacob – were together somewhere. She only wished she knew exactly where.

Meanwhile, somewhere not too far away, Dixie Carmichael's soul was celebrating once more. *Result*, Dixie thought, as he looked on at Susan, hoping that she would sustain her footing on the road to happiness this time. It had taken a lot of careful organisation and cooperation to arrange the 'coincidence' with the flowers earlier. Dixie was only glad that Amanda Morgan hadn't decided at the last minute to buy Susan Carmichael a box of chocolates instead.

As Dixie began to contemplate the next stage of his journey, he was at least contented to know that Susan Carmichael's thoughts were moving in the right direction at last.

It was now up to Dixie (and others) to encourage the thoughts of the other participants in the plot to do the same.

-CHAPTER FOURTEEN-

A Manic Monday Morning

Amanda Morgan's phone rang at 6.30 a.m. on Monday 10th October. She had been sleeping soundly, so the loud chimes of her ring-tone had a very unsettling effect on her at this very early hour of the day. Amanda reached over for the phone beside her bed. She couldn't think who the call might be from. She looked at the screen, but didn't recognise the number. Amanda answered the call, feeling very concerned. 'Hello? Who is it?'

'Amanda – it's Mike Gordon. I thought I'd probably better let you know – but I've had to take Steve to hospital.'

Amanda hardly knew how to react in response to this news. She sat upright in bed and attempted to focus her thoughts and feelings, before she eventually said something. 'Why? What's wrong with him?'

'We don't know yet. He's been complaining of a bad stomach all weekend. We thought it might have been my vindaloo at first. He's been like an elephant with sore ears. It all came to a head this morning, when he wasn't able to get out of bed. He was in so much pain, Amanda; Steve really isn't in a good way. The medics are running tests on him as we speak.'

'Where are you?'

'Memorial Hospital. Just up from my clinic.'

'Have they said what they think it might be?'

'No. They haven't really said anything yet. But I'm phoning to let you know because I'm leaving the hospital now. I have to go home to get ready for work.'

'OK. Thanks Mike.' Amanda ended the call. She put her head back onto the warm pillow, and pulled the bed covers around her again. What was she supposed to do? As far as Amanda was concerned, her life with Steve was well and truly over – aside from the fact that a divorce would have to be arranged and settled soon, and their business concerns sorted. Nevertheless, she still realised that Steve was Charlotte's father – at least biologically-speaking. If something bad were to happen to Steve, Amanda would never forgive herself if she hadn't told Charlotte beforehand. Charlotte was probably entitled to know that her dad was ill in hospital. Goodness knows just how ill he was. And yet, what if Steve was pulling everyone's leg? He certainly had it in him to play sick jokes on people – for his own amusement – but surely he wouldn't stoop this low: would he?

Amanda was suddenly furious. She could really do without this today, and so too could Charlotte, she thought. Amanda had arranged to meet Eva this morning, for coffee, but that would probably have to be called off now. Charlotte and Amanda had also hoped to spend the remainder of the day together, shopping and talking, before

Charlotte would have to work tomorrow in Amanda's father's department store. Trust bloody Steve to throw a spanner in the works again. If Steve didn't die naturally today, Amanda thought, she would probably be tempted to end his life for him.

Amanda looked up Memorial Hospital's number on her phone and dialled it. The hospital receptionist (eventually) put Amanda through to Admissions, who then put her through to Steve's Ward. A nurse began to speak to Amanda. 'Mrs Morgan? I'm Staff Nurse Michelle Barlow. We have your husband, Steve, with us now.'

'Hello there. Have you any idea what's wrong with him, Nurse?'

'No. The doctors are still running some tests on your husband, Mrs Morgan, so it's too soon to suggest anything specific quite yet. We should have a clearer picture about his condition later today.'

'Thank-you, Nurse. In your expert opinion though, do you think his condition could be serious – or life-threatening? I'm asking because I don't really know whether I should tell Steve's daughter, Charlotte. She's already been through quite a lot of trauma this weekend. I don't want to alarm her unnecessarily.'

'As I said, Mrs Morgan, we're running tests. We should have a clearer picture about his condition later today.'

Amanda Morgan realised that Staff Nurse Barlow was not in a position to tell her anything more about Steve's health at the moment. Amanda would therefore have to consider the worst – that Steve might actually be seriously ill: she would have to tell Charlotte, therefore. 'OK. Thank-you, Nurse.'

After ending her call to the hospital, Amanda got out of bed and began to get dressed. She really couldn't believe this was happening to her today. It was as though Steve Morgan was a nasty rash that Amanda couldn't shift. How would she begin to break this news to Charlotte – without upsetting her daughter too much? What a bloody disastrous start to the week this was.

Amanda suddenly realised that she needed to contact Ray and Susan Carmichael, to let them know that Steve was in hospital, and that he wouldn't therefore be going into work at the Dental Spa. She would text Susan, she thought, instead of starting a long and complicated discussion about the topic. Amanda was confident that Ray and Susan would be more than capable of running Epsilon's affairs in Steve's absence: it wasn't as if Steve ever really did much at the Dental Spa when he was there anyway.

As she walked towards Charlotte's bedroom, a few minutes later, Amanda dreaded the thought of upsetting her daughter - again. She knew that she would have to down-play the situation as much as possible, if Charlotte wasn't to become too upset. She walked over to Charlotte, as she lay asleep in bed, and began to shake her lightly, whispering her daughter's name at the same time. After a few seconds, Charlotte Morgan woke up, looking and feeling very disgruntled. It was just after seven. 'Charlotte,' Amanda said quietly. 'I'm sorry to have to wake you like this, but it's about your dad – '

Amanda Morgan tactfully proceeded to inform her daughter about Steve, impressing upon her that Steve would very likely get better soon. Mother and daughter then went downstairs for breakfast, before Charlotte got dressed, and the two women eventually left their address in TW9, to make their way to Memorial Hospital nearby. They had already decided to leave home by foot, and take the tube to Steve's hospital: the parking charges were astronomical at Memorial, Amanda had heard. It was now 9.30 a.m.

*****

Amanda and Charlotte were directed to Steve Morgan's private side ward upon their arrival at the hospital. Amanda thought it ironic to be entering a hospital today. The chrysanthemums she had purchased for Susan Carmichael, yesterday, hadn't appealed to Amanda, for the simple reason that these particular flowers had always reminded her of hospitals and death.

As Amanda entered Steve's ward, she was shocked to see her husband looking so terrible. She looked at Charlotte's face, which had turned a shade of grey. Steve was lying in his hospital bed, linked by tubes to oxygen and a feeding drip. He was extremely pale and frail-looking, and he appeared to be unconscious. 'It's OK, Charlotte,' Amanda tried to reassure her daughter, as she linked arms with her.

A nurse now entered the ward. 'Mrs Morgan? I'm Staff Nurse Jane Maltman. I believe you were talking to one of my colleagues on the phone, earlier.'

'Yes,' Amanda replied, still a little taken aback by the sight of Steve, lying in his hospital bed. 'Do you know what's wrong with him yet?'

'Not quite yet. But we should have a better idea in the next few hours. We're querying a few possibilities at the moment.'

'Will he be OK?' Charlotte asked, very shocked and concerned.

'Hopefully. Although he'll more than likely have to stay with us for a while. Until we're satisfied that he's OK.'

'What do you think might be wrong with him?' Amanda was still more worried about Charlotte, however, than she was about Steve.

'As I said, Mrs Morgan, it's a little too early to say. But you shouldn't think the worst just yet. He's on strong pain medication at the moment, and he has been linked to oxygen because he was having a little difficulty breathing when he was admitted. He won't be permitted to eat until we have a clearer idea what's wrong with him. You can try to talk to him, although don't get worried if he seems a little drowsy or unresponsive: that's simply the effects of the pain medication.'

'Thank-you, Nurse Maltman,' Amanda replied, looking over at Steve.

'I'm just going to complete my Ward Round. Let me know if you need anything in the meantime.' Staff Nurse Maltman exited the side ward.

'It's going to be OK, Charlotte. Don't worry. You heard what Nurse Maltman said.' Amanda Morgan desperately wanted her daughter to leave the hospital now – to get away from all of this sickness and worry.

'What if he dies?' Charlotte asked, looking over at Steve.

'He won't. Now. I want you to go into town and go shopping – just like we'd planned. I'll stay here a little while longer, and then I'll meet you for coffee later.' Amanda was determined to keep this day as 'normal' as possible for her daughter.

'Will you let me know if anything happens to him?'

'Of course I will. Come on – it's just after nine. Go and get yourself a skinny latte in town, and then treat yourself to something nice – '

Steve Morgan began to move and open his eyes in his hospital bed. He had been roused by Amanda and Charlotte's voices. 'Skinny latte, shitty nappy,' he said profoundly.

'Steve?' Amanda walked over to her husband's bedside. He looked doped-up to the eyeballs. 'Steve. How are you feeling? It's Amanda and Charlotte. We've come to visit you.'

'Shitty nappy,' Steve replied, falling unconscious once again.

Amanda rolled her eyes to heaven. 'You see, Charlotte. He's fine. Your dad's completely out of it. There's no point in you being here at all. Go into town and I'll follow you in as soon as I can. I'll phone Sally and tell her not to prepare dinner tonight. Really, Charlotte – your dad will be OK.'

'OK.' Charlotte was still a little stunned by the sight of her sick father, although she was more than relieved to be leaving Memorial Hospital: Charlotte had felt very strange, ever since she had entered its doors, several minutes ago. 'I'll call you when I get to Fateful.'

'Bye, sweetheart.' Amanda kissed Charlotte on the forehead. She watched, as her daughter walked out of the side ward, and along the hospital corridor, towards the lift.

Amanda took her phone out of her pocket. She called Eva's number, as she continued to stare at her unconscious husband. 'Hi!' Eva's voice said.

'Hi! Listen, but I can't really talk at the moment. I'm in Memorial Hospital. Steve's been taken quite ill, so I'll have to hang around here for a bit – for Charlotte's sake.'

'God – is it serious?'

'Maybe – but I'm not sure. They're still running tests – although I must admit, he's not looking particularly well. Anyway, the bottom line is, unfortunately I won't be able to meet you for coffee this morning. I'm so sorry.'

'Hey – don't worry about it! I can meet you again tomorrow – or whenever else suits.'

'Thanks for understanding. I could almost swear that something's conspiring against me at the moment.'

'Stop worrying, Amanda. Just look after yourself – will you? And let me know if I can do anything.'

'OK. I'll call you later. And sorry again.'
'No worries. Talk to you later.'

Amanda put her phone back in her pocket. There was absolutely no point staying at the hospital with Steve, she suddenly decided. Amanda had put enough of her life on hold for him in the past, and she was determined to move on from all of that. She briefly thought about contacting Steve's family in Kent, but Steve's parents had died when he was in his early twenties, and he had never been close to his older sister, Samantha. Anyway, Amanda knew that Steve had always preferred not to associate himself with any of his family members – ever since he had married into the Montgomery clan. Steve's working class roots did not fit in with his new life or image – he had once told Amanda, drunkenly.

Amanda had a choice to make now, and she chose to leave Steve alone. She walked out of his side ward and went immediately over to the Nurses' Station, where she left her mobile number with Staff Nurse Maltman. Amanda explained that she needed to be with her daughter today, but that she would return to the hospital if her presence was required. She would purchase some toiletries and other essentials for Steve in town, which she would bring along to the hospital later. Staff Nurse Maltman thanked Amanda, and wished her a good day.

Dixie Carmichael clearly recognised that Steve, Amanda and Charlotte Morgan had finally reached the crossroads they had been destined to encounter for a very long time. Their lives were about to change profoundly during the forthcoming days, weeks and years; although the exact path they would each follow would only be determined by the individual choices they made.

As Amanda left Memorial Hospital, she felt as though she was escaping from a prison. She hated hospitals – especially Memorial Hospital, which was where Charlotte and Matilda were born, over nineteen years ago. Dixie Carmichael knew, however, that Amanda Morgan had some important memories she needed to come to terms with, inside Memorial; some ghosts she had to lay to rest. Indeed, if things went according to plan, it was hoped that Steve and Charlotte Morgan would also be permitted to join Amanda on her journey into the Morgan family past.

But that was for another time.

Dixie watched on, as Amanda Morgan began to make her way into Central London to meet her daughter. It was five-past-ten in the morning, and a lot was still to happen today.

*****

Dixie's attention suddenly switched to Unity Park, only a short distance away from Memorial Hospital. There, sitting alone at a picnic bench, Matthew Rourke was busy contemplating his first full week of unemployment, after being made redundant from Snaub's Foot Boutique, the previous Tuesday. Matthew had been compelled to visit one of his crime scenes from last Friday. Although he had felt very apprehensive about bumping into the female, from whom he'd stolen the dead dog at the tube station, Matthew wanted to come here anyway, to convince himself that the events of three days ago had actually happened.

As he sat now, looking around Unity Park, Matthew was eventually satisfied that it was safe to disappear into the wooded area where the flowery bag and its grim contents were buried. He walked towards the by now familiar area of Silver Birch trees, Rowans and Oak, where he had constructed the impromptu rocky tomb for the white dog last week.

Matthew crouched down beside the tomb, as if in reverence. The weather was much warmer and drier today than it had been last Friday, and Matthew was dressed much more casually, in jeans and a jacket. Matthew closed his eyes tightly. He hoped that he might see Christian again today. He wanted to test and see if he could relive his last moments with Christian, one more time.

After several minutes, Matthew opened his eyes again, disappointed. He looked around at the wooded area, and noticed remnants of the breakfast cereal and sugar he had scattered on the ground. Matthew knew for sure now that the events of last Friday had been real, after all.

Dixie Carmichael was puzzled. What was it about human beings? he wondered. Why did they always question things; go over things again and again in their heads; worry unnecessarily about almost everything from their past? Why weren't they able to just take the things that happened in their lives - and move on? That's what a dog would do, Dixie thought confidently, as he sat looking on at Matthew Rourke, from his dog perch inside the invisible realms.

Indeed, it had often frustrated Dixie, when he had lived with Susan Carmichael, in London, England, that she had so often missed out on the good things in life, because she had been too frequently preoccupied with the bad. Why did Matthew Rourke have to come back to this place today, Dixie wondered; when Matthew's brother, Christian, had already told him that he was happy? Surely Matthew Rourke realised that he needed to start thinking about his own life now – instead of hanging around with a dead dog, inside a flowery bag, under some rocks and soil.

Dixie knew that Matthew had spent all of the previous day avoiding his surly, hung-over wife, and vice versa. Matthew was still hopelessly holding onto the idea that his life with Ruth could possibly improve. While those in the invisible realms acknowledged that the impossible could sometimes happen on earth, it was highly unlikely in this particular case that Ruth Rourke would ever change her ways of thinking and behaving now.

Dixie stepped back down from his dog-perch-on-high. He had lost himself in his new state of consciousness. Dixie knew that he had to begin to think physical and human again. He had always known that working alongside humans was never going to be a straightforward task – that's why he had chosen to undertake that role in the first place, after all.

Dogs did their best to comprehend the complexity of human beings. It was a privilege to ride the waves of human thoughts and emotions, even though the journey often seemed so unnecessarily perilous at times. Dixie had to give Matthew Rourke a lot of credit for coming through so much during the last week; in the same way that Dixie greatly admired and loved Susan Carmichael for enduring the terrible grief she had suffered for much of her adult life. But Dixie just wanted the best for all the individuals he had come into contact with, during his most recent trip to the earthly, physical realms.

Dixie wanted Susan Carmichael to reach forward and grab her future – in the same way as Jacob, her son, wanted his mum to be happy.

Dixie had been enlisted by Jacob (and others) to guide Susan. It had been Jacob's idea to introduce Susan to Matthew Rourke. Jacob had known that Matthew's soul was perfectly positioned to say the right thing to Susan, at exactly the right time in her life. Jacob had also arranged the flower situation yesterday (he had always been very good at working with electricity) – ensuring that Amanda Morgan brought Susan Carmichael the bunch of yellow and violet chrysanthemums, which Jacob had known would speak to Susan's soul, in exactly the right way, at exactly the right time. Jacob had always felt certain that Susan knew he was still around her – somewhere – but he also realised that it was time she knew about his existence for certain; so that Susan would be able to embark on the next stage of her earthly existence. Jacob was also aware that Susan would soon find out that she was to become a mother, again. She needed to focus positively on this new beginning. It had been important that Susan was able to say 'goodbye' to Jacob's Box last week, thanks mainly to her encounter with Matthew Rourke. Jacob would always be around for Susan – and for his future siblings on earth – whose souls had already successfully fused with the two blossoming embryos inside Susan Carmichael's womb. But Jacob also needed to tend to other things in his particular dimension, in the meantime.

Jacob had worked alongside Dixie Carmichael on numerous occasions in the past, ever since Dixie first met Susan, three earthly years ago. Jacob and Dixie had met up again, immediately after Dixie re-entered the invisible realms, last Friday morning, and the two had conferred over their progress with Susan to date. Both agreed that Susan had made wonderful headway, and it was greatly hoped that she would continue along her current chosen path, even if it meant that further prompts and moments of enlightenment had to be sent her way, via 'magic'.

As Dixie Carmichael now began to focus once more on the confused figure of Matthew Rourke, crouched down on the ground, inside the secluded area of woodland in Unity Park, he knew that he would have to enlist the assistance of another one of his latest connections.

Dixie had struck up a friendship with Christian Rourke – ever since the moment Matthew Rourke stole Dixie's body from Charlotte Morgan, last Friday.

Christian had become upset in recent years by his brother's increasingly unhappy and unfulfilling life. He had thought it an excellent thing that Matthew was made redundant from his managerial position at the designer shoe store, in London, although Christian wished that Matthew could see it that way too. Although Matthew often claimed to be a firm believer in fate, and in invisible forces, he had too often ignored the prompts that were sent his way in the past. Dixie knew that Christian, along with several others residing in the invisible realms, had frequently attempted to land particular people, objects and ideas in Matthew's path before; to push him in another direction in life - such as when Matthew was 'mistakenly' sent pamphlets about the Lake District and Cumbria through the post, or when a customer of Matthew's, from the designer shoe store, had mentioned to Matthew that he'd just watched an old film about spiders (although, to be fair to Matthew on that occasion, the male customer hadn't been able to remember the actual title of 'The Spider Mystery'). Christian knew that if Matthew was ever to be truly happy again, Matthew had to return to his former home in the Lake District, to make peace with himself, as well as with his parents, who had never recovered from losing Christian *or* Matthew.

Christian had never truly been able to fathom why Matthew had chosen to blame himself for Christian's 'death'. Christian knew that he had simply left earth as the result of a freak accident. It had been a massive shock to Christian's soul, when it had entered the invisible realms, almost sixteen earthly years ago. Nevertheless, Christian had been carefully guided through this soul transition by his many companions in the invisible realms. In so many ways, Christian acknowledged that he had been the lucky one – compared to Matthew and his parents, back on the physical realms. While Christian was able to enjoy happiness, lightness and insight in his new state of consciousness, he recognised that Matthew's soul was still constricted by the density and uncertainties of human, earthly time and ego. From Christian's perspective, no time at all had passed by since his departure from the earthly realms. Christian's existence was now timeless and eternal. The concepts of time and age did not exist where Christian's soul currently resided – and that's what Christian had attempted to demonstrate to Matthew, on Friday, inside The Rising Dawn. Christian could be everywhere at once: his soul experienced no past, present or future, as human souls did on the physical realms of earth. Christian's existence was a constant *now*. He could be old or young, depending upon his mood or purpose at any given moment – like when he had appeared to Matthew as the six-year-old boy, inside The Rising Dawn, simply because Christian knew that this was how his brother would best recognise him.

Christian had also appeared to his heartbroken parents, John and Linda, in recent times – again, in the figure of the six-year-old boy they had known on earth. He was determined to reunite his brother and parents: Christian would never be able to fully tend to other things in his current dimension unless this happened. He had to encourage Matthew to go back to the Lake District.

That's why Dixie Carmichael had been chosen to assist Christian in his earthly mission. Aside from shocking Matthew's soul into travelling to Christian's dimension,

Dixie's dead body had also led Matthew back to *nature*. Dixie had always been particularly fond of parks and woodland when he was Susan Carmichael's dog on earth, so it only made sense that Dixie would compel Matthew Rourke to enter a nature location, similar to those Matthew had frequented as a child, but rarely as an adult. Eva Kelly, being a true friend of nature, had (unwittingly) helped steer Matthew towards the large Oak tree in Unity Park, where Matthew eventually buried Dixie's body. Matthew was able to experience peace and Oneness with nature, as he knelt beside the Oak, and this subsequently allowed his soul to reach out and encounter Christian's.

But Matthew's encounter inside The Rising Dawn, and his experiences as he watched 'The Spider Mystery', had evidently not hit home hard enough. Matthew needed to put some of his earthly future plans into action soon, or risk remaining stuck for a long time in his current sludgy, depressing life with Ruth.

Dixie's soul stepped back for a while now, and let Christian take charge.

Christian had always had a way with animals and nature, so Christian was hopeful that he would be able to do something now, to shake Matthew's soul into action, to compel his brother to leave this place now, and go to another location. Matthew needed to be elsewhere, even though Matthew didn't realise this yet.

Christian needed to do something meaningful, that would speak clearly to Matthew's soul; and yet, he didn't want to overly startle or disturb his brother, to such an extent that Christian's message would get lost. It was well understood by those inside the invisible realms that many humans had been damaged by signs and symbols revealed to them by other dimensions of consciousness (Madeleine Singleton, for example, had teetered into alcoholism and paranoia, ever since her departed daughter had appeared to her, two years ago: Madeleine's current earthly predicament had still to be addressed by those residing inside the invisible realms).

Christian thought now about what he should do – and his plan came into immediate effect.

Matthew Rourke continued to look down at the spilled cereal and sugar on the ground around him. He was disappointed at not having encountered Christian again.

Just as he was about to rise from his crouched position beside the dog's tomb, there was a sudden commotion above his head. Matthew looked up to see lots of small birds flying away, as a huge bird swooped into the wooded area, and rested beside Matthew.

Matthew was very taken-aback; shocked.

He stared at the bird. Matthew could clearly see that it was a peregrine falcon. It stood quietly, staring intensely into Matthew's eyes. The bird was clearly not there to feed. It remained still, all the time staring into Matthew's eyes.

Matthew felt mesmerised by the sight before him.

He suddenly recalled his brother, Christian. Matthew and Christian had once searched for peregrines through their binoculars, when they were young. There had been so many of them in the Lake District.

The peregrine falcon continued to look into Matthew's eyes. It was majestic. Matthew gazed at its dark head, yellow-rimmed black eyes and yellow-based grey beak. He could see its broad and bulky pale chest and throat, and its strong yellow legs.

As Matthew stared at the magical figure of the bird before him, he suddenly began to perceive that its black eyes were changing in colour. It was unmistakeable: the falcon's eyes had turned a vibrant shade of *green*.

Matthew continued to stare into the bird's eyes. He felt as though he was being hypnotised. Matthew began to experience the same sensation of timelessness he had encountered during his vision of Christian, inside The Rising Dawn. Matthew couldn't believe it, but he suddenly realised that he was not staring into the peregrine falcon's eyes: he was staring into *Christian's*.

Matthew tumbled backwards onto the ground, in shock at his awesome realisation. As he did so, the peregrine falcon swooped out of the wooded area, and disappeared, leaving Matthew alone again with nature.

Matthew began to breathe very heavily. His heart was thumping inside his chest. He needed to get away from here – now.

He stood up, brushed himself down, and began to stagger past the Oak, Rowans and Silver Birch trees, until he met the section of long grass that led him out of the wooded area. Matthew wandered onto the open area of parkland, beyond the wooded area, with its grass and picnic areas. He walked quickly onto the familiar driveway that led him through Unity Park's large double gateway, and back out onto the crossroads outside.

Matthew walked in the direction of the tube station. He came to The Rising Dawn and thought briefly about calling in for a drink. It was closed. Matthew looked at the time on his phone. He couldn't believe that it was still only ten-thirty in the morning. Matthew could have sworn he had been in Unity Park for much, much longer. Where could he go now?

He walked on, thinking again about the peregrine falcon he had just encountered, inside Unity Park. It wasn't really unusual for that type of bird to be seen in this area of London. The hotel Matthew had meant to attend for the Recruitment Fair, last Friday, was called 'The Peregrine', after all. That was it! Matthew could go to The Peregrine, order some tea, and sit in the lobby to gather his thoughts.

Christian looked at Dixie, and smiled.

Matthew proceeded onwards until he reached The Peregrine. He walked into the lobby, ordered some tea, and sat on one of the large sofas.

A few minutes later, the waiter approached Matthew's sofa, and placed the tray with Matthew's tea and complimentary biscuits on the low-rise oak table in front. Upon thanking the waiter, Matthew suddenly thought that he may as well enquire about the Retail Management Recruitment Fair he had missed on Friday. The waiter agreed to ask at Reception if any leaflets or information sheets had been left behind. Matthew thanked him.

As Matthew took his first few mouthfuls of hot, black tea from The Peregrine's white china cup, he began to look around at the hotel lobby. It was decorated with numerous paintings of peregrine falcons, all in their natural habitat. The scenes reminded Matthew of the Lake District.

Matthew continued to look about him, and he immediately spotted a huge painting of the head of a peregrine. Matthew's eyes were instinctively drawn to the bird's black, piercing eyes. Matthew began to think about Christian again. He could almost swear that Christian was looking at him again. Matthew couldn't have been mistaken - inside Unity Park today, or in The Rising Dawn, on Friday – not twice. Matthew was certain that Christian must be trying to contact him, but he couldn't think why. Matthew had always believed in invisible forces.

The waiter approached Matthew's table. 'Hello, Sir,' he said. 'There doesn't seem to be anything left from the Retail Management Recruitment Fair on Friday. But we do have these leaflets. They were left behind by a tourism recruitment group, after their exhibition – last Wednesday afternoon.'

'OK,' Matthew replied, disappointed, as the waiter walked off again.

Matthew took another drink of hot tea, as he looked down at the two leaflets in his hand. The first was for a flower-arranging company in the New Forest. Needless to say, Matthew placed *that* leaflet straight onto the oak table, directly in front of him.

He looked at the other leaflet.

It was an advertisement for tour guides in the Lake District.

Matthew Rourke took in a gasp of air. The world appeared to freeze around him. He felt shivers running up and down his spine, as he recalled Christian's green eyes, staring at him, from inside the yellow-rimmed eyes of the peregrine falcon, inside Unity Park.

Matthew felt surreal. He immediately finished his tea, and walked straight out of The Peregrine, taking with him the Lake District leaflet. He had to go home now. Matthew realised that Christian was definitely trying to tell him something.

*****

Christian Rourke now left Dixie Carmichael, as Dixie's attention immediately switched to Amanda and Charlotte Morgan, drinking skinny lattes together, in Fateful, in Central London.

Dixie was contented that Amanda had already begun to take the first few steps towards a new future, although Charlotte still had much to discover, within a very narrow earthly time-frame. If Charlotte was to achieve her elusive dream, of discovering 'the point' of her life, a lot would depend on her visiting The Peregrine, where Matthew Rourke had just left.

Dixie realised that Charlotte's twin sister, Matilda, would work alongside him, to ensure that Charlotte went to that hotel – tonight.

-CHAPTER FIFTEEN-

Passing Ships

Susan Carmichael was having a terrible Monday. She hadn't slept a wink the previous night, thinking about Dixie; wondering where he was. Ray had been doing his best to console Susan since finding out about Dixie's death and theft, but neither Ray nor Susan had really had the chance to catch breath since their arrival back from Buckinghamshire, yesterday. Susan was still furious with Ray for convincing her to go there in the first place. Susan had attempted to contact Mike Gordon last night, after Amanda Morgan left the Carmichaels' house, but Mike's phone kept switching to voicemail. When Susan received the text from Amanda Morgan this morning, explaining that Mike had taken Steve to hospital, Susan decided that she would leave it a while before she would try to contact Dixie's vet again.

Both Susan and Ray were relieved not to have to speak to Steve Morgan today. Aside from the fact that they both blamed him for the Dixie situation, they had arrived at work in Epsilon Dental Spa this morning to find the place in complete disarray. Not only did they discover Susan's prize umbrella plant lying on its side in Reception, with soil spilled everywhere on the carpet, but the practice's customer brochures were strewn all across the Reception Desk, along with several half-filled mugs of black coffee. Then, when Ray had switched on the computer to check for this week's appointments, he soon realised that Steve Morgan had not fulfilled his promise to take at least some of Ray and Susan's appointments from last Thursday and Friday. Now that Steve would likely be off sick for the foreseeable, Susan and Ray knew that they would be working like mules for the next several days at Epsilon.

As if all this wasn't bad enough already, when Fiona the Receptionist went on to Epsilon's website, later that morning, she came across Steve Morgan's hashed tabloid re-jig of the site. Susan Carmichael had to be physically restrained by Ray and Fiona, as Susan threatened to go to Memorial Hospital, to personally re-arrange Steve Morgan's private parts – irrespective of whether Steve was dead or dying. Susan was only relieved that she had succeeded in ensuring that Epsilon hadn't set up MyVaneSpace or Twopenniesworth accounts, a few months back. Steve had been eager to do this – to promote the dental practice, and to reach out to celebrities and commoners alike – but Susan had feared that Steve's messages and posts would have been too much of a liability for the Dental Spa: she knew that too many of them would have been sent after Steve had drenched himself with alcohol.

Dixie Carmichael was relieved that Susan had so much going on in her life today. She didn't really have the time to think about her dead and missing dog (much).

All morning, Dixie had been busy working alongside Christian Rourke, who had successfully managed to drop the hint to his brother, Matthew, that Matthew should return to the Lake District and his parents, as soon as possible. Dixie now arrived back at Epsilon Dental Spa, just in the nick-of-time to catch Susan Carmichael grabbing her first spare minute of the day. It was eleven o'clock, and Susan had just lifted the phone in Reception to call her local police station, to enquire if anyone had located Dixie's body yet.

'Hello. My name is Susan Carmichael. My business partner – Amanda Morgan – reported my dog missing to your officers on Friday. His name is Dixie.'

'Sorry, Madam, but we don't do missing dogs here.'

'Oh yes you do, Officer. You see – my dog is *dead*, and he was *stolen* on Friday. That's why my friend called your Officers round to her house on Friday evening – to report that a *crime* had been committed.'

'Please hold the line, Madam.'

Susan Carmichael waited for a few minutes, impatiently, before another voice spoke to her on the phone.

'Hello, Madam. My name is Officer Mark Steele. I think I know the case you're referring to, Madam – '

'Good. Have you found Dixie's body yet? Did you look at the CCTV images from the tube station – and find the man who stole him?'

'Listen, Madam. We're very busy at this station. We have to look at cases in order of priority, Madam. Cut-backs and that. I'm sure you've heard them talking about them on the news, Madam.'

'Now. You listen to me!' Susan's internal boiler was about to burst. 'Get out there *now* and find my bloody dog – or I'll report you – '

Ray Carmichael grabbed the phone out of his wife's hand. He had heard her raised and emotional voice from inside his surgery room, and realised that something was very wrong. 'Who are you talking to on the other end of this line, Susan?' he demanded, holding the phone away from his mouth.

'Some *COCKY* police man!' Susan shouted, feeling strangely emotional and weepy.

'Shit!' Ray shook his head in disbelief, before he began to speak to Officer Steele on the phone. 'I'm very sorry about this, Officer. My wife is feeling very upset at the moment – '

Susan was furious. 'Don't bloody patronise *ME* – Ray Carmichael – '

Ray attempted to speak to Office Steele again. 'As I said, Officer, I'm sorry. It won't happen again. Goodbye!' Ray hung up the phone immediately. 'What are you playing at Susan?' he shouted.

'I'm not *playing* at anything. This isn't some sort of *game* for me, Ray.' Susan was crying hysterically now - much to the bemusement of Fiona the Receptionist, Epsilon's two dental nurses, and a well-known T.V. presenter, who had just arrived to have his teeth whitened (again). Ray Carmichael immediately ushered the well-know T.V. presenter into his private surgery room, in an attempt to diffuse the situation.

Fiona the Receptionist sprinted for cover into the tea room, along with Susan Carmichael's dental nurse, who giggled over at Ray's dental nurse, as she closed Ray's surgery room door behind Ray and the well-known T.V. presenter.

Susan tearfully lifted the phone again. She was livid. She dialled Mike Gordon's Veterinary Surgery to let off some more steam.

'Hello! Gordon's Veterinary Surgery. Lisa speaking. How may I – '

'I want to speak to Mike,' Susan growled.

'May I ask who's speaking?' Lisa, Mike's receptionist, was beginning to think she might start looking for another job soon – given the amount of verbal phone abuse she had been subjected to recently.

'Susan Carmichael.'

'Please hold.'

After a few seconds, Mike Gordon's voice spoke to Susan. 'Hi Susan. I'm sorry I didn't get back to you last night or this morning, but – '

'Just cut the crap, Mike. Tell me, in your professional opinion, why do you think Dixie died?'

Mike was only slightly taken aback by Susan's open aggression. 'I really honestly don't know, Susan. And by the way – I'm very sorry – '

'You mean – you haven't a clue why he would have died – so young?'

'No. He had no underlying health issues – I went over his notes again this morning, Susan – so until we are able to examine Dixie's body, we really have no way of knowing what happened to him.'

'Great. Thanks for nothing.' Susan hung up, and ran towards Epsilon's staff toilets. She thought she was going to be sick; and on top of that, she had a full schedule of work today – right up until evening-time.

Back at Gordon's Veterinary Surgery, Mike Gordon handed the phone back to his receptionist, Lisa. 'The next call for me – say that I'm out,' he ordered, before walking into his surgery room. Mike had listened to enough grief this weekend, without being subjected to the rough end of Susan Carmichael's tongue. He was still recovering from his ordeal with Steve Morgan, not to mention the disturbing incident with the mad bunny woman, inside Abandonment, on Saturday night. Mike still couldn't get the image of Steve fighting with Madeleine Singleton's insane, animal-print sister out of his head. He just wanted to wash his hands entirely of Steve Morgan now. Steve's affair with Madeleine Singleton, his involvement in Dixie Carmichael's death and theft, and his current health issues, were not something Mike Gordon would choose to willingly associate himself with.

Mike's biggest concern, however, was still the bunny woman with the 'shed salon'. He had frantically looked up Deborah Silvestri's name when he came into work this morning, and he instructed Lisa, the receptionist, never to accept any of this woman's calls, or let her into his surgery, unannounced. Mike didn't know what he would do, however, if he was ever confronted by this woman again – bunnies or no bunnies.

*****

A few miles away, in W5, Ruth Rourke was thinking along very similar lines to Mike Gordon. Ruth was sitting alone, in her psychotherapy office, above The Cookie Jug bakery. She had just finished with her first client of the day, and she was dreading the other two clients she still had lined-up in her Appointment Book.

Ruth had spent all the previous day quietly mulling over her incident-filled Saturday night in Abandonment. She had spoken briefly to Clare Silvestri by phone, yesterday, to conduct a post-mortem on the events inside Abandonment – but Ruth still couldn't really believe the madness she had become embroiled in. She was beginning to finally tire of her antics with Clare, and Clare's mother, Deborah. Ruth couldn't believe it yesterday, when Clare had told Ruth about the insane lifestyles of Deborah Silvestri and Madeleine Singleton (Clare's aunt). Clare informed Ruth that Deborah and Madeleine were both obsessed with ghosts and fortune-telling. Deborah Silvestri's life was apparently heavily influenced by the 'teachings' of Chinese Astrology. Clare's mum's rabbit obsession had started when Deborah discovered that she was born during the 'Year of the Rabbit'.

Clare's Aunt Madeleine, Clare informed Ruth, had started to go slightly mad, ever since she claimed she saw her dead daughter's ghost, a couple of years ago. Clare's mum, Deborah, frequently held séances in her shed (when she didn't have any clients), during which Deborah tried to facilitate lines of communication between Madeleine and her departed daughter, Victoria.

On one occasion, recently, Deborah informed Clare that Madeleine had received a message from the spirits, which told Madeleine that she would soon come into contact with a psycho. Madeleine immediately decided, last Friday, when she overheard Steve Morgan talking about murder and dead dogs in Epsilon Dental Spa, that Steve must be the psycho. Madeleine immediately phoned Deborah, after telling her husband, Douglas, about her affair with Steve; whereupon Deborah confirmed Madeleine's worst fear about 'Psycho Steve', after Deborah did a quick tarot card shuffle in her shed.

When Deborah Silvestri later encountered Steve Morgan, in Abandonment, she couldn't contain her anger at him – not just because he had treated Madeleine so shoddily in his surgery on Friday; or because Steve had let slip to Deborah inside Abandonment, that he like to please more of his clients than Madeleine; but because Steve Morgan had murdered a poor defenceless dog.

The thing that had *really* disturbed Ruth Rourke about Clare Silvestri's family anecdotes yesterday, however, hadn't necessarily been the anecdotes themselves, but rather the fact that Clare appeared to view them as so average and run-of-the-mill. Clare Silvestri was evidently better-placed mentally to deal with these types of crazy beings and situations: Ruth Rourke realised now, that she, Ruth, was definitely not.

Ruth didn't think she could do this any longer. She had to keep clear of Clare Silvestri, as well as Clare's insane mother and aunt – forever. Not only this, but it suddenly dawned on Ruth Rourke, as she stared down at the dead, cobwebbed cactus plant on her desk, that she no longer wanted to be a psychotherapist. Ruth began to sob loudly. She felt dead. She didn't know what to do anymore. She felt as though everything was over. She had ruined everything in her life. She didn't even know who she was anymore. She couldn't even remember who she used to be. Ruth couldn't cope with any more psychotherapy clients today – or ever. She had to get out of this office – or she would explode. She never wanted to come back to this office again.

The phone on the desk began to ring. Ruth couldn't bring herself to answer it, so she let the call go to voicemail. She pressed the button on the phone now, and listened to the person leaving the message:

'Hi Ruth! It's Amanda Morgan. I'm just calling to let you know I won't be attending my appointment with you on Wednesday. In fact, I'll be giving my psychotherapy sessions a miss for a while, I think. Something pretty big has happened in my life this weekend, and I'm happy to go it alone for a while. I think things are finally working out for me. Thanks a million for all your help again, and I'll let you know how I get on. Bye!'

Ruth suddenly remembered where she had heard the name *Steve Morgan* before. The drunken, dog-killer, sex-mad dentist was Amanda Morgan's *husband*. Ruth stood up. She began to cry again. She had endured as much of this crap as she was able to: dead people, dead dogs, stolen dogs, sex-obsessed dentists, ghosts and rabbits – the world was full of crazy people, and Ruth didn't want to have to deal with any of them, any longer. She had to think about a new career path. One that would take her away from all of this lunacy. One that would earn her more money, and allow her to meet wealthy *and* sane individuals – although Ruth was beginning to wonder if there were any sane individuals out there at all.

Ruth grabbed her handbag and coat and ran out of her office; down the narrow flight of stairs; out the door; past The Cookie Jug bakery; towards the nearest tube station. She had to go home now – although she didn't have a clue what she would do when she got there.

*****

Amanda and Charlotte Morgan returned to Memorial Hospital at 6.30 p.m. on Monday 10th October. Amanda had not received any phone calls from the hospital since she left it earlier, so she presumed that Steve's life must not be in danger. Amanda had tried to persuade Charlotte to go straight home that evening, but Charlotte had felt strongly inclined to return to Memorial – even though it gave her the spooks.

Mother and daughter entered Steve's side ward to discover him awake, and talking to a doctor and nurse. He glanced up at his wife and daughter, still looking very weak and very out-of-it. Charlotte stood behind Amanda, as her mother introduced herself to the doctor and nurse, and enquired whether the medical staff had discovered what was wrong with Steve.

The doctor, a male in his late thirties, responded to Amanda's question. 'Mr Morgan has *Acute Pancreatitis*. We've just been explaining to him that he appears to have a mild case – although this still means that Mr Morgan will be in a lot of pain for the next few hours. He'll therefore continue to receive opiate-based pain relief.'

'Is it serious?' Amanda enquired curiously.

'We hope not,' the softly-spoken doctor continued. 'Although Mr Morgan will have to stay with us for a few days until the inflammation in his pancreas subsides. He won't be permitted to eat in the meantime, so he'll remain on a feeding drip. Due to the pancreas's proximity to the lungs, he will also require oxygen – until he is more comfortable.'

'Right,' Amanda said, absorbing all the medical jargon.

'We're still running some tests on your husband – just to rule out anything more sinister – but we're hopeful that they won't turn up anything new.'

'Will he likely make a full recovery?' Amanda asked, looking down at Steve in bed.

'Yes – but only if Mr Morgan looks after his health. We are in little doubt – going on what Mr Morgan has informed us himself - that his particular case of Pancreatitis has been caused by his excessive alcohol intake in the past. We advise with cases like this that the patient refrains completely from alcohol for at least six months after the illness clears – preferably even longer.'

'OK. Thank-you, doctor,' Amanda said gratefully, holding Charlotte's hand.

'Right, Mr Morgan. We'll be back to check on you later. Goodbye everyone!' the doctor announced, as he walked out of Steve's side ward, with the permanently-smiling young female nurse.

'Fancy meeting you two here!' Steve Morgan joked, with evident discomfort.

Amanda sat on one of the seats beside Steve's hospital bed, and Charlotte sat beside her. Amanda was determined to make this visit as short as possible – now that she knew that Steve was OK. 'Right, Steve,' she said. 'I've brought you some toiletries and a couple of changes. I'll bring more things if you require them, some other time.' She placed two bags beside Steve's bedside locker.

'Super Dooper!' Steve whispered; smiling to himself, as his eyes began to shut.

'Charlotte and I won't hang around for too long here tonight. You obviously need lots of sleep.' Amanda was relieved to have a plausible excuse to leave the hospital soon.

'Top of the Leader Board!' Steve mumbled: he was floating in a lovely game-show bubble, without a care in the world. Steve's troubles with Susan Carmichael and Madeleine Singleton felt a million miles away right now.

'OK Charlotte. Let's go,' Amanda said, standing up.

'Do you think it's OK to leave now?' Charlotte was taken aback by the brevity of this visit.

'Of course it is. You heard what the doctor said. You dad will make a full recovery – if he chooses to. There's nothing more you or I can do for him at the moment.'

Charlotte stood up. She was secretly glad to be leaving this place. She had felt cold and shivery ever since she first entered her dad's side ward, a matter of minutes ago. Charlotte couldn't really figure it out, but it almost felt as though somebody was watching her. This feeling was giving Charlotte the complete creeps.

Amanda linked arms with Charlotte, and began to walk out of Steve's side ward. 'Do you fancy going for a little drink, Charlotte – before we go home?'

'OK,' Charlotte replied, glancing around at her unconscious and frail father, before stepping onto the hospital corridor with Amanda. Charlotte still felt a little spooked and surreal for some reason.

'Great! We can go to The Peregrine. It's just down from the hospital, and not far from the tube station – although I think we should maybe just get a cab home tonight.' Amanda didn't touch alcohol very often, but she thought she could really do with a scotch-on-the-rocks right now. It was 7.05 p.m.

*****

Around twenty minutes later, Amanda and Charlotte Morgan were sitting together on a sofa inside the lobby of The Peregrine hotel, sipping their drinks. Amanda had ordered her much-anticipated scotch-on-the-rocks, while Charlotte was having her usual Mojito. Charlotte didn't want to have too much to drink this evening, because she was working behind the cosmetics counter in her grandfather's department store tomorrow. She didn't really do hangovers anyway: they weren't good for the complexion.

Amanda began to talk to Charlotte about their day shopping in town. They hadn't really bought much – except a couple of new lipsticks and some perfume – but they had spent a lot of quality time together, having their nails done, drinking skinny lattes and talking. Amanda was determined for Charlotte to forget about Steve now, so she swiftly moved the conversation on to the current trends in autumn/winter coats.

As Amanda now chatted to her daughter, inside the majestic yet cosy lobby of The Peregrine, Charlotte suddenly felt inclined to look around at the paintings on the wall. It was 7.29 p.m.

All of the paintings appeared to be of the same type of bird – and Charlotte found them all very creepy for some reason, even though she normally loved looking at art. A lot of the paintings showed birds flying about, or catching rabbits, or other small birds and animals. But one painting was particularly weird-looking, Charlotte thought. It was a painting of the head of one of these birds, and it was massive.

Charlotte stared closely at this picture. It made her feel very, very eerie, all of a sudden – like she was drifting off somewhere. Charlotte looked into the bird's black eyes, which were surrounded by large yellow rims. She began to feel as though she was getting sucked closer and closer into the darkness beyond the large bird's eyes. Charlotte couldn't see or hear anything else at the moment – not even Amanda – and she soon realised that she was floating in pitch-black darkness. She felt as though her body was drifting off inside the bird's staring black eyes. She felt warm, but not really frightened at all. Charlotte knew instinctively that she didn't have anything to fear. She continued to drift deeper and deeper inside the bird's eyes, until she came to a STOP.

Charlotte's body remained still for a very short time, until it began to pull backwards again, as though it was about to exit the bird's eyes, the same way it had entered, moments ago. As Charlotte drifted backwards, inside this dark but warm void, she fully expected to pull back to discover the large bird staring out at her again, from inside the picture. Instead, however, Charlotte had to wait a while before she realised what was actually staring at her.

Charlotte's body drifted backwards and backwards, until it began to exit one of the bird's eye sockets. She travelled further, until she was staring at two black eyes. As her body continued to reverse, Charlotte was able to perceive a small human nose; a tiny mouth; skin; a round head; a hand; a tiny body; *a baby*.

Charlotte was still floating in darkness, staring at the peachy-coloured, curled-up baby, who was staring back at her. The baby smiled at Charlotte, and gave her a little wave of its hand. Charlotte smiled back, delighted to be in the company of this tranquil, awe-inspiring figure. She could tell that it was a baby girl. Charlotte didn't want to leave this baby. She wanted to stay with it – forever.

'Charlotte!' Amanda Morgan said, shaking her daughter beside her on the lobby sofa. Charlotte stared blankly at Amanda. It was still 7.29 p.m. 'I just asked you if you liked the new season House of Dune blazers?' Amanda repeated, taking another sip of her scotch-on-the-rocks.

'I haven't seen them,' Charlotte replied, still gazing up at the large bird staring down at her on the sofa inside The Peregrine.

'Oh you must! The raspberry colour would really suit you!'

'Mum.'

'Yes darling.'

'Was I out-of-it for long, just then?'

'You weren't out-of-it at all, Charlotte. I just shook you because you didn't hear my question about the blazers when I first asked you it. Why – are you feeling OK?'

'Yes.' Charlotte didn't understand what had just happened to her. She took a large drink from her Mojito, in silence.

'Look at this, Charlotte!' Amanda said, handing Charlotte a leaflet she had just lifted from the low-rise oak table in front of their sofa.

Charlotte glanced down at the leaflet in her hand, still feeling very strange and otherworldly. She couldn't even begin to absorb the meaning or implication of her encounter with the baby, inside the bird's eyes; or, come to mention it, her visit to the dark, enchanted lake, at the top of the flight of stairs, at home, on Saturday morning. Charlotte began to read the leaflet in her hand now. It was a recruitment leaflet for a flower-arranging company in the New Forest.

'Do you think you might be interested in something like that, Charlotte?' Amanda asked. 'You've always said you'd like to do something artistic.'

Charlotte flicked through the leaflet, still feeling surreal from her encounter with the baby, a few moments ago. She suddenly began to get very excited. Charlotte looked at the pictures of the beautiful flower structures and bouquets. She knew nothing about flowers – but for the first time in her life, she noticed how beautiful they were. 'Oh my God, mum!' Charlotte said, beaming. 'That's it!'

'What's it?' Amanda was confused.

'That's what I'd like to do!'

'Seriously?' Amanda had only really shown Charlotte the leaflets for something to talk about. She couldn't even imagine why it had been placed on the table inside The Peregrine in the first place.

'Yes!' Charlotte said happily. 'Do you think I could study to do something like this in London?'

'Of course you could!' Amanda was pleased, but she was still also very taken-aback by Charlotte's sudden and unexpected interest in flower arranging.

'I could set up my own business – couldn't I?' Charlotte enthused: for the first time in her life, she could actually see 'the point' in doing something.

'That would be wonderful, darling!' Amanda was genuinely amazed at the expression on her daughter's face. Something now unexpectedly 'clicked' with Amanda. This suddenly seemed the perfect opportunity to raise a subject that Amanda had been dreading discussing with her daughter: Eva. 'You know – ' Amanda continued. 'I know someone you could perhaps talk to about flowers – and about setting up your own business in that sector.' Amanda could hardly believe that things were moving so quickly in her life all of a sudden.

'Really?'

'Yes. She owns her own gardening business in NW1. You may have seen her working in our garden occasionally. She's called Eva.'

Charlotte thought for a second. 'Ah yes! The pretty lady gardener?'

'Yes!'

'Do you really think she'd be able to advise me on courses and things?'

'Definitely!'

'OK – so when can you arrange for us to meet and talk?'

'What about this week? I can ask Eva what day suits best.'

'Great! Thanks mum!' Charlotte lifted her Mojito glass towards Amanda's scotch-on-the-rocks. 'Cheers!'

'Cheers, Charlotte! To the future!'

Amanda Morgan felt very strange inside – as though fate had somehow played its part in landing the flower-arranging leaflet on the table she was sitting at, inside The

Peregrine. Amanda knew that the most difficult part had yet to come, and she did feel slightly guilty about setting up the meeting between Charlotte and Eva under a slightly false pretence – but at least it was a start.

Amanda and Charlotte eventually ordered a taxi to take them home from The Peregrine. The two women began to walk towards the door of the hotel, arm in arm, and a little light-headed, after the Porter gave them the nod that their taxi had arrived, just after 9.00 p.m.

As Charlotte Morgan was about to exit, she glanced around once more at the massive bird painting that had so captured her attention, earlier. The bird's black eyes stared back at Charlotte, as Charlotte smiled up at the bird, and then down at the flower-arranging leaflet in her hand. Charlotte Morgan had sensed all evening that someone invisible was watching her – ever since she had entered her dad's side ward at Memorial Hospital.

As Charlotte climbed into the back seat of the taxi, outside The Peregrine, she realised that something magical had occurred to her tonight – and on Saturday morning, when Charlotte had sat curled in darkness at the top of the flight of stairs at home, listening to her parents rowing. Charlotte did not feel alone or scared any more. She knew there was a strange and invisible presence around her now. Charlotte dared not think who this presence was, but she had a feeling that she might just know.

As Charlotte travelled home with Amanda in the taxi, Charlotte's twin, Matilda, travelled home with her. She had fully understood Charlotte's fascination with art in the past. Matilda had used the spirit of the painting of the peregrine falcon, inside the hotel lobby, to connect with her sister's soul. Matilda, just like Christian Rourke, wanted the best for her family on the physical realms. It was amazing, Matilda thought, to behold how a small white dog had finally begun to move life forward for those she loved the most on earth.

-CHAPTER SIXTEEN-

More Discoveries

Matthew Rourke awoke in the spare room of his apartment at 7.00 a.m. on the morning of Tuesday 11ᵗʰ October. He lay for a while, alone, contemplating what he would do today: Matthew had nothing in particular lined up.

Matthew had arrived back from his morning in Unity Park and The Peregrine hotel, yesterday, to discover his wife, Ruth, already at home. He had found her lying curled on top of the sofa inside their lounge, sobbing, and still dressed in her work clothes – coat and all.

'What's wrong?' Matthew had asked Ruth.

'Nothing,' she snapped back at him.

'What are you doing at home?'

'I needed a break for a while. I didn't feel well.'

'Do you need to see a doctor?'

'No. Just leave me alone.' With this, Ruth then got up from the sofa, grabbed her handbag from the hallway, and left again. Matthew didn't manage to get to the bottom of Ruth's latest episode – not even yesterday evening, when she arrived back home at her usual time, presumably from work again. She barely spoke to him all evening after this, and she went to bed very early.

Matthew had spent all yesterday afternoon, up until Ruth's (second) arrival home, looking at Internet sites of the Lake District. He hadn't dared look at anything relating to his former home since he left there, more than fourteen years ago. Matthew had always blanked out any literature that came his way relating to the Lake District and Cumbria in the past – such as when junk mail was mistakenly forwarded to him. He had no desire to know, read about or visit that area in his life again. That was - until Christian told him otherwise, in The Peregrine, yesterday. All of a sudden, Matthew couldn't resist the idea of returning to his childhood home. He wanted to go there as soon as possible. Matthew knew that this was what Christian wanted him to do.

As he lay looking at the ceiling in the spare room now, Matthew suddenly heard Ruth walking into the kitchen. A tiny part of Matthew still wished that things were the way they used to be with Ruth. He had always believed that someday Ruth would revert back to the person he had once thought she was, and that they would live happily ever after – together. Matthew knew that this would never be the case now. While this cold and harsh realisation would have been too much for Matthew to accept before – even as recently as this time last week – he was suddenly able to accept the fact that Ruth did not love him in the way Matthew wanted or needed her to. He didn't blame Ruth, however. She was an unhappy individual, Matthew realised. He could never give Ruth what she needed or wanted – nor was Matthew sure that anyone could. All Matthew knew was that he had to go back to the Lake District. He was done with London. Matthew knew that Christian wanted him to go back home, even though the thought of going back home terrified Matthew. He hadn't a clue why he had to go back to Cumbria, but the driving force inside him now was overwhelming – as though it had been borne by magic.

Matthew began to think about his parents, John and Linda. He wasn't even sure if they were still alive – and he didn't want to find that out until he actually returned home. He had detached himself so much from his parents since leaving the Lake District, at the age of nineteen. Matthew didn't really expect them to want to see him at all. Yesterday, while Matthew had been searching through Internet sites about the Lake District, it dawned on him that he should look up his old address on the *FindaStreet* site. Matthew couldn't believe it when he found himself staring directly at a picture of the house he had grown up in. It didn't look much different to when he last remembered it – except perhaps that it was a little more overgrown. Matthew didn't recognise the red car in the driveway. He couldn't be sure if it belonged to his parents, or to the house's new occupants.

Matthew had felt very sad looking at his old home. He recalled helping his dad mow the lawn; wash the family car in the driveway; play football with his mum, dad and Christian in the garden on warm days.

But most of all, Matthew remembered Christian.

Matthew had to trust in his instincts. He knew that Christian had shown him signs, telling Matthew to go back to Cumbria. Matthew had recognised the signs, ever since he discovered the body of the white dog inside the flowery bag, last Friday. He had encountered the signs in The Rising Dawn, and in the eyes of the peregrine falcon, in Unity Park. But how long would he be able to remain in Cumbria? Would his family want to know him? What about Ruth? Matthew couldn't bring himself to think about all of these issues right now. He was still terrified that the police might knock on his door, any time soon, and arrest him over the theft of the dead dog. They could be trawling through CCTV images from the tube station - right now.

Matthew would wait until Ruth left the house for work, and then he would sit and gather his thoughts, alone. Matthew would decide what to do with the remainder of his life – soon: and Christian Rourke and Dixie Carmichael would help him, they now resolved, from their dimension inside the invisible realms.

Matthew heard movement outside his bedroom door. Ruth was thumping about the apartment – deliberately, and for dramatic effect, Matthew knew – getting ready to depart for work. Ruth hadn't allowed Matthew to forget about what a disappointment and a failure he was, ever since he had broken the news of his redundancy. Only yesterday, when Ruth had arrived back from work for the second time, Matthew enquired about Ruth's health, only to be told that she only felt sick because she was 'sick' of being the sole breadwinner. At the moment, it didn't even surprise Matthew to think that he'd stolen a young female's bag to placate his wife.

Ruth Rourke eventually slammed the front door of her apartment, and began the short walk to her nearest tube station. She was going to work as normal, in her psychotherapy office, in W5.

Yesterday, Matthew's wife had re-evaluated her decision to completely walk out on her job. She had realised how silly and impractical this would be, given that Ruth needed to get money from somewhere: her credit card statements showed that she owed more than she cared to admit to. Ruth would therefore have to endure the unbearable demands of her job – at least for now.

She also decided yesterday, however, that she would re-invent herself again. She had successfully done this before, when she swapped from being a hospital receptionist to a psychotherapist - so she would simply do it again. This time, however, Ruth would think much more strategically about her future career path. She would ensure that her new job fully tied in with all her dreams, aspirations and expectations – not to mention that it should pay an excellent wage. Her change of mind would also mean that Ruth would have to retain her relationship with Clare and Deborah Silvestri. But Ruth was prepared to do this: her future happiness and security were at stake. In the meantime, Ruth would swallow hard and endure the boredom and predictability of living with Matthew, as well as the despair of listening to crazy tales of sex-mad dentists, ghosts, and dead and stolen dogs.

*****

As Matthew and Ruth Rourke continued to mull over their futures on the morning of Tuesday 11th October, Charlotte Morgan had just arrived at Montgomery's Department Store to begin her first five-hour shift of the week. It was 8.30 a.m.

Those in the invisible realms had kept a very close eye on Charlotte, ever since her recent encounters with her past. Just like Matthew Rourke, Charlotte had been permitted access to the timeless, invisible realms, where she had been able to experience earlier moments in her life. Although Charlotte Morgan had never been a believer in the invisible, timeless realms, she had a soul, nevertheless. Charlotte could not escape the realities of what she had experienced on Saturday morning, as she sat at the top of the flight of stairs at home; or yesterday, as she stared into the penetrating eyes of the peregrine falcon, inside the hotel lobby, near Memorial Hospital. In fact, Charlotte didn't want to escape from any of these experiences. She had felt a strange kind of inner peace and stillness, ever since her encounters with the timeless realms. Not only this, but Charlotte didn't feel alone any longer. She felt as though there was somebody experiencing life alongside her now. Charlotte Morgan knew that this 'somebody' was her twin sister – Matilda.

As Charlotte hung her coat on the peg in Montgomery's staff quarters, she could hardly believe everything that had occurred in her life, ever since she left work, last Wednesday. She almost felt like a different person (albeit that she still liked the same clothes etc. as before). It was as though she was looking at the world through different eyes. Charlotte had actually begun to see 'the point' in things. She had mysteriously and unexpectedly discovered that she had a sister – the one she had longed for all her life. Charlotte had also discovered that she wanted to be a professional flower-arranger and businesswoman (where had *that* idea come from?), and she even knew that her mum, Amanda, had promised to introduce Charlotte to Eva, her mum's gardener, to discuss Charlotte's future career. It was unbelievable, but everything in Charlotte's life had suddenly begun to click in place magically.

Even though Charlotte was still rather sad that her mum and dad had split up, and that her dad was still ill in hospital, all the positive and weird things that had happened to Charlotte – ever since she found Dixie Carmichael's dead body in his basket last Friday morning – more than compensated for the bad stuff that had gone on. She didn't even mind going into work today. Charlotte knew that she wouldn't have to work in her grandfather's department store for much longer, nor would she have to tolerate all the O.M.P.s she was always subjected to there. She didn't even care that she would have to listen to Pippa Parsons' mind-wrecking stories about her weekend with Andrew Singleton. Charlotte would be able to tolerate Pippa today – mainly because Charlotte had so much to think about regarding her own future. And because Charlotte had a brilliant new business proposition for her best friend, Ebony Glazier.

As Charlotte approached her usual position behind one of the cosmetics counters in Montgomery's, she was correct to believe that she was not on her own today. Matilda, her twin, had not left her side since yesterday, inside The Peregrine. Matilda knew that Charlotte still had an eventful and defining few days ahead of her (not to mention years), and she was determined to stand by, to ensure that Charlotte sailed through these events, knowing that she had company. Matilda had always been around Charlotte; but it hadn't been until Charlotte learnt about Matilda's existence properly, last Friday, that Charlotte had really been able to connect to Matilda's presence. Matilda and Charlotte's souls could work more as a team now, Matilda thought. Matilda was keen to help Charlotte realise just how much Charlotte could achieve in her life – starting with the flower-arranging and business courses Charlotte would (hopefully) attend in the New Year.

In the meantime, Matilda would remain close by her sister; in the same way as Dixie Carmichael would continue to connect to the many ripples he had left behind, on the earthly, physical planes.

'Hi Pippa,' Charlotte Morgan said to Pippa Parsons behind the cosmetics counter in Montgomery's. It was 8.55 a.m., and Charlotte's grandfather's department store had just opened for business. Pippa immediately turned her back on Charlotte and walked away. Charlotte stood for a moment, not really knowing which way to turn. She had fully expected Pippa to start blabbing on about her weekend with Andrew Singleton. 'What's wrong with *her*?' Charlotte asked Julie Smith, another of the very attractive, glamorous assistants employed by Charlotte's grandfather.

'Andy's squeezed the *Pip* out of *AndyPip*,' Julie replied.

Charlotte was none the wiser. 'In English, please?'

'Andrew dumped Pippa this weekend,' Julie clarified with a glint in her eye.

Charlotte's jaw visibly dropped. 'Shit. Did he finally tire of the MyVaneSpace stuff?'

'She's blaming *you*, actually.' Julie walked off – very enigmatically.

Charlotte stood dumbfounded, at a complete loss as to why Pippa Parsons could possibly hold Charlotte responsible for her break-up with Andrew Singleton. 'How can she blame *me*?' Charlotte was pursuing Julie Smith around the cosmetics counter now.

'I don't know,' Julie replied (she was loving the drama of all this: working in Montgomery's was usually so bloody boring). 'She said it was something to do with your family.' Julie looked directly at Charlotte for some feedback. Anything. Charlotte was clueless. Julie continued. 'Pippa's even gone so far as to request that your grandfather allow her to move to another floor. She said she doesn't want to work with you any longer. In fact – she says she wants nothing to do with your entire family again. She's going to start looking for a new job.' Julie was itching for an explanation, a snippet of insight from Charlotte.

Charlotte immediately marched off in the direction of Pippa Parsons, directly pursued by a very animated Julie Smith.

Matilda knew what was coming next. Charlotte wasn't one to mince her words when she was angry. Whereas Matilda would be more inclined to chicken away from confrontation, like Steve Morgan, Charlotte had always preferred to take the giraffe by the neck, just like Amanda. Luckily, no customers had entered Montgomery's – yet.

'OK Pippa,' Charlotte stomped. 'What's this about you blaming me for your break-up with Andrew Singleton?'

'I'm not speaking to you,' Pippa replied petulantly, turning to walk away.

'Yes you are!' Charlotte pulled Pippa back by the arm.

'Don't touch me – or I'll sue you!'

'Cut the crap, Pippa. I'll ask you again. Why are you blaming me for – '

'Because Andy said that he couldn't go on seeing me – because I work for your family!'

'What have *we* got to do with your relationship with *him*?'

Pippa was on the edge. 'He said his dad and him are taking legal action against your family! He wouldn't TELL ME WHY!'

'What a load of C-R-A-P!' Charlotte shouted back, prompting her grandfather, Sir Horace Montgomery, to pounce across the shop floor towards Charlotte, Pippa, and the small gathering of employees now gathered around them. 'What the hell is going on here?' his voice boomed angrily: Sir Horace's voice was almost as round and large as his belly. Matilda Morgan had always thought her grandfather a bit of a grump. For a very wealthy man in his early seventies, he certainly never appeared to be very happy. Although Matilda knew exactly why this was the case. As for Charlotte, she could barely tolerate them man. She knew he had never taken much to do much with her mum, Amanda. Charlotte began to shout at Sir Horace. 'She just said that Singleton solicitors are taking legal action against our family! Do you know anything about this?'

'Get round to my office now – the pair of you. Before any customers have to hear any of this nonsense.' Sir Horace Montgomery's large face was the colour of a ripe tomato (he liked to drink a lot of whisky). He was not in the mood for any trouble today – although Sir Horace was rarely in the mood for anything that wasn't positively related to the efficient running of his business empire. Amanda Morgan had always thought her dad wore a permanent scowl on his face – like he pushed all of his troubles ahead of him. He used to frighten Amanda, when she was younger.

Sir Horace marched towards his office, his granddaughter and employee in tow. Charlotte could really do without this today – although the only thing that was keeping her calm was the thought of leaving her job in her grandfather's department store, as soon as possible. Julie Smith's face crashed to the floor as she realised that she wouldn't be able to listen in to any more Montgomery scandal or gossip.

'NOW,' Sir Horace roared, as he shut his office door behind Charlotte Morgan and Pippa Parsons. 'I don't know what is going on between you two ladies – and frankly – I don't give a damn. But I will NOT tolerate common behaviour like that in my department store. At least not from my staff.'

'Have you asked her why the Singletons are supposedly launching legal proceedings against our family?' Charlotte threw another filthy look in the direction of the beautiful and glamorous Pippa Parsons.

'What's this you've been claiming, Ms Parsons?' Sir Horace demanded (he never requested information).

Pippa Parsons felt very intimidated. She couldn't really believe that she had suddenly found herself in the boss's office. She started to blub like a girl. Pippa knew what she was up to. She wanted to get home early – to see if she could contact Andrew Singleton, in an attempt to patch things up with him. 'Oh, Sir Horace!' she cried. 'This is nothing to do with me. All I heard from my boyfriend – ex boyfriend – Andrew Singleton – was that his dad's legal firm are suing your family. And Andrew didn't want anything more do to with me - because I work for you.'

'Is this true?' Sir Horace shouted at Charlotte. 'Because I am certainly not aware of any legal case.'

'How should I know if it's true?' Charlotte answered defiantly.

'Really, Charlotte. Your manner and turn-of-phrase is really so common.' Sir Horace was disgusted at his granddaughter.

Charlotte suddenly turned to Pippa. 'Did Andrew Singleton say this legal case against our family was anything to do with a dead, stolen dog?'

Pippa looked at Charlotte and pulled a face that said *you're mental*, before Sir Horace Montgomery addressed the two women again. 'Please stop talking such nonsense, Charlotte. This is not funny. Now. I want you two ladies to get back onto the shop floor, and behave like Montgomery's staff – not like extras from some working-class soap opera (Sir Horace secretly *loved* watching 'working-class soap operas' - as he referred to them). Ms Parsons – you can work at the Letterbury counter today, as you requested earlier. Charlotte – get back to your usual position. I have a phone call I need to make.' With this, Sir Horace chased Charlotte Morgan and Pippa Parsons from his office, and banged the door behind them.

Charlotte and Pippa walked to opposite corners of Montgomery's Department Store, firing each other looks of disgust, as Charlotte began to count the hours to home-time.

In the meantime, her grandfather had just lifted the phone to his daughter – Charlotte's mum, Amanda Morgan.

'Hello?' Amanda's voice said. She couldn't understand why her father was calling her today. Sir Horace rarely ever called Amanda – unless something was wrong with the family business. What Amanda *did* know, however, was that her father certainly wasn't contacting her to spread any paternal love in her direction.

'Amanda?' Sir Horace was checking to make sure that he'd got his only child's name correct.

'Yes,' Amanda confirmed.

'What is this your daughter's work colleague has been saying about Douglas Singleton bringing legal action against our family?'

'My daughter's name is Charlotte.'

'Don't get lippy with me, Amanda. I phoned for an explanation – not a conversation.'

'Well if it's an explanation you're looking for, I'm afraid I haven't a clue what you're talking about.'

'This is probably something to do with that educated idiot you're married to – isn't it?'

'Unlikely this time. Steve's ill in hospital at the moment.'

'Well, let's just hope that it's something and nothing then – shall we? But - if you *do* happen to hear anything about this – let me know.' Sir Horace hung up, leaving Amanda Morgan to ponder her father's strange phone call. It was true: Amanda knew nothing about any legal action against her family, although she did have to admit that if anything like this *were* to happen, she too would automatically assume that it was something to do with Steve.

'Everything OK?' Eva Kelly asked Amanda. The two women had met for drinks in a little French café in NW1, near Eva's business. Eva had arranged to take some time off work this morning to meet Amanda – considering that their plans had been put on hold all over last weekend, and yesterday morning, due to the business with Steve, Charlotte and the stolen dead dog.

'I hope so,' Amanda replied pensively. 'It's hopefully something and nothing.'

'So – go on. What were you telling me about Charlotte deciding that she wanted to do *flower arranging*?' Eva was greatly amused by the idea that Amanda's daughter could possibly consider working with bug-ridden things like flowers.

'Oh my God, Eva. My life has gone from mad to madder over this last week.'

'You were saying she just hit on the idea when she saw a leaflet in The Peregrine?'

'Yes. And it was all my fault too. I was the one who suggested it to her – because she's always been into art, but she was never able to draw. Charlotte used to get frustrated during art classes in school. She always ended up in trouble for deliberately destroying her landscape paintings, by drawing UFOs in the sky. She said she did it on purpose – because she got pissed off that her paintings always looked so awful.'

Eva laughed. 'Flower arranging should be right up her street then! God help the flowers if they don't behave themselves!'

'So you don't mind talking to her about gardening, and flower courses – or whatever else you people do?' Amanda was teasing. She knew that Eva was very chilled – in a warm sort of way. Amanda admired the fact that Eva was so cosy in her own skin.

'God, Amanda. You're going to have a very difficult time over the forthcoming months – dealing with all those bug-infested flowers inside your house – and all the killer germs they bring with them!'

'Ugh. Don't remind me. As long as it doesn't involve any soil or cat or dog poo in the house – I don't mind. I suppose it could be worse: Charlotte could be asking to become a gardener!'

'Perish!' Eva replied, laughing. 'Anyway – talking about *dog* poo – any more on the dead dog situation?'

'Well, of course, Steve conveniently got ill and absconded to hospital – leaving me with the task of going round to Susan Carmichael's house to explain the details of how and when her dog was stolen. Honestly, Eva, I feel like doing a double-take every time I think about the whole crazy situation. Not to mention everything that's come about as a result of it: my marriage with Steve finally ending, and Charlotte finding out about Matilda.'

'You've certainly had an eventful time.'

'That's an understatement.'

'So did Charlotte remember much about the man who stole the dog?'

'Not a lot. Just that he was good-looking, foreign and wearing a suit.'

'Narrows things down – not-a-lot!'

'I know! Although he did probably stand out a bit – running about with the flowery bag the dog was lying in!'

Eva Kelly suddenly froze. 'What time did you say the man stole Charlotte's bag?'

'Em – Friday morning. Some time around eleven, I think. Why?'

'Oh, nothing!' Eva began to feel queasy, as she recalled meeting her brother-in-law, Matthew Rourke, at around eleven, on Friday morning. Matthew had been carrying a flowery bag. Eva had thought there was something wrong with Matthew at the time. 'When Charlotte said that the man was foreign – what nationality did she say she thought he was?' Eva was trying not to sound too curious.

'German – or Scottish!' Amanda laughed. 'Any accent other than a London or south-of-England accent is foreign to Charlotte!'

'Ha Ha Ha!' Eva didn't want to show that she suspected something: Matthew's soft Cumbrian accent could easily have been mistaken by Charlotte as foreign, Eva realised. 'And at what station was her bag taken?'

'Unity Park Station.' Amanda took another drink of her skinny latte.

Shit, Eva thought.

Poor Matthew. Eva was in a quick-spin over this information. Should she do the honest thing, and tell Amanda about her suspicions about her brother-in-law and the flowery bag? Or should she keep quiet, and say nothing to anybody? Why the hell would Matthew have wanted to steal a girl's bag anyway? Eva cared deeply about Amanda; but she still thought the world of Matthew Rourke, in spite of the possibility that he had committed a crime. Eva would have to think about this situation, alone. She would have to think about giving Matthew the benefit of the doubt at least. Perhaps this was all just one big co-incidence, she hoped.

'Are you OK?' Amanda asked suddenly.

'God – yes!' Eva replied, a little flustered by the thoughts racing through her mind. 'I was just thinking about going back to work. So how is Steve anyway?' she asked quickly, changing the subject.

'OK. I think.'

Eva paused for a while. She couldn't stop thinking about Matthew Rourke. 'Listen, Amanda. I'm going to have to go soon. I have a delivery arriving at around ten – I'm really sorry.'

'No worries. Thanks for taking time out to meet me in the first place. So you don't mind if I call to arrange a time for you and Charlotte to meet – later this week?'

'Of course not. It will feel a bit weird though.'

'I know. We'll just stick to the flower arranging subject, I think – shall we? See how things go?'

'OK. Whatever you think.'

Amanda Morgan and Eva Kelly embraced, before going their separate ways.

Meanwhile, Dixie Carmichael and Matilda Morgan's attentions had already been drawn to the two women's conversation. Matilda realised that her mum would soon have to face up to some difficult experiences from her past, not to mention the impending crisis with Steve and Sir Horace Montgomery. Dixie, however, was more concerned about the decision Eva Kelly would make, over what to do with her knowledge about Matthew Rourke, the flowery bag, and Dixie's dead body. Eva's decision would determine many futures – including Matthew's.

As he contemplated all of this, Dixie's attention suddenly switched to Epsilon Dental Spa, where his thoughts now focused on Susan Carmichael. It was just after ten in the morning.

While Ray and Susan Carmichael worked in the dental practice, as normal, a private courier unexpectedly arrived with a letter, simply addressed to '*The Management of Epsilon Dental Spa*'. Susan Carmichael took receipt of the letter in Reception, and went quickly into her private surgery alone, to open and read it.

She had spent all morning with a client who was having some implants fitted; but whenever she had been able to catch a spare moment, Susan was busy searching for the phone numbers and contact details of private detective agencies. Susan had resolved, last night, at home, that she would secretly hire her own private investigator to locate Dixie's body. She was satisfied that her local police officers had no intention of searching for her dog, but Susan knew that she would never be happy until she retrieved Dixie. Her quest for a private investigator was also useful, Susan thought, because it helped her feel like she was actually doing something positive for Dixie – after she had let him down so badly.

Dixie had to admit that he was very flattered by all the attention he was still receiving from Susan - although he was desperate to let her know that she needn't bother spending money on a detective. Dixie was hopeful that his body would be located soon enough. And anyway, Dixie thought; the contents of the letter in Susan Carmichael's hand would soon take her mind off his dead body – for a while, at least.

Pippa Parsons had been correct: Singleton and Singleton Solicitors had prepared legal papers against Charlotte Morgan's family - but more specifically, against Epsilon Dental Spa and Steve Morgan.

Susan Carmichael opened the letter and read it. While on the one hand Susan was not at all surprised at the charge of 'inappropriate conduct' against Steve Morgan, she knew that this could have a devastating effect on the practice she had built up with Ray, over the last ten years and more. Susan looked up at her notice board in her surgery, which was still filled with photos of Dixie, and began to cry. Susan wasn't just crying for her recently departed, stolen dog, however: she was crying at the thought that she had ever agreed to go into business with Steve Morgan in the first place.

Susan went immediately over to Ray's surgery and knocked at the door.

'What do you want, Susan?' he whispered, after his dental nurse went and fetched him. 'I have a client.'

'You have a *problem,* Ray. That's what you've got,' Susan said angrily, shoving the Singleton letter into her husband's hand.

'Shit,' Steve said, after he had absorbed most of the letter's meaning. 'What do we do? Tell Amanda?'

'Yes. Although there's no point in letting her know yet. I'm full up all day – and so are you. We may as well keep as much business going as we can.' Susan paused before speaking again. 'This could ruin us – you know?'

'I know.'

'I told you about that bloody Singleton woman.'

'I know.'

'*You* get Fiona to contact Amanda to arrange a time when we can meet her later – after work. I just can't cope with any more of this crap right now.'

'OK.' Ray took the Singleton letter into his surgery and closed the door behind him.

As he did so, Dixie Carmichael and Matilda Morgan looked at each other in anticipation – curious about the future events that would unfold between their two families back on earth.

-CHAPTER SEVENTEEN-

Facing the Past

Amanda Morgan had spent most of Tuesday evening talking to Susan and Ray Carmichael. They had arranged to come around to Amanda's home to talk 'business' – although the reality had been much worse for Amanda.

As Amanda got ready to leave her home at 9.30 a.m. on Wednesday 12th October, to visit her husband Steve at Memorial Hospital, she was still reeling from the news that Singleton and Singleton Solicitors were launching legal action against Epsilon Dental Spa – thanks to Steve's infidelities with Madeleine Singleton, matriarch of the Singleton clan. Amanda hadn't intended to visit Steve in hospital this morning. Charlotte had stated to Amanda the previous day that she wanted to go and see Steve on Wednesday afternoon – but she had insisted that Amanda accompany her to Memorial (Charlotte hated hospitals, nearly as much as Amanda). Charlotte still didn't know anything about the business with the Singletons, so Amanda wanted to hit Steve with the news alone.

While Amanda wasn't really the slightest bit surprised by the news of Steve's most recent extra-marital activities, she was nevertheless dumbfounded that her husband could have been *so* stupid and *so* naive, choosing to have an affair with the wife of a solicitor. And not just any old solicitor. Oh no – Steve had really hit the jackpot this time by picking Douglas Singleton's spouse to have his little 'fix'. Even the dogs on the street knew about *Dastardly Douglas* and his so-called professional reputation – not to mention his personal reputation.

Susan Carmichael had been in a complete state at Amanda's house, last night. Amanda couldn't have apologised enough to Susan and Ray over Steve's involvement with their dead and missing dog; not to mention his reckless behaviour with Madeleine Singleton. Amanda knew that Susan had been correct when she suggested that the Singletons had the potential to completely destroy Epsilon. Douglas Singleton had ruthlessly brought many private dental practices, G.P. practices and schools to their financial knees in the past – and he had shown zero mercy in doing so. Amanda knew that Douglas would look upon the case against Epsilon with relish – given Steve's connection to the Montgomery family. Sir Horace, Amanda's father, had mysteriously fallen out with Douglas several years ago, and the two men had never spoken since. Amanda knew that Douglas Singleton would not only have financial reasons for pursuing Steve and Epsilon; he would also have *personal* reasons.

*****

Amanda arrived at Memorial Hospital just after 10.00 a.m. Once again, she had taken the tube, so as to avoid paying the hospital's exorbitant parking fees.

As she approached Steve's side ward, she could hear him talking and laughing with one of the nurses – the one with the permanent smile on her face. At least Amanda knew that Steve was more compos mentis today – meaning that she could really lay into him over the Singleton case.

'Amanda!' Steve exclaimed as his wife entered his side ward. 'I didn't expect to see you until later!'

Amanda remained silent, as the permanently-smiling nurse left the side ward. Amanda shut the door behind her, and turned directly to Steve, holding the Singleton letter aloft in her right hand.

'Do we have peace in our time?' Steve joked.

'Put your teeth away, Steve,' Amanda said angrily. 'They may impress your nurses, but I've seen quite enough of them. In fact, I'm in the mood right now to knock them down your throat.'

Steve stopped grinning like a horse. He knew something was seriously up. 'What's up?' he asked – a little wary. 'Did you hear they're maybe going to let me out of hospital tomorrow?' Steve (wrongly) thought that this piece of information would cheer Amanda up.

'Do you know what's inside this letter, Steve?'

'Em – a bill?'

'It will be a bloody bill – by the time this is all over. And a damned hefty one too.' Amanda was shaking with anger. She had begun to think recently that her life was working out at last – until Steve's behaviour had stepped in again, to potentially ruin everything for her.

Steve sat quietly, feeling a little vulnerable, as he lay in his hospital bed, still attached to a feeding drip.

'Does the name *Madeleine Singleton* ring any bells – Steve?'

Steve Morgan's face slumped. He had somehow been able to forget all about Madeleine Singleton (and Susan Carmichael's dog) ever since he was admitted to hospital. Steve thought it a pity that his pain relief had been reduced so significantly in the last few hours: he could do with a bit of a lift right now. '*Madeleine* – I think I may have heard her name *somewhere*.'

'You've heard a lot more than her name recently, according to the contents of this letter.'

Steve felt a bit like an eel that had just been grabbed out of a water tank. 'Really?'

'Oh, give me a break! Do you know what, Steve? I don't even give a shit about your inability to control your primitive urges. What I do care about is the fact that you're dragging everybody else's livelihoods into your dirty little past times. The whole dental business could go bust – thanks to your selfishness.' Amanda wanted to scream and yell at Steve right now. The only thing that was preventing her was the fear that she'd be ejected from Steve's ward before she'd had the chance to speak to him properly. 'So – give me a straight answer, Steve. As if I don't already know the answer. Are these allegations about you and Madeleine Singleton true? Did you have an affair with her in your surgery? Oh – and, by the way – this is the best bit – did you tell her that you'd *murdered a dog* – causing poor Madeleine to have *a mental breakdown?'*

Steve couldn't believe this was happening. 'Do Susan and Ray know about these allegations?'

'Of course they do! This affects their lives too! Susan even began to question last night whether you *did* actually murder her dog! *Did* you, Steve?'

'Of course not!'

'Did you have your way with Madeleine Singleton inside Epsilon?'

'Yes. Not very often though.'

'Oh! – that's fine then!' Amanda shouted sardonically: she couldn't contain her anger at Steve any longer. 'Sorry, Your Honour. But we didn't really do it that often, Your Honour. I didn't fancy her *that* much, Your Honour!'

'Amanda – stop shouting!'

'Oh – sod off, you prick! You make me sick!'

Steve always liked to crack a joke when he was nervous or in a bit of a tight spot. 'Hey, Amanda! -That rhymes!'

*****

Amanda suddenly found herself getting hauled from the top of Steve's bed by two nurses. She didn't know what had just happened, but it was as though Amanda had blacked out.

'Are you OK, Mrs Morgan?' the permanently-smiling nurse asked, as the other nurse began to fix Steve Morgan's feeding tube, which had somehow become dislodged from Steve's arm during Amanda's tumble.

'Yes. I'm fine. What happened?' Amanda felt surreal.

'You fainted,' Steve said from his hospital bed.

Amanda looked at her husband from the armchair the permanently-smiling nurse had placed her in. 'Is it any bloody wonder?' Amanda shouted at Steve, before she got up, grabbed her bag and the Singleton letter, and staggered out of Steve's side ward, as the permanently-smiling nurse called after her to rest for a while.

Amanda began to make her way out of Memorial Hospital. As she did so, Steve Morgan suddenly experienced a terrible pain in his chest. 'Nurse,' he said. 'I have a terrible pain in my chest.'

Before the permanently-smiling nurse and her companion had time to tend to Steve Morgan's latest health scare, he had passed out in his hospital bed. It was 10.36 a.m.

*****

Charlotte Morgan was just over two hours into her second and last five-hour shift of the week. Charlotte preferred to work in Montgomery's on a Wednesday because there always seemed to be a bit more of a buzz on that particular day of the week (not that Charlotte knew what Montgomery's Department Store was like between a Thursday and Monday – inclusive).

This morning, when Charlotte had arrived at work, just after 8.30 a.m., she was pleased to discover that Pippa Parsons had phoned in sick for the day. Although Pippa no longer worked alongside Charlotte at the cosmetics counter at Montgomery's, thanks to Andrew Singleton, Charlotte didn't even want to be under the same roof as Pippa at the moment. Charlotte had been really annoyed, yesterday, when Pippa had made up a load of lies about Singleton and Singleton Solicitors taking legal action against Charlotte's family – and all because Pippa was annoyed that Andrew Singleton had dumped her.

At 11.25 a.m., Charlotte was just about to nip off to the ladies for a change of scenery – when she suddenly felt her phone vibrate inside her skirt pocket. She lifted it out, glancing over to ensure that no one was looking in her direction (it was Montgomery's staff policy not to use mobile phones while they were on duty). Charlotte could see that Julie Smith, her work colleague, was still purring over the counter at the same O.M.P. Julie had been flirting with for the last half hour (although Charlotte detested O.M.P.s, Julie lived for their attention). Charlotte didn't recognise the number coming up on the screen of her phone, but she decided to answer the call anyway. 'Hello?'

'Is that you, Charlotte?'

'Yes. Who's that?'

'It's Mike Gordon. Your dad's mate. I was given your number by your grandfather's secretary, Jo. I'm vet to her hamster. She gave it to me after I told her why I needed it. It's about your dad, Charlotte. He's had a turn for the worse. The hospital have been trying to call your mum – but for some reason, she hasn't wanted to accept their calls. She won't accept any calls from me, either. I'd just like you to let her know what's happened.'

'OK,' Charlotte said, very taken-aback. 'Is he bad?'

'I'm not sure. Just let your mum know as soon as possible – will you?'

'OK.' Charlotte hung up, in shock. What could possibly have happened to her dad now? And why wasn't her mum answering the hospital's calls all of a sudden? Charlotte's hands were visibly shaking as she began to call Amanda to let her mum know about Steve's 'turn for the worse'. She was anxious, but for some reason, Charlotte knew that Matilda was nearby her now. It was 11.29 a.m.

*****

As Charlotte successfully managed to contact her mum, Mike Gordon was left wondering about Steve Morgan's most recent health crisis. The hospital had only contacted Mike this morning because he had left them his phone number on the day he admitted Steve.

Steve had seemed fine, yesterday afternoon, when Mike had nipped out briefly to service one of Steve's hospital bed requests. Steve had phoned Mike to beg him to place a bet for him at Harper's Bookmakers. There was horse racing on T.V., and Steve was desperate for some excitement – given the fact that he had been deprived of the Game Show Channel for over half a week now. Mike did as he was asked - only really because he wanted Steve off his back for the day. He delivered Steve's betting slip to the hospital, just as the first race was about to be shown on the small T.V. inside Steve's side ward.

Steve had looked OK, Mike thought – much better than he had last Monday, when Mike first admitted him to hospital. There hadn't been much conversation between the two men yesterday, however – except a brief recap on the Madeleine Singleton situation (thankfully for Steve, there hadn't been any news on that front), and a message of love and support for Steve from Harriet Harper – which had put a massive grin on Steve's face, as he absorbed himself in the horse racing. Mike had returned to work at the vet's only a few minutes after his arrival at Memorial.

As he worked on Mrs Green's tabby cat now, Mike was only glad that he hadn't encountered the mad bunny woman in the animal print since last Saturday night's encounter in Abandonment. The further away *she* stayed from everyone, the better, Mike thought.

*****

At this time, Dixie and Jacob Carmichael's attention switched to Susan Carmichael.

Susan was staring at a photo taken of the happy scene outside Paws for Thought, last Wednesday. As she stood in Epsilon Dental Spa, Susan's thoughts became infused with sadness. It was just after half-past-eleven in the morning, and Susan began to reflect that it was only a week ago that she encountered the handsome stranger in the dog-friendly café. She recalled again how happy she had been on that occasion; how her soul had filled with hope and lightness when the handsome stranger had spoken to her about Jacob; how mischievous and determined Dixie had been.

Susan felt strangely close to both Jacob and Dixie today. She had felt like this since Sunday, when Amanda Morgan had presented Susan with the bunch of yellow and violet chrysanthemums. Susan wanted to return to Paws for Thought today. She could go during her lunch break. A client of Susan's had cancelled his early afternoon appointment, so this meant that Susan had an extended lunch break today. She would have plenty of time to catch the tube, there and back, and still be able to stay in Paws for Thought for a short time.

*****

Susan arrived in Paws for Thought at around twenty past noon. The café was quiet – as it was normally – and Susan was able to order a coffee and a sandwich, and sit at the same table she had been at last Wednesday, with Dixie and the handsome stranger.

She took out her phone to keep her company, and immediately began to stare at the photo taken by the tourist, last week. Susan looked at Dixie's face. She missed her dog terribly. Susan desperately wanted to know where he was, but Ray had talked her out of the private detective idea last night, after they had returned home from their meeting at Amanda Morgan's house. Ray had been able to convince Susan that they would have to pay a private detective too much money, without any real guarantee of locating Dixie's body. As much as this saddened Susan, however, and as much as Susan adored her dog, the terrible loss she felt over Dixie did not compare to the overwhelming grief she experienced when Jacob died.

Susan looked at the face of the handsome stranger in the photograph, and began to think about Jacob. She recalled that the man with the Cumbrian or Yorkshire accent had shared the same birthday as Jacob. Susan also gratefully remembered how the handsome stranger had referred to her as *Jacob's mum*. Susan would never forget the pride she had felt whenever he said that. She had always wanted to feel like Jacob's mum in the past, but she sometimes found it difficult. Susan had often wondered why Jacob had to leave her. Did someone, somewhere, think that Susan wasn't good enough to be Jacob's mum? She had frequently questioned if she could or should have done something differently during her pregnancy to ensure that Jacob was OK. Even though Susan's medical knowledge and background meant that she fully understood when her obstetrician informed her that Jacob had been born with a chromosomal condition that was 'incompatible with life', Susan still beat herself up, thinking that she should have perhaps done something differently around the time of Jacob's conception, to ensure that her son was fit and well. It broke her heart to think that her son might have had to suffer or experience pain inside her. Susan felt guilty that she hadn't realised there was something wrong with Jacob. She had been so busy being happy and pregnant. She was angry that this had happened to *her* son. Why not somebody else's? What had *she* done so wrong that Jacob had to be taken from her? Why couldn't she just have been allowed to have a normal life, like other women? Why had she been forced to endure the agony of the last few years, when she could so easily have been enjoying life with her son? Why had her bubble of love and happiness been so cruelly destroyed?

Susan recalled how, in the days and weeks following Jacob's loss, she felt so low, so sad, and so empty. Her life was like one big void, redundant, irrelevant, cold and endless moment. Susan kept thinking that she should be pregnant. She had lived only for her baby when he was growing inside her. Jacob had absorbed Susan's every heartbeat; every thought; every emotion; every experience, and every moment of her life. Jacob and Susan had functioned as *One*. For the first time in Susan's life, she had learnt the true meaning of *love*: for her baby, and for herself. When she lost Jacob, those lovely feelings were replaced by despair and a lot of self-loathing: the focus of

Susan's existence had been stolen from her, after all. Life became a painful and meaningless experience. It didn't even feel like 'life' now. Susan felt as though her life was suddenly parallel to everyone else's around her. She was there, existing in a silent black-and-white limbo, while everyone else appeared to be operating in a universe filled with technicolour, noise and meaning. She didn't feel part of the real world, and she actually began to feel more comfortable in her new, detached existence. Susan had no time for anybody's nonsense now – such was the pain and anger pent up inside her.

Susan suddenly recalled walking out of the hospital the day after her 'miscarriage' with Jacob.

She was waiting in the hospital lobby for Ray, who was bringing round the car from the parking zone, when Susan suddenly spotted a pregnant woman walking in the direction of the Obstetrics Unit. Susan knew the woman was going for a scan of her unborn baby. Susan should have been having her second scan of Jacob that day too. Susan couldn't help feeling resentful, sick and angry. She wanted to groan aloud with pain.

Susan's life was crushed. She became scared of living, and thought that people wanted to avoid her because they couldn't think what to talk to her about now. She felt as though she had a big card around her neck, saying: 'I lost my baby'; and yet no-one wanted to talk about it. It was almost as though Susan had to pretend to the outside world that Jacob hadn't happened. Other people didn't know Jacob; they had never spoken to him or been close to him; they hadn't shared their soul with him, like Susan had. She wasn't even sure if she wanted to talk about Jacob to other people – she just knew that she didn't really have the option. She had to smile and get on with normal life, feeling all the time that her life was all now a big act. Anyone who did say something to Susan about Jacob always seemed to say the wrong thing. Such as, 'you can always try again'; 'it's just nature's way'; 'it was probably all meant to be'. They were talking about Susan's *son*. Didn't they realise that she couldn't simply go out and get a replacement? Whole pages of Susan's future had been stolen. Whole future chapters of her life story had been violently torn out of their book. Susan couldn't stop thinking about what she should be doing with Jacob *now* – at any given moment in time. She just wanted to curl up and disappear with her son. She wanted to think about him all the time. It became too awkward and difficult to socialise with other people; too hard to put an act on for their benefit. It was easier to stay away from others, so splendid isolation became a self-imposed way of life for Susan. The only ones she could talk to now were Ray and Dixie.

Susan enacted the remaining seventeen weeks of her pregnancy inside her head – right up until Jacob's birth – on 5th October. Susan recalled looking with envy at all the other women and babies after this date. It felt like every day was sent as a punishment. Susan kept telling Jacob how sorry she was that he couldn't be here now. Susan hoped that she hadn't let her son down. Her life became a series of 'what ifs'.

But Susan couldn't really blame people for not knowing what to say to her about Jacob's loss. Susan wouldn't know what to say to someone in her position now. It was all too painful. Too unspeakable. Too uncomfortable. Too *sacred*.

Susan looked around at Paws for Thought. She suddenly recalled Amanda Morgan's bunch of yellow and violet chrysanthemums. She began to smile. Susan knew that Jacob must have played a part in sending those flowers on Sunday. She hadn't even meant to think about Jacob today, but she could feel him around her now. Susan knew that he was OK. And even though these last few days had been nightmarish for her, she still somehow felt that her life had begun to move in a new direction.

A light bulb suddenly blew above Susan's table.

As a male member of staff began to fuss around her, attempting to change the bulb, Susan decided that she would make her way back to the tube station – but not before she had purchased something she realised she might need, in the nearby pharmacy. Susan paid for her coffee and sandwich and left Paws for Thought at ten-to-one.

Three minutes later, Matthew Rourke entered the premises.

He had just purchased a one-way ticket to the Lake District, at a nearby ticket station. Matthew's train would depart this Sunday morning, 16th October: the day Christian had died, sixteen years ago.

Matthew walked directly over to the seat he had occupied in Paws for Thought, at exactly the same time last week. He shifted out of his way a half-drunk mug of coffee, and the remnants of a cheese and pickle sandwich on wholegrain bread, as he said 'hello' to a waiter who was changing a light bulb beside his table.

'Can I order you something, Sir?' the waiter asked.

'Just a black tea – please,' Matthew replied with a warm smile, as the waiter took away the used coffee mug and sandwich plate, and walked over to the counter.

Matthew Rourke had felt strangely compelled to return to Paws for Thought today. He had enjoyed the solace and anonymity he experienced there last week – even during the crazy period, when Matthew encountered the tourists, the lady with the warm smile, and her cheeky West Highland Terrier. Matthew still felt disgusted at himself for stealing the other dog last Friday. He stared at his train ticket for the Lake District now. Matthew knew he was doing the right thing. Christian had told him to go home.

The waiter suddenly placed Matthew's tea on his table. After Matthew thanked the man, he took a long, satisfying drink, before looking around at the virtually empty café. He wondered briefly if he would bump into the lady with the dog today – although Matthew realised that that would probably be *too* much of a coincidence. He immediately recalled the woman telling him that her son shared the same birthday as Matthew. Matthew hoped that the lady's son - Jacob (Matthew clearly recalled the name) – was around to help his mum, just in the same was as Christian was around to help Matthew now too.

*****

Dixie Carmichael breathed a sigh of relief. Jacob had only just managed to ensure that Matthew Rourke and Susan Carmichael did not meet for a second time in Paws for Thought. Matthew had been on schedule to enter the dog-friendly café several minutes before Susan left the premises, but he was unexpectedly delayed by a freak three-minute power cut at the ticket office. Happily, this had ensured that Matthew and Susan's paths didn't cross this time.

Jacob Carmichael laughed. He only hoped that Susan would pick up on his *next* prompt, better than she had the one he sent her way today, inside Paws for Thought.

*****

Charlotte and Amanda Morgan arrived at Memorial Hospital at 2.30 p.m. on Wednesday afternoon. They went immediately to the floor of Steve's side ward, not really sure if he would still be there.

Upon going first to the Nurses' Station, a middle-aged nurse, eating a piece of toast and drinking tea, advised them that Mr Morgan had been taken briefly to another section of the hospital this morning for observation, but that he had only just been returned to his former side ward again.

Amanda and Charlotte entered the side ward, as the middle-aged nurse followed them and began to speak. 'We don't really understand what happened to Mr Morgan this morning. We think that his Pancreatitis perhaps flared up again – causing acute pain, and making him pass out. His heart and other vitals have been monitored and appear to be OK. But we'll probably have to keep an eye on him for at least another day. His pain relief has been increased in the meantime.'

'Thank-you, Nurse,' Amanda Morgan responded, as the middle-aged nurse left the side ward.

Amanda looked at Steve. He looked exactly as he had this morning, when she confronted him with the Singleton letter – except perhaps a little drowsier. Steve also had a stupid grin on his face, which Amanda supposed was due to the pain medication. She wanted to leave the hospital straight away now. Amanda realised the whole 'emergency' over Steve had been a huge storm in a teacup. 'Steve,' Amanda said firmly to her husband. She simply wanted him to speak for Charlotte's sake – so that Charlotte could go home without any worries.

Steve opened his sleepy eyes as wide as he possibly could. He stared at Amanda and Charlotte, but did not say anything.

'Steve. Please tell Charlotte that you're OK.'

Steve looked at Charlotte and smiled – although he didn't have the energy to flash his veneers. 'I'm OK,' he said.

'What happened?' Charlotte asked him.

'Your mum made a pass at me earlier,' he grinned.

'Oh – Please. You sad, pathetic man,' Amanda said angrily, before she stopped herself from saying anything else in Charlotte's presence. 'Sorry Charlotte. This is just your father's silly idea of a joke.' Amanda didn't want Charlotte to know that she had visited Steve earlier.

'I got you this,' Charlotte said matter-of-factly, placing a blue plastic bag containing a 'Best of the 80s' magazine on his hospital bed: she had bought it in a nearby convenience store.

'What is it?' Steve asked curiously. He looked like an excited puppy when Charlotte explained to him.

'OK. Well – considering everything's OK, I don't suppose there's any point in us staying here any longer,' Amanda stated firmly: she had phone calls she needed to make today regarding the Singleton legal case and Epsilon Dental Spa.

Steve didn't really mind if his wife and daughter left now. He had his pain relief, his 80s magazine – and he also knew that Harriet Harper was nearby if he needed anything. Yesterday afternoon, when Mike Gordon informed Steve that Harriet Harper had enquired after Steve's health in the bookie's, Steve phoned her later and asked her to pop up to Memorial to visit him, to keep him company for a while. Harriet brought Steve a very large baguette with meatballs, and a fizzy energy drink, which she had purchased in the convenience store beside her betting office. Steve had gratefully scoffed down the lot (he was starving) – in spite of the fact that he was still on a strict nil-by-mouth regime. Steve supposed that the baguette and energy drink could perhaps have caused his little turn this morning – although he wasn't going to tell the medical staff that. *God bless Harriet*, Steve thought now. *At least she got me back onto the decent pain relief.* 'No problem, Amanda,' Steve said quietly. 'But will you just open the blinds before you go. I'd like to read the magazine Charlotte brought me.'

Amanda swished open the horizontal blinds on Steve's side ward window, which ran the full length of the wall, to the right-hand-side of Steve's bed.

Amanda gasped.

She thought she might choke on the air inside her mouth.

She had seen the view from this window before – but surely not?

Amanda looked out at the view again. She hadn't been mistaken – or at least she thought she hadn't. There was the large campus belonging to a local comprehensive school; the playing fields; the swimming pool; the petrol station; the car repair centre; the car dealership. Amanda knew this scene off-by-heart. She had stood by this window before. Just over nineteen years ago. But it had been a maternity ward back then. The ward she was put in after Charlotte and Matilda were born.

Amanda turned around and excused herself, before she left Steve and Charlotte in the side ward, and approached the middle-aged nurse sitting at the

Nurses' Station. 'Excuse me,' Amanda interrupted the nurse as she worked busily on a pile of paperwork.

'Yes,' the nurse smiled up at Amanda from her seat.

'I was just wondering. Did this part of the hospital ever function as a Maternity Ward?'

'Oh yes! Up until about fifteen years ago. I remember it well!' the nurse replied. 'I had all of my children here!'

Amanda shuddered. 'Do you happen to know if the side ward my husband is currently in used to be called E-52?'

'Well, to be honest, I can't really. But it more than likely was. It's now called 5EB. The hospital was renovated, and the rooms were re-numbered. But yes – it probably was E-52 in the good-old-days: E for Block E; 5 for floor five; Room 2. Now it's just 5th floor, E Block, Room B.

Amanda's face turned pale. 'Thanks,' she said quietly, as she walked away and re-entered Steve's side ward.

Amanda walked over to the large window again, and stared outside. She felt as though she had just been visited by a ghost from her past.

'Are you OK, mum?' Charlotte was sitting on the end of Steve's hospital bed, checking for Twopennysworths on her phone.

'Yes,' Amanda stated blankly, still staring out at the view she had memorised by heart, all those years ago. Amanda remembered how she had spent hours by this window, after Matilda's death, holding her daughter's body in her arms, and talking to her. Matilda had been so small. So quiet. So perfect. Just *asleep*.

Amanda wrapped her arms around her body now, as though she was still holding Matilda. She remembered, back then, telling her daughter how much she loved her. How sorry she was that she hadn't been able to save her. Amanda had been devastated at the thought that she would never get to know Matilda – and that Charlotte would never get to know her sister. Amanda recalled looking out the window and thinking that Matilda would never be able to go to the swimming pool, just outside the hospital window. For some reason, this silly little thing had made Amanda cry inconsolably at the time. Matilda would never be allowed *to be. Why*? Amanda had asked herself angrily, over and over again. Why had Matilda come so far – only to be snatched away from Amanda again? It was all too cruel; too unfair; too unbelievable. Why had this happened to *Amanda's* daughter? What had *she* done to deserve this? Amanda recalled wanting to curl up and scream and die when Matilda died. It was as though a huge part of Amanda's soul had died and gone away too. She felt cold and frozen inside – and yet, Amanda was forced to move on, for the sake of her other baby, Charlotte. It had been a very difficult choice at the time, but Amanda threw herself into her role as Charlotte's mother: it was the only thing that had kept Amanda going. But everything that Amanda did with Charlotte as a child, she also did it inside her head with Matilda. Her two daughters were identical twins. Amanda saw Matilda in Charlotte every single day – even though she knew that they probably would have had different personalities, had Matilda lived. Amanda poured all her love into Charlotte, imagining that Charlotte and Matilda were still *one*. When Charlotte was a baby, people rarely ever talked to Amanda about Matilda – even though they knew that Amanda had been expecting twins. They always focused on Charlotte. Although in one sense, this had helped Amanda get on with everyday life, she sometimes felt like she was betraying Matilda's memory by not talking about her more. Why had Amanda felt the need to undermine her own grief and loss like this? The reality was, Amanda had felt as though she would appear a little too self-indulgent or eccentric if she ever referred to Matilda; although at the same time, she felt like she had betrayed Matilda by not telling Charlotte about her twin sister sooner. Apart from Amanda, everyone else appeared to have forgotten about Matilda. It had seemed better not to tell Charlotte. Amanda knew now that her decision had been wrong.

'Mum!' Charlotte said, as she approached Amanda at the hospital window. 'What's wrong?'

Amanda hadn't realised it, but she had begun to cry. She couldn't speak. Amanda reached out and grabbed Charlotte and hugged her tightly. Charlotte was scared. She felt very strange all of a sudden. She pulled away from Amanda, who wiped her eyes with her bare hands.

Matilda was now present.

Amanda stared over at Steve. He was staring back at her. For some unknown reason, Steve knew exactly what Amanda was thinking about. He felt it. He recalled staring at Amanda like this, as Amanda had held the baby's body in her arms, over nineteen years ago.

It suddenly dawned on Steve that it had all happened in this very room. Steve recalled freezing on the spot back then. He couldn't take it in. It was too awful to get his head around. He wasn't capable of looking at Amanda or the baby in her arms. He had a choice to make. And he made it. Steve left the hospital that day, and never really spoke properly to Amanda again. He hadn't wanted the subject of the baby to come up again. He didn't want to talk about it. So he stayed away. As often as possible. Steve just wanted things to continue in the same way they had always done. But Amanda was never the same again. His wife devoted herself to their daughter – Charlotte – and Steve never felt like he was able to be a part of all that. It only reminded him of the other baby. The one Amanda called 'Matilda'. Steve didn't even feel like smiling or grinning now – and Charlotte suddenly realised why.

Charlotte could feel the energy of her parents' present thoughts and past experiences – right now; as though Charlotte was still a baby, lying in the corner of the room, listening and watching the events of the day Charlotte and Matilda were born, over nineteen years ago.

The room was thick with silence. Matilda was everywhere around her family now. She wanted to hold them in this moment for as long as possible.

*****

After a time (no one knew how long), the middle-aged nurse entered the side ward, to find the Morgan family together, in silence. 'Well, Mr Morgan,' she said. 'Everything OK?' The nurse felt a bit awkward for some reason – as though she was disturbing something. 'I just want to check your temperature and pulse. It's nearly four-o'clock.'

Steve was silent and stone-faced – still staring at Amanda's pain-filled eyes, from over nineteen years ago.

'Mum – should we go now?' Charlotte wanted to go home.

'Yes.' Amanda grabbed her bag, as Charlotte said goodbye to Steve.

Amanda walked out of the ward after Charlotte. For some reason, she was compelled to turn around and look at Steve again. He was still staring at her, as the middle-aged nurse worked alongside him.

Steve was crying. Amanda had barely ever seen her husband without a cheesy grin on his face – let alone crying; with tears streaming down both sides of his face.

Amanda looked at Steve. And said *nothing*.

She turned and walked out of the side ward, as the middle-aged nurse left now too.

Leaving Steve and Matilda.

Alone.

-CHAPTER EIGHTEEN-

Talking Business

When Amanda Morgan arranged for Eva Kelly to meet Amanda's daughter, Charlotte, on Tuesday, she had no idea that so much would have happened in her life in the meantime.

Not only had Susan and Ray Carmichael confirmed Amanda's worst fear – that Singleton and Singleton Solicitors were launching legal action against Epsilon Dental Spa – but Amanda had also discovered, yesterday, that her husband, Steve, was lying in the hospital ward where Charlotte's twin, Matilda, had died, over nineteen years ago.

It was now 9.30 a.m. on Thursday 13th October, and Amanda was preparing for Eva to arrive at her home in TW9, to meet Charlotte, to discuss flower arranging and 'business'.

Amanda had been unable to sleep, most of last night, thinking about Steve, Charlotte and Matilda. She still couldn't believe that Steve had finally shown an emotional response to Matilda's death. Amanda almost felt as though her whole family had been transported back to the time of Matilda's death, yesterday afternoon. It was strange, but she almost sensed that Matilda had been present in Steve's side ward. While Amanda had felt very emotional at the time, she realised she had already experienced all of those feelings of grief and loss before. It was only really Steve who hadn't. Charlotte had shown a lot of maturity since finding out about her sister's existence. Amanda even sensed that Charlotte had become more grounded and focused in her thoughts in recent days. But Steve had never been forced to face up to the reality of Matilda's death – until yesterday. While Amanda always knew that her husband had completely and deliberately blanked out Matilda's memory, she had always presumed that he would remain frozen as his nineteen-year-old self, for the remainder of his so-called adult life. She couldn't really believe that he had shown such humanity yesterday, as he lay crying in his hospital bed. Amanda found it hard to believe now, as she prepared for Eva's arrival at her house, but she was actually worried about Steve. She didn't know if he would be able to cope with all the emotions she had been processing for over nineteen years. Steve had to face them all head-on now – like he'd just crashed into a brick wall of realisation.

And yet, Steve only had himself to blame, Amanda told herself now. She had attempted on numerous occasions in the past to confront Steve with the reality of Matilda's loss – but she had never been able to get anywhere with him. Steve had blown his chances; and, not only that, his irresponsible behaviour over the years had caused the break-up of the Morgan family, as well as the impending crisis over the family business. Amanda found it difficult to forget about all of that. So why was she still worried about her husband?

Amanda had been forced to swallow her pride, last night, and arrange a meeting with her father, Sir Horace Montgomery, to discuss the Singleton case. Amanda was dreading having to tell her father about the predicament Steve had got Epsilon into (Sir Horace had always detested Steve); but even more than this, Amanda hated the thought that she was being compelled to ask for her father's financial and business clout to get her out of this potential legal mess. She felt like such a fool for not having dealt with Steve's stupidity earlier. Amanda was dreading the meeting with her father, later, this afternoon.

The front doorbell rang. It was just before ten on Thursday morning.

'Charlotte! That will be Eva!' Amanda called to her daughter upstairs, as Amanda ran to the door and opened it. 'Hi!' she said, a bit nervously.

'Hi!' Eva replied, as she entered the Morgan's hallway.

Charlotte came bounding down the stairs, dressed to impress; her head filled with exciting thoughts about the business idea she wanted to run past Eva Kelly. Charlotte couldn't wait until she met Ebony Glazier, in PolkaPolka, tomorrow night, to (hopefully) get Ebony to come on board with her idea.

'Hi!' Charlotte said to Eva. 'Do you want a coffee?'

'Thanks!' Eva replied, smiling at Charlotte.

'Mum?'

'Yes please, Charlotte.'

Amanda and Eva followed Charlotte into the Morgan's kitchen, where Charlotte proceeded to fix everyone up with coffee and cookies.

'So,' Eva said to Charlotte. 'What's this about your new-found interest in flowers?'

Eva was very impressed by Charlotte's business idea. She proceeded to tell Charlotte all that she knew about Charlotte's specific interest in flowers and the business side of things. Even Amanda began to relax as Eva and Charlotte's conversation progressed. Amanda really couldn't believe just how alive Charlotte seemed all of a sudden. 'You're going to have to get used to having a few more flowers around the house, mum! Although your admirer has probably got you used to flowers by now!' Charlotte was referring to the vase of pink roses, sitting on the kitchen work surface. Amanda began to blush, as she looked awkwardly at her feet. Eva broke the silence. 'I can sort your mum out with protective clothing if it all gets too much for her. Although from what I can gather, she already has the world's largest collection of latex gloves and dust masks!'

Charlotte laughed. She liked Eva. She could also sense that her mum liked Eva. It seemed as though Eva was somehow meant to be part of Charlotte and Amanda's life right now.

'OK, everyone,' Eva said, getting up from her stool at the large breakfast bar inside the Morgan's kitchen. 'I guess I'd better get back to work now.'

'Thank-you so much for coming here today,' Amanda said to Eva, slightly formally.

'Yes. Thanks Eva!' Charlotte added.

As Eva Kelly left the Morgan household at eleven, Charlotte strangely began to feel like somebody was trying to tell her something. She had felt as though messages were being placed inside her head, ever since last Saturday morning, when Charlotte had sat at the top of the flight of stairs, listening to her parents arguing. Amanda looked over at Charlotte after she shut the front door behind Eva. Charlotte smiled at Amanda. 'I think Eva is great mum. But can we go and visit dad again soon?'

Charlotte had suddenly recalled the staring black eyes of the large bird in the painting, inside the lobby of The Peregrine.

*****

Amanda Morgan got into her car at 2.00 p.m., later that afternoon. She was still very taken aback by Charlotte's remarks, inside the hallway, earlier. Surely Charlotte couldn't have guessed about Amanda's relationship with Eva? And why did Charlotte suddenly ask to go and visit Steve?

Right now, however, Amanda had more pressing concerns on her plate. She was dreading telling Sir Horace, her dad, about the mess with Singleton and Singleton Solicitors.

As she pulled into the executive car park at Montgomery's Department Store, she dreaded the confrontation that lay ahead. Amanda's father was like a gorilla with a toothache on a good day: God knows how he would react when Amanda informed him about her predicament over Steve and Epsilon.

Amanda left her car, and began the short trip to her father's office, inside Montgomery's. As she approached his office door, she inhaled heavily, before finally knocking the door. After a brief pause, Sir Horace bid her to enter. It was just after three in the afternoon.

Amanda looked at her father's large and angry frame as he sat behind his huge desk. 'Amanda,' he boomed like a fog horn. 'What can I do for you?'

Amanda took a seat across the desk from her father. She always felt as though she was visiting the school principal when she was in Sir Horace's company. 'Well,' she replied. 'I suppose I may as well get straight to the point. It's Epsilon. Your suspicions were correct on Tuesday. Singleton and Singleton *are* intending to take legal action against the family. Except it's *my* business they're after – not yours.' Amanda awaited her father's reaction. It felt like a stay of execution.

Sir Horace took off his half-moon glasses, and sat back formidably in his large leather reclining chair. 'So why are you coming to me?' he asked coldly.

'Believe me, father. I don't want to be here right now. But unfortunately, I am forced to ask for your advice on this issue. Be it your influence, or your money – can you somehow help me stop the potential damage the allegations in this letter could mean for my business?' Amanda handed Sir Horace the Singleton letter.

He took several minutes to read it, before he finally gave a response. 'I'm sorry, Amanda. I can't help you.' He handed her back the letter.

Amanda was very taken aback - and very angry. 'What do you men – you can't help me? Of course you can help me.'

Sir Horace remained quiet. He looked angry.

'What would stop you wanting to help me?' Amanda continued.

Sir Horace looked over at Amanda. 'It's your own fault, Amanda. For marrying that ill-bred fool.'

Amanda was furious. She began to shout at Sir Horace. 'And why do you think I married Steve? Who else did I have at the time? *You* certainly weren't around for me – when Aunt Matilda died. You weren't even around for me when my *mother* died!'

'Stop it now, Amanda!'

'NO! I won't stop it now. Just what is it with some people? How come people like you and Steve are so incapable of facing up to your responsibilities?'

'I want *nothing* to do with Douglas Singleton.'

'Neither do I. But I don't have that luxury – do I?'

'If you only knew –,' Sir Horace began to mutter under his breath angrily.

Amanda looked over at him. 'What's that supposed to mean?'

'Nothing.'

'No – come on. It obviously means something. What exactly is it that I should know?' Amanda yelled.

'Stop it now, Amanda.'

'NO! I'm not leaving here until you properly explain why you won't help me out with Douglas Singleton.'

'Why don't you ask *him*?'

Amanda stopped in her tracks. She was completely taken aback. 'Because I have nothing to do with him. That's why,' she shouted again.

Sir Horace remained quiet. His face was blood-red in colour; his eyes were filled with fury.

'Tell me!' Amanda ordered.

'He's your father!' Sir Horace blurted out in rage.

Amanda swallowed hard. She thought she was going to vomit.

She stared into Sir Horace's angry eyes; and Sir Horace looked immediately away from her gaze.

'Why would you say that to me?' she asked, begging for his mercy. Amanda wanted Sir Horace to retract his last statement immediately, and apologise to her.

'Because it's true, Amanda,' he stated indifferently, as he began to pace furiously around his office.

'How can it be true? I'm Amanda *Montgomery.*'

'You were brought up as Amanda Montgomery – that's all.'

'But I don't understand.'

Sir Horace was trembling with anger now. 'You mother had *an affair*, Amanda. With Douglas Singleton. You were the likely product of that affair.'

Amanda thought she was going to pass out. 'The *likely product*? Is that how you see me? A *product*?'

'Maybe you should leave now, Amanda. Before we say anything else we regret.'

'No. I'm not going anywhere – until I get to the bottom of this. So unless you're going to call your security guards in – I'm staying right here. You owe me an explanation.' Amanda could hardly believe what was happening. Her head was in turmoil.

Sir Horace sat down on his chair again. There was silence for a few minutes, before he eventually began to address Amanda in a serious tone. Sir Horace proceeded to tell Amanda how – just over forty years ago – Amanda's mother, Lydia, had embarked on a very short 'fling' with Douglas Singleton, then a single go-getting solicitor in his early thirties. Sir Horace was only thirty-four at the time – just like Amanda's mother – and the Montgomery marriage had been under severe strain, due to Sir Horace's hectic business schedule, which meant that he was forced to stay long periods away from the family home – which had been in Bournemouth, back then.

Douglas and Lydia's affair was over as nearly as soon as it had begun; but Lydia had felt so guilt-ridden, she confessed everything to Sir Horace. Sir Horace forgave Lydia. He knew that her affair had been partly his fault – for neglecting their marriage so much in the past. But he never forgave Douglas Singleton. He despised the man deeply.

When Amanda's mum, Lydia, discovered she was pregnant with Amanda, shortly after her brief liaison with Douglas Singleton ended, Sir Horace always feared that the baby was not his – even though he never expressed this doubt to Lydia at the time. He chose to go along with the idea that he was Amanda's father – both for Lydia's sake, and for the sake of the Montgomery family name. When Lydia died from a short illness, when Amanda was only six, Sir Horace immediately sent his daughter, and only child, to live with Lydia's sister, Matilda.

'So that's why you've never given a damn about me – is it?' Everything suddenly began to make sense to Amanda now.

Sir Horace remained silent.

Amanda wanted to pursue this further. 'Are you *sure* I'm not your daughter?'

'As sure as I can be.'

'So you're *not* sure?'

'Not entirely sure – if that's what you mean.'

'And you really think that's good enough? You never thought to find out if you were sure? I mean – is Douglas Singleton aware that he might have a long-lost-daughter?'

'No. The subject was never broached.'

Amanda sat back in her seat. She couldn't live the remainder of her life like this – not knowing who she was. Everything was such as mess. Her whole life had been turned upside down. 'I have to know,' she stated, rising to her feet. Amanda grabbed the Singleton letter from Sir Horace's desk, and ran out of his office, stiff with rage. It was just before five o'clock.

*****

Matilda Morgan had known this family revelation would be one of the likely outcomes of the Morgans' involvement with Dixie Carmichael's death and disappearance: she had hoped it would be so. Matilda had always fully understood the reason behind Sir Horace's indifference towards Amanda – not to mention his permanent angry mood.

It had once been hoped that the death of Amanda's youngest daughter would have compelled Sir Horace to draw closer to Amanda, nineteen years ago; but things had unfortunately not worked out this way. The Montgomery family secret now needed to be confronted head-on, if lives were to be lived harmoniously once more. Unfortunately, for Matilda's mum, Amanda, this would mean an ill-tempered confrontation with Douglas Singleton – as well as a further heated exchange with Sir Horace Montgomery.

*****

Eva Kelly had been troubled – ever since her conversation with Charlotte Morgan, this morning. She couldn't help feeling very angry at Matthew Rourke for stealing a bag from such a young woman. As much as Eva genuinely liked Matthew, and as much as she sympathised with everything he had been forced to tolerate during his marriage to Ruth, Eva was disgusted and ashamed at the thought that Matthew could have behaved so despicably.

Although she had tried to give Matthew the benefit of the doubt, since having the conversation with Amanda in the coffee shop, Ruth couldn't realistically believe that all of these factors were mere coincidences (the dead dog, the flowery bag, Unity Park Station), when she considered them alongside her encounter with Matthew and the mysterious flowery bag, last Friday, near Unity Park Station. Eva had to talk to Matthew soon. She had to confront him with what he had done. She needed to convince her brother-in-law that he had to make amends for his rash, stupid and reckless behaviour – one way or another. Matthew at least needed to return the body of the dead dog to its heartbroken owners – Amanda's business partners, Ray and Susan Carmichael. Amanda had informed Eva all about the Carmichaels – as well as the potential legal case against Epsilon Dental Spa.

Eva took her mobile phone out of her coat pocket and began to search for Matthew's number. It was just before five in the evening, and Eva was still at work in her gardening business in NW1. It was beginning to get cold and dark, and Eva was keen to get home soon.

'Hello,' Matthew's voice said.

'Matthew. It's Eva.'

'Hi Eva!' Matthew was taken aback slightly by the fact that his sister-in-law was calling him. 'What's up?'

'We need to meet, Matthew.'

Matthew paused. Eva sounded quite serious. 'OK. Is everything alright?'

'Yes. But I need to meet you. Can you manage tomorrow morning?'

'Yes.'

'OK. Then meet me at Unity Park. I have some work there again tomorrow.' Eva was telling Matthew the truth, but he became immediately suspicious. 'Is everything OK?' he asked her again.

'Of course,' Eva replied: she didn't want Matthew to suspect anything. 'I just want to talk about Ruth.' Eva hated lies, but she felt that she needed to tell this one – for the sake of a lot of people – including Matthew.

'Oh – right. OK. I'll see you at Unity Park then, Eva. What time?'

'Let's say about eleven-thirty. Would that suit?'

'Yes. See you then. Bye, Eva!'

'Bye, Matthew.'

Matthew hung up.

He had been a little wary of Eva's tone of voice at the beginning of the phone call. Matthew had almost begun to think that Eva knew something about the dead dog at Unity Park. But that would just be silly: how could she possibly?

As he began to ponder exactly why Eva Kelly would want to talk to him about Ruth, Matthew continued to secretly pack away some of his things into a suitcase in the spare room of his apartment. Ruth had been out shopping with Deborah Silvestri all day, and the two women had arranged to meet Clare Silvestri for drinks, after Clare finished work, around now. Matthew only knew all this because he had overheard Ruth arranging her plans with Deborah Silvestri, this morning, over the phone. Ruth must have decided to cancel all her psychotherapy clients for the day, Matthew realised – so maybe that's why Eva was worried about her sister. Matthew was still confident that he had made the right decision about returning to the Lake District, this forthcoming Sunday. His only dilemma now was whether he should tell Ruth.

Or so Matthew thought. Dixie Carmichael and Christian Rourke also knew that Matthew would be confronted with a dilemma of a different kind, tomorrow. It would not be long before Susan and Ray Carmichael were reunited with Dixie's earthly body once more.

CHAPTER NINETEEN

And Nothing But the Truth

It was exactly a week since Dixie's body had made its way into the hands of Charlotte Morgan and Matthew Rourke. Dixie was laying thinking, underneath his favourite Oak tree, in Susan and Ray Carmichael's back garden. It was Friday 14th October, and Dixie could see Susan getting ready to leave for work, as she stood at the large window near his favourite armchair, inside the Carmichaels' spacious kitchen.

It was another cold autumn day, and Dixie noticed that the leaves had begun to fall quite significantly from the trees in Susan's garden. Even Susan's Jacob's Ladder plants had died back substantially – ready to conserve their energy, in time for another busy season, next year.

Dixie had always been happy in this place - but he knew that it would soon be time for much of his energy to move away from here too. Although Dixie would have many more tasks to fulfil, and lives to assist, away from here, his soul's imprint would nevertheless remain forever with the places and people whose lives he had already touched on earth. Fortunately, the flexible laws in the invisible realms permitted this kind of manoeuvrability and ease of movement; so Dixie had no doubt that he would be able to keep in touch with Susan and Ray Carmichael, as their futures unfolded in the years to come.

As Dixie looked over at Susan from under the Oak tree in her back garden, Susan began to look back at him. She couldn't believe it was Friday. Susan had just been thinking about a dream she'd had, the previous night. It was the same one Susan had dreamt on two occasions before; when she had met the young couple in the park; the young boy; Dixie; the handsome stranger from Paws for Thought; Amanda and Charlotte Morgan; and the rose and lily fields. This time, however, Susan's attention had been particularly drawn to the young boy. He was about seven or eight years old, Susan thought. He had beautiful dark curly hair; brown smiling eyes; an enchanting smile, that didn't reveal any teeth; and sun-kissed skin. The boy had smiled at Susan for ages. He had made her feel very happy and at ease. He looked like *Susan*. After a while, the boy ran off towards the others, skipping and enjoying the brightness and warmth of the sun-lit park. Just before the dream had ended, Susan also recalled seeing two more figures in the park: two women. They were both in their late thirties, Susan thought. They were walking arm-in-arm, giggling, and clearly enjoying each other's company.

Susan looked out at Dixie's Oak tree in her back garden. She was exhausted and overwhelmed by everything that had happened since her return from the Eden Resort in Buckinghamshire, last Sunday. Susan was so exhausted and overwhelmed, in fact, she had agreed with Amanda Morgan and Ray, last night, to shut Epsilon Dental Spa on Monday. She needed some respite. Susan had never really taken time off work like this in the past, but she somehow knew that she needed to on this occasion. Ray was more than delighted at Susan's idea: he needed a day off too. He agreed to personally call all the clients already booked for Monday, and rearrange alternative appointments for them, at a later date.

Amanda Morgan had been rather distant on the phone, yesterday evening, Susan thought; almost as though Amanda had been affected by everything that had happened this week. Amanda had said very little to Susan during their conversation – except to inform her that Epsilon would likely have to undergo some restructuring soon, in light of the potential legal wrangling with Singleton and Singleton Solicitors, as well as Steve Morgan's inability to work right now.

'Are you ready, Susan?' Ray Carmichael called to his wife, as he opened the front door of their house to depart for work: Ray knew they had another arduous day ahead at Epsilon.

'Coming!' Susan shouted back, before she turned to look out at her back garden again. She thought she might do some gardening tomorrow. Susan wanted to plant the rose bush and lily bulbs she had bought for Dixie in Buckinghamshire – before the weather would turn too cold to work outside. She also wanted to tidy up the bed containing all her Jacob's Ladder plants, although it made her sad to think that Dixie wouldn't be around next summer to enjoy them.

Dixie therefore knew that he would have to do something - to convince Susan that this would not necessarily be the case.

*****

As Susan and Ray Carmichael continued to work at their dental practice in W8 that morning, Matthew Rourke couldn't believe he was returning to Unity Park, exactly a week after he had stolen and buried the dead dog there.

It was almost eleven, and Matthew couldn't help feeling a bit anxious about meeting his sister-in-law, Eva, inside the gates of Unity Park, just as they had agreed on the phone, yesterday. Matthew had taken the bus to Unity Park Station today. He hadn't wanted to potentially bump into the female he'd stolen the dead dog from, last Friday, inside the tube station. He had spent most of his time on the bus, thinking about Ruth. Matthew's wife had spent all the previous day and night away from their apartment in TW9. She had texted Matthew briefly at eight in the evening, to inform him that she would be staying at Clare and Deborah Silvestri's house that night, in SW12; and that she would 'likely' be back home some time today.

Ruth appeared to have given up nagging Matthew about finding a job. It was almost as though she had something more important to think about at the moment – although Matthew didn't quite know what yet (perhaps Eva would be able to tell him something, this morning). At this moment in time, Matthew had no intention of informing Ruth about his decision to leave for the Lake District, on Sunday. He knew that Ruth didn't give a damn about him; and as far as he was concerned, she could keep their apartment in TW9, and everything in it.

Matthew's mind was still racing with thoughts as he approached the familiar double gates to Unity Park. He entered the park from the direction of the crossroads, and immediately began to look about for Eva. It was a cold day, and Matthew could see that it would not be long before most of the trees in Unity Park had lost their leaves. He felt rather anxious right now - not just because he was curious to know why Eva wanted to speak to him – but because he was suddenly filled with thoughts about the dead dog and Christian.

'Matthew,' Eva's voice called, as she walked towards her brother-in-law, who was resting beside a picnic table, just inside the gates of Unity Park.

'Eva – hi!' Matthew said, as he got up from the seat at the picnic table: he had been staring at the area of woodland where he had buried the dead dog, and encountered the peregrine falcon, last week.

'It's a little cold,' Eva said. 'Would you like to join me for a drink in the little shop attached to the Visitors' Centre? It's just over there,' she said, pointing towards Unity Park's wide driveway.

'That's a good idea,' Matthew said. He could sense that Eva must be in a hurry to get back to work soon: she was dressed in her gardening clothes, and she appeared to be in a rather business-like mood.

Once Matthew and Eva had ordered their hot drinks in the Unity Café, and sat at a table overlooking Unity Park's sprawling areas of woodland and grass, Eva was the first to speak. 'How are you, Matthew?'

'I'm fine. Although I'm a bit curious about why you want to speak to me today.'

Eva didn't see the point in wasting any time getting directly to the point. She had to return to her gardening business in NW1 as soon as possible. 'Matthew,' she said seriously. 'I have to ask you a question. And I need you to promise me that you'll answer it honestly.'

'OK,' Matthew replied, as he nervously took a drink of hot black tea.

'When I met you, last Friday, in the convenience store, nearby here – what were you carrying inside the flowery bag?'

Matthew nearly choked.

He immediately began to feel his face reddening; his heart thumping; his mouth freezing. He looked at Eva, as she stared intently back at him. 'Tell me *the truth*, Matthew,' she said very softly and kindly.

Matthew simply looked at Eva. He couldn't find any words right now. 'OK,' Eva continued quietly. 'Then let me ask you a simple question – and just answer me with a nod, or a shake-of-the-head.'

Matthew looked at his sister-in-law, dreading her next question; hoping that it somehow wouldn't be the one he knew it was going to be.

'Matthew,' Eva said. 'Did you steal a dead dog - last Friday?'

There was a pause of several seconds, as Matthew Rourke attempted to absorb Eva Kelly's brutally direct question. He nodded in the affirmative. Matthew knew that he couldn't tell Eva lies. She evidently knew something already.

'OK, Matthew,' Eva said, taking a deep breath; perhaps of relief, perhaps of despair. 'Do you realise what a terrible thing you've done? I mean – what the hell possessed you, to take a young woman's bag?'

Matthew looked up at Eva, feeling thoroughly ashamed. 'How did you know about it?' he asked, panicking. 'How did you know I took the bag from a young woman?' Matthew Rourke thought that the police had perhaps finally discovered his identity.

'Don't worry.' Eva knew what Matthew was thinking. 'The police don't know. Nobody else knows it was you. Except me.' Eva Kelly proceeded to explain the strange set of coincidences that had led her to know that Matthew stole a dead dog, last Friday (she was careful, however, to tell Matthew that Amanda Morgan was her 'employer').

Matthew could hardly believe what he had just heard. 'Why did you want to talk to me about this?' he asked Eva. 'Do you think I need to tell Ruth?'

'Of course not! It's got nothing to do with her! It's the dog's owners you need to tell. I know for a fact that they've been demented all week – wondering what's happened to their dog.' There was a pause, before Eva began to speak again. 'What *did* you do with the bag and its contents, Matthew?'

'I buried them.'

'Where?'

'Over there.' Matthew pointed towards the specific area of woodland, inside Unity Park.

Eva began to think that she had just entered another realm of existence – she could hardly believe what Matthew had said.

'What are you laughing at?' Matthew asked.

'I don't know, Matthew. Maybe it's because I've heard Ruth describing you as *boring* and *unpredictable,* so many times in the past.'

'She doesn't know anything about me,' Matthew said angrily. 'And anyway. I won't be around for her to find out anything more about me – after Sunday.'

'What's that supposed to mean?'

'I'm going back to Cumbria. For good.'

Eva was very taken-aback. 'And have you told Ruth?'

'No.'

'For God's sake, Matthew! You have to tell her! You can't just run off on people like that!' Eva thought she knew Matthew, before now.

'Eva – Ruth is hardly ever in the apartment. She stays out most of the time now. She hasn't spoken to me properly in ages. She didn't even come home last night!'

'I know. I spoke to her briefly on the phone, yesterday evening. She phoned to tell me that she was on a promise of a job as a secretary, with some solicitor type. Apparently, her friends, Deborah and Clare Silvestri, have put her in contact with Deborah's sister, who's married to some hot-shot city type. Ruth's delighted. She just wants to work and play alongside the wealthy set right now.'

'You see! I told you! Ruth hasn't even told *me* that yet – and I'm meant to be her husband!'

'It doesn't matter, Matthew! You can't just disappear on Ruth. You still own an apartment together. You still have a certificate to say you're married to each other! Have you lost your mind?'

'Maybe,' Matthew mumbled. He began to think about the dead dog and Christian.

'No you haven't!' Eva scolded Matthew, bringing him to his senses again. 'Now. You need to work out how and when you're going to tell Ruth that you're leaving her. And you need to think of a way to tell the owners of the dead dog where his body is.' Eva paused and shook her head in disbelief. 'My God, Matthew! How have you been living with all of this inside your head?'

'Don't ask, Eva. Don't ask.'

Eva Kelly and Matthew Rourke continued to talk for a while longer. Matthew even told Eva about his family in the Lake District – including Christian. Matthew explained the reason why he first came to London, years ago; *and* why he chose to keep it a secret from Ruth for all this time. Eva swore never to reveal Matthew's secrets to anyone – including Ruth – and Matthew trusted her infinitely. Eva advised Matthew to write a letter to Ruth, explaining that he had ended their marriage – but Eva told him only to post this letter *after* his departure for the Lake District, on Sunday. Eva also advised him to write a letter to the Carmichaels, c/o Epsilon Dental Spa in W8, telling them about their dog's whereabouts.

Eva Kelly eventually had to leave to return to work in NW1, at noon. She was astounded by all she had discovered about Matthew Rourke. She needed to go away and think about everything.

Meanwhile, Christian Rourke would remain beside Matthew – at least until Matthew was able to reach a definite decision about what to do regarding Ruth, the Lake District and the dead dog's body. Christian realised that Matthew would almost certainly need a companion to help him through the dilemmas he was now faced with; and Christian was determined to give Matthew all the prompts and assistance he could. He wanted to ensure that his brother did not make any wrong or foolish choices during the next few crucial hours and days.

*****

Although Dixie Carmichael was also very curious about Matthew Rourke's current predicament (he had always been a nosey dog), his attention was nevertheless drawn to a slightly more dramatic scene, about to unfold elsewhere.

Amanda Morgan's life had been thrown into complete disarray, yesterday afternoon, since discovering that Douglas Singleton, the most unscrupulous solicitor in England, was possibly her father.

Amanda had spent all of Thursday evening in tears. She didn't go to the hospital to visit her husband, Steve; and neither did Charlotte, who instead chose to visit Ebony Glazier to talk 'business' – ahead of another meeting they had already scheduled for tonight, at PolkaPolka nightclub, in Central London. Although Charlotte had wanted to visit her dad in hospital, earlier on Thursday, she could clearly see that her mum was not in the mood to go anywhere that evening – although her mum would not tell Charlotte why. Charlotte would therefore wait until another time to see her father – and she hoped that Amanda would go too.

Amanda had spoken briefly on the phone to Susan Carmichael, on Thursday evening, to confirm that Epsilon Dental Spa should remain closed this coming Monday. Amanda had no idea what was going to happen with her business now. Her father (or step-father – or whatever he was to Amanda), Sir Horace Montgomery, had flatly refused to help Amanda with her legal problems with Singleton and Singleton Solicitors. She had no idea where she stood with anything right now. It was as though Amanda was being denied the chance to live an uncomplicated life. Not only was her husband (or, soon-to-be ex-husband) just beginning to come to terms with the death of his daughter, Matilda, for the first time; but Amanda wasn't entirely sure whether she could be open with Charlotte about Amanda's new companion, Eva; and then, on top of all this – Amanda's business was potentially going to crash, thanks to a man who may or may not be Amanda's father.

Amanda had decided to phone Singleton and Singleton Solicitors, first thing on Friday morning, to enquire if Douglas Singleton would be at his office today. Amanda didn't give her name to Douglas Singleton's secretary, who therefore refused to tell Amanda anything about Douglas's whereabouts. Amanda made the decision, nevertheless, to go to Singleton and Singleton's office in W11, on the off chance that Douglas would be there, so that Amanda could challenge him – unannounced.

Amanda entered the impressive Singleton and Singleton offices at just after noon, on Friday 14th October. Her daughter, Matilda, accompanied her there.

Amanda was dressed formally, yet glamorously, for the occasion, and she had in her hand the letter, sent by Singleton and Singleton Solicitors, to Epsilon Dental Spa, on Tuesday.

'May I help you?' the suit-clad, hooked-nosed, blonde receptionist asked Amanda.

'Yes. I was informed that Mr Douglas Singleton would be here today. I have some business I need to discuss with him.'

'I'm sorry – but if you don't have an appoint – '

'JENNIFER!' a male voice called from an office door, just down the corridor from Singleton's Reception Area. 'Did we receive any correspondence from *The Daily Messenger* yet?'

'Is *that* Douglas Singleton?' Amanda asked the receptionist.

'JENNIFER!' the unpleasant voice demanded; at which point, Amanda Morgan dashed towards the corridor it had emanated from, and confronted its owner directly. 'Are you Douglas Singleton?' she asked, facing the man in the corridor.

'I beg your pardon?' the man replied, extremely annoyed. Amanda looked at him. She could see the thirty pieces of silver glistening in his eyes. He held his mouth in a permanent grimace. He had teeth like a paper shredder.

The flustered receptionist now joined Amanda in the corridor. 'I'm so sorry, Mr Singleton. She just rushed past me.'

'Who are *you*?' he demanded loudly, looking directly at Amanda Morgan.

'I'm Amanda Morgan. I own Epsilon Dental Spa. We have business to discuss, I believe, Mr Singleton.' Amanda was feeling very confident – albeit that she was anxious about what she might discover from her conversation with Douglas Singleton.

'Well then. Make an appointment!'

'And I have to talk to you about my mother. *Lady Lydia Montgomery.*'

Douglas Singleton looked as though he had just discovered he had seconds to live. 'Get into my office,' he ordered Amanda. She desperately hoped that this ignoramus was *not* her father.

*****

Douglas Singleton's office was presidential in size and décor. He took a seat behind his majestic mahogany antique desk, and stared intensely over at Amanda Morgan, who took a seat opposite him. Amanda found it easy holding Douglas Singleton's stare: she had met his type on many occasions before. She thought he looked much older than his seventy years. He was overweight, and still had a full head of white hair. In fact, it looked as though several inches of snow had just fallen on him.

'Now,' he said. 'Tell me why you are here.'

'I'm here because I need to ask you about my mother – first and foremost. But I also want to discuss the contents of this letter.' Amanda placed the Singleton letter onto Douglas Singleton's desk.

'Go on,' he said, trying not to sound interested.

'I want you to tell me if my mother – Lady Lydia Montgomery – ever alluded to the fact that you might have conceived a daughter with her.'

Douglas Singleton's bulbous eyeballs nearly popped from their sockets. 'She most certainly did not!' he shouted furiously.

Amanda was unfazed. 'Well then – I'm afraid you're going to have to give your consent for a paternity test to be carried out. Quite simply, because the man whom I always believed to be my father – Sir Horace Montgomery – thinks that you might be my father. I don't think I need to remind you of the reason why he would think this.'

Douglas Singleton was appalled; genuinely appalled. 'How dare you come in here and suggest such a thing! Get out of my office – now!' He stood up, pushed back his seat, and walked around to Amanda's side of the desk. 'Get up!' he shouted down at her.

Amanda sat still, and continued to hold Douglas Singleton's stare. 'No. I won't get up.'

'I'll call the police!'

'I'll call the press. *They* would be interested to know that the most notorious solicitor in London might have a daughter he never knew, or wanted to know about.'

'You wouldn't dare do that. What would that gain?'

'The truth. It would also ensure that Epsilon Dental Spa wasn't destroyed by *you*.' Amanda lifted the Singleton letter from the mahogany desk. 'So. Do we agree that we keep this little secret between us – and that you arrange for your 'client' – your wife – to drop all the allegations outlined in this letter?'

Douglas Singleton continued to stare angrily at Amanda. He had never been affronted like this before in his life – and he certainly didn't like how he felt right now. 'I can see what I can do,' he said firmly.

'You can do much more than that, Mr Singleton. You can guarantee – in writing – that all the allegations in this letter are now dropped. I expect to receive confirmation in the post – by Monday, at the latest.'

Douglas Singleton almost recognised himself in Amanda Morgan. He really couldn't afford, or be bothered with, a revelation like this emerging at this late stage in his career: he was hopeful that he might be knighted soon. 'You have my guarantee, Ms Morgan. Now please leave my office.'

'Well. Since you asked me so politely this time, I will leave,' Amanda said firmly, as she got up from her seat. 'I will expect my letter by Monday morning. Send it to Epsilon Dental Spa – for my attention. Hopefully – if you do as I request – we will never have to revisit this conversation again.' Amanda walked out the door of Douglas Singleton's office, past his receptionist, and onto the street outside.

It was strange, but Amanda knew she had done it. She knew she had saved her business from Douglas Singleton. She hoped she would never have to encounter that man in her life again. Amanda had intuited a very heavy and dark air in the Singleton office suite. In fact, the only thing that had held Amanda together in the presence of Douglas Singleton had been the knowledge that her daughter, Matilda, was beside Amanda the entire time.

Amanda's phone suddenly began to ring inside her handbag. She took out the phone and looked at the screen: it was Steve's number. 'Hello?' she said, as she continued to walk along the busy street in W11: Amanda hadn't spoken to her husband since she left his hospital ward on Tuesday evening.

'Amanda. They're letting me out of here tomorrow morning. Do you think you could come and pick me up maybe? Mike said he's busy.'

Amanda actually felt compassion for Steve right now: maybe because she was in such a good mood after dealing successfully with Douglas Singleton. 'OK,' she said; 'What time?'

'Around elevenish – tomorrow?'

'OK. Are you feeling better?'

'Yes. Thanks.'

'OK. I'll see you then.'

Amanda hung up and put her phone back inside her bag.

She began to think about Matilda again – and how her daughter had made her presence so clearly known to Steve, the last time Amanda spoke to her husband, inside the hospital ward, where Matilda died, over nineteen years ago. Amanda needed Matilda's support more than ever right now, and she had never been more conscious of her daughter's presence than during the last week. Although Amanda was happy that she had practically stopped Douglas Singleton's legal action against Epsilon, she still needed to know if he was actually her father. But this would only happen if Amanda secured Sir Horace Montgomery's cooperation.

In addition to this, although Amanda did not necessarily want to *murder* Steve any longer, she still found it difficult to forget all the hurt he had caused over the years – and especially since the whole dead and stolen dog incident, recently. Amanda needed to sort out all her business and personal relationships this weekend, if her life was finally to move on. Steve would wait until tomorrow, Amanda knew; but Sir Horace Montgomery would not. Amanda would go to Montgomery's Department Store now, and confront Sir Horace – in the same way she had just confronted Douglas Singleton.

Matilda Morgan was in no doubt that her mum would be successful on this occasion; and, after watching her impressive performance in front of Douglas Singleton, a few minutes ago, neither was Dixie Carmichael.

-CHAPTER TWENTY-

In the Post

It was the morning of Saturday 15th October, and Matthew Rourke had finally made a decision over what to do about his wife, Ruth. While he realised now that he couldn't just leave for the Lake District, tomorrow, and say nothing to Ruth about his whereabouts, Matthew nevertheless resolved to tell his wife in a letter, as opposed to face-to-face – just as his sister-in-law, Eva, had advised.

Matthew had convinced himself, all last night, that there was no point in trying to talk to Ruth any longer. The truth was, Matthew hated confrontations, almost as much as he hated goodbyes. He didn't have the energy to think about what to say to Ruth. He knew that if he told her why he was leaving London, she would simply tear him to pieces with her reaction. Matthew didn't feel like he knew Ruth any more, and Eva Kelly had confirmed this to Matthew, yesterday, when she told him about Ruth's decision to change careers; that Ruth suddenly wanted to become a solicitor's secretary.

Matthew was mortified that Eva knew he had stolen a bag from a young female. He just wanted to get away from this whole sorry mess for good. While Matthew still deeply admired and liked Eva, he felt like a fool now. He felt stupid and ashamed. He knew that Christian had been correct to tell him to return to the Lake District. Matthew was excited about the fact that he would be spending his last night in his TW9 apartment, tonight. He would leave early tomorrow morning with his suitcase (which he would secretly finish packing today); but just before catching his train, he would post two letters: one to Ruth; and one to the owners of the dead dog, whom Eva had told him could be contacted at Epsilon Dental Spa, in W8. These letters would both reach their destination on Monday – *after* Matthew had left London. He never wanted to have to think about their recipients after this time.

Christian Rourke and Dixie Carmichael were not disappointed that Matthew had resolved to leave Ruth without addressing her in person – nor were they surprised. In fact, Christian understood Matthew completely. He recognised that his brother had a vulnerable and gentle soul, which had never coped well in a crisis. At this stage in Matthew's soul development, he would not be in a position to fend off another of his wife, Ruth's, ruthless verbal attacks. Those in the invisible realms could not afford for Matthew to be manipulated into changing his mind over his decision to leave for the Lake District, tomorrow morning. There was a high probability that Ruth would become suddenly interested in Matthew again – if he suddenly began to display his ability to behave dramatically, selfishly and unpredictably. Ruth would undoubtedly be attracted to these qualities, and she would definitely enjoy the challenge of conquering and overwhelming her husband once again.

Although many souls residing on the physical, earthly dimensions would undoubtedly label Matthew Rourke a coward and a cad for leaving his wife in such a manner, Dixie, Christian and others in the invisible realms did not judge him like this. For them, the most important thing was that Matthew gave Ruth an explanation (as Eva Kelly had urged Matthew, yesterday). The fact that the explanation would appear in a letter (as Eva had suggested to Matthew), *after* his departure for the Lake District, did not matter. In fact, it was actually preferable in Matthew's case. That's why Christian and other souls from the invisible realms had spent all last night infusing Matthew's head with dreams. Matthew had been able to watch, as he wrote a letter to Ruth, explaining the reasons for his departure. He would be able to finalise things with Ruth at a later date – when Matthew felt stronger and more able.

Matthew had also been advised in this dream to write a letter to *'The Owners of Epsilon Dental Spa'*, in which he would carefully describe the whereabouts of Dixie Carmichael's body, inside Unity Park. Matthew would type and address these letters today, and post them tomorrow morning, just before he would catch his train to the Lake District. It was hoped that Matthew would not change any of these well-laid plans in the meantime.

As Matthew began to spend his final full day at his London apartment, his wife, Ruth, was completely oblivious to her husband's private intentions and activities. It was just after ten in the morning, and Ruth had awoken after another night socialising with Clare and Deborah Silvestri. Ruth had learnt about Deborah's *Shed Head* activities; but although Ruth was a bit disgusted by Deborah's choice of 'career', she was prepared to look beyond her negative judgement, for the sake of her own career.

Ruth had managed to persuade Deborah Silvestri, to persuade Madeleine Singleton, to persuade Douglas Singleton, to give Ruth a job – as one of Douglas's many P.A.s. While Ruth's past secretarial skills and qualifications had been moderately helpful in securing her new job, it was her photograph that had clinched it. Douglas Singleton liked to surround himself with as many attractive blonde females as possible, and Ruth Rourke's 'look' fitted the bill perfectly.

It had already been agreed that Ruth would begin her new job at the end of this month – once she'd had time to sort things out with her remaining psychotherapy clients, and as soon as she'd sorted out the lease on her office in W5: she never wanted to look at its filthy cobwebs again. Ruth informed her sister, Eva Kelly, about her decision to return to secretarial work, on Thursday evening, but Eva hadn't seemed particularly impressed. Ruth wasn't bothered about this, however. It wasn't likely that she would be seeing as much of Eva in the future – given that Ruth would be operating in new social circles.

Ruth was absolutely delighted with herself. At last, she felt like she had achieved something in her life. Ruth knew that she would soon be socialising with the wealthy sections of society, whose psychological problems she had been dealing with for the last several years. Ruth felt as though she knew them all already. All Ruth had to do now was end her miserable marriage to Matthew Rourke – but that would wait until Ruth had settled into her new career, she thought now, as she prepared to get ready for a day's shopping with Deborah and Clare Silvestri.

Ruth had agreed to stay over at the Silvestri's house tonight. Deborah had arranged for her sister, Madeleine Singleton, to come around, for drinks and a séance, before all four women would go on to a night club. They had already decided not to go to Abandonment, as they had, last Saturday night. Deborah realised that she wouldn't likely be admitted, after the debacle on that occasion. Unbeknown to Mike Gordon, the vet who had been the focus of much of Deborah Silvestri's interest in Abandonment, Deborah had decided that she would no longer pursue his attentions. She had come to the conclusion, with the help of her son, Benito, that Mike must be tight with his money – given the fact that he hadn't jumped at the opportunity to visit her shed this week. Deborah had already begun to research other (male) London vets to service her rabbits and bunnies; and anyway, Deborah didn't want to associate her shed with a person whose dentist friend murdered dogs – not to mention the fact that Steve Morgan's name would soon be plastered all over the London Press, as a result of the impending legal case Singleton and Singleton were launching against him. Ruth Rourke couldn't wait to work with Douglas Singleton on *that* case: she felt as though she already knew Steve Morgan personally, given the work she had done with Steve's wife, Amanda. Ruth had always prided herself on her professionalism as a psychotherapist: she had never broken a confidence. Her new career, however, as Douglas Singleton's P.A., might require that Ruth divulge a bit of her knowledge about some of the psychotherapy cases she had dealt with in the past – but only if this was done professionally, and in the interests of Ruth's career development, as a solicitor's P.A. Ruth was sure she would never let her new employer down.

*****

Amanda and Charlotte Morgan arrived at Memorial Hospital at 11.00 a.m. on Saturday 15th October. As they parked their car outside the main hospital doors, Charlotte was still in the process of telling Amanda about the new business idea she had discussed with Ebony Glazier, last night, at PolkaPolka nightclub. Amanda was very impressed by her daughter's idea – not to mention heart-warmed by Charlotte's infectious enthusiasm for her new-found interest in flowers and flower arranging.

The two women left their car, and proceeded to make their way to Steve Morgan's side ward on the 5th floor. Amanda had spoken to Steve, this morning, by phone, and her husband had confirmed he would be discharged today, but he told Amanda that he still felt very poorly. Reluctantly, Amanda had agreed to let Steve come back to the Morgan family home in TW9 today, instead of leaving him off at Mike Gordon's pad. Amanda had insisted to Steve, however, that this would only be a temporary arrangement; that Steve could only stay with her and Charlotte for a few nights (although Charlotte secretly hoped it would be for longer); and that Amanda expected Steve to find his own place, as soon as he was well enough. She still needed to discuss Steve's future at Epsilon Dental Spa with her husband – not to mention their impending divorce.

Amanda's head had been filled all morning with thoughts about everything that had occurred in her life, yesterday. She hadn't told Steve yet about the fact that she had likely resolved the crisis over Epsilon. Amanda hadn't even informed Susan and Ray Carmichael about everything that had gone on, inside Singleton and Singleton Solicitors' offices; nor indeed was Charlotte even aware of the crisis. Amanda would not let anyone know that the crisis was over until she had Douglas Singleton's letter in her hand, on Monday morning, when she would visit Epsilon's premises, alone, to collect it.

Amanda was even more concerned, however, about another envelope she would be opening on Monday. Sir Horace Montgomery had (eventually) agreed, yesterday, to Amanda's request for a paternity test. They had used their contacts and money to arrange for a test to be carried out during the course of this weekend, after Amanda dropped off their samples to the clinic, yesterday evening. Amanda hadn't discussed her paternity crisis with anyone. In every respect, Amanda hoped that she would never have to.

'Mum,' Charlotte said, as they were about to enter Steve's side ward.

'Yes, darling.'

'Do you think dad will be OK? I mean – after everything that happened here – on Tuesday evening?'

Amanda and Charlotte had not discussed Matilda's presence in Steve's ward on Tuesday: neither of them had thought they needed to. 'Of course he will be fine! You know your dad, Charlotte. He never takes anything too seriously in the end – does he?'

'No,' Charlotte replied, as she turned and walked into her father's ward, and Amanda followed.

Steve was already sitting dressed, and ready to leave, at the end of his hospital bed. He looked so frail, Amanda thought. 'Are you ready?' she asked, as Charlotte lifted her dad's case.

'Yes. I've got my medication to take home and everything. I can't wait to get out of here, actually,' he said soberly, as he looked at Amanda, and held her gaze for a few seconds.

'OK then,' she said brusquely. 'Let's go.'

'Amanda,' Steve said suddenly.

'What?'

'I'm sorry.'

Amanda and Charlotte paused and looked at one another for a while. Amanda felt very awkward and uncomfortable – much more than she had yesterday, inside Douglas Singleton's office. 'Sorry for what?' she asked, puzzled. Steve had never apologised to her like this in his life.

'For everything,' he said seriously – not even flashing his veneers. 'And you too, Charlotte. Sorry.'

Matilda's presence was palpable once more in the side ward.

'OK, Steve,' Amanda said, breaking up the sombre mood: she had noticed that Charlotte had begun to cry. 'It's all in the past now. Let's just get out of here.'

Charlotte and Amanda pulled Steve up from his sitting position at the end of the hospital bed, and began to walk him out of the side ward. As they reached the corridor, all three instinctively turned around to look back at the room they had just exited – before Amanda shut the side ward door firmly and confidently behind her.

*****

As Amanda, Steve and Charlotte were getting into Amanda's car, outside Memorial Hospital, Susan Carmichael had just finished putting on her gardening clothes. It was 11.27 a.m.

Susan had uncharacteristically slept in this morning. She felt exhausted and a little light-headed, but she was determined, nevertheless, to plant the lily bulbs and rose bush she had purchased for Dixie, in Buckinghamshire – near his Oak tree in their back garden, today. Ray had also decided to cut the lawn for the last time this year, too; given that the weather had become much colder during the last number of days.

'You look a bit tired,' Ray said to Susan, as they were both putting on their gardening overcoats in the small cloakroom at the back of their kitchen. 'Are you sure you wouldn't like me to plant the bulbs and the rose bush?'

'No. I need to do it myself. But thanks anyway.'

As Ray wandered off to the corner of the Carmichaels' back garden, to fetch his lawnmower from the shed, Susan put on her gardening gloves, lifted the packet of lily bulbs, the rose bush, and the gardening tools Ray had already assembled for her – and walked towards Dixie's Oak tree, at the bottom of the back garden.

Susan set the plant, bulbs and tools gently on the ground, and looked around for a while. It was a bright and sunny day so far, but it was cold enough that Susan could see her breath when she exhaled. Everything was very quiet, and Susan soon became completely oblivious to Ray's presence in the garden, as he fumbled and fought with his lawnmower, beside the shed.

Susan knelt underneath Dixie's Oak tree, and *listened*.

All she could hear was the sound of her own thoughts, which were strangely calm today, given that Susan felt sad that she had to plant Dixie's bulbs and rose bush, without him by her side. She looked at her Jacob's Ladder plants, which had become rather tattered by the recent cold weather. Susan would have to cut them back today, she remembered; in time for next summer.

She lifted her trowel and decided upon a spot to plant her lily bulbs first – quite near her Jacob's Ladder plants. Susan began to dig deeply into the cool, moist soil. She wanted to plant all the lily bulbs together, in a large group, so that when they grew, they would resemble the beautiful fields of lilies she had seen in her dreams recently.

Susan placed each bulb carefully inside the large, round trench she had diligently created. Once she was contented that she had arranged them correctly, she spoke to the bulbs, before she covered them with their soft brown winter bedding. 'Night,' she said. 'See you next summer.' Susan recalled the names of the bulbs she was concealing with soil: 'Stargazer' lilies. She looked up at the sky briefly, before she had to turn her gaze away from the bright sunlight.

Susan lifted the rose bush out from its black plastic pot.

She began to dig another trench, between where she had planted the lily bulbs, and beside her Jacob's Ladder plants. She placed her rose bush into the trench, surrounded it with some fertilizer, and filled the trench with soil.

Susan stood back, pleased at the work she had done so far. All she needed to do now, she thought, was tidy up her Jacob's Ladder plants, put her tools away, and relax for the remainder of the day.

She took out her secateurs from one of the pockets of her gardening coat, and carefully began to snip back the dead sections of plant. Susan suddenly began to recall many happy memories from the summer that had just passed. She remembered Dixie, rolling about on the grass, on warm evenings; snapping angrily at bees as they dared to come near him, as he lay snoozing under his favourite Oak tree. Susan had loved looking at Dixie, when he attempted to chase the butterflies and the small birds that often converged around the blue flowers on her Jacob's Ladder plants. Dixie had always been a bit of a drama king, Susan thought now, as she laughed to herself. He loved mischief, too. Susan began to recall the day Dixie dragged her towards the handsome stranger, inside Paws for Thought. Dixie was a very smart dog, Susan realised. Irreplaceable, in fact. She wondered where he was now. Susan just wanted to place Dixie's body in a safe place – where she could go and visit him, whenever she wanted. That had been important to Susan, when she lost Jacob, over eight years ago.

Susan suddenly began to think about the day she went to the hospital to collect Jacob's body, to bury him. It was four days after Jacob was delivered, and she and Ray had been instructed to go to the hospital mortuary, where they would be reunited with Jacob, and where a chaplain would accompany them to the small burial ground, inside the hospital grounds.

When Susan and Ray arrived at the mortuary, just after 5.00 p.m., on 12th June, over eight years ago, Susan had kept thinking: *it shouldn't be like this*. Inside her mind, Susan was still expecting a baby. Her body and her mind were still pregnant with Jacob. She couldn't process the thought that her baby was inside the small, neat, white box the chaplain now handed to her. Susan screamed and cried, as she thanked the chaplain; and Ray held her tight and cried too. This simply couldn't be happening, Susan had thought at the time. *This wasn't meant to happen.*

Susan, Ray and the chaplain buried Jacob's body in the infant plot, within the grounds of Memorial Hospital. Susan was distraught – leaving her baby behind. Jacob should still be growing inside her. Susan just loved her baby boy so much. That's all there was to it. She didn't know how she would ever pick herself up after this. She felt so terrible about Ray. He had lost his baby too. Susan knew he was devastated, but she couldn't even help him – she was destroyed herself.

Susan looked at her Jacob's Ladder plants again. It was Susan's garden, and Dixie, that had helped her to start to heal, during the years since Jacob's death. She began to think about the bunch of chrysanthemums Amanda Morgan had brought her, last Sunday. Susan had heard that Amanda once lost a baby too – but she wasn't sure of the details. Nobody ever talked about these things. Somehow, Amanda's bunch of flowers had suggested to Susan that Jacob and Dixie were both OK – although Susan would love to be *sure* of that fact.

'Susan!' Ray shouted over. He had just finished cutting the lawn.

'Yes?'

'Do you want some lunch? I'm going to heat a tin of chicken soup.'

'OK. What time is it?'

'It's almost one,' he said, walking into the house.

'I'll be there in a minute.'

Susan looked one more time at Dixie's Oak; her newly-manicured Jacob's Ladder plants; her 'Dream Time' rose bush; the patch where she had just buried the Stargazer lilies.

Everything fell silent again.

Susan felt warm currents of air – sparks of electricity – flowing through her body. She closed her eyes, and allowed the heat the sparks had produced to warm her soul. She smiled, and thought about Jacob. Susan knew he was close by her now – and she knew that Jacob would take care of Dixie, too.

'Susan!' Ray shouted from above his wife's head.

Susan looked around from her kneeling position, very taken aback.

'I've been calling you for ages!' Ray said, laughing. 'It's nearly half-past-one! Your soup is freezing!'

'God,' Susan said. 'I must have dozed off.'

'Here – let me help you up,' Ray said, lifting his wife gently by the arm. 'This just arrived for you in the post.' Ray handed Susan her monthly instalment of 'Lovely Garden. Lovely Home' magazine.

'Thanks,' she said, as she began to walk alongside Ray towards the house.

'Did you get everything planted?' he asked.

'Yes. We just need to sit back now - and wait for everything to flower again – next summer.'

Susan entered the kitchen, and sat down at the table, as Ray proceeded to re-heat the chicken soup. She glanced down at her magazine, which was still inside its clear plastic cover. Susan smiled when she saw that 'Lovely Garden. Lovely Home' was suggesting ways to brighten up the home, this winter. She looked more closely at the cover now, and gasped.

Under the headline, 'Spring into Winter!' - was a glossy photo of a cottage-style living room, decked in shades of violet and yellow.

Right in the centre of the living room, was a cosy-looking violet, velvet sofa; and beside it, an oak table.

On top of the oak table was a bunch of violet and yellow chrysanthemums; while lying cuddled on the violet, velvet sofa, was a West Highland Terrier.

Result, Dixie thought, as he looked over at Jacob Carmichael; and Jacob Carmichael smiled confidently back.

-CHAPTER TWENTY-ONE-

Going Home

Matthew Rourke awoke just after six on the morning of Sunday October 16th. He was going home. Today.

He got out of bed and looked across the room at his packed suitcase, which was still lying open, waiting for Matthew to pack the remainder of his things, before he would leave his apartment for the train station, later. His train to the Lake District was due to leave Central Station at 9.32 a.m.; but Matthew had to catch another train to Central before this – and he didn't want to be late.

He got washed and dressed, before he walked into the kitchen at the back of his apartment for some breakfast. Matthew's wife, Ruth, had stayed over at Clare and Deborah Silvestri's house in SW12 last night, and she wouldn't be back until much later – long after Matthew would have left.

Matthew finished his breakfast quickly and tidied away his dishes. He looked into the kitchen cupboards and drawers to ensure that he hadn't forgotten any of his personal belongings, and then he proceeded to check the other rooms in the apartment.

Satisfied that he had everything he needed, Matthew placed his remaining items of clothes, as well as his laptop, inside his suitcase, and zipped it closed. He was ready to go. Or – almost.

Matthew walked back into the kitchen and took a pen and some paper out from the drawer. He wrote a quick note:

> *Dear Ruth,*
> > *Have gone away for the night. Will explain more tomorrow.*
> > *Matthew.*

He dated the note, and placed it on top of the kitchen table, before walking out of the kitchen, back into the bedroom to collect his suitcase, and out the front door of his TW9 apartment. He closed the door behind him, without looking back. Matthew began to walk in the direction of his nearest train station with his suitcase, trying not to think much about what he was doing. It was a cold day, and it was raining steadily.

Matthew reached his local station at 7.46 a.m. It would take him approximately forty-five minutes to reach Central from here – and he would have to change trains once. Matthew was anxious for the 8.00 a.m. train to arrive on time. He didn't want anything to ruin his plans today.

The train obliged; pulling into Matthew's station only a couple of minutes late. He boarded and took a seat; intent on keeping a close eye on all the stations the train would stop at; adamant that he would not miss his change-over station.

The train moved off. There were very few people on Matthew's carriage.

After a few minutes, the train stopped at the station where the young female had boarded, over a week ago, with the flowery bag. Matthew was relieved she didn't get on the train now. At least he understood now why she had been carrying a dead dog about with her, but he didn't really want to think about that at the moment. Matthew suddenly realised that this was also the station near Paws for Thought, where he had sat contemplating how to tell Ruth about his redundancy, almost two weeks ago. Matthew recalled the lady with the West Highland Terrier. He wondered what she was doing now.

The train moved off again; until it stopped at Unity Park Station. As a tiny handful of passengers got on and off the train now, Matthew immediately began to think about burying the dog at Unity Park. He recalled the peregrine falcon with the green eyes. The Rising Dawn. Eva. He had thought a lot about Eva, last night. Matthew was so angry that Eva would think so little of him now.

After several more minutes, Matthew's train eventually reached his change-over station. Central was only minutes away now; the Lake District only a few hours.

*****

At Central Station, Matthew got off his train, and began to walk in the direction of the platform he needed to reach in order to catch his train home – to the Lake District. It was 8.52 a.m. Matthew could feel his heart thumping excitedly – or nervously – inside his chest: he wasn't exactly sure how he was feeling at the moment.

Just as he was about to reach an escalator, a voice suddenly called out his name. Matthew turned around to find Eva Kelly rushing towards him. She looked drenched from being out in the rain. 'Eva!' he said, very shocked, but very pleasantly surprised. 'Is everything OK?'

'Yes,' she said, smiling – and a little out-of-breath. 'I just wanted to come and say goodbye. I thought you deserved to have *someone* wave you off.'

Matthew placed his suitcase on the ground and embraced Eva tightly. He had tears in his eyes – and so had Eva. 'Are you sure you're doing the right thing, Matthew?' she said, wiping her eyes.

'Yes,' he replied, looking intensely at Eva. 'I can't stay here any longer. I've messed up everything.'

'It hasn't all been your fault, Matthew.'

'Maybe not. But I know I've been told to go back to the Lake District. Don't ask me why – but I know I have to leave London.'

'Did you write the two letters?'

'Oh – shit,' Matthew said, as he reached into the inside pocket of his jacket, and pulled out two envelopes: one addressed to Ruth Rourke at her TW9 address; and the other addressed to '*The Owners of Epsilon Dental Spa*' in W8. 'I wrote them – but I forgot to post them.'

'Don't worry. I can do that for you.' Eva reached out and took the letters from Matthew.

'Thanks Eva.'

'OK. I guess I'd better go now – and let you catch your train.' Eva smiled at Matthew.

'I'm so sorry – that you must think so little of me now, Eva.'

'I don't, Matthew. I don't at all. I just wish it could all have been different – that's all.'

'I know,' he whispered, as he pulled Eva close to him again.

Matthew didn't know how long he held Eva like that. 'I'll call you when I get there,' he said, releasing Eva, and picking up his suitcase. 'We should try to keep in touch – even though I know we won't be family for much longer.'

'I'd like that,' Eva smiled through her tears. 'Bye Matt,' she said; before turning and walking away.

*****

Around three hours later, Matthew Rourke reached his station at the Lake District. It was 12.52 p.m.

He got off his train, alone, and began to look around at the station he remembered from his youth. Matthew knew that he had to catch a bus from here, which would take him the short twenty-minute journey to his family home, just outside the village of Empyrmere.

He had a short wait at the station, before he finally boarded his coach, and took a seat near the back. Matthew's ears began to tune into the sound of home. He could hear the babble of Cumbrian accents on the coach. He didn't feel like an outsider any longer. Matthew felt as though he had never been to London in his entire life.

As the coach pulled out of the station, Matthew briefly thought about Eva's unexpected appearance at the train station, this morning – before his attention was suddenly grabbed by the stunning scenery that surrounded him now. It was a beautiful autumn day in Cumbria – much sunnier and brighter than the weather had been in London, when Matthew left there, this morning. Matthew gazed in awe at the houses, hills, woods and people he encountered, as his coach passed steadily through the Cumbrian countryside. Nothing appeared to have changed since Matthew left here, fourteen years ago. He recalled today's date: 16th October. It was the sixteenth anniversary of Christian's death. Matthew began to think about his parents – John and Linda. He would (hopefully) be meeting them again soon.

Matthew was suddenly able to see his old village ahead – just down to his left. He knew he had to get off the bus soon. His old home was near here, he remembered. Matthew stumbled to the front of the coach, and asked the driver to stop wherever was convenient.

A few seconds later, the coach pulled in on a lay-by; and Matthew got off, and collected his suitcase from the luggage hold-all.

The coach pulled away.

Matthew was standing alone with his suitcase. He knew exactly where he was now. He looked down at the valley beneath, and across at Empyrmere village in the distance. Matthew could see the local river, flowing towards Empyrmere; and he couldn't begin to think why he had ever chosen to leave this place. He picked up his suitcase, and looked a few yards up ahead, towards a two-storey, detached, white-washed house, which was surrounded by nearly an acre of mature, private gardens.

Matthew began to walk towards this house, becoming intensely emotional with every step he took. He kept looking upwards, towards the house. It was just as it had looked when he was a child – albeit that it appeared old and tired now – and perhaps even a little sadder-looking. Matthew recalled looking at the house on the FindaStreet website, and thinking at the time that it had seemed overgrown, and slightly neglected. As he looked at the house closely now – in the flesh – Matthew realised that the house hadn't experienced happiness in a long time. The house and its garden's spirit had changed – that was all.

Matthew reached the gateway. He looked at the house, and at the car in the driveway, and he felt sick with nerves. He knew he had to approach the door now – or risk turning away forever.

Everything disappeared from sight now; except the red, wooden front door of the white-washed house. Matthew stood in front of the door, and knocked on it with his knuckles. He stood and waited, with his suitcase on the ground.

*****

It took a few seconds for the person on the other side of the door to eventually unstuck it from its closed position. Matthew could sense them pulling and tugging on the door – as though it always caused problems like this. A troublesome door.

With a final tug of effort, the door opened; and a perplexed face peered around at Matthew – a face that said: *Who could this be? We never get any visitors here.* It was Matthew's father, John. He stared and squinted at Matthew for a few seconds, as though he was trying to focus with soap suds in his eyes. 'Matthew?' he asked.

Matthew couldn't speak. He thought he was going to choke.

'Matthew!' his father shouted, beginning to cry. 'Linda! – Linda! – Come here! – it's *Matthew!*' John Rourke stepped forward onto the front step of his home, and embraced Matthew. Matthew began to sob heavily: with sadness; with shame; with regret; with relief; with love; with happiness.

'Matthew!' Linda Rourke said, as she reached the front door, in a state of bewilderment mixed with sheer delight. 'Oh my God!' she cried, as she looked to the sky.

Matthew stepped forward, and his mother embraced him; welcoming her son into her world, just as she had, over thirty-three years ago.

*****

Matthew Rourke talked to his parents for just over two hours, inside their oak-beamed living room. Matthew's father lit the fire inside the room's huge, stone fireplace, and Matthew was shown to the armchair that had been his favourite as a child. Although a lot of the décor had changed since Matthew was last here, the house itself was exactly as Matthew remembered it.

Matthew spoke to his parents at length about why he had decided to leave them, fourteen years ago. They couldn't stress enough, again, how they had never blamed Matthew for Christian's death; how much they loved and admired Matthew; and how much they wanted him to stay with them, in the Lake District.

Matthew could hardly believe the extent of his parents' love. Even when Matthew told his mum and dad about how his marriage had failed and how he had lost his job recently – they still didn't judge him: they simply told him it was 'all for the best now'. Matthew had never felt so secure and at ease in his life.

'Why don't you go upstairs to your room, Matthew? Unpack some of your stuff and freshen up – before dinner.'

'OK, mum. Thanks.'

John Rourke stood up. 'I'll help you up with your suitcase.'

'No. I can do that,' Matthew said, rising from his seat. He looked at his dad, and suddenly recognised how old he had become.

'Your room is still as it was,' Linda Rourke said, smiling warmly at Matthew; her face much softer and sallower than it was years ago. Matthew smiled back at his mum – although he immediately began to feel unworthy of his parents' love. 'Matthew,' his mum continued, as though she had just read his thoughts. 'You're going to be OK here. Everything is going to work out for you now.'

Matthew didn't know how to respond. He walked out of the living room, and back into the front hallway, with its quarry-tiled floor. Matthew lifted his suitcase and began to ascend the oak staircase. He reached the top of the hall landing, and breathed in heavily. Matthew wanted to become part of the spirit of this place again.

He walked down the short corridor, and into his bedroom. Matthew closed the door behind him, and began to cry tears of happiness and relief. He was *home*. He had forgotten what home felt like. Although he owned his apartment with Ruth, in London TW9, Matthew had never felt at home there. He was almost glad he had stolen the dead dog now – as absurd as that seemed to Matthew.

Matthew walked over to his bedroom window, which looked out over panoramic views of Empyrmere – its valleys, waters, fells, countryside and village. He opened the window, and breathed in the fresh, cold, pure, sunlit air. Matthew could feel Christian everywhere. 'Thank-you, Bud,' Matthew said out loud, as he began to cry again: tears of gratitude, this time. He had forgotten what if felt like to be happy – until now.

*****

Once Matthew and his parents had finished their Sunday dinner, just after 4.00 p.m., Matthew's father nervously made a suggestion. 'Matthew. Your mum and I always visit Christian – on this day – every year. You don't have to, of course. But would you like to come with us?'
　'Yes. I'd like that.'
　Linda and John looked at one another. They could barely believe that their family had been reunited today. It felt like a miracle.

They got ready to leave for St. Saviour's Church graveyard, even before they had cleared away all their dinner plates.
　Matthew knew that he would find the next few moments of his life difficult – but for some reason, he was happy. He felt that his life was just about to re-start, after a sixteen-year blip.

*****

It was only a five-minute drive to the small rural graveyard at St. Saviour's, on the outskirts of Empyrmere village. John Rourke parked their car alongside the main road, and all three proceeded to walk along the graveyard's narrow gravel pathways, towards Christian Rourke's grave.
　They stood in silence at the grave for a while, as Matthew re-familiarised himself with the simple inscription on Christian's gravestone: *Christain Rourke. Beloved Son and Brother. Died 16th October. Aged 6. Always Loved. Always Remembered.*
　Matthew's mother walked forward and placed a wreath of yellow and violet chrysanthemums on the grave.
　'Are we ready to go now?' John Rourke asked.
　'Yes,' Linda replied; and Matthew concurred with a nod.
　Matthew followed his parents slowly out of the graveyard, all the time looking at the fells and surrounding countryside.
　'Look!' John Rourke shouted proudly, pointing at something. 'I bet you haven't seen one of those in a while, Matthew!'

Matthew looked towards the sky, just as his father had instructed. 'No. I haven't,' he replied; as he smiled at the peregrine falcon, flying above his head.

*****

Eva Kelly had spent all day alone, at home in NW1. It had been raining all day, and Eva, uncharacteristically, hadn't felt like going outdoors for a long walk.

She had spoken briefly on the phone, yesterday afternoon, to Amanda Morgan, who had informed Eva that she would be tied up with family business for the foreseeable. Eva recognised the traumatic time Amanda had endured recently – with her husband, her daughter, her business, and not forgetting, the dead dog incident. Eva had told Amanda not to worry about her; that they could meet up at any time in the future – but only if it fitted in with everyone's plans. Eva had a feeling that she wouldn't be seeing very much of Amanda in the future. Their companionship had been important; meaningful; spiritual – for *both* women, Eva realised. It had sprung up very unexpectedly – a bit like when a bird would drop a seed on a barren piece of land, and up would grow an apple tree – as if by magic. Eva had reached something of a dead-end in her life, when her relationship with Amanda first began; and so, it seemed, had Amanda. Through their early conversations, they were each instinctively able to pick up on the other's predicament. Eva realised that Amanda had been through a very difficult time with her family – ever since Amanda was a child; while Eva explained to Amanda that she felt she had missed out on life – in spite of loving her career, working alongside nature.

Eva's relationship with Amanda had developed very slowly, but very surely; and Amanda had even contemplated telling her daughter, Charlotte, about their growing friendship. But Eva and Amanda's apple tree would never blossom, Eva realised now. The season of their companionship had come and gone, but both women were stronger emotionally because it had happened. Eva had learnt to love, and to feel love in return; while Amanda had told Eva that – for the first time in her life – she had learnt to trust in her own feelings and abilities.

But what would Eva do now? Amanda had her family, Eva realised; whereas Eva could never rely on her one remaining direct family member in England – Ruth Rourke. Eva and Ruth's parent's had moved to Australia, over ten years ago, to work as teachers; but their two daughters had only visited them once during all that time.

And now, *Matthew* had gone too - .

Eva's phone began to ring. She picked it up excitedly, and looked at the screen – only to see that it was Ruth's number calling. It was 4.45 p.m.

'Hello,' Eva said.

'Eva? Do you know anything about Matthew's whereabouts? He's just left a note on the kitchen table – saying that he's *gone away for the night*. And that he'll *explain more tomorrow*.'

'No. I don't know anything,' Eva replied flatly.

'What's wrong with *you*?' Ruth demanded, dissatisfied at Eva's distinct lack of interest in her latest drama: Ruth liked to think that the world revolved around *her* foul moods.

'Absolutely nothing. Why? What's wrong with *you*?' Eva was in dreadful form. She hadn't felt this miserable in years.

'Well – you have absolutely no need to be like that,' Ruth snapped angrily. 'It's just that I've been away all day – and all last night – so I thought he might have left a message with you. I've tried to phone him, but his phone went straight to voicemail. That's all.'

'Well he hasn't left a message with me. And if he told you he'll explain tomorrow – then I guess you'll just have to accept that he will.'

'Well – stuff you, Eva,' Ruth hissed, as she ended the call immediately.

Eva Kelly turned off her phone and set it on top of the arm of her chair. She began to laugh to herself. Eva had always prided herself on being straight and truthful with people in the past, and she had always treated everyone with as much respect as she thought they deserved. She had chastised Matthew Rourke for being so dishonest – for stealing a dead dog, and for burying it secretly. But Eva had been dishonest too, and, most of all, with herself. At least Matthew had done something to make his life better now, Eva thought. He had also been honest enough to try to explain his actions to Ruth, and to the owners of the dead dog.

Eva had always admired and cared deeply for Matthew. The question was – could she take a leaf out of his book, and begin to live her life according to her *own* truth?

-CHAPTER TWENTY-TWO-

Revelations

Amanda Morgan arrived at Epsilon Dental Spa at 8.30 a.m. on Monday 17th October. She was relieved she had agreed, last Thursday evening, for the practice to remain closed today.

Amanda had spent all weekend with her husband, Steve, and her daughter, Charlotte. It had been a strangely quiet, calm and uneventful couple of days – given the chaotic nature of Amanda's life recently. Steve had been very mellow and polite towards Amanda and Charlotte. He had stayed in bed most of the time – recovering after his illness – but he had been very sociable and pleasant to his wife and daughter, in spite of his continuing discomfort, after his bout of pancreatitis. Neither Steve, Amanda nor Charlotte had felt the need or the inclination to discuss anything that had occurred between them, inside Steve's side ward, at Memorial Hospital, last Tuesday evening. It was as though they had finally got through that episode of their lives, Amanda thought. Matilda, Charlotte's twin, had at last been acknowledged by *all* of the Morgan family.

Amanda desperately hoped that today would see a continuation of the spell of calmness and harmony her family was enjoying at the moment. As she sat alone, anxiously, at the Reception Desk, inside Epsilon Dental Spa, Amanda began to think seriously about the implications today could have for the remainder of her life. The thought that Douglas Singleton could be her father terrified Amanda – much more than the possibility his legal firm could put an end to her dental business. Amanda would hopefully discover the outcome of both these dilemmas this morning. She still hadn't confided to Steve, Charlotte or the Carmichaels about any of these things – nor indeed had Amanda told her companion, Eva. For some reason, Amanda sensed that her relationship with Eva was about to take a back seat. Although this saddened Amanda, she had so much else on her mind at the moment, she barely had time to dwell on the subject. Eva, as ever, had seemed very easy-come, easy-go, when Amanda had spoken to her on the phone on Saturday afternoon. Amanda recognised that Eva had a lot going on in her life at the moment, too.

At 9.06 a.m., a private courier entered the Reception Area of Epsilon Dental Spa. He handed a letter over to Amanda Morgan at the desk, and she duly signed for it. When the courier left the premises, a few short minutes later, Amanda looked at the envelope in her hand for a while, before she tentatively began to open it.

Amanda read the short letter from Singleton and Singleton Solicitors, slowly and carefully. She put it back inside its envelope, and smiled broadly. Douglas

Singleton had been true to his word: he would no longer be pursuing a legal case against Epsilon – or against Amanda's husband, Steve Morgan.

Amanda rose to her feet and put the Singleton letter carefully inside her handbag. She began to walk towards Epsilon's front door, to leave, when a postman shoved several letters through the letter box. Amanda lifted the post without looking at it, put it in her handbag alongside the Singleton letter, and left the premises – locking everything up carefully behind her.

Instead of feeling total relief at this stage, however, Amanda was filled with an impending sense of doom. She was about to go to the clinic where she had dropped off the samples for the paternity test, last Friday. Amanda had been reliably assured that the test results would be ready to collect first thing this morning. She got into her car and began the short, nerve-wracking journey to Delta Clinic, which was owned and managed by one of Amanda's many wealthy contacts.

When she arrived at Delta, Amanda parked her car outside the clinic, and entered its plush Reception Area, where she gave her name and explained her reason for being there. Amanda was asked to take a seat in Reception, while Delta's receptionist walked off to locate Amanda's test results. It was 10.30 a.m.

*****

After about ten minutes, Amanda was called to the Reception Desk, where she was handed an envelope, which she was asked to sign for. Amanda took the letter and walked back to her car.

She looked at the envelope for a while, before eventually opening it and reading its contents.

Amanda phoned Sir Horace Montgomery at work.

'Amanda,' he stated, upon answering her call.

'Hi. I've got the test results in my hand.'

'Go on.'

'Well, I'm sorry to disappoint you. But it seems very improbable that you are *not* my father.'

There was a pause before Sir Horace said anything. 'I can't lie to you, Amanda. But I am genuinely surprised at this news. And genuinely happy. May I ask how you feel?'

'Hugely relieved. So where do we go from here – dad?'

'I think I owe you an apology, Amanda. Many apologies, in fact. I know my treatment of you over the years has been very much determined by my belief that you were *not* my daughter.'

'It's just a pity you didn't think to check your facts a bit sooner.'

'I know. And again, I apologise – genuinely so.' There was another pause before Sir Horace spoke again. 'Amanda. I'd like to ask you to meet me for lunch – or dinner – so that we can discuss this – in person.'

'OK,' Amanda said. 'But I can't make today. It will have to be tomorrow – at the earliest.'

'That's fine. Just let me know what suits; and I'll be there.'

'OK. Bye then.'

'Bye, Amanda.'

Amanda Morgan detected softness in Sir Horace Montgomery's voice; softness she had never detected before. She was very relieved: not just because she had discovered that she wasn't related to Douglas Singleton, but also because she suspected that her father – Sir Horace – might actually begin to treat Amanda like his flesh-and-blood – for the first time in her life.

This had been a day of wonderful revelations for Amanda; things could not have possibly worked out better for her. In spite of all the upheaval during the last couple of weeks, Amanda somehow sensed that her life was finally moving in the right direction.

As she slipped her test result envelope into her handbag, ready to leave for home, Amanda suddenly decided to sift through the other mail she had lifted from the floor of Epsilon Dental Spa, this morning. The only letter that grabbed her attention, which appeared to be potentially significant to Amanda, was addressed simply to '*The Owners of Epsilon Dental Spa*'. Amanda opened the letter – hoping that its contents would not spoil her wonderful start to the day. It was neatly typed, and dated 16th October.

Amanda took only a few minutes to read Matthew Rourke's letter. She sat agape for a few minutes, in the front seat of her car. Amanda looked at the letter again, in an attempt to make sure she had read what she thought she had read. A million questions entered her mind: Who wrote the letter? How did they know who owned the dead dog? How did they find out about Epsilon Dental Spa? Was this all a sick joke?

Amanda was baffled – and very spooked. It was probably the strangest letter she had ever read in her life. She didn't even know if she should show it to Susan and Ray Carmichael – in case they thought Amanda was making fun of their loss. Surely *Steve* wouldn't even have stooped so low – to pen a prank letter like this? No; Amanda thought: he had been too ill in hospital – even if he'd *wanted* to write such a letter.

Amanda considered what she should do now. In spite of the distress this letter might cause for the Carmichaels, she knew she had to show it to them. Perhaps it *was* true; perhaps the person who wrote the letter *was* the person who stole Dixie Carmichael's body; perhaps they *had* buried him inside an area of woodland, inside Unity Park. This last part certainly seemed to tally – given the fact that

Charlotte was mugged at Unity Park Station. Amanda's adrenalin levels were soaring now, as she began to think angrily about the arrogant moron who had stolen her daughter's bag – and then had the audacity to send a letter, outlining where he (or she?) had buried it.

Amanda put the keys into the ignition, and sped off immediately in the direction of TW9: she would visit Susan and Ray Carmichael - now.

*****

Amanda pulled up in front of the Carmichaels' detached Edwardian residence at 11.25 a.m. She walked to the door, and knocked confidently on it – even though she was dreading the outcome of the conversation she was about to have.

Susan Carmichael came to the door first. 'Amanda. Come in – is everything OK?' Susan had noticed the worried expression on Amanda Morgan's face.

'Susan,' Amanda replied, stepping onto the parquet floor of the Carmichaels' front hallway. Susan shut the front door, and led Amanda into the kitchen. 'I think you'd better read this.' Amanda handed Susan the letter, and Susan began to read it immediately. Ray entered the kitchen. 'Hi Amanda! Everything OK?'

Nobody spoke for several seconds, much to Ray Carmichael's discomfort.

'Oh my God!' Susan cried. 'Who the hell sent this?'

'Susan – I have no idea. I just picked it up with the other post at the practice. I wasn't even sure if it was a sick joke. And – before you ask – I really don't think Steve would have been capable of sending it.'

Ray took the letter from Susan and read it.

'It must be some sicko,' Susan said, holding her head in her hands.

'Do you really think this is our foreigner friend – writing to us? The one who stole Charlotte's bag? His written English is very good – for a foreigner, that is,' Ray added.

'I don't know who wrote the letter. But we have to check it out Ray – don't we?' Susan asked.

'Yes. Get your coat.'

Amanda Morgan was determined to get off the scene now. 'I hope this doesn't turn out to be a joke, Susan. I really genuinely hope you both find your dog.'

'Thanks, Amanda,' Ray said: Susan was distraught; caught up in her thoughts.

'I know this isn't exactly a brilliant time,' Amanda hesitated, as she began to walk towards the Carmichaels' front door. 'But I thought you'd both like to know anyway. I received a letter, this morning, informing me that Singleton and Singleton won't be taking a case against Steve or Epsilon, after all.'

Ray and Susan both stared at Amanda, agog. 'How the hell did that happen?' Ray was in complete shock.

'It's a long story, Ray. But everything's going to be OK with the business. I just have to sort things out with Steve's position now. But I don't think that should be a problem.'

'OK,' Ray said, still in shock. Both he and Susan knew that this was fantastic news – but they couldn't absorb it right now: all they were thinking about was Dixie.

*****

Ray and Susan Carmichael arrived at Unity Park at 12.45 p.m.

Susan stood at a picnic table, as Ray followed the directions in the letter Amanda Morgan had presented to them, just over an hour ago.

Ray located the flowery bag easily. It was under some rocks and soil, just over from a large Oak, and near a group of Silver Birch trees. Ray also (strangely) discovered a blue plastic bag nearby, containing an empty breakfast cereal packet, and an empty bag of sugar, under some other rocks and fallen tree foliage.

Ray covered his mouth, put on some protective gloves, and looked inside the bag. He immediately recognised Dixie's blue collar and lead, which he unfastened and put into his coat pocket, before he zipped the flowery bag closed again.

Ray began to walk out of the wooded area, towards Susan. To his curiosity, he noticed bits of breakfast cereal and sugar scattered on the ground. He was sure they must be connected to the empty packaging he had just uncovered, inside the blue plastic bag, beside Dixie's tomb. Ray thought the person who stole Dixie must have camped here for some time – and that was also perhaps why Ray had discovered a pair of used latex gloves, inside the flowery bag. Whatever the case, Ray thought, this was one strange and disturbed individual they were dealing with.

Susan glimpsed Ray walking towards her, solemnly; carrying her favourite weekend bag. 'Dixie!' she cried in agony, as she fell to her knees on the ground, heartbroken.

*****

Susan and Ray did not speak during the journey home from Unity Park, except to agree that they wanted to bury Dixie's body straight away now: they didn't want to involve Mike Gordon, Dixie's vet.

The Carmichaels arrived home just before 2.30 p.m.

Ray carried Dixie's body into the back garden. Susan sat with Dixie, while Ray prepared a grave, underneath Dixie's favourite Oak tree.

Ray placed Dixie and the flowery bag into the grave, and covered it with earth.

Susan and Ray did not speak to each other during all this time. There was nothing to say. Susan was crying, but she felt strangely relieved: she hadn't thought she would ever get the chance to bury Dixie at all.

Ray re-placed the slabs of turf over Dixie's grave, and trod them neatly into place. He stood back and put his arm around Susan's shoulder.

'Dixie always loved this place – didn't he, Ray?'

'Yes,' Ray said, wiping a tear from underneath his right eye.

After a short while, Susan and Ray turned and walked into the house.

As Ray proceeded to busy himself in the kitchen, tidying away the Sunday newspapers for recycling, Susan stood beside Dixie's favourite armchair, and looked out at his favourite Oak tree.

Dixie was *home*.

Dixie Carmichael looked back at Susan, as he lounged underneath the Oak tree. He desperately hoped that Susan would remember to do one more thing today.

Dixie watched on, as Susan turned, and began to walk upstairs.

*****

At exactly this time, Ruth Rourke arrived back at her TW9 apartment, a few miles away from Susan and Ray Carmichaels' home.

Ruth had only dealt with three psychotherapy clients today. She had already started to pack up her office in W5, ready to move out of the premises at the end of the month. Ruth had agreed a way to end her lease with her office landlord, and had also begun to tie up things with her remaining psychotherapy clients. She couldn't wait to start her new position as Douglas Singleton's P.A., in a few weeks' time.

Ruth picked up the post, inside the hallway of her apartment, before she walked into the kitchen. There was no sign of Matthew. She walked into the two bedrooms, but he wasn't there either. Ruth had checked yesterday evening, and she realised that Matthew had taken some things away with him on Sunday; she just didn't know exactly how much. Ruth was furious with her husband – for disappearing like this – unannounced.

Ruth walked back into the kitchen, and sifted through her post.

Her attention was immediately drawn to an envelope, addressed in Matthew's handwriting. She opened the envelope with a heightened sense of alarm:

Dear Ruth,

I don't really know how to begin this letter, because I know that by the time you are reading it, I will already be miles away.

I don't need to point out to you how unhappy our marriage has been recently – and if any of that was my fault – then I am very sorry. I do, however, realise what you clearly knew a long time ago: our marriage is over. For that reason, I have decided to leave London for good. I have gone back to Cumbria, to live with my family.

I realise that we still have things to sort out between us, Ruth, but please know that I am willing to sign over everything to you, as soon as possible, so as to avoid any more unnecessary conflict between us.

All my redundancy money and some of my savings have been transferred over to your account. These should cover the mortgage payments on the apartment for a few months, until you perhaps sell the property.

I have left the address of my solicitor at the end of this letter. Please pass any paper work you need signed, via his office.

I am sorry for not saying all of this in person to you, Ruth, but I thought it was probably best to leave things like this.

I wish you all the luck in the world in your new career, and I hope you find everything in life that makes you happy.

Matthew.

Ruth was shaking with emotion. She couldn't believe what she had just read. She didn't think Matthew had it in him, to behave so impulsively. She thought she had meant everything to him. How *dare* he do this to her. Where did he find out about her new career anyway? What was this about him having savings? Who the hell was his family in Cumbria?

She called his mobile, hysterical now: 'Matthew!' she screamed, as his phone switched to voicemail (again). 'What the hell are you playing at? Who do you think you are? How dare you send me a letter like this! Get back here immediately - so that we can talk about this properly!'

Ruth wanted to scream at the top of her voice, but she couldn't think what to scream. She hung up. Her head was about to explode with fury and confusion. She dialled Eva Kelly's number: *she* would know what to do. 'Eva!' Ruth shouted frantically, as Eva's phone switched to voicemail. 'You have to call me back! It's Matthew. He's gone AWOL. Please, please call me back. You have to meet me. It's only four o'clock. We could meet for drinks....'

*****

Eva Kelly chose not to answer her sister's call, as she stood inside one of her greenhouses, at work, in NW1. Eva watched the screen of her phone now, as it flagged up Ruth Rourke's voicemail message. Eva deleted the message, before she made another call.

'Hello!' the pleasantly surprised voice said at the other end.

'Matthew. I need to talk to you about something,' Eva said: she had been contemplating making this call all day.

'OK,' Matthew Rourke replied seriously. 'I was hoping you would call. I was trying to get through to you – all last night.'

*****

Susan Carmichael walked downstairs, in her detached Edwardian residence in TW9. She entered the kitchen, where her husband, Ray, was staring out the window, towards the large Oak tree at the bottom of their back garden.

Susan walked across the kitchen floor. She looked down at the magazine sitting on the kitchen table - the one with the photo of the yellow and violet chrysanthemums and the West Highland Terrier. 'Ray,' she said.

He turned around and looked at Susan. 'Hi. Are you OK?'

'Yes,' she replied, smiling broadly. 'I've just found out I'm pregnant.'

-CHAPTER TWENTY-THREE-

The Kids Are Alright

Forty (earthly) years later, to the exact moment, a thirty-three-year-old Matthew Rourke was sent in the direction of an idyllic park, bedecked with trees, shrubs, flowers and grass.

Up above him, the sun shone brightly, in a perfect pale-blue sky. It was warm, but not uncomfortably so. Matthew was dressed in casual summer clothes: a pair of light-coloured trousers, and a blue T-Shirt.

He looked around, and saw that the park was filled with many people whose faces he knew. Matthew felt instinctively and blissfully happy.

He began to walk in the direction of a picnic table. His parents, John and Linda Rourke, approached Matthew with beaming smiles on their faces. Matthew hadn't seen them in over thirty-five years. They embraced him, and went off for a walk together.

Matthew proceeded to walk towards the picnic table. He began to smile warmly at a woman sitting on a bench beside the table. 'I heard you were coming,' she said, as Matthew took a seat beside her.

'You look exactly as I remember you,' Matthew replied. 'How long have you been here?'

'Just four years longer than you. I was seventy-five when I arrived.'

'You don't look any different from the last time I met you.'

'I know. I like being this age. It was the happiest age of my life. I knew you would recognise me like this.'

'Everything worked out for you then?'

'Perfectly. I wanted to meet you. To thank you for meeting me that day. My life started from that moment.'

'I knew it would.' Matthew replied. 'I felt it. It was as though someone had just told me you would be OK – even before I spoke to you, inside the café.'

'Yes. When I first arrived here, I discovered you were sent to meet me that day. It had all been arranged – without us realising it at the time. You'll begin to understand how things work here, soon enough.'

'You had more children?'

'Yes. Two girls. Twins. I called them Rose and Lily.'

'Your daughters: what age are they now?'

'They turned thirty-nine, on June 8th, just four months ago. They were born on the same date Jacob went back, nine years earlier. It was the happiest of times for my husband, Ray, and I. And all the flowers were blooming at the same time, when we brought our daughters home from the hospital: the Jacob's Ladder plants; the lilies and the rose bush.'

'Where is Ray?'

'Still there. He only has a few years left. He's enjoying being granddad to Lily's two sons, and Rose's son and daughter. They give Ray a great excuse to stock his cupboards up with sweet things! I look in on all of them frequently. They know I'm still around. They recognise when I use the signs Jacob taught me.'

'Eva – my wife – is still there. In the Lake District. We had two sons – James and Philip.'

'I heard.'

'I'm afraid they're all hurting.'

'It's still very early days. Give them time. Let them know that you're still around. You'll learn how. You won't feel time passing by here at all. You'll simply blink one moment, and they'll be beside you once again.'

'They'll hopefully immerse themselves in the family gardening business in Empyrmere. Eva loves it there. She came to join me at my parents' home, six months after I left London.'

Matthew Rourke proceeded to tell Susan Carmichael about how he and Eva Kelly finally admitted their feelings for each other, forty years ago. Matthew had always been drawn to his sister-in-law – but he had obviously suppressed his feelings, in the interests of his marriage to Ruth. When Eva confided to Matthew, just after he left London for the Lake District, that she had feelings for him, they decided to see if they could work together as a couple. Eva sold her gardening business in London, and moved to the Lake District to be with Matthew – just as soon as his divorce with Ruth was completed.

Eva told Matthew that she had spent several years hiding her love for him. She had almost given up on meeting another man like Matthew. She told Matthew that it had felt as though sweet honey had been running down her back for years – but Eva simply hadn't been able to lick it: Eva couldn't stop loving Matthew Rourke.

'What about Ruth – the one you didn't want to tell about your redundancy - the day I met you?' Susan asked.

'We divorced very soon after I left London. She married a wealthy solicitor, and got to live the life she craved. Ruth and Eva never really spoke much to each other again. Except when their parents died – in Australia – some years ago. Ruth was livid when she discovered that Eva and I got married. She told Eva that we deserved each other. Eva said she could sense that Ruth was not happy – in spite of the fact she was the wife of a very wealthy man.'

'Would you like some food?' Susan Carmichael asked, as she gestured to the huge picnic now spread out on their table.

'Yes. Will others be joining us?'

'Look over there,' Susan said, pointing towards a large area of lush green grass.

Matthew Rourke looked. Walking towards the picnic table was a male and a female – aged roughly in their early sixties. As they got closer, the male and female became progressively younger in age – until Matthew recognised the male.

It was Matthew's six-year-old brother, Christian.

Matthew suddenly felt and looked like his seventeen-year-old self. He rose from his bench, and walked over to embrace his brother. 'Hi Bud!' Christian said, his green eyes twinkling in the sunlight. 'You want to come play over here?'

Matthew Rourke walked off ecstatically with Christian, towards some trees. The two boys ran and climbed together; and chatted forever.

Susan now glanced at the female who had accompanied Christian Rourke. The female looked nineteen years old now. She took a seat beside her nineteen-year-old identical twin, Charlotte Morgan.

Charlotte had been reunited with Matilda, in this place, over twenty years ago. Charlotte arrived, after a disease claimed her earthly physical body, at the tender age of forty. She had fulfilled many of her dreams during her time on earth, however. Charlotte had established a very lucrative business, called 'Made in Heaven', with Ebony and Melody Glazier. The three women organised flowers and music for every special occasion – like weddings, funerals, Christenings and birthdays. They used their extensive MyVaneSpace and Twopenniesworth connections to create a UK-wide concern, which became hugely popular and successful. They were even under 'Royal Appointment', at one stage. Matilda Morgan had relished watching her sister succeed in life, and she looked over her, every step of the way.

Ebony and Melody Glazier continued to run 'Made in Heaven' for five years after Charlotte's untimely departure – but they eventually sold the business – and made enough money to afford them a very affluent existence for the remainder of their earthly lives.

Charlotte met a lovely man – Jeff – during her last years on earth. Charlotte loved him dearly; but they never got married, and Charlotte never wanted to have children. Jeff had now moved on: he had a family with another, back on earth.

Charlotte was simply glad she could spend all her time with Matilda now. The two sisters often talked about the time they had shared together, on earth, inside Amanda's womb. Charlotte was able to recall how she hadn't wanted to leave Matilda's side, when the time came for them to be born. Charlotte had somehow sensed that Matilda wasn't going to survive for very long – and Matilda was forced to persuade Charlotte to move forward – without Matilda – during the last drawn-out stages of Amanda's arduous labour.

When Matilda's soul was eventually able to re-connect to Charlotte's, as Charlotte had sat curled at the top of the flight of stairs, at home, one Saturday morning, and inside the lobby of The Peregrine hotel, Charlotte had suddenly been able to move forward purposefully with her life at last.

Charlotte and Matilda were reunited with their mum, Amanda Morgan, when Amanda arrived here, three years ago, at the age of seventy-two. Amanda, however, had now reverted to her nineteen-year-old self. She was in her absolute prime.

When Matilda first introduced herself to Amanda, three years ago, she did so as a newborn baby. Amanda was finally able to fulfil her dream of holding her youngest daughter's vibrant body in her arms. Amanda loved being back with her daughters: she had especially missed Charlotte's company, after Charlotte left earth, at such a young age.

Amanda looked over now, and watched two women – both in their thirties – walking towards the picnic table. They were linked together, giggling and laughing. 'Any food for us?' one of them asked, smiling. 'Of course,' Amanda said, before she introduced her mother, Lydia, and her Aunt Matilda, to Susan Carmichael.

'Pleased to meet you,' Susan said, as Charlotte Morgan began to speak.

'Was that the man who stole the dog from me?'

'Yes,' Susan answered, laughing. 'That's why I'm here at the moment.'

Charlotte looked in the direction of Matthew Rourke. She had gained a little more experience with dogs since her fateful dog-sitting episode at Susan Carmichael's London home, forty years ago. While Charlotte was not completely averse to the canine race by now, she still stopped far short of letting any dog lick her on the face.

Charlotte began to speak to Amanda. 'We should thank that man some time, I guess – shouldn't we, mum?'

'Definitely, Charlotte,' Amanda replied.

Amanda suddenly began to reflect on her husband, Steve Morgan.

Luckily, after the whole Dixie situation, and the Madeleine Singleton crisis, Amanda had been able to force Steve to leave Epsilon Dental Spa. This had meant that Susan and Ray Carmichael were able to run the business alone, for many years, with Amanda Morgan as a sleeping partner. Amanda had been such a sleeping partner, in fact, she may as well have been in a coma (she was sick to the back teeth of all things dental). Amanda was more than happy to let the Carmichaels run the dental business as they saw fit – and profits continued to soar for many years.

Steve remained at the Morgan family home after his bout of acute pancreatitis. He and Amanda were able to pick up their marriage, the way they had left it, before their daughter Matilda's untimely departure (much to Harriet Harper's distress). Steve never had another extra-marital affair. He never really socialised with Mike Gordon again (much to Mike's relief). Steve couldn't have done enough to say sorry to Amanda (and Charlotte) for all the wasted years he had spent straying away from his family. He reassured Amanda that he hadn't just stayed in their marriage because it had been the 'easy' option. Steve had always secretly loved his wife – he just didn't know how to talk to her any longer. Steve had found it easier to cut his family off, and belittle them – in order to make himself feel better about his own inadequacies and shortcomings. Steve and Amanda had been able to discuss (at last) how Matilda's death had affected Steve so badly, he hadn't been able to face life's realities at all. He was finally able to convince Amanda that he hadn't blamed her for Matilda's death.

Amanda could barely believe she was able to re-kindle her relationship with Steve Morgan. She came alive again as a woman. She wasn't as obsessed with cleanliness. Steve was even able to make his wife laugh again – without her wanting to ram his veneers down his throat. Amanda was able to remember why she had fallen for Steve in the first place. Steve began to show more consideration for Amanda and Charlotte. Amanda was able to have a decent conversation with her husband once more. It was as though Steve had gone through some sort of unexplainable transformation – ever since Matilda, Steve's daughter, visited him, inside his side ward in Memorial Hospital, forty years ago.

Amanda Morgan was also able to forge a new kind of relationship with Sir Horace Montgomery – who finally began to acknowledge Amanda as his daughter, and Charlotte and Matilda as his grandchildren. Sir Horace even had a special plaque made in Matilda's memory, which he placed on her grave, beside his wife, Lady Lydia's resting place, on the Montgomery family plot. Sir Horace was reunited with Lydia only ten years after he finally discovered that Amanda Morgan was really his daughter. He remained close to his wife – although he tended to do his own thing most of the time. As well as finding it difficult to grab Lydia's attention away from her sister, Matilda, Sir Horace had always enjoyed flitting about from place to place on earth – and nothing was going to change that now. He frequently popped in to keep an eye on Montgomery's Department Store, in Central London, which had been bought over by a wealthy Chinese family. Sir Horace was very intrigued by how this new family operated the business – which he still considered to be his. He was hugely relieved that Amanda had chosen to sell the Montgomery business, instead of signing it over to her imbecile husband, Steve Morgan. Sir Horace still thought of Steve as an educated idiot.

It took Steve a few years to move completely away from his silly, immature ways; Amanda reflected now. She often referred to him as her 'late developer'. The only thing that had really saved Steve – was Charlotte. Charlotte was delighted that her parents had remained together. She employed her father as an advisor, delivery man and chauffer for her 'Made in Heaven' business – but not before Steve had fulfilled his promise to grant Charlotte her bedroom makeover; computer colonic; hair extensions and Mediterranean holiday.

Steve delighted in watching his daughter do well: he realised now that paper qualifications alone didn't necessarily denote intelligence and ability. Steve recognised that he had wasted his talents and intelligence by resting too smugly back on his laurels, when he had married into Amanda's wealth. He regretted not having made more of his dental career, although he largely made up for this by throwing himself fully into Charlotte's business. Ironically, Charlotte often admitted to herself that 'Made in Heaven' would not have succeeded so easily without Steve's insights and hard work over the years.

Steve gave up alcohol altogether – but he flatly refused to sacrifice his beloved Game Show Channel addiction. Amanda agreed to let her husband indulge in this particular past-time – but only when he promised not to use any game show cheesy catch-phrases in Amanda's presence.

Steve's wife and daughters still looked in on him a lot. He was eighty, and still healthy and strong. Steve Morgan had grown very contented as he got older – although his shiny-white, youthful-looking veneers did look a bit ridiculous amongst all his wrinkles and age spots. He missed Amanda and Charlotte desperately. Steve knew how much he had underestimated his wife and daughter's intelligence and loveliness at one stage of his life – and he deeply regretted that, too.

Steve always thought about his daughter, Matilda.

Steve had outlived Mike Gordon, his 'mate', by several earthly years. Mike left earth after he suffered a heart attack, while he was weight-lifting at Elite Physique Gym: he was fifty-five years old at the time. Mike had always liked to think that he was younger than his age – although this belief almost certainly cost him his physical body.

Mike Gordon didn't frequent the park Amanda and Susan were part of, however. He preferred a nearby safari park, which reminded him of the time he had spent in Kenya, during his veterinary training. Mike had always preferred animals to humans. His only regret was that he hadn't remained in Africa during his youth. Cosy domesticity and domestic animals didn't really do it for Mike, as much as lions, tigers and zebras. (Mike never kept contact with his earthly wife and daughters). When Mike heard that Deborah Silvestri - the mad bunny woman, dressed in wild animal print - had entered this realm, very shortly after Mike (and only a year before Deborah's sister, Madeleine Singleton), Mike was sure she was still stalking him – in spite of the fact that he never saw her after the infamous night in Abandonment.

This was another reason why Mike Gordon preferred to stay in his safari park: he knew Deborah Silvestri would steer more in the direction of rabbit sanctuaries and Chinese-themed parks. Deborah had never given up her earthly fascination with rabbits, sheds, men, Chinese Astrology and the invisible realms – although she was a bit taken aback when she discovered that the laws of the invisible realms operated slightly differently than she had supposed, while she was on earth.

Deborah continued to look out for her earth-based daughter and son – Clare and Benito. Neither Clare nor Benito had married. Clare was in her late seventies now, while Benito was a decade younger. Deborah knew that Benito would pass over and see her soon - and Clare wouldn't be far behind. Benito smoked and drank heavily (just as his father had: Deborah had certainly avoided *him* ever since her arrival here). Clare suffered terrible bouts of depression – even though she had given up her job as a psychotherapist several years ago. Clare hadn't remained friends with Ruth Rourke (now Ruth *Singleton* – after Ruth's marriage to Andrew, Douglas and Madeleine Singleton's eldest son). Ruth quickly disposed of her 'friendship' with Deborah and Clare, once she had settled nicely into her new career as Douglas Singleton's P.A.

Douglas and his wife, Madeleine, had remained married, while they were both on earth – but only until Douglas died, at the age of seventy-five.

After this time, Madeleine continued to scramble frantically for signs of her departed daughter Victoria's presence – thanks to Deborah and Clare Silvestri's frequent alcohol-fuelled séances, inside Deborah's shed. Madeleine never saw Steve Morgan again, after their brief fling ended. It disgusted her to think that she'd shared a dental surgery with a man who murdered dogs. When Madeleine suffered a second nervous breakdown, two years after Douglas's departure, her two sons, Andrew and Tom, bought her a Golden Labrador puppy, to placate their mother. Madeleine named her dog Mr Jitters – in honour of her nervous disposition. Mr Jitters was obtained from Candy Pups Kennels, in Buckinghamshire, which was still owned by Phil and Jill Candy at the time. Madeleine collected Mr. Jitters on a sunny day in early October, along with her son, Andrew, and daughter-in-law, Ruth.

Mr Jitters encouraged Madeleine to steer away from her sister Deborah's shed. Madeleine began to walk her dog in nearby parks. She discovered a peaceful earthly existence – until she too departed earth, eight years later. Mr Jitters joined her the very next day.

Madeleine was finally reunited with her daughter, Victoria. As Madeleine approached the warm, bright, sunny park, all those years ago, her three-year-old daughter jumped into her arms, and Madeleine became the vibrant, happy, twenty-nine-year-old woman she had been before she 'lost' Victoria on earth. Mother and daughter had been inseparable since – and Mr Jitters was their constant companion.

Douglas Singleton, however, never met up with his wife and daughter. He preferred to stalk the outskirts of the warm park, looking in on his two earthly sons, as they continued to play the 'legal' system like musical maestros. Douglas admired how his eldest son, Andrew (now in his late sixties), continued to attract the younger ladies: Ruth, Andrew's wife, certainly didn't look as good as she used to, Douglas thought.

Douglas desperately wanted to go back down to earth. He recalled how he had eventually been awarded his knighthood – but he died suddenly, the week before he got to go to the Palace to collect it. He was still furious that he had missed the opportunity to destroy Horace Montgomery's daughter's business, all those years ago. Douglas had remained under the illusion that Amanda Morgan was *his* daughter, for the remainder of his earthly life, and this was the only reason why he hadn't gone in for the kill with Epsilon Dental Spa. Douglas had feared that any revelation over his private life would have killed off his chances of a knighthood. If he had known Amanda Morgan was not his daughter, Douglas could have gained massive publicity over the Epsilon case – given the dental practice's celebrity-based client list. This would surely have given Douglas the extra exposure he would have needed to gain a mention in the Honours List, a few years earlier in his career. How he would do it all differently now! He should have agreed to Amanda Morgan's request for a paternity test! He should have stuck to his guns! He should have got to the Palace before his death! If only he could go back again – he would *really* know which legal cases to pursue...

Susan Carmichael looked across the sun-lit park. She saw a young boy walking towards her. The boy was playing with a West Highland Terrier pup. Susan smiled and watched, as the boy and the dog approached her at the picnic table. 'Hi Jacob,' she said, as the boy leapt onto her knee. Susan gazed into the boy's dark brown eyes. She ran her long fingers through his dark, curly hair. The boy looked just like Susan.

Jacob smiled at Susan: a warm, enchanting smile; a smile that did not reveal teeth. 'Will you come for a walk – with Dixie and I?' he asked.

'Yes,' Susan answered, as she bent down and stroked Dixie's head tenderly with her hand. Susan loved nothing more than walking with Jacob and Dixie.

Ever since her arrival here, four years ago, Susan had been able to experience a whole lifetime with her son. He had greeted her, upon her arrival, as a baby. Susan had held her son in her arms, just as she had always envisaged, ever since the day she first saw him, waving and smiling at her, from the screen on her obstetrician's scanner. Susan dressed Jacob in his penguin baby-gro. She walked him around the sun-lit park in his pram, with Dixie tottering alongside, just as she had walked with her daughters, Rose and Lily, around Unity Park, many earthly years ago. Susan was able to experience Jacob's toddler years; his childhood years; his teenage years; and his adulthood, in an instant: such was the timeless nature of life in the invisible realms. She was able to reclaim all the lost pages of her life story. Jacob was able to show Susan that although his soul had not been able to occupy his weak, physical body – it had always been with Susan, nevertheless. That's why Jacob had arranged for the lady to sell Susan the Jacob's Ladder plants in Unity Park that day. Susan knew now that she hadn't been punished when

Jacob left earth. Her son had always remained the biggest and most important part of her soul.

Susan enjoyed Jacob's eight-year-old self a lot. It reminded Susan of the time when she met the handsome stranger, inside Paws for Thought. Jacob reassured Susan that she had been right to put Jacob's Box away for 'a little while' – back then; although Susan did return to it on many occasions, after her daughters were born. Jacob's memory enabled Susan to truly relish her role as Rose and Lily's mother, even though this was the most demanding and difficult work Susan Carmichael had ever undertaken. She never forgot about Jacob, and she still experienced pangs of anger and loss over her son, on many occasions, throughout the remainder of her earthly life.

As for Dixie, he had also reassured Susan that she had been right to leave him behind when she went to Buckinghamshire with Ray. He informed her that he had definitely *not* died from a broken heart.

Matthew and Christian Rourke approached the picnic table again.

Matthew smiled, and scooped Dixie into his arms. 'Hello boy!' he said, as Dixie licked Matthew's face with his gristly pink tongue. 'Don't *you* have a lot to answer for?'

'Woof!' Dixie acknowledged.

Matthew knew exactly what Dixie meant. It was somehow right that Matthew had stolen Dixie's body, at Unity Park Station. It was the only thing that would ever have enabled Matthew to move on with his life. 'I almost expect some tourists to walk by now!' Matthew joked.

'I think that would be a little silly – don't you?' Susan laughed.

Susan and Matthew laughed for a while, before Susan spoke again. 'I looked at the photo of you on my phone for the remainder of my earthly life. Little did I know then that you were the strange individual who had stolen my dog – and written those bizarre instructions about where to find his body, inside Unity Park.'

Matthew laughed again. He couldn't think how else to respond.

'Hello,' Charlotte Morgan suddenly said to Matthew. 'Remember me?'

Matthew laughed again, as he placed Dixie Carmichael on the ground. 'You haven't changed at all,' he said to Charlotte.

'How is Eva?' Amanda Morgan interrupted suddenly.

'Great,' Matthew replied. 'She always thought a lot of you, Amanda.' Matthew knew instinctively who Amanda Morgan was. His soul was suddenly infused with information. He was told that Eva and Amanda's relationship had helped pave the way for his relationship with Eva.

Amanda continued to talk to Matthew. 'I thought about Eva every spring-time, when the bulbs she planted flowered in my garden.'

Amanda Morgan and Eva Kelly only met each other twice after Dixie Carmichael's earthly body was found, inside Unity Park. Eva later informed Amanda that she was leaving London. She told Amanda that she wanted to create a new life, elsewhere. Amanda had wished Eva well – and told her that she was going to spend more time with her family. Amanda later contacted her psychotherapist, Ruth, to let her know that she wouldn't be continuing with her counselling sessions; but when she had dialled Ruth's office, Amanda was told that the premises now operated as a tattoo parlour.

Amanda laughed, before speaking to Matthew again. 'Eva helped me move on – even more than your other wife – Ruth.'

Amanda and Matthew both laughed, in recognition of the irony, before Christian spoke to Matthew. 'Let's go and watch *The Spider Mystery*, Matthew!'

'OK!' Matthew replied.

'Come on - now, Matthew!' Christian said, tugging at his brother to leave; before the two of them ran in the direction of some trees again.

Susan Carmichael got up now, and took Jacob by the hand.

They began to walk towards beautiful fields of roses, lilies and chrysanthemums, with Dixie by their side. Susan talked to Jacob, and her son beamed happily back at her. Susan looked forward to the day when Ray would join them – soon.

As mother and son sat down to enjoy the sunshine on some soft grass, Dixie wandered off in another direction. He approached a group of several other dogs - all his former kennel mates on earth (including his parents, Jupiter Sue and Spartacus III, and his siblings, Millie, Billy and Angelica) – who were playing beside a huge Oak tree. Dixie began to join in; rolling and messing about like a puppy.

'Hello Dixie!' a female voice said.

'Woof!' Dixie replied happily.

'You coming to play with your brothers and sisters? You love to play, my Dixie, don't you? It's great fun – isn't it?' Jill Candy cuddled Dixie and wrestled playfully with him, as he licked her face with his gristly pink tongue. 'Phil!' she said. 'Get Dixie one of his favourite treats!'

Phil Candy brought Dixie over a doggie biscuit. 'Here you go, boy!' he said, placing it underneath the large Oak.

'Woof!' Dixie replied, in gratitude, as he bounded out from Jill Candy's arms, and lay under the shade of the Oak, and ate his favourite doggie treat.

While his parents and his brothers and sisters continued to play with Phil and Jill Candy, Dixie lay back, very satisfied. His tale could have gone any way – at any time – given the fickle nature of the human mind. It had never been a foregone conclusion that the lives of the individuals Dixie had connected with on earth would have made the choices they eventually did. Unfortunately, human beings didn't always respond to the magical prompts frequently sent their way during their earthly lives, resulting in too many people losing their footing on their life journey. Luckily, for Susan Carmichael, Matthew Rourke and the Morgans, they had grasped the opportunities placed in their paths (eventually), and they had been able to reach their desired destination in life.

Eva Kelly had recognised the need to grab *her* opportunity with Matthew Rourke – before her sister, Ruth, would work her way into his life again. Ruth Rourke had, in fact, fleetingly contemplated making things work again with her husband, Matthew, on the Monday after her catastrophic Saturday night out at Abandonment with the Silvestri women. Ruth had momentarily questioned the direction her life was headed in, but she later chose, nevertheless, to continue pursuing the path to wealth and riches, in the belief that this would secure her happiness: Ruth was subsequently never able to fathom why her life with Andrew Singleton was no more contented or fulfilling than her life with Matthew Rourke had been.

Eva Kelly knew exactly how her sister Ruth ticked. She knew that Ruth would have been instantly enticed by Matthew's secret, impulsive, unpredictable side – had Ruth discovered this sooner. Eva therefore deliberately told Matthew to let Ruth know that he was leaving her in a letter – *after* his departure for the Lake District. Eva had feared that Ruth might change her mind and seek a reconciliation with Matthew, if Ruth had discovered her husband's plans earlier. When Eva later discovered that Matthew *had* decided to write to Ruth, explaining his intentions, Eva was hugely relieved. She knew it would be too late for Ruth to have a second chance with Matthew now – and Eva was determined to fill the void in her brother-in-law's life.

Dixie began to smile. The drama and intrigue of human life was confusing yet compelling, he thought. It had been a very eventful period; but it had all worked out as well as could be expected in the end.

Dixie curled his tail around his warm body, and drifted into a magical sleep.

www.ingramcontent.com/pod-product-compliance
Lightning Source LLC
Chambersburg PA
CBHW050517260626
47157CB00004B/1356